MONSTER MENU

MONSTER MENU

Terrell Garrett

Podium

This book is dedicated to the author of the tale you are about to read. Terrell Thomas Garrett died tragically and unexpectedly, shortly after finishing this book. His story led him ahead of us to lands beyond. May his words live on.

All rights reserved. No part of this publication may be reproduced, stored in a retrieval system, or transmitted in any form or by any means electronic, mechanical, photocopying, recording, or otherwise without prior written permission from Podium Publishing.

This is a work of fiction. Names, characters, places, and incidents are either products of the author's imagination or used fictitiously. Any resemblance to actual events, locales, or persons, living, dead, or undead, is entirely coincidental.

Copyright © 2023 by the Estate of Terrell Garrett

Cover design by Podium Publishing

ISBN: 978-1-0394-3329-8

Published in 2023 by Podium Publishing, ULC
www.podiumaudio.com

MONSTER MENU

— CHAPTER ONE —

Octopus Al Pastor

She didn't remember storing the carcass of the creature that tried to kill her in the mini-cooler.

When Nay first woke up and saw one of the tentacles hanging down the side of the cooler, she had jumped in fright. But then her memories of her near-death experience the previous night came rushing back to her. At first, she was trying to figure out why she put the body on ice. What was the initial plan?

I was drunk last night, and this monster with tentacles tried to strangle me in an alleyway; better save the body so I have proof in case no one believes me. Call the authorities and say, "Yo, I was attacked by a tentacle abomination, officer. Don't know how I survived. But here's the body, which proves I'm not a drunk liar. Maybe you can show it to the local Cryptozoological Society or something."

But after she was fully awake, recovering from her hangover, she was struck with a crazy and sick idea. She could be a vindictive person, but this was something on another level. It was maybe a little too spontaneous and reactive. She had never tried to hurt someone with her food before, but she had taken a bad hit from that terrible review. She had felt the reviewer to be particularly cruel, and it had put a dent in her business. Against her better judgment, she took the lifeless monster out of the cooler and got to work.

Now she had it impaled on the vertical spit in the back of her taco truck, Taco the Town. She had soaked the thing in vinegar for the remainder of the morning to remove whatever funky taste it might have. She figured the more palatable she could make it, the better. She didn't need the reviewer to know he had consumed something questionable. Her knowing about it would be enough satisfaction for her. In her mind, it was a twisted sense of justice.

Then she had moved the carcass to a pineapple-based marinade for a few more hours, and now it sat on the spit looking like al pastor octopus. Some sort of black foam bubbled out of the rubbery flesh under the heat lamp.

"The fuck is this?"

Remi arrived, climbing into the truck, smelling like too many Natty Lights and fresh-baked donuts. He held a cardboard tray with cups of espresso and a paper bag from Simone's Donuts nestled on top. Nay could see one side of the bag was wet from moisture, which told her the donuts within were placed inside while still steaming.

She wasn't hungry but now felt herself jonesing for something sweet and fluffy.

"That's gnarly," Remi said. He untangled himself from his backpack and handed Nay the drink tray and bag of baked goods. He took a closer look at the thing on the spit. It looked like he had had a late night too. From Nay's experience, most of her comrades in the food industry were night owls. The type of people who truly awaken once the sun is down and the moon is up.

"Octopus al pastor?" he asked. "It's genius. What's this black marinade?"

Nay grabbed her cup of espresso and took a whiff. Steam rose off the foamy surface. A triple shot. Her go-to every day. Simone's always used dark roast beans, and she loved the intoxicating aroma. She threw her head back and downed it in one go, letting the hot, bitter liquid wash over her tongue. It filled her body with warmth, and already she could feel the rush of caffeine in her bloodstream.

"Just something I threw together," she said. "Pineapple juice and balsamic."

"I can dig it," he said. "Wait, where'd you get the octopus from?"

There was no way she was going to tell him the truth. No way to explain that it wasn't an octopus but some *thing* she had fought to the death. And she certainly wasn't going to explain that she was going to serve it as a dish of revenge for the social media influencer who had given their truck a bad review. Foodie TikTok could be a harsh place.

"I picked it up at the new market," she said.

"Which one?"

"It's in Little Tokyo; bunch of vendors are out there all hours of the night."

"Sounds dope."

Remi sipped his espresso like it was an aperitif, the stark opposite of how Nay consumed her caffeine. He savored the taste when she would inject it if it were a choice. Even before COVID-19 had wrecked her taste buds, she consumed her coffee more for the effect than the flavor. It didn't mean she didn't care about the flavor or the quality. She wasn't a fan of shitty coffee; she just rarely took the time to enjoy the journey as opposed to the destination.

He pulled his phone out and snapped a pic of the spit.

"Don't post that," she said.

"Why not?"

"I want it to be a surprise for the festival today."

"Whatever."

He pocketed his phone and began preparing his station for prep work. As her sous-chef, Remi's job was to get all the vegetables chopped, the tortilla batter mixed, and the sauces made.

Nay had a flash of one of the thing's tentacles trying to coil around her neck. She wondered if it would have been her on some kind of spit if she hadn't managed to stab it multiple times with her Konosuke knife.

She began making a list in her little Moleskine notebook of ingredients and possible flavor combinations. A list for a pico mixture with Cherokee Purple tomatoes and pickled okra and a tartar sauce with lemon juice and fresh dill. She had the perfect vehicle in mind for how she was going to serve this monster meat.

The food festival was in full swing, and already news of her truck was spreading via word of mouth thanks to a social media post making the rounds.

As Nay shaved some more of the meat off the strange-tentacled creature, she glanced at the TikTok playing on her phone. The TikToker was her target. He was one of the more popular foodie influencers in Los Angeles, a Pakistani guy whose account was called, *How Dev Eats It*.

He was showing off a burrito the size of a brick. The burrito that she gave him. "Hey, fam, it's yo boy *How Dev Eats It!* Tonight, I'm at the Anaheim Food Festival and I'm about to try the new El Diablo burrito from Taco the Town! Listen, I know I was a bit harsh the last time I tried their food, and I like to think of myself as a fair-but-honest critic. So, that's why I'm giving them a second chance."

Next, there were brief glimpses of Nay's food truck from different angles. Then a close-up of the logo she designed, which was a chupacabra with a taco in one hand and a burrito in the other.

"Look at this big boy," Dev said. He held the massive burrito up and slapped the end of it. It jiggled. "It's massive!"

Finally, the money shot. A close-up of the El Diablo burrito, glistening in all its moist and meaty glory. Dev split it open for his viewers to see. The cross-section of black-tentacled mystery meat oozed creamy tartar sauce and red pico de gallo. It actually looked tasty. "Get a peep at this cross section. Look at the drip. Now let's see if it's the real deal. I'm about to get my mouth pregnant!"

Dev took a bite and chewed. His eyes widened in surprise, then they closed and he softly moaned, swallowing. He took another bite. A more ravenous one. A bigger one. He opened his eyes so his viewers could see them roll into the back of his head as the flavors triggered some type of ecstatic experience. His whole body quivered like Meg Ryan in *When Harry Met Sally*.

"Jesus Christ," Nay said. "He's loving it."

She wondered if the initial euphoric experience would lead to something more diabolical. Would the flesh of the dead creature try to kill its eaters just as it had tried to kill her when it was alive? This was supposed to be a form of revenge, but it was backfiring in a spectacular but not wholly unwelcome way.

She remembered that first video he made and how he had shit on her street tacos that everyone else in town had seemed to love. He called her, her cooking, and her truck mediocre. The spread and fallout of that review had really done a number on her business. It didn't really affect her regulars who visited her truck for lunch like clockwork every day, but when it came to the potential of new customers, Dev had really screwed her over. His TikTok had left a bad taste in her mouth.

But this new one more than made up for it.

It had only been two hours since he made the video, and now the special ingredient for her El Diablo Burrito was almost gone. Either she had poisoned all the foodie influencer attendees at this fest, or she had made them ravenous for more. Her revenge scheme transformed into something else.

Remi called her over to him. He was gawking at his phone, amazed. "The El Diablo burrito went viral, Nay."

She looked over and he scrolled through all the posts people had made. Hell, the burrito even had its own hashtag, and the photo of the octopus-looking creature on the spit was all over Instagram, TikTok, and Twitter. "Looks like you got Dev to finally say something good about us," Remi said. "Maybe he'll take his first review down."

Nay wished she could feel elation instead of dread. It was always her dream for Taco the Town to go viral, and now that it finally had, she had run out of the one ingredient that had made it possible. How would she explain to people that the meat came from an otherworldly creature that might not be of Earth? The El Diablo burrito was a once-in-a-lifetime event.

Unless she could find another monster, survive the encounter, and kill it for its flesh.

Later that night, unable to sleep, Nay found herself outside the Potions & Poisons bar in Koreatown. She figured her best bet at finding another one of those creatures and harvesting its meat would be retracing her steps from the night before. Only problem was, she had been on the precipice of blackout drunk that night, so her memory was super hazy.

She remembered going to Potions & Poisons after a long shift to unwind. It was her place to go to nurse a cocktail and eat French fries. Their basket of fries was the perfect nosh, fried to a crispy perfection and sprinkled with parmesan, garlic powder, and the ingredient that took it to another level, a light sprinkle of curry powder. She couldn't taste much since COVID, but Nay was a creature of habit.

She figured the alleyway where she was attacked was near the restaurant, so she sparked up her Zippo and lit an American Spirit Black as she observed the street and the crowd. It was a Saturday night, so the place was packed with casuals trying to impress their dates.

She noticed a red light emanating from the alleyway across from her. A memory flashed in front of her eyes then. A red neon light in Korean script burned in her mind. She headed across the street and entered the alleyway. There seemed to be a temperature change as she entered the corridor. She suddenly wished she had brought her jacket or at least her long-sleeve flannel that she usually took with her to the beach. But the source of the red glow was at the end of the alley.

It was a neon red cross with flowing Korean script. She couldn't read Korean, but she knew it was a church sign. She felt called to it like a moth to the flame.

She got to the side of the building, finding a door underneath the neon cross. She was surprised to find that it was unlocked. She stepped in.

She entered what looked to be a Korean community center. It was one of those multipurpose rooms that could serve as both a gymnasium and a meeting center. Stacks of metal folding chairs were pressed against the walls. There was a podium on one end. Flyers and ads were hung on a large bulletin board, but the feature that was currently holding Nay's attention was what appeared to be a pentagram-like symbol scrawled on the floor.

It wasn't quite a pentagram, but it definitely looked occult-like in nature.

"What the hell?" Nay muttered. The sight of it alarmed her, and that's when she noticed the forms on the floor. There were three people lying on the ground, their bodies mostly covered by robes and cloaks. There was an open book between the three of them. As she got closer, she saw blood and other wet matter stained on the floor around their heads, as if there was an explosion resulting in a red and crusty halo.

These people were dead. These were corpses.

Nay was struck with the uneasy sensation that she was being watched. She looked around and noticed half of the room across from her was in total darkness. She thought she saw something there. She rose to her feet, squinting into the dark. She thought she could make out a shape that reminded her of a leg, cut out in the darkness.

Not a human leg, either.

A jointed appendage, long, thin, and dark red as it moved into the moonlight coming in through the window. Nay could feel the hair on the back of her arms rising. The skin on her neck hackled, crawling. A primal instinct, a response collectively etched into her DNA as a member of the human race long ago when every person had to worry about predators. As her stomach twisted into knots, every nerve in her body was sending the same message.

Run.

Another crimson leg emerged out of the shadows. It too was segmented and jointed. More legs emerged, the torso they carried swaying into the blue moonlight shining in through a window. It was a giant spider, skin a slick red like it was covered in blood. But its head was not arachnid in origin but human. A human infant head. An extra set of hooked appendages hung below its face like butcher's chains ending in hooks.

Nay heard herself scream.

She turned to run but felt something cold and rope-like go taut against her shins. She tripped and fell forward, caught herself with the heels of her hands on the floor.

Something slippery and serpentine scrambled over her and squeezed ahead of her. She looked up to see the bulbous body of a land octopus. It squirted a dark green ink at the spider, and the air filled with a gaseous cloud of the stuff. Nay coughed, sputtering. She dragged herself forward, out of the edge of the ink cloud. It was like being blasted in the face and breathing in a broccoli-and-asparagus smoothie. She sputtered for air.

She pushed herself up and ran for the exit. She glanced behind her to see the spider recoiling from the cloud and having to skitter around it. Tentacles coiled around her ankle again, pulling her back. She got the distinct feeling that this new creature was trying to throw her at the spider so it could get away too. She didn't have time to dwell on it, but she was pretty sure it was also operating purely on fear.

She wrestled with the purple tentacles coiling around her, her hands unable to get a grip. It was like trying to grab at rubber and muscle. She caught a glimpse of eyeballs and beaks on these stalks. She drew her Konosuke chef's knife from its leather sheath and went to hacking. She could feel the edge of the blade cutting into the muscular flesh, and for a moment, she swung with such frenzy, the creature must have felt it was like on the wrong side of a Cuisinart. Nay used her other hand to draw her taser, and she deployed the button, jolting the thing with electricity while she severed one of the appendages.

The air filled with purple ichor that must have been its blood, and then another spray of that green ink surrounded both Nay and the monster. Her eyes burned and her airways filled with the revolting ink. Through her own tears and the cloud she caught a glimpse of the underside of the spider's hourglass torso appearing above them. A neon red outline formed underneath it, like the outline of a door. Then her vision was blinded by a burst of the red light, and then the chaos stopped.

There was stillness in her going unconscious.

Nay woke up coughing and cold, and extremely disoriented. She heard the howling wind around her and could feel it on her skin. She vomited green bile onto the snow. When her vision cleared from the red afterimage of the light, she caught glimpses of white, as if she woke up in the midst of a blizzard. And something else appeared in her vision, some glowing text that hovered in front of her, at the center of her vision.

[Quest Detected]
[Quest: Find Shelter from the Cold]
[Accept Quest Y/N?]

— CHAPTER TWO —

Worldtripping

Nay thought she must be dreaming. Or stuck in a nightmare. One moment, she had wandered into what was supposed to be a meeting place for a Korean church only to stumble upon some occult ritual gone wrong and two alien or otherworldly creatures that wanted to kill her. Now she was inside of a snowstorm on what appeared to be a mountain pass while hallucinating text prompts.

Did she want to find shelter from the cold? Hell, yes, she did. She mentally clicked on the *Y* and a new prompt appeared.

[Quest Accepted!]
[Find Shelter from the Cold]

"Is this a nightmare?" she said, teeth chattering. She also discovered that she was naked, which just made the whole situation worse. What happened to her clothes? Before she was sucked into the red door, she was definitely wearing clothes. "This is definitely a nightmare. *Please* be a nightmare."

She hugged herself as the snow and wind battered her bare skin. She could feel herself going numb, the icy cold pressing into her bones. If she didn't find warmth soon, she was going to be turned into a popsicle. "Which way to go?"

Was she supposed to instinctually choose? It was hard to see through the swirling snow and wind.

That's when something else appeared in her vision like it was part of a HUD from a first-person shooter game. It was a glowing and translucent grid map. There was a glowing white dot. *Does that signify my location?* she thought. There was a blinking gold dot that appeared to be in the southwest. She didn't have any better ideas of where to go, so this blinking spot on this map she was clearly hallucinating was as good as any. As she mentally accessed the map, she discovered she could zoom in and out, but she could only explore what was shown. The rest was covered in a gray fog. She didn't have access to it because she hadn't explored it.

But as she stumbled down the path to the southwest, she noticed the gray fog clearing in that direction on her mini-map as she walked. If she explored in a specific direction, it was being added to her mini-map. Still, she didn't know why it was showing her the blinking spot. Maybe it was because she was in the vicinity of something helpful.

"This is all a hallucination, anyways," she said, trying to convince herself. "So, it's not like it really matters. Now I better get moving before I freeze to death."

A glowing purple dot appeared on the map. It was smaller than her own white dot. As she walked, it was keeping pace with her. She turned around but couldn't see anything in the storm. If something was following her, she would worry about it when she found warmth. She'd deal with whatever it was after she found a safe place from this storm.

As she stumbled down the snowy mountain pass, the pain she felt on her feet went away as the cold numbed any sort of sensation. She carried on, accepting the fact that she was probably going to die out here. Through the snow and wind she caught glimpses of alpine trees and mountain peaks all around her. She was in the middle of a treacherous mountain range. With the dark color of the sky, she surmised nightfall was approaching, which would probably make everything that much colder. She was wheezing. Snot running out of her nose, and the tears running down her cheeks froze upon contact with the frigid air.

She lost track of time, but as she came around a bend, she caught glimpses of a cave entrance through the haze of snow. It was an opening in the rocky mountainside, and its location corresponded with the blinking gold dot on her mini-map, which also confirmed she was standing in front of it. She trudged towards the cave entrance, which appeared like a dark maw before her, but at least it was shelter of some sort.

She stepped inside and immediately felt a temperature change. The surface of the floor had warmth, and the stone walls were covered in condensation. She was pretty sure it was from the steam that she could feel against her face and body. It was coming from deeper within the cave. She stepped on something sharp and fell against the wall. It was just the uneven and rocky surface of the cave floor. The pain was worse because sensation was returning to her extremities thanks to the warmth.

She crouched there, clutching the warm rock, moisture dripping around her. The howling wind was muffled there, and she took a few moments to catch her breath. Her skin felt like it was being plucked with needles as she warmed, hot blood flowing underneath.

She noticed the purple dot on her mini-map coming into view again. According to the map, it was right outside the cave entrance. She turned her head towards the opening of the cave. All she could see was the snowfall. There was no one else there that she could see. Yet she still looked around for something she could use as a weapon in case whatever the purple dot was meant her harm. She had lost her Konosuke knife as well as her taser in the tussle with the monsters and the resulting chaos. She found a hefty rock she could hold in one hand. With it in her hand, she felt some comfort that she wasn't completely naked.

Well, that wasn't true. She was still naked. But at least she had something she could use as a weapon.

"Hello?" she yelled at the entrance. "Who's there?"

The only answer was the howl of the wind cutting through the mountain pass.

She noticed that the quest was still in her quest log.

[Quest Log]
[Find Shelter from the Cold]

"All right, then," she said. "Let's find the source of the heat. But I wish there was a quest to find some clothes or at least a blanket." She chuckled to herself, thinking she had gone half-mad, and continued deeper into the cave.

It was a hot spring.

Nay had walked into a chamber with a natural domed ceiling, finding it after following the steam that floated through the tunnel that took her deeper into the earth. Below were pools of hot water in pockets of the rock. It looked like there were multiple individual tubs to soak in. Nature's hot tubs. Standing in the large chamber felt like standing in the middle of a sauna. Nay thought of the sauna in her gym where she used to have a membership, but this was better. Way more impressive.

There was a chime in her mind.

[Quest Complete!]
[Find Shelter from the Cold Completed!]
[Congratulations!]
[You have been rewarded Vigor Points]

The Quest Log section in her HUD was now clear.

She shook her head. "This nightmare just keeps getting stranger." Was she unconscious and dying in real life? Was her body being dissolved in the belly of the spider and this video-game dream was just her brain's response to death? The last firing of neurons between the synapses before she succumbed to death? What were Vigor Points? Who knew?

As she approached one of the hot spring pools, she paused. She remembered a story about some campers or hikers finding what they thought was a hot spring in Yellowstone. But when one of them entered it, he melted. It turned out the pool was a toxic combination of chemical elements that could dissolve matter. And that's exactly what it had done to him. Was this such a pool? Was it a trap? Just because this was a dream or a nightmare still didn't mean she wanted to die in the midst of the nightmare.

She inched close to the pool and sat on the side of it, cautious but basking in the warmth. Her shivers had disappeared, and she was glad she made it here without her fingers or toes getting frostbitten. She didn't want to lose bits of her body, either. So, she was glad she had made it out of the blizzard with all her limbs still attached.

Curious, she tossed her rock in the water. Other than a splash, there was no other reaction. She could see it sink to the bottom of the pool. As far as she could tell, it wasn't dissolving. There was no violent explosion of matter, like pouring soda over pop rocks. There were hardly any bubbles. The warm water called to her. She couldn't help but think of the soak sucking out the rest of the cold that had settled and found home in her bones.

She held her hand over the surface of the water, felt the steam rising off the surface and touching her hand. Slowly, she touched the water with the tip of her finger and pulled back. She didn't feel any pain, and her skin didn't burn or slough off. It had just felt nice. She touched the water again, longer this time. Still no sign of it being a pool of acid. So, next she slid her hand in and held it under. No reaction except for the feeling of hot water relaxing her blood flow.

It was safe.

So, she spun and, bit by bit, lowered herself into the hot-spring pool. She groaned in relief as the warm water worked its magic with her body. She sat there like she was soaking in a hot tub, letting the water and warmth heal her body from the effects she had suffered from being naked in the middle of a snowstorm. She relaxed.

As she pushed her worries out of her mind for the time being, allowing herself a moment just to be warm, she thought about the HUD system she had been seeing and using in her vision. She realized she could pull it up with just a thought. In the upper right corner was the mini-map. In the bottom left was a symbol she didn't recognize. It looked like a glyph. When she swept over it with her mind, a menu opened up.

[Worldtripper Interface]
[Quest Log]
[Inventory]
[Delicacy Stats]

She explored the Quest Log. After finding warmth, the log was empty. She checked her inventory. That, too, was empty. So, next she looked at the Delicacy Stats screen.

[Delicacies: 0/3]
[Delicacy Skill Trees: 0/3]
[Marrow Abilities: 0/36]
[Rank: Base]
[Vigor Points to Next Rank: 1%]

She felt herself getting sleepy as she contemplated what Delicacies, Marrow Abilities, and Vigor Points were. Now that she was safe, warm, and comfortable, she let her guard down and dozed off.

Soon she was gently snoring, her head resting on the edge of the natural spring.

The blinking purple light on her mini-map woke her up. She had no idea how long she had been out for. A warning chime sounded off in her mind. Whatever the purple dot was, it was in the hot-spring cavern with her. She looked off in the direction indicated on her map; still, she couldn't see anything.

She remembered her rock and felt it at the bottom of the pool with her feet. She used her foot to scoot it closer, then she went under the water and grabbed it with her hand.

She pulled herself out of the pool and stood there naked on the stone floor, water dripping off her body. The rock in her hand.

"I know you're in here," she said. "Show yourself!"

There was no answer.

The only sound was her own nervous breathing and the dripping of water. *Drip drip drip.* She took a step towards the entrance of the chamber, being careful not to slip. There was a flash of movement up ahead. She swore she could see something slither behind one of the large rocks.

"Stop!" she cried out. "This is your last warning! Show yourself and I won't hurt you!"

Again, no answer.

But she could hear the sound of something sliding across the surface of the cave floor. Something was up ahead behind that large rock.

"All right, that's it!"

Nay rushed over, holding the rock over her head. She made it around the side of the rock and stopped in her tracks.

There was a single purple tentacle here, standing on one end like a stalk. It was one of the tentacles she had severed from the creature in the Korean church. One of the appendages of the monster she had cooked up and served in the El Diablo burrito. It wavered before her. Green protuberances curved off its body like rubber fins. Near the top of the stalk was a single cyclopean eyeball, and below it was a beak.

"Wait, no!" Nay heard a voice. The tentacle wavered like it was cowering in fear. The single eyeball blinked frantically. "Please don't hurt me!"

Nay looked closer and realized the voice came out of the beak on the tentacle.

The tentacle could speak.

— CHAPTER THREE —

Nzxthommocus III, Third Whip of the Pain Lord

"I'm not trying to hurt you," the tentacle said. "I'm just here because it's warm."

Nay stared at the tentacle, her eyes not believing what she was seeing. Her ears not believing what she was hearing. She shook her head as if to shake herself out of a bad trip. "I've really lost it, haven't I?"

"Lost what?" the tentacle said. It curved itself, contorting its stalk into the shape of a question mark.

"You're just a figment of my imagination, aren't you?" Nay muttered. "Just like everything else I'm seeing."

"I assure you, lady, that I'm no figment. Now, would you put down the rock? It's making me nervous."

Nay looked at the rock she was holding in her hand like she was going to club the creature with it. "All right, let's play this game, then," she said to herself. Then she looked back at the tentacle. "How do I know you're telling the truth? Last few times I saw tentacles, I was fighting for my life."

"That's because I was just an appendage," it said. "I had no control, none of my own autonomy except for my own thoughts. But I always had to answer to the body that controlled me no matter how much I didn't want to."

"Are you saying you're one of the tentacles I severed?" Nay asked. She remembered slicing through a couple when she was fighting the land octopus.

The tentacle shook, curving and nodding its top end like it was shaking its head. "For that, I have to thank you."

"Thank me? For what?"

"For freeing me, of course. I was stuck to a most disagreeable taskmaster who just wanted to strangle everything in sight."

"And you're not like that?"

"Of course not!" Its color morphed from purple to a light green. Its hue reminded Nay of lime jello. It was translucent, and for a brief moment, she could see the thing's strange organs and circulatory system. It had quite a large brain. "I'm a lover, not a fighter."

Nay then realized she was standing in front of this sentient tentacle while completely naked. She was suddenly self-conscious. She crossed her arms, trying to cover herself.

"Now that you're not going to try to bludgeon me to death," the tentacle said, "our first matter of business should be finding you some clothes."

"Don't think that I've made up my mind."

"Suit yourself," it said. Then it slinked into one of the hot-spring pools. Bubbles rose to the surface as it plunged. Then it reappeared, bobbing back up like a buoy. Its color morphed again, but this time to a gentle blue. It was relaxed. "Oh, now that's the ticket."

Nay stared at the thing in utter bewilderment as it let out little moans of pleasure.

Nay had lowered herself back into the water, but mostly because she felt less naked with her body submerged. The tentacle showed her some courtesy by turning so that its single eyeball wasn't pointing at her when she lowered herself in. She set the rock on the edge of the spring within hand's reach in case things went south with the creature. She wasn't comfortable parting with the stone just yet.

"What are you?" Nay asked.

"My name is Nzxthommocus III, formerly the Third Whip of the Pain Lord Ormandius," it answered. "But now I'm just Nzxthommocus. Since you freed me."

Nay shook her head. "I meant . . . what kind of mon—creature are you?"

"Oh." It submerged its beak, taking in some water. Then it sprayed it out, like a child playing in a pool. "Ormandius, the host I was formed from, is called a shoggoth. Humans also call his kind chthonic kaiju."

"Where did you, and it, come from?"

"Flayers and others of their ilk were spawned in the Roiling Celestia in the rings of Tindalos."

"What?"

"It's in the dark pocket of the cosmos where those called the Dread Ones or the Hounds of Tindalos slumber. I've never seen it myself and couldn't give you an exact location, but sometimes I dream of it like I've been there before. It's as they say, roiling with giant squirmy things. You would probably find it unpleasant. But I always think it's kinda nice."

"Christ," Nay said. She didn't know what to make of any of this, yet she had no other choice but to confront it. "Do you remember, before I freed you from your host, a giant spider thing? In a church?"

"I remember that one minute, Ormandius was feeding on the mind of a prisoner in the cells where we were employed, and the next we were in a strange world surrounded by three cultists dabbling in spells beyond their skill level. I'm pretty sure they botched one of the pronunciations of their incantations and that's how it summoned us in addition to the riftway spider."

"Riftway spider?"

"Sure, big red bastard. Lots of legs. Glowing red door on its tummy?"

"Oh, yeah. The giant spider thing."

"We both world-hopped again when it sucked us into its door. That's what they do, mostly. Provide doorways between worlds. Also, they like to eat people. Probably an unforeseen side effect when they were bred by the Architects. I don't know about you, but all the dimensional hopping gave me a serious case of whiplash."

"Dimensional hopping? Is that where I am? Another dimension?"

"I'm pretty sure that explains what happened to your clothes. The fabric didn't survive the trip. I hear it's been known to happen. People tumbling naked out of riftway spiders, spit out into some strange new world like they're being spat out of a womb again. Just carrying the skin on their back, just like the first time they emerged."

Nay looked around and considered the implications with wide eyes. She felt dizzy all of a sudden and a little sick to her stomach. "Is that where I am? Another world?"

"I think we're both in another world. Some other place different from our own respective dimensions."

"I thought this was all a hallucination. A nightmare. A bad dream at best."

"No, it's real. Didn't you feel the bite of the cold out there? We both almost died from hypothermia. If it wasn't for following you, I would have turned into an icicle. Trust me, I don't do well in extreme cold. Or extreme fire. Extreme fire is probably worse, though. What do you think would be a worse way to die? Cold . . . or fire? I think I'd have to go with fire, because with cold, it seems like, yeah, there would be a lot of discomfort. But ultimately it's like falling asleep. But with fire—"

"Please stop. I can't hear myself think."

The tentacle stopped talking. It grew quiet. It submerged itself again, taking more water in its beak. It gurgled and sprayed it out in a stream.

"So, if this is another world . . . or reality . . ." Nay was thinking out loud. "Whatever this is, wherever this is . . . I still need to find clothes before anything else."

"Except maybe food," the tentacle said. "At some point, probably sooner than later, we will need food."

"You need food?"

"Well, yeah. Food and water. Doesn't every living thing?"

"Forgive me, I'm still coming to terms with a talking tentacle."

"Sheesh. Get used to it now. We're probably both going to see all sorts of strange shit that's out of our norm. It'll be easier if we just go with it."

Just go with it. Easy for you to say. You're a talking tentacle."

"Your judgmental nature is going to get tiresome, I can tell. I guess it's not your fault, though. You seem to come from a pretty basic world. I mean, you didn't even know about the rings of Tindalos! Not every world has advanced civilizations yet, I suppose."

Nay almost retorted, but then she realized she'd be in an argument with a tentacle. And now probably wasn't the time. "What do you like to eat?"

"Fried xchien is my favorite." He flailed enthusiastically, excited about the thought of tasty treats. "Well, really, anything fried is pretty good. I like crispy things on the outside, juicy in the middle. But for now, I'll settle for anything. Beggars can't be choosers, after all."

Great, she thought. The tentacle was also a foodie.

"What do *you* like to eat?" it asked her. It blinked, excitedly waiting for an answer. The tentacle seemed passionate about this topic.

"Lots of things," she said. "Where I come from, I'm a cook. A pretty damn good one, too. But for now, any sustenance that will help me survive will do. You're right. We currently don't have the luxury of being picky."

"A cook!" The tentacle wiggled back and forth, practically buzzing with happiness. "The Dread Ones must be gracing me with luck that I should find myself in the presence of one who can cook!"

She suspected that entities called Dread Ones probably had nothing to do with grace or good luck, but she didn't want to kill his vibe. They were already in enough of a dire situation that was cause for increasing alarm as the minutes passed. The longer they were here, the more they would need food. And, most importantly for her, clothes. She was pretty sure she could live with being hungry longer than she could live with being naked in a strange new world.

She pulled up her mini-map to see if there was anything nearby they should explore. She could see some of the cave system around her, and there was a whole area that appeared to be another chamber, marked with a question mark symbol.

"What are you thinking?" the tentacle asked. "You still with us? Looks like you zoned out or are staring off into space."

She blinked and the mini-map disappeared. She found the corresponding exit in the chamber that would lead in the direction of the question mark symbol she saw on the map.

"I'm thinking we should see what else is down in this cave."

* * *

As Nay and her new tentacle companion made their way through the network of winding passages, the tentacle slithering on what Nay came to think of its wider base or hindquarters, they started to notice some type of moss or fungus on the walls and ceiling that emitted a bluish-green glow. Perhaps it was lichen. Nay wasn't sure. The light was bright and it illuminated the way well enough for Nay to avoid stubbing her toes. It reminded her of the bioluminescence in ocean creatures.

She occasionally had to brace her hand on the wall for support, because walking on a cave floor in bare feet hurt. To make it even more inconvenient, the ground was also slick with condensation. The last thing she wanted was to crack her skull open by slipping naked on a rocky floor or impaling herself on a stalagmite.

"How far is this place up ahead?" the tentacle asked.

Nay glanced at her mini-map. "Not far. It should be coming up on our right side."

"I still can't believe you have a map that only you can see. How come I didn't get one of those?"

"If I had a nickel for every question I have right now, I'd qualify as a member of the billionaire oligarchy."

"What's a nickel?"

The wall moss grew brighter up ahead, and as they drew closer, they could both see a huge archway. Nay stopped. "Hold up; do you think this is dwarven architecture?"

"I don't know what *dwarven* means."

Nay looked at the tentacle and frowned. Why was there crossover with some things across their worlds but not others? The concept and nomenclature of dwarves should be a universal thing, she thought. "You know, like Helm's Deep? Black Rock Mountain? Cities built inside of mountains by short kings?"

"When I think of subterranean cities, I think of the Dread Ones and their magnificent necropoli underneath the Derleth Strait."

Nay heard humming up ahead. She motioned for the tentacle to be quiet. She put her finger to her lips—"Shhh"—pointed at her ear, and then gestured at the chamber beyond the arched entrance.

The tentacle swayed in that direction. Nay took that as a sign of his listening in that direction.

She was right.

Coming out of the chamber was someone humming a song.

She motioned at the tentacle to move quietly and then she started creeping along, putting down her heel first, then shifting onto her toes. A careful way of walking to create stealth. When she reached the archway, she cocked her head to peer inside.

The chamber within took her breath way. It was a huge pocket within the mountain, large enough to contain pillars carved from stone that shot up hundreds of feet to the ceiling. Buildings and statues were hewn out of the rock. It was the ruins of a stone city, illuminated by the blue-and-green light glowing from the moss on the ceiling high above. as if a moon within the mountain was shining down on the city.

Close to them, near an area of stone slabs, a black-cloaked figure crouched on a rock, their back to them. This person was stirring a pot over a small fire as they hummed a song. On a stone slab next to them were what appeared to be ingredients, herbs and cut-up root vegetables. And some type of large shell.

At that moment, a glowing text prompt appeared in Nay's vision.

[Quest Detected]
[Quest: Challenge and Defeat the Delicacy Forager]
[Accept Quest Y/N?]

— CHAPTER FOUR —

But I Have Zuppa

Nay scooted away from the archway and crouched with her back to the wall. She motioned for the tentacle to get closer. "There's someone there. They have a campfire going."

The tentacle got low and slithered towards the archway.

"Make sure you're not seen," Nay whispered.

Nay thought the tentacle nodded in acknowledgement before slowly peeking around the corner. It stretched its body taut and pressed itself to the archway before hooking around so its single eye could take a peek. Nay thought of a periscope in a submarine.

It retracted and came back to her.

"I don't like the looks of that person," the tentacle said.

"What makes you say that?"

"I'm not one to trust strangers."

"I'm with you there."

"What should we do? I think we can get the jump on them. We'll have the element of surprise."

"Are you suggesting attacking them?"

"Well, yeah. Why, what are you thinking?"

"I don't know. My mind doesn't go straight to killing, though."

"Then what else are we supposed to do?"

"We can just avoid them."

"We don't have to kill them; we could just tie them up and rob them."

"I don't know about you, but I don't really have experience in hand-to-hand combat. Plus, I don't even have any clothes—"

At that moment, a male voice interrupted them.

"You know, I can hear you out there. Why don't you come on in and join me? I could use the company."

Nay and the tentacle froze, staring at each other wide-eyed.

Nay was still pressed against the wall, but she had moved closer to the entrance.

"Go on, don't be shy," the voice said. "Show yourself."

Nay closed her eyes and debated with herself on what the play was. It still wasn't too late to run. But what if this person was friendly? It was a possibility, wasn't it?

"I know you're still there. Come on, now. It's rude to keep a gent waiting."

"I think we're okay out here, stranger," Nay said, projecting her voice.

"We don't have to stay strangers." The figure lit up some type of tobacco rolled up like a cigarette. They held a wick up to the rolled-up paper and started puffing, then shook out the ember and took a hit of their tobacco or whatever it was. "They call me Piero."

"Well, Piero," Nay said, "I think we'll be moving along. Places to go, things to see, you know?"

"But I have zuppa."

Zuppa? Nay thought. She knew that as an Italian dish. A winter soup, to be exact. Was she in Italy or somewhere nearby? Her stomach rumbled at the thought of a hot, hearty soup.

"Is he talking about food?" the tentacle said. "Would someone who meant us harm offer us food?"

"Made with tazoroot, too," Piero continued. "Which you know is out of season. Come on; surely you'll want to warm your belly with Piero's zuppa? Take some respite from the blizzard and this cold. Join me by my fire."

"Come on," the tentacle said. "Maybe we should at least try this zuppa."

"All right, quiet!" Nay hissed at the tentacle.

"I'll join you, but I have a caveat," Nay said.

"A caveat," Piero mused. "Well, now I'm intrigued."

"You don't happen to have an extra blanket or cloak, do you? I'm in a bit of a predicament."

Nay could feel Piero raise an eyebrow. "Something about your tone tells me you're not just cold. Can I ask how one comes to lose their clothes in the middle of a snowstorm near the peak of the Spineshards?"

Nay didn't recognize the name of that mountain range. But granted, her sense of international geography wasn't exactly Loremaster-level.

"It's a rather long and boring and probably confusing story," Nay said.

Nay peeked around the corner and saw Piero ruffle through his bedroll and grab what appeared to be a folded-up blanket. He looked up and she retreated back against the wall. She could hear him slowly approach, his boots scuffing the stone floor. Then the blanket landed in the entryway. "As you requested, my lady."

Nay reached out and quickly grabbed the blanket. It was soft and fluffy, and she realized it was a woolen blanket, and underneath the moss-light she could see it was dyed blue. She wrapped the blanket around her, feeling relief that she could cover herself. She whispered down at the tentacle, "You should stay invisible. Let me feel him out first."

"But," the tentacle said, "but the zuppa—"

"We still need to keep the element of surprise."

"But I want to try it—"

"I'll save some for you. Now hush. Stay unseen."

"Who are you talking to?" Piero said.

"Myself," Nay replied, stepping out through the archway. "It's a habit of mine."

She finally got a good look at Piero. He wasn't quite six feet but still taller than Nay. He had dark eyes, scruffy black hair, and thick stubble covered his lower face, just a day or two away from becoming a beard. He was dressed in a black fur coat that looked like it was stolen from a wolf and what appeared to be leather armor covering his chest and torso. She also noticed a dagger hilt sticking out of a leather scabbard.

It looked like he either walked out of a Renaissance festival or a cobblestone-laden back alleyway bathed in torchlight. Either way, there was something about him that Nay didn't like. She couldn't put her finger on it.

He looked at her quizzically, the hint of a smile at the corner of his mouth, and he studied her. This was a dangerous man. She regretted not walking away, no matter how much her stomach grumbled.

He turned and walked back towards his pot on the fire, only pausing to say over his shoulder, "Well, come on, then. Let's get a warm meal in you."

Nay glanced around, trying to see where the tentacle went. *What even is my life, right now?* she thought. *I feel more safe around a talking tentacle than another human being.* She got to the campfire and sat down on a large rock. He ladled hot broth and its contents into a wooden bowl and handed it to her with a wooden spoon. "Thank you," she said.

He sat across from her and took another hit of his cigarillo.

"What are you smoking?" she asked.

He exhaled a fragrant cloud of smoke that reminded her of burning cedar. "You are not familiar with brightleaf?"

"I'm not from around these parts."

"Where are you from?"

"Los Angeles."

He mouthed the words to himself. "I've never heard of it. Are you from the other side of these mountains?"

"You could say that."

His eyes glinted like black agates, reflecting the campfire, as he considered her words.

She looked down at the soup in the bowl. The fragrant steam wafting off the surface of the broth reminded her of minestrone. It was milky with chunks of what looked like potato, but it had more of a red tint. It was probably the tazoroot he mentioned. It was also sprinkled with a green herb that reminded her of parsley. She dipped her spoon into the soup and glanced up to see Piero watching her. Was it the watchful eyes of a cook excited to see her reaction to the taste? Or was that the look of darker intentions? She couldn't tell.

Her tummy grumbled again and she threw caution to the wind. She was already in dire straits, so she might as well not go hungry. She brought the spoon full of hot broth to her lips and took a taste. The receptors on her tongue had been fried since she got COVID. Her sense of taste was pretty much nonexistent, so she had to rely on her other senses to get some idea of the flavor.

Her vision, sense of smell and touch, combined with her memory and knowledge, played a role in helping her scry the quality of a dish.

From the consistency and texture of the broth, she could tell it was salty and creamy. The chunk of tazoroot she chewed on was soft, and she knew by the sensation that it was starchy. It reminded her of potato chowder, and her stomach practically moaned from the sheer pleasure of being fed something that was actually good. If her numbed tongue was ever confused, her gut could reliably provide her with answers when all else failed. The green herb must have been dill or whatever its similar analogue was in this world.

"It's good, isn't it?" Piero said. He took another hit of his brightleaf. "It's a recipe I picked up from my favorite tavern. Keeps you full and warm when you're hemmed in by snow and ice."

He smoked and she ate in silence save for the crackling fire. Soon her bowl was empty and his cigarillo was down to the nub. "You can have some more if you're still hungry."

She wanted more, but she also remembered she told the tentacle she would save it some. She held her bowl in her lap and gestured at the ruins around them. "What is this place?"

He gave her a curious look. "You mean you don't know?"

She shook her head. "Like I said, I'm new around here."

"This used to be a maugrim city before the Scar appeared. Now, it's just ruins."

Maugrim? The Scar? She wasn't sure what he was talking about. And although she wanted to ask, she wasn't sure how much to tip her hat that she was *really new* to the area.

"You don't happen to have extra clothes, do you?" she said.

"My turn to ask questions," he said, crushing the nub of his cigarillo, extinguishing the ember into ash. "How does one end up completely nude in the ruins of Paleforge?"

"Would you believe me if I told you I got into a tussle with some monsters that resulted in my current state of affairs?"

"It's believable, yes," Piero nodded. "These mountains are full of strange beasts, especially this close to the vicinity of the Scar. But what fascinates me is how you were able to survive."

"I'm a resourceful gal. So . . . how 'bout those clothes?"

"You've tasted my hospitality. My zuppa, my warm fire. My blanket. Perhaps I could procure you garments in exchange for some of your hospitality. It has been too many moons since Piero has experienced the hospitality of a woman."

Her back straightened and her hand went to the stone she had set next to her underneath the blanket. She took a breath and tried to appear still while she used her peripheral vision to try and find the tentacle.

"On second thought," she said, "I think I should be going."

"If that is the case," Piero said, "then I'll be needing my blanket back."

Nay chuckled to herself. It was a grim chuckle. She shook her head and knew this turn of events shouldn't be surprising to her. She stood to her feet, clutching the stone in her hand, the wool blanket still wrapped around her.

"Fine," she said. She whipped the blanket off her and threw it at him. She didn't stop to watch it enfold him but instead darted for the archway.

The quest prompt returned over her vision with a cheery chime.

[Quest Accepted!]
[Quest: Challenge and Defeat the Delicacy Forager!]

"What?" she exclaimed. "No! I don't want to defeat the Delicacy Forager! I want to escape!"

She ran for her life.

Behind her, Piero extricated himself from the blanket and leapt to his feet. He drew his dagger and pursued her.

Adrenaline surged through Nay, making her ignore the pain she felt on her bare feet as she traversed the sharp and rocky stone floor. She could sense Piero chasing her, and she didn't want to peek behind her and lose her momentum. But then she tripped and went crashing and sliding across the moist chamber floor.

The adrenaline rush didn't numb her from the pain of sliding headfirst into the base of a stalagmite. She felt the pressure on her head and she saw stars. She groaned in pain. The entire side of her body stung. She didn't have time to gain her senses when Piero appeared above her, brandishing the dagger.

Her eyes found his and she saw desire burning in his darkened eye-sockets.

"Yes," he said, breathily. "Piero will be taking from you some hospitality."

He lowered himself on top of her, and she felt his brightleaf-strong hot breath. He also reeked of alcohol and sweat. Her hands searched for the stone she had been clutching, but he pinned her wrist down with his hand. He put the tip of his dagger at her cheek. It stung like a bee sting. A bee sting that drew blood.

"The Celestia must be smiling down on Piero to find such an offering in this place."

As he crushed her, trying to force himself on her, his lips mere millimeters away from hers, he let out a cough like a wet sneeze, his face contorting in pain and freezing in a grimace. A wheeze came out of him like a slow whine. He vibrated on top of her like he was fighting some type of inner battle.

"Take his dagger and use it on him."

Nay looked over and saw the tentacle focused on Piero. Its entire body pointed at him like a tuning fork, engaged in some kind of mentalism. It was practically buzzing with some sort of psychic energy.

"Hurry," the tentacle said through gritted teeth. "I can't hold him still for much longer."

She found her hand was free as his grip loosened. His dagger clattered to the floor. She stared at the weapon as Piero tried to resist the tentacle's psychic attack. They were engaged in a battle of wills.

"What are you waiting for?!" the tentacle shouted. It let out a cry, and suddenly Piero collapsed on her, gaining control of his body again.

Nay grabbed the dagger and drove it into his side.

As a cook, Nay had butchered her fair share of animal carcasses. Cow. Deer. Rabbit. Chicken. Fish. Turkey. But she had never stabbed a human being. Much less a human being that was alive. But the sensation of cold metal penetrating flesh and muscle and bone was a familiar one. Except this time there was resistance.

Piero let out a terrible cry. Nay twisted the blade and jerked the weapon upwards, and she knew she had bisected a kidney. Sticky, warm blood spilled over her hand and between her fingers grasping the hilt. She kept the blade jammed in him until he stopped breathing, releasing a final pained wheeze into her face. His body fell atop her, totally limp.

There was a congratulatory chime and the quest prompt appeared again.

[Quest Complete!]
[Challenge and Defeat the Delicacy Forager Completed!]
[Congratulations!]
[You have been rewarded Vigor Points]

Nay wondered who was screaming when she realized it was her.

— CHAPTER FIVE —

Delicacy Detected

When Nay came out of her fugue, driven into shock by killing Piero, she was wrapped in his wool blanket, her arms wrapped around her knees, which were pulled up to her chest, and she was rocking back and forth.

The tentacle had its beak deep into the pot of zuppa and was making slurping noises and moans of pleasure. Piero's belongings were untouched, and she saw his feet poking out behind the boulder where they had left him, his body now growing cold. His blood had dried on her fingers, hand, and forearm. It was still sticky to the touch, and she shuddered at feeling the congealed blood clinging to her skin.

Her mind kept going to the moment the dagger had entered him. At how the writhing of his muscles quivered down into the blade and into her palm. Was there any other option she had? Was there any outcome where his death could have been avoided after he made his decision to attack her?

Then she realized if it wasn't for what the tentacle did, some kind of mind or psychic attack, it would probably be her body growing cold on that floor.

She rose to her feet, walked over to Piero's belongings, and grabbed his waterskin. She poured water onto her hand and tried to scrub the blood off. It did little except remove some of the top layer of dried blood. Mostly, it spread it around. She could feel her tears well up in frustration.

"It's not coming off!" she cried, violently scrubbing but just smearing the red onto her clean hand.

The tentacle poked its head out of the pot, its top half covered in the zuppa and dripping off its beak. "You're back! This zuppa is better than I thought it would be! Kind of reminds me of the birthing fluid and formula baths from back home when I was just a tendril. Yes, such creaminess and heartiness. A fine broth for a young flayling to fatten up!"

Then it realized Nay was in some distress. It spoke in a calming tone. "We can go back to the hot springs. You need hot water to wash that off. In the meantime, we should loot."

"Loot?" Nay said.

"Yeah, see if he has anything we can use," the tentacle said.

"Isn't that the same thing as robbing him?"

"Does it look like he still needs any of this stuff? He's shuffled off to the nether life. This stuff will be useless to him."

Nay was taken with a dark thought. "We've turned into murderers . . . and thieves."

"He was going to do the same thing to us. He forced our hands. Well, your hands, but my Mind Shiv."

"Mind Shiv?"

"It's one of my spells. It's what I used on him before he was going to cut you."

"You . . . have spells?"

Nay felt overwhelmed. First with this new reality she found herself in. Second with taking Piero's life. And now third this idea that the tentacle had spells, which meant he was using magic. "Magic is real?"

"You don't have magic where you come from?" the tentacle asked. A long, green tongue emerged from his beak and licked the zuppa off its body. "Oy, your world really is a basic one."

Nay couldn't tell if he was washing himself or merely eating the soup off its body. But after a moment she realized, apparently, it was both. He was multitasking.

"We have science and math," she said. "We don't have spells; we have knowledge and algorithms. Not . . . incantations and what did you call it? Mind Shivs?"

"Mind Shiv," the tentacle said. "If you think about it, magic is just another form of knowledge. Maybe your world just hasn't come across that particular knowledge yet."

Nay exhaled and said to herself, "One reality-shattering revelation at a time, Nay. One at a time."

She moved to Piero's pile of stuff. His belongings included his rolled-out bedroll, his cooking kit, which was next to the fire, and his leather pack. She began taking items out of the pack. Smaller rolled-up bags and kits and also what appeared to be dried meat and biscuits wrapped in cloth.

But no extra pair of clothes.

She looked over at his corpse, knowing she was going to have to strip him.

"What's wrong?" the tentacle asked.

"I'm not exactly excited at the prospect of wearing a dead man's clothes."

"Would you rather be naked and cold?"

"That's the fucking problem."

The tentacle started to rifle through the various kits, inspecting Piero's stuff. "Let's see if there's anything good in this loot."

Nay walked back to Piero's corpse and began the unpleasant task of stripping him of his clothes. The human body was weird when it was lifeless. The man had died with his eyes open, so the first thing she did was close his eyes. She shuddered as her fingertips touched his eyelids. But, all in all, in principle, it wasn't that much different from a handling the carcass of a large animal.

She was a trained butcher. Her grandfather had made sure of that, and she had learned how to harvest the meat off poultry, pork, beef, and wild game in his shop before she had even gained a large knowledge of cooking.

It took her some time to figure out how to remove the man's leather tunic and how to undo and unbuckle his scabbard. She set those and his dagger to the side. She removed his cloth shirt and saw the silver chain around his neck. There was a small key on the end of it. She removed it and stared at the chain and key in her hand.

Then she slipped it around her own neck. Could be useful if they found the corresponding lock.

She removed his boots, then wrestled his pants off his legs. She drew the line at his undergarments. She'd rather go commando then wear someone else's dirty underwear, especially his.

She wished she could at least wash the shirt and pants before having to wear them but then decided she'd take care of that back at the hot springs. She shimmied into his pants, which were made out of a sturdy material that wasn't quite leather. She had to roll up the legs, as they were too long for her. She used the dagger to cut away the part of the shirt where the stab wound was, cutting away the bloody cloth. She slipped it on and it hung off her, loose and baggy. Then she put on his boots. A little big, but they would do.

She picked up the scabbard and dagger and carried them back to the campfire.

"Well," the tentacle said, making an appraisal of the loot, "we didn't come out rich, but I think there's some useful stuff here."

It had nudged the items so they were spread out across the floor. "There's enough dried meat and cheese here to last us a while. He's got some seasoning mixes and salt in these containers. Basic upkeep for his gear, oils and sharpening stones. There's a journal or notebook here, but I'll let you take a look at that."

It tapped an item with one of its spiky green protuberances. "This is a badge of some sort; looks to be made from bronze or something similar to it. Could be worth something. Not sure what the symbol signifies."

"Then there's this." It was a wooden chest with metal locks, about a foot long. "You didn't happen to find a key on him, did you?"

Nay's hand went to the key dangling on the chain at her neck. She pulled it out of the shirt to show the tentacle.

"Bingo!" the tentacle said. "Now we can find out if this loot isn't a total bust. Well, other than some basic necessities we found. But it would be nice if there's something more exciting than salt and seasoning in this chest!"

Nay took the chest and sat in front of the campfire. She ran her hands across the wood grain. Then there was a ding, and a text prompt appeared in her vision.

[Delicacy Detected]

"What is it?" the tentacle asked.
"You don't see those words?" Nay replied.
"What words?"
"I get this text I can see hovering in the air." She pointed in front of her. "You don't see that?"
The tentacle shook its top half. "Nope. What does it say?"
"It says 'Delicacy Detected.'"
"Curious," the tentacle said. "Very curious."

Nay removed the chain from around her and fit the tiny key into the lock. She turned it and there was a *click*. The top cracked open and glowing yellow motes drifted into the air like fireflies floating through an open window during a violet summer night. She pushed the lid up, revealing an object nestled in a velvet case like it was fine jewelry.

At first, Nay had no idea what she was looking at. There was something plump and grayish-pink emitting a yellow glow. Motes swirled in the air within the aura. The object was about half the size of a cucumber. It conjured up images of cow tongue before Nay transformed it into lengua tacos.

"What in the Endless Nether Hell fuck is that?" the tentacle said.

There was a crescendoing series of notes that reminded Nay of opening loot boxes in video games. Or like when Link finds a good item in *Zelda*. A victorious tone that hit right in the dopamine center of the brain. And another text prompt appeared, but this time with a lightshow visual flair.

[Delicacy Discovered!]
[Delicacy: Tongue of the Hierophant]
[Delicacies Unlocked 0/3]
[Would you like to Consume Delicacy Y/N?]

It looked like a tongue severed at the base and ripped out of someone or something's mouth.

"It says it's a Delicacy called Tongue of the Hierophant," Nay said.

"That's what your magic words say?" the tentacle said.

Nay nodded. "I mean, I don't know if they're magic per se . . ."

"What else would they be? You're seeing words floating in the air that are providing you with information I'm not privy to. And probably no one else is privy to, either. Look at you, evolving. You can do magic, too! Whether you know it or not."

"Well, then it's more of a Passive Ability. It's like . . . seeing reality's underlying menu screen if life were a video game."

"What's a video game?"

"You don't have video games where you're from?"

"The only games I'm familiar with involve death and eternal enslavement."

"That sounds . . . awful."

"Depends which side you're on."

Nay continued to stare at the tongue. She didn't know if she would consider tongue a delicacy, not cow tongue at least. Maybe an organ from another, more exotic creature. But lengua was a pretty common food in Los Angeles. Especially in street taco culture. Was it the Hierophant part that made it rare?

"What's a Hierophant?" she said.

"A hierophant?" the tentacle said. "Do you know what a priest is?"

"Of course I know what a priest is."

"How am I supposed to know what your world has and doesn't have? We're all just trying to survive here."

Nay rolled her eyes.

"A hierophant is like a priest, someone who deals with mysteries and esoteric rituals," the tentacle said.

"Cult shit."

"I mean, or religion. In my world, Dread One worship is the main religion and it's not considered cultish at all. But now, the All-Seeing Omnipotent and Loving God Worshippers?" Its eyeball rolled around in its socket. "You want to see a crazy person? Deal with one of those guys.

"So, we have the tongue of some kind of priest or shaman here," the tentacle continued to say. "What else are your magic words saying?"

"It's asking if I want to consume it."

"What? The tongue?"

"I think so."

"Gross."

"Probably," Nay said. "Wait, you never use tongue in dishes in your world?"

"I've heard of it but it personally grosses me out."

Nay just stared at the tentacle, perplexed. What an odd creature it was. "I'm also seeing information that I have zero Delicacies unlocked. And there's three total Delicacy slots."

The tentacle thought about this puzzle for a moment. "It sounds like more magic of some kind. Maybe you can only consume three Delicacies? It's hard to know. Maybe you should just consume it so we can explore this further. But I have to admit, the fact that you can see this magic and I can't is starting to make me jealous. I wonder how I can see these magic words too."

Nay sniffed the Tongue of the Hierophant. Despite its unappealing appearance, there was a fragrant smell to it that made her think of beef jerky. Even though COVID had ruined her sense of taste, she was thankful her smell was mostly intact, or at least trustworthy.

"I mean, if you consume it," the tentacle said, "what's the worst that could happen? It tastes terrible? That's assuming that's what *consume* means. Although I do have a cousin who consumes his food through his skin. But he's special."

"My sense of taste has been destroyed, mostly."

"Destroyed? How?"

"There was a sickness going around in my world. A flu of sorts. It was new, and many people's bodies didn't know how to deal with it. I recovered, but it did something to my taste buds and my tongue. I haven't really been able to taste anything since. It sucks but I'm glad I was one of the ones who survived."

"You have no sense of taste and you're a cook?"

Nay nodded. "I still have my memory and my instincts. You'd be surprised by how much knowledge, routine, and technique can get me by."

"Still, that's quite the handicap for a chef."

"I manage."

She pulled up the Tongue Delicacy menu again and stared at the text. "Well, I think you're right about this. There's only one way to find out." She mentally selected *Yes* to consume the Delicacy. Another text box appeared:

Congratulations on your Delicacy, Tongue of the Hierophant! There's some Hierophant out there who has been rendered mute (or dead!), either a willing or an unwilling sacrifice, so that you may unlock a Delicacy, the first prerequisite in acquiring Marrow Abilities.

Either way, for best results, you'll want to give the Epicurist of your choice these instructions for proper preparation. The ingredients you will need are:

Oil.

Water.

Salt.
Garlic.
Onion.
Bay leaves.
Peppercorns.

Note: It is not recommended to consume the tongue raw, but if you're a savage with no time to savor your Delicacy, at least make sure the Epicurist seasons the tongue with salt to meet proper ritual cooking requirements. But if you're a Marrow Eater with taste and sophistication, let your Epicurist boil and simmer the tongue in the water with onion, bay leaves, peppercorn, and garlic for three hours. Once done, make sure they remove the skin-like covering before slicing into strips and sautéing. Enjoy it wrapped in a tortilla of flour or mais with a nice pico or salsa with condiments of your choice. We recommend pickled red onions and crumbled goat cheese.

If you're not a fan of tortillas, it is also acceptable to prepare a pita, flatbread, or bing. In these instances of preparation, a purple cabbage slaw or some chopped scallions would work well as condiments.

Or feel free to let the Epicurist surprise you! All sanctioned Epicurists are trained in the proper ritual cooking techniques to activate the Delicacies!

Enjoy!

— CHAPTER SIX —

The Tongue of the Hierophant

Nay had the Tongue of the Hierophant simmering in a pot of water. The tentacle demanded that she prepare it as best as they could. Despite her chef's sensibilities, she had considered consuming the tongue raw. She wouldn't really taste it, anyways, and she wanted to learn more about what a delicacy was. But in the end, she opted for patience and succumbed to the menu's demands.

Piero's cooking kit surprisingly had both onions and bay leaves. He did have salt on him. In the other seasonings she found, she discovered peppercorns, onion powder, and a few cloves of garlic. She had tossed it all into the pot, which the tentacle had made sure to lick clean of the zuppa.

She had taken the dirty pot back to the hot springs, where she rinsed it in one of the smaller pools. She didn't want to use any of the freshwater from Piero's flask, which she used to clean her hands, because she realized they would still have to locate a freshwater source. She thought she saw a stream when she zoomed into her mini-map, but she couldn't tell. There were no labels. She wondered if that would ever change, if there was like a magical upgrade or something.

She had decided to bathe again in the hot springs, feeling unclean after fighting and killing a man. But there was no washing away guilt. She had cleaned the rest of Piero's dried blood off her arm, and she even decided to soak and scrub his dirty shirt, even though she didn't have any soap. She figured scrubbing it in the hot water was better than nothing. She hung his shirt to dry on a rock and returned to the large cave that gave way to the ruins of the old subterranean city. The tentacle had already seen her nude. He was a tentacle, after all, and not some horny man or woman. She had a feeling he wasn't horny. If he had any carnal desires, she was pretty sure she wasn't really his type. Plus, she didn't want to spend the next few hours with a wet shirt clinging to her.

The tentacle was hovering around the pot, basking in the aroma wafting out of it.

"What do I call you, anyways?" Nay said.

"What do you mean?" the tentacle said.

"Like, Nazxth—sorry—your full name, it's a mouthful. What's something that's easier to say I could call you?"

"Easier?"

"There's other, more practical reasons other than just convenience. If we're ever in a situation like . . ." She nodded at Piero's corpse, ". . . you know. And I have to get your attention or communicate with you. I need something easy to say on the fly. And I'm tired of thinking of you as *the tentacle* in my head."

"Let me think on it."

And think he really did. The tentacle grew silent for the rest of the time the tongue simmered. Nay could hear him muttering to himself, but she couldn't make out anything concrete he was saying.

As she stirred the pot with the wooden spoon, her mind went back to her life when things were normal. Which, she figured, was just a few days ago. Before the horrific events in the Korean church. Before the El Diablo burrito. Even before the encounter with the first tentacled creature in an alleyway that night she almost died.

She wondered if Remi, Taco the Town's sous-chef, had called the police to report her missing. He would be the first to know that something was wrong, as the taco truck and her employees depended on her, as she was head chef and owner. It was unlike her to neither show up for a shift nor be in touch with them. So, her absence would be immediately noticed.

The taco truck was her life. She had poured all of her savings in it when she had fled New Orleans for Los Angeles after her fallout with Chef Jean at Café Melville. After her experience there, pouring years of her life into her craft, after what he did, there was no way she was going to stay in New Orleans. The city became tainted for her and she had needed a fresh start. So, Los Angeles it was.

It was not just her dream to have a successful taco truck, but it was how she survived. Profits had slowly been growing, and she forecast that within a year, she'd be able to purchase and set up another truck. And since they had been about to go viral after the El Diablo burrito fiasco, that goal would have been a quicker reality. The truck and her coworkers were her life.

The only family she had was her mother, who was back in Louisiana, but they talked every other week at best. Her mother worried over her choice to go somewhere like Los Angeles, but she had a busy life of her own with her bakery.

Nay didn't have a boyfriend or girlfriend. No lovers other than drunken or high one-night stands with people she met in the bar. These people might have just as well been warm bodies. These encounters ticked off a physical craving.

No strings attached. Which meant no emotions. She never caught a case over these brief flings. There was never time for anything serious. The restaurant worker's life was a hectic one. They were creatures of the night, and the schedule wreaked havoc on relationships, especially if the partner was someone with a normal schedule.

So, other than her Taco the Town people and eventually her mother, there would be no one really missing her. She'd just become another missing-persons statistic or unsolved mystery, which Los Angeles already had thousands of. She was sure she'd be barely a blip on the radar.

She wasn't quite sure how she felt about it.

"Is it done yet?" the tentacle asked, pulling her out of her thoughts.

She rolled the tongue around in the water with the spoon, inspecting the color. The glowing yellow motes continued to sparkle in the water and drift into the air with the steam. The color resembled the brown of cooked pork, and the skin-like covering on the appendage had turned yellow, making it look like it was encased in a condom. The onion had grown translucent and the bay leaves swirled around the edge of the pot. She fanned the steam into her face.

"Looks done," she said. "Smells done."

She took the pot off the fire and set it to the side. She fished the tongue out with her spoon and Piero's dagger. She shuddered at the thought of using it to handle food, but she had spent a good amount of time cleaning it, and there was no trace of blood left. She convinced herself the hot spring had sanitized the blade. She didn't want to scald her hand in hot water, either, which was another reason to use the knife.

She set the steaming tongue on a rock to let it cool. Then she went towards a depression in the cavern floor, where she poured out most of the broth. Before she fully emptied it, she wondered if she could use it as stock. She set the pot back down, walked back to find an empty clay pot in Piero's kit. Which, she figured, was now her kit. She used it to store some of the broth.

She poured some of the cooking oil into the pot. She sniffed it. It smelled exactly like olive oil. She put the pot back on the fire and went to the task of removing the skin-like covering on the tongue. She perforated it with the tip of the dagger and peeled it off, tossing it to the side. It clung to her fingertips for a second, like used sausage casing. Then she proceeded to slice the Tongue of the Hierophant into thin slices. The meat was soft and it parted, smooth and buttery as velvet.

She knew from its texture it was a quality ingredient.

If the tentacle had hands, she was sure it would be clapping in anticipation. "For tongue, that looks pretty good! I actually can't wait to try it!"

She gingerly dropped the slices into the hot oil in the pot. It immediately started to sizzle. She was hit with a pleasant aroma that actually made her salivate. She let it cook for a minute on one side before flipping each piece with the dagger so it would evenly cook. She took some of the flatbread from Piero's pack and cut into two pieces, forming a pocket, creating flatbread pouches. She took a nibble of the flatbread, but other than the dry texture and the hint of wheat, she couldn't really taste it.

The seared and cooked tongue now emitted an even brighter glow, as if the preparation process had activated the dormant magic within. There was some satisfying char to each side and it looked tantalizing. She took each piece with the dagger and tucked them into the two pieces of flatbread.

Nay set the tentacle's serving on a stone next to the creature. "It's a shame we don't have any condiments or sauce, as I think a good purple cabbage slaw would go great with this, but maybe it'll still be good."

The tentacle hummed with hunger and excitement. It moved to devour it, but then stopped. "Wait. Since you're the chef, you do the honors."

"I think you're just afraid that it's poisonous or something," Nay said. She held up her serving. "Well, down the hatch!"

She took a big bite, and the first thing she noticed was that her tongue was hit with an explosion of flavor. It had been almost half a year since she had been able to taste anything, so the sudden activity in her palate almost bowled her over. She closed her eyes and had to lean on her hand as the waves of taste rolled over her.

The tongue melted like butter in her mouth, releasing a savory and rich umami flavor. The slight sear on both sides created a crispy char that gave way to a juicy bite. The flatbread sang of olive oil and dough, and was the perfect carb-laden counterpart to the tongue itself. Together, the harmony of mouth-feel and taste was simply debilitating in its power of pleasure.

It was pure ecstasy.

She wasn't sure if her problem with her taste buds had finally been cured, if the Delicacy had awakened the sleeping nerve receptors. She didn't know if it was a magical temporary thing, or if it was a permanent effect. Either way, she was enjoying the moment. She wanted to hold on to it forever, in case the effect was fleeting.

As that first bite hit her gut, a warm feeling birthed in her stomach and began to spread throughout her body. She imagined a gold light going super-nova in her belly and following the trail of her veins and painting everything gold. Waves of dizziness made her lie down as the light made her circulatory and nervous system glow so bright, it was visible through her skin as if she was translucent.

"Uh"—the tentacle backed away—"what is happening?"

Nay saw stars and a galaxy before her eyes as if she was given a glimpse to the heavens like she was having a celestial visitation or experience. She was aware of a series of dings before more prompts floated into her vision, the letters exploding like part of a galaxy being born.

[Delicacy Unlocked!]
[Tongue Delicacy Unlocked!]
[1/3 Delicacies]

Then another menu opened up beneath it:

[Marrow Ability Path Unlocked]
[Prerequisite: Yes]
[Marrow of the Tongue]
[Rank: Base 2%]
[0/12 Ability Slots in this Tree]

1. Congratulations, you have unlocked a Delicacy [1/3] and have activated Marrow Abilities. Since you meet the Prerequisite for Marrow Abilities, you may now consume Marrow to awaken Abilities [0/12] within the Marrow of the Tongue Ability Tree.
To help you find and identify Marrow, you've been granted the Passive Ability of Detect Marrow.
Detect Marrow means your senses have been awakened to the existence of Marrow.
You've also unlocked the Tongue of the Hierophant Delicacy Passive, Chef's Kiss, Rank 2. (It appears you possessed Chef's Kiss, Rank 1 as a Traveler Passive Ability.)
Chef's Kiss gives you the ability to prepare Delicacies for proper consumption.
Note: Only Delicacies prepared by those with the Chef's Kiss Ability can be properly unlocked and harnessed for consumption.

Nay sat up, overwhelmed. "Holy shit."

The tentacle looked at her, jealous, and immediately bit into its serving. He released little grunts of delight and glee. It sounded ironically like *Nom nom nom!*

Dazed, Nay had another revelation in this series of awakenings as she watched the tentacle eat.

"I got it," she said. "I know what I'm going to call you."

He looked up at her as he ate.

"I'm going to call you Nom!" she said.

"Nom?"

"As in *nom nom nom*."

The tentacle devoured the rest of its tongue flatbread with gusto and shrugged.

"Works for me," Nom said between bites.

— CHAPTER SEVEN —

Hunting Marrow

Nom started to change colors as his digestive system started to break down the tongue-flatbread meal. The purple-shaded tentacle began to turn yellow, but not in a sickly way. The new shade and color spread throughout his stalk like a droplet of ink spreading as a cloud through water. The yellow began to brighten and morph into a golden glow that sparkled underneath his skin. He looked kind of like a lava lamp that just got turned on, the yellow, gold, and purple colors all mixing together and glowing.

"Whoa," Nay said. "Looks like the Delicacy is doing something to you, too."

"The taste," Nom said. "I would have never thought that tongue could be so delicious. You are a fantastic chef!"

"Thanks, but I think I owe a lot to the quality of the ingredients."

"Don't sell yourself short. You definitely worked some magic in your preparation and execution of this dish."

Nay wondered how much the Chef's Kiss Passive played a part in this meal. She had a feeling that it allowed her to level up with her cooking. But all in all, it was a pretty simple dish to prepare.

"How are you feeling?" Nay asked. "Is it normal for you to change colors when you eat?"

"This is the first time anything like this has happened. I'm telling you, you worked some magic."

"But do you feel any different?"

The gold glow settled and Nom's skin returned to the normal purple. "It's hard to explain but my senses feel heightened. Especially my sense of smell and taste. They feel . . . sharper."

Nay wondered if the Delicacy had given him the magical changes it had unlocked and activated in her. "You don't see any magic words or prompts in your vision? Like screen menus?"

Nom sighed. "I wish. No, no magical prompts. Just a strange feeling something is different now."

"Weird."

"That's certainly one way to put it. Things have been weird ever since we met."

As they relaxed after their magical meal experience, Nay rifled through the rest of Piero's belongings. Of particular interest to her was the leather journal. It was battered from traveling in the harsh elements, its leather cover creased and worn. The interior pages seemed fibrous, the pigmentation brown and gray. Examining the ink scrawl of Piero's handwriting provided her with a strange experience.

Underneath her mini-map in the upper right corner of her vision, a line of small text blinked. She zoomed into it:

[Worldtripper Passive: Rosetta Stone]
[In Use]

She was aware the glyphs and symbols that were written on the page weren't English, and while they were obviously a foreign alphabet and language to her, she could still read it. Whatever a Worldtripper Passive was, she was sure the Rosetta Stone Ability was translating the foreign language for her in her brain.

More magic.

The journal seemed to be a travel log of jobs he was on. He was hunting Delicacies and something called Marrow.

She read part of the latest entry aloud to Nom:

"To the nether hells with it. I've finally made my decision. I'm traveling north, beyond the Spineshards, to forage the ruins of Paleforge for the one Marrow that can completely change my fortune. I have it on good authority the Steksis dwells there. There's a guide from Skullcap who will help me traverse the mountain range to get there. His expertise is costing me everything, but like my father, I'm a gambler."

He had also sketched out the map he was working on of the cave system and ruins. Up ahead, the remains of the city itself were unmapped.

In his pack, clipped to the back of his badge, was a folded-up piece of paper that was a license of sorts. It said:

Piero Del'Ami.
Authorized Delicacy Forager Licensed by the Delicatessa Marrow Authority.
Authorized Agent of the DMA.

The bottom half of the page was a large wax stamp of the DMA, which Nay interpreted as the *Delicatessa Marrow Authority*.

"What the hell is the Delicatessa Marrow Authority?" Nay said.

Nom perked up. He scooted over to take a look for himself. "If Delicacies and Marrow are a type of magic, it sounds like someone has a finger on them. Where I come from, there's a lot of money in whoever controls and governs magical resources. Sounds like someone is smart here, too, and has the same idea."

"So, he was here because he was looking for a Marrow," Nay said. "I suppose now is as good a time as any to discuss next steps. It's probably not wise for us to stay in this mountain forever. We only have so much food. And I don't know about you, but I'm not exactly a hunter or trapper. We'll have to find a freshwater source. That's probably the first thing we should do."

"I want to know more about this Marrow," Nom said. "And what is the Steksis he mentioned?"

"I think we can worry about that once we find a stream or something."

"Why don't we just take some of the hot-spring water in the pot and flasks and let it cool?"

"That's a start. If it turns out it's good to drink, we'll use that, then. But I also think, when the weather permits, we try to find civilization. We know there's people in this world, so there has to be towns, villages, even cities."

Nom shuddered. "I don't do so well out in the cold."

"You're telling me you want to stay down here?"

"I like subterranean spaces. Where I come from, it's where me and my kind dwelt mostly. In the dark and moist places underneath the earth."

"Yeah, I love that for you. But that's not really my vibe."

"What if we find food down here, though? If we have a source of food in addition to water, then we won't have to leave."

"Yeah, I don't think that's the play."

Nom looked around, then lowered his head. He sighed. "You're probably right. Aren't you . . ." He trailed off.

"Aren't I what?" Nay asked.

"Aren't you afraid of what might be out there?"

"I'm terrified. I'm also afraid of what might be down here, too. But I want to survive and figure out what this world is. And for that, we need to find people. Maybe even someone might be able to help us get back to where we came from. Our homes."

"I don't want to go back to my world, though."

"You don't?"

Nom's green protuberances quivered in agitation. "Hell, no. I go back there, they're going to try and reconnect me to a host body. That's the last thing I want. Do you know what it's like to have some douchebag monster making all of my decisions for me? That just needs to use me as an appendage, that needs me to be a leg or an arm or a hand? It's the worst. I'd rather perish here than go back to that."

Nay thought of working for Chef Jean as his sous-chef at Café Melville. She knew a little too much what it was like to be used solely as a tool or a means to an end, to have someone in power try to assert their control over her. "Point taken," she said.

They had decided to set up base in the hot-springs chamber. They had filled the pot and one of the waterskins with hot water and left them there to let them cool. Nay had scraped some of the bioluminescent lichen off the wall and created makeshift torches by tying them to some sticks Piero had in his pack. They had also used the glowing lichen to mark the path from the hot spring to the entrance of the cave so they could check every day to monitor the conditions outside. When the blizzard was gone, they would trek out and explore.

Nay rationed out what was left of the dried meat, cheese, and flatbread, and calculated they had maybe a week's worth of food before they would have to acquire some more.

In the days while they waited for the weather to get better, they spent their time exploring the ruins of Paleforge. All the structures of the former city were hewn out of the stone, and lumber and timber had been brought in to supplement the scaffolding of what had been under construction before the place was abandoned. Nay had also identified iron amongst the cogs, chains, and giant discs she glimpsed up above or deep in the carved-out walls of the stone architecture. Which meant the city dwellers here probably mined the ore deep in the mountains Piero referred to as the Spineshards. Every quarter of the city seemed to revolve around giant forges that had grown cold over the long passage of time.

In their exploration, they had found wide stairs that led to some sort of mead hall, a long, squat structure that was probably a gathering place of note, because it was decorated with statues of the maugrim carved out of the stone. They were muscular and stout creatures, and almost exactly like the concept of dwarves Nay was familiar with. But their arms were long, the knuckles almost dragging the ground. And they barely had any necks. Their torsos seemed to be comprised entirely of chiseled muscle.

Nay stood in front of one of the statues, looking up at it in awe. "I wonder what happened to them."

"Piero mentioned something called the Scar," Nom said. "The way he said it, it sounded like there was a connection between it and the fate of this city turning into ruins."

At that moment, a green dot blipped on Nay's mini-map at the corner of her vision, getting her attention. A text prompt blinked under the map.

[Tongue of the Hierophant Delicacy Trait]
[Detect Marrow]
[Status: In Use]

She got a glimpse of the green dot, but then it moved north and disappeared off the map. She zoomed in and saw that there was a spiral-shaped chamber up north.

"I just felt something," Nom said.

Nay looked down at him, his whole body craning towards the north as if he was trying to get a better look. But since the only thing in this section was the mead hall they were in front of, he was just looking at the stone wall beyond. They'd have to go back up the stairs and head north through the city.

"You did?" she asked.

"It was like a cold wind passing through me, nudging me in that direction. But it's gone now."

So, it appeared consuming the Delicacy did leave Nom with something other than a pleasant bite to eat. Seems like he could Detect Marrow as well, but he just experienced it in a different way. His interface was more feel, while hers manifested in video-game prompts and menu screens.

"I think the Marrow Piero was hunting for is somewhere north of us," Nay said.

Nom was already slinking back up the stairs like a slinky in reverse.

Nay wielded the stick with the glowing lichen like it was a torch, holding it in front of them so the eerie green eldritch light illuminated their path through the city ruins.

The north side of the city appeared to be some sort of religious or spiritual quarter, as every block in the hexagonal grid seemed to contain a temple or building meant for a place of worship. Each one had a small statue set into an alcove above the entrance archway.

It was of a maugrim holding an ornate blacksmith hammer in one hand and what appeared to be a diamond in the other. Shafts of blue light emanating from the lichen above illuminated this quarter, and the blue light reflected off the diamonds in such a way to suggest that these temples and the placement of the alcoves were designed this way, to catch the light.

Nay saw what looked like runic markings below the figurines. Her internal Rosetta Stone translated it into the name *Voreheim*.

"Must be some type of deity or holy personage for them," she said.

"Doesn't look like he tried to help them, unless it was escaping the calamity here," Nom mused.

Nay couldn't shake the feeling that they were being watched. What if it was another person? Would she have to kill again? She wished she had a gun instead of a dagger. Not that she was trained in firearms; far from it. The most she carried in her purse for protection back in Los Angeles was a taser and bear mace. Guns had frightened her, made her nervous. There was no going back if you shot someone with a gun. There was a permanence to it she didn't like, no reset button. But she wanted one now. There was something more personal about stabbing someone. It meant she had to get close. It was disturbingly intimate.

She realized that from inadvertently traveling from her world to this new one, a shedding of skin would be required to survive. In a way, it was a fresh start. She could possibly become anyone she wanted. That person she was, too timid or afraid to be back in Los Angeles, even back in New Orleans? What was stopping her from becoming it here? Seemed like there was nothing in the way except her own morals and code of honor. But did those concepts matter here? She wasn't sure. But it was something to ponder.

Oddly enough, the desire that she'd had all her life still burned within her here: to change people's lives with the food she cooked.

With that thought, the blinking green dot appeared again on her minimap. It was in the northern outskirts. They had walked into the radial range of the Marrow.

"I feel it," Nom said. "The whisper of a breeze. It's up ahead. It's calling to me."

— CHAPTER EIGHT —

Remnants of a Last Stand

Nom moved so quick, Nay struggled to keep up with him. He lowered himself to the ground like a snake and slithered ahead, his body hypnotically winding from side to side, propelled by his sheer musculature and his green protuberances, which acted like springs and treads, thrusting him ahead like a rocket.

"Nom! Wait!" Nay said. She hurried after him, her breath already ragged. "Jesus Christ."

She caught up to him at the entrance of what was the spiral-shaped chamber on her mini-map. Nom perched there, poised like a hunting dog who had cornered a fox. His body trembled like an antenna, his head looking down at the bottom of a humungous hole bored into the rock. Stone stairs spiraled down the walls.

Nay stood next to him, holding her lichen light, peering into an abyss. In that moment she felt miniscule at the sheer scale of the architecture, an insignificant human who had stumbled onto a wonder of the world. It was like being inside of a massive snail shell and gazing into the depth of its spiraled chambers.

Her mini-map indicated that the Marrow was somewhere down below.

"Well, what do you think?" Nay asked.

"We go down," Nom said.

"What if it's a trap?"

"I think it's something valuable that could help us."

"Why do you think that?"

"Think about it. We know a Delicacy is a valuable magical resource. Consuming one changed us. Look at your magic words again. What do they say about Marrow?"

"There's nothing explaining them. Just that I have open slots for Marrow Abilities . . ."

"That, coupled with how Piero mentioned that this was a valuable-enough Marrow to change his life, should tell us everything we need to know. It's a magical resource."

"Yeah, but is it worth endangering our lives for?"

"Anything worth having is going to involve risk. Listen to me. Consuming the Delicacy was the prerequisite you needed to have access to these abilities. Now you just need to find a Marrow to confirm what happens next. But my guess is that it's going to lead to enhancements for you in some way. Which will give you more tools to survive, which also means you'll be more effective at helping me stay alive, too."

"So, everything ultimately leads to you in the end, huh? It's all about you and your well-being?"

"Glad you're realizing that," Nom said. "Now, let's go find that Marrow."

It took almost an hour for them to traverse the spiral staircase to get to the bottom. At least, Nay thought it took around an hour. Perhaps it took more. It felt like more, but it was hard to be sure, because they didn't really have a way to tell time. Her legs ached, especially the top of her thighs, from keeping her stabilized and balanced as she traveled down the stairs.

The bottom was like being inside a silo, but one curved side had a set of massive iron double doors. They were ajar and Nay felt uneasy about what was beyond, lurking in the blue lichen light that fell in angular shafts like moonlight in the area beyond. Her mini-map indicated that the Marrow was in the center of a large, rectangular-shaped zone.

She took a swig of water from their waterskin. She held it out to Nom, offering him some, but he was eager to rush ahead, ignoring the waterskin in front of him. Nay wondered how much water and food he needed, as she noticed she had to eat and drink on a consistent basis but he seemed fine for going longer than a day without nourishment or hydration. Good news for their rations, but she was intrigued by the metabolism of the tentacle.

She followed him through the doors and found that they were in a tomb. Rows of stone coffins filled the area, which was easily the size of a few football fields. There were pillars every thirty yards in every direction, affixed with empty sconces meant for torches. The only light in here was the pale glow from the lichen. It was a giant mausoleum.

But even worse was the mountain of bones on the opposite end. Even from where they stood, they could tell what it was. The skulls poking out from the piles of skeletons gave it away.

This was where the citizens of Paleforge had made their last stand against the thing or things that ended them. They had wondered where the people who had occupied the city had gone. This was the answer. It had been an extermination. Nay wondered what possibly could have done this.

Part of her wanted to turn around and flee this place. Death had been here to collect souls, and now only the skeletons remained. But another part of her was filled with morbid curiosity. Not only did she want to locate the Marrow, she wanted to investigate the tragedy of Paleforge.

"Why did they decide to make their last stand in their cemetery?" Nay asked.

"Maybe it was the best-defendable place for them. By coming down here, they forced their attackers into a bottleneck down the pit. Then they would have to funnel through those double doors. They could bunker here and slaughter their attackers until they were overwhelmed."

"Yes, but that's not exactly it."

Nom thought for a minute, but didn't add anything.

"This is where the women and children and probably all those not fit for battle hid. The men tried to defend the city and this place from their attackers. They only retreated here as a last resort."

Nom nodded. "I wonder why they didn't give themselves a defendable place with an escape route, though."

"That's easy. Escape wasn't an option for them. The maugrim weren't cowards. This was their home. They would defend it until death."

Nom grew quiet at the somber thought.

They continued forward, the blinking green dot on Nay's mini-map growing closer.

"Whatever did this is long gone," Nom said.

"How do you know?" Nay said.

"Because I have the feeling we would already be part of that pile if they weren't."

Nay referenced her mini-map and noticed something odd. "The Marrow is somewhere in that mountain of skeletons."

"I know, but I didn't want to be the first to break that news. I was hoping my instincts would be wrong."

The next disturbing clue greeted them as they realized something had constructed an entrance into the mountain of maugrim bones. The archway of skulls was held together by some type of congealed jelly that had hardened around the skeleton heads like dried mortar the color and translucence of tree sap. It was the entrance of a dark tunnel that led into the funeral mound of bones.

"Didn't Piero's journal mention some type of creature . . ." Nom trailed off, trying to recall the name.

But Nay identified it for him. "He mentioned something he called the Steksis."

"I think we're about to find out whatever that is."

The bones of the maugrim towered over them, a grim warning.

Nay stood in front of the tunnel, the eyeless sockets staring back at her. It felt like the darkness within those sockets was staring holes into her soul. It smelled of must and mold.

Nay shouted into the tunnel. "Hello?"

"What are you doing?" Nom hissed.

"Whatever might be in there, I'd rather face it out here."

But there was no answer.

Nay drew her dagger from its leather sheath. It wasn't the gun she'd rather have, but it was better than nothing. "Let's get this over with."

She walked into the mountain of bones.

She held the lichen light in front of her, the dagger in her other hand. Sweat beaded on her skin. She observed the tunnel. More skulls looked out at them from the walls and the ceiling, held together by the strange jellied substance serving as mortar.

Nom stayed not behind her but at her side. Whatever they faced, they would face it head-on together.

Soon, the entrance behind them was no longer visible, and the deeper in they went, the closer they got to the green dot on her mini-map. After a few minutes, the tunnel opened up into a chamber.

According to Nay's mini-map, the Marrow was in here.

The chamber was decorated in strange bone-sculpture designs, the skeletons of maugrim fashioned into bizarre calcium mega-centipedes. They curled around the chamber and arched into the air, giving it the appearance of some sort of grotesque art installation designed by some goth-obsessed artist.

There was a table constructed from bones in the center of the room, but there was something else here in the dark.

A pair of yellow orbs burned in the darkness here. Then the sound of something sniffing, as if nostrils were flaring to take in a scent.

The voice was inhuman and wet. "I smell soft tissue."

The yellow orbs rotated, facing them, and a bone-white smile formed in the air above, revealing sharp ivory teeth. It seemed like an upside-down face, but Nay couldn't really scry the shape in the dark. They could only see the eyes and the teeth glowing in the dark. "It has been too long since I have nibbled on flesh."

The rest of the Steksis descended from a hole in the ceiling, revealing an iridescent carapace. The rest of its body was in the bones above them, coiled in the network of tunnels it had fashioned in the remains, its head hanging down into the room like a sleeping bat. The body that emerged was long, like a giant millipede scrabbling into the chamber, so long, its body coiled around the circumference of the ceiling. That heebie-jeebie feeling that arises when one sees a spider or an insect, something that dwells in the dark with multiple legs with flagellating antenna and pincers and alien eyes, that primordial instinct that prickles the skin behind the neck, behind the knees, that transforms forearms into gooseflesh, that physical warning that tells a human to either take care or run, well, it hit Nay in full force.

"That many legs on a creature is never a good thing," Nom said, already squirming deeper into the tunnel they were in. "I once knew an acolyte of the Dread One *Exterphaganmodius*, known for their multitude of legs. The stories he told me about his master were scandalous to say the least."

"Nom, now is not the time," Nay hissed. She backed deeper into the tunnel as well, white-knuckling her dagger. She had doubts if the dagger would be even useful against this thing. As she took another step back, she met resistance against the back of her leg.

There was something behind them.

She looked behind her and down to see part of the thing's long body was blocking their exit. It slid from one wall into the next, parting the bones, as its body coiled around the chamber like a giant serpent.

Those yellow eyes appeared in front of them, and the upper half of its body, its torso, rose before them in the chamber outside the tunnel. The iridescent carapace looked like it was fashioned from the armor of thousands of beetles. The scale-like segments fluttered like wings, revealing a pale and long and withered humanoid form within. It wore the carapace like a suit of armor.

Its face pushed into the lichen light as it revealed its visage. To Nay's surprise, despite its glowing yellow eyes and needle-sharp teeth, it had the head and face of an old human woman. Strings of unwashed gray hair hung in front of its face. The skin was wrinkled, but it was also translucent, which created the odd effect of seeing glowing eyes and teeth hanging in the air. Was this another perversion of the human form, meant to frighten her and make a mockery of her kind? Or was this someone who was once human who had transformed into a monster?

"Trying to leave so soon?" it said. "We haven't even had time for introductions."

As it cackled like a crone, the carapace around its torso opened like an iron maiden, and a human arm emerged, flicking out and slapping the lichen torch out of Nay's hands, casting them all in darkness.

— CHAPTER NINE —

The Steksis

Nay felt the hand grab her by her tunic and pull her forward. She drove the dagger forward, but the Steksis caught her arm, blocking her. Something latched on to her wrist and twisted, forcing her to drop the dagger. Then she was airborne and hanging upside down. There was a rush of momentum and she sensed she was in the chamber.

Those yellow eyes appeared in front of her again, glowing bright enough to show Nay that one of the many millipede-like appendages was locked around one of her ankles, holding her upside down from the ceiling. Suddenly, the eyes narrowed and darted at the ground.

Nom was there, standing straight up on his hind stalk, his eye focused on the Steksis. The tentacle trembled, indicating he was in the throes of casting Mind Shiv.

"And what do we have here?" the Steksis said, studying the tentacle.

Nom focused harder and the Steksis chuckled.

"I can feel you, but your little trick isn't strong enough to work on me. But come closer so I can get a good look at you."

Its torso moved towards the floor, but Nom gave up on the Mind Shiv and fled towards the wall. He moved so fast that when Nay blinked, the tentacle had already disappeared into the gap between bones.

The Steksis turned back to look at Nay. "What strange company you keep!"

It closed its eyes, and then the torso and top part of the millipede dove into the wall. Nay felt the mountain of bones shuddering around her. As the Steksis moved through the bones, its serpentine body created a tectonic shift in the skeletons. The bones rattled and rumbled around them. Pieces of bones fell from the ceiling, and motes of dust and decay filled the air.

Then the wall across from Nay exploded and the head, arms, and torso of the Steksis appeared in the chamber. It was clutching the squirming Nom in its hands. "Got you! You're quite the slippery thing, aren't you?"

The Steksis held the tentacle out before it, taking in Nom with its eyes. It held Nom close to its face and sniffed at his body. "You smell of the water depths. It's been so long since I've fed on something that dwells on the riverbeds or in the depths of the brine water. It appears I haven't been forgotten down here after all. They've sent me morsels to help me get by until they return."

It held Nom closer to its face and a tongue slipped out of its mouth and licked the tentacle.

"Ew! Stop it! Gross! Also, that tickles!" Nom cried.

The Steksis opened its mouth, its glowing teeth lighting up the darkness as it was about to bite into the middle of the tentacle like he was a piece of fried cod.

Nay heard herself shouting, "No! Nom!"

She reached for something in her pockets to throw at the Steksis, but the piece of dried meat she grabbed fell out of her hand and hit the floor, catching the attention of the creature. It pulled away from Nom and looked at the piece of jerky on the floor.

Curious, it grabbed it and sniffed. Then it took a bite and chewed, its face lighting up in excitement. "Even the food has food!"

It swallowed; its glowing yellow eyes rolled into the back of its head in pleasure. It took another bite of the dried meat, its entire body shuddering in satisfaction. As it ate, the tremors in its coiled body shook the chamber around them.

Its carapace fluttered in rhythm to its bites, and both Nay and Nom glimpsed a green glow on its back underneath its outer shell. For a brief moment, Nay saw the strange growth on its pale body. She squinted and tried to get a better look, but the text prompt blocked her view and took up all her vision.

[Marrow Detected!]
[Truffle Marrow of the Steksis]

More of the magic words pressed that prompt down.

[Quest Detected]
[Quest: Separate the Marrow from the Steksis]
[Reward: Truffle Marrow of the Steksis]
[Accept Quest Y/N?]

Nay mentally accepted the quest and the prompt disappeared.

"This is really quite delicious," it crooned.

"And there's more where that came from," Nay said. Her voice trembled. It was impossible to hide her fear. But if they couldn't fight this thing, maybe they could negotiate. "All you have to do is not kill or eat us, and we can give you the best meal you've had in . . . well . . . I'm guessing a very long time."

The Steksis studied Nay. She tried not to look away from its gaze, to show resolve and that she wasn't trying to deceive the monster. She needed it to trust her.

"What are you talking about?" it asked her. It had taken the hook.

"I'm a chef," Nay said, and she nodded at Nom. "And that's my sous-chef. If you let us, we can prepare you a delicious meal. Something that will taste much better than us."

"How do I know you're not trying to trick me?"

"If you're displeased with the meal, then you can do with us as you will."

"So, what do you get out of it if I do like your food?"

"Our lives."

The Steksis looked between them both, examining the two with scrutiny.

"It's not like we could get away from you if we tried. You're much faster than us. And stronger. You could eat us . . . but in the end, I think you'll find as a meal, we're rather disappointing. And you'll have missed out on some of the best food you've ever had."

The Steksis considered Nay's words for a long moment, presumably weighing the options and outcomes in its head. Nay held her breath, expecting the worst. This was it. She had survived this long to finally meet her end at the hands of an actual real monster in an alternate reality where magic was real. Different regrets flashed through her mind, not getting to say goodbye to her mom, not getting her brick-and-mortar restaurant up and running, not getting to cook ever again. And strangely, not getting to survive this ordeal to eventually return to her own world to tell people that the multiverse and alternate realities were real.

The Steksis finally spoke again. "No one has actually ever cooked for me before."

The Steksis was so excited about the prospect of someone cooking for it that it carried both Nay and Nom close to its torso, its two human arms wrapped around them as its serpentine-millipede body carried them back to the outskirts of Paleforge proper, where their camp was set up.

"I can't remember the last time I left my Bone Dolmen," it said. "But you promise me a meal and I can't think of a better reason to leave my dwelling."

Nay and Nom exchanged a look. She wasn't sure how comfortable they should get with The Steksis, especially when death was as imminent as a change in its mood. Better to focus on the task at hand and worry about their relationship status with it later. At that thought, more text appeared at the center of her vision.

[Reputation Menu]
[Factions]
[The Scar: Unfriendly]

A status bar appeared, indicating her reputation with the Steksis: Unfriendly. It was nearly filled with green progress, and now she was close to the Neutral bar. Interesting. Nay wondered where they would stand if it liked her cooking. She was hoping it would push them into the Friendly bar.

"What are you even going to make?" Nom whispered. "We barely have any ingredients."

Nay shushed him. "I'll show you when it's time."

When they were back at their camp, the Steksis deposited them back to the ground and coiled around the camp, forming a circle around the area with its body. If they tried to make a run for it, they would have to climb over its insectoid-snake body.

"If you try anything," the Steksis said, "then I will be eating both of you raw."

Nay nodded. "Understood."

She nudged Nom towards the ashes of their last fire. "Get the campfire going; I'll handle the rest."

"What do I do after it has started?" he whispered.

"Follow my lead and make yourself look busy."

"If this goes south, I'm going to have words with you when we're in the belly of that thing."

She shushed him again and went to the cooking kit. She took out their remaining flatbread, the quarter of dried cheese they had left, and more of the dried meat. She set them up on the flat rock, which she had made her cooking station. She reached for the dagger in her scabbard and realized it wasn't there. *Dammit.* She needed that blade.

She walked over to where the Steksis was sitting.

"You don't happen to have my dagger, do you?" Nay asked. "I need it. It's my chef's knife. And as you know, a chef cooks best with their knife."

The Steksis let out what sounded like a purr and then just stared at Nay. Then Nay sensed movement and looked across the campfire at the creature's body. Its segmented legs were passing her dagger from one leg to the next, until it finally reached the human-like hands. It had probably hidden the weapon in one of what must be many compartments within its carapace. It held the dagger out hilt-first to Nay. But when Nay grabbed it, the Steksis did not let go.

"Remember, try anything and it's you I'll be nibbling on." The Steksis let go of the blade, and Nay nodded and hurried back to her cooking station.

Nay took some of the flatbread and sliced it down the pocket, creating two pieces. She drizzled some of the olive oil on each piece and set them to the side. Next, she carefully cut through portions of the cheese, creating thin slices. She placed these on the oil-drizzled sides of the flatbread. She said to Nom, "Give me a low-flame setting, Nom."

"Yes, chef!" Nom had the tinder lit and was fanning it into a bigger flame with undulations of his body.

Nay wondered where he had learned that etiquette. Were restaurants a thing in his world? She would have to remember to ask him. "Go ahead and get a teakettle going, too." They still had some of the tea Piero had on him. They haven't had a chance to drink it. It would be best to pull out all the stops now.

Nom positioned the pot on its holder so there was some distance between the fire and the bottom of the pot, which was how they would get a low-flame setting. He slithered back over to Nay's side, hooked one of his green fin-protuberances through the kettle handle, and brought it to the fire.

Nay joined him and filled the kettle with water from one of the waterskins. Next, she crushed up some of the tea leaves and sprinkled it into a wood flagon. She was curious what plant the leaves were actually from and what it was called here. From her experience drinking it, it contained a caffeine boost.

The Steksis watched their activity with interest, occasionally clearing its throat. It held its two human arms out in front of it, the fingers moving as if it was an old crone crocheting a quilt. It was talking to itself but Nay couldn't hear what it was saying. But it seemed both pleased and entertained. With a little luck, maybe they would be out of unfriendly territory with it soon, so they wouldn't have to worry about being on its murderous side anymore.

Next, Nay drizzled more of the olive oil in the bottom of the pot and then placed the two pieces of flatbread with cheese on top into the pot. The oil sizzled upon contact with the bread, and soon enough, they would be crispy. She closed the pot with its lid so the steam would melt the cheese.

Nom sidled up to her and pretended to fan the flames. He lowered his voice. "What is this curious dish called?"

"You've never had a grilled cheese sandwich before?" Nay said.

Nom seemed like he was in awe. "Grilled . . . grilled cheese? I must try this dish."

"No, we don't know how much it's going to want to eat, and we only have so much."

"But—"

"No *but*s! We're trying to stay alive here."

That shut him up.

Nay lifted the lid and peeked in the pot. The cheese had melted on top of the flatbread. She grabbed one side of the sandwich and flipped it over, placing it on top of the other half, making the sandwich whole. Then she spent the next minute making sure each side was evenly grilled.

She removed the sandwich and set it on the flat stone. She took her dagger and cut the sandwich in half diagonally, creating two beautiful halves of a flatbread grilled cheese sandwich. It kind of looked like a panini with just cheese. Not exactly the best presentation, but it was simple and Nay knew it would taste delicious.

Nom poured the hot water from the kettle into the flagon, making the tea. He carried the flagon and set it down on the flat stone next to the sandwich. Nay scooped out the soaked tea-leaf detritus with the wooden spoon, wiped the side of the cup, then positioned it all together on the stone. She was pleased with this simple yet effective presentation. She and Nom shared a look, then they both backed away to give the Steksis room.

Nay motioned at the Steksis and bowed. "I present to you, a flatbread grilled cheese and tea."

"This better work, or this might be our last moment before we're unalived," Nom whispered out of the side of his beak.

"Shut up," Nay hissed, kicking him with the side of her foot.

"Ow!"

The Steksis extended and wrapped around so that its torso was in front of the flat stone. Its yellow eyes flared with brightness upon the sight of the sandwich and tea. There was a greedy hunger contorting on the face of the crone.

It slowly lowered one of its withered human arms and wrapped its fingers around a half of the sandwich. It held the grilled cheese up to its face and examined the texture of the bread, scraping a fingernail across the goldenbrown crispy surface. It sniffed at the gooey cheese leaking out of the side and grew a tad more excited upon smelling the sharp, tangy cheese.

Then it leaned in, its sharp teeth glowing like pearls, and it took a bite out of the sandwich.

Both Nay and Nom leaned forward, scrutinizing the creature's face and reaction as it chewed. It swallowed, not saying anything, but took another curious bite, its teeth crunching into the perfectly grilled bread.

A tear rolled down its cheek as it finished the first half of the sandwich.

"Is everything okay?" Nay said.

"This is the first time someone has cooked for me." It began to weep, its shoulders shaking with each sob.

"Please let those be tears of joy; please let those be tears of joy," Nom chanted, bracing for the worst.

"This is the first time I've been happy in a long, long time," the Steksis said. "I never thought I would experience joy again, at least not until the return of the Shrilling."

Nay wanted to ask what *the Shrilling* were, but she suspected they had something to do with the Scar and the fall of the city of Paleforge.

The Steksis picked up the wooden flagon and took a sip of the tea. Its face lit up even more, if that was possible. There was a ding as Nay received a notification.

[Reputation Menu]
[Factions]
[The Scar: Unfriendly]

The bar filled with green and the Unfriendly bar disappeared, replaced with Neutral.

[The Scar: Neutral!]

All of Nay's tension deflated out of her. She immediately felt relief. Her gamble worked. The Steksis liked her meal so much, it put them on better terms. This monster now considered her and Nom non-threats. Looked like they wouldn't be dying yet.

It picked up the other half of the sandwich and took another bite but more slowly this time, savoring the experience. Then it sipped more of the tea, its eyes closed as it continued to eat and drink. Soon, it had finished the sandwich and had slurped up the last of the tea, taking its final smack of the lips and swallow.

[Reputation Menu]
[Factions]
[The Scar: Friendly!]

The reputation meter leveled up to the next degree, which was Friendly. Nay was flabbergasted.

Nom nudged her and said, "What's going on in that magical head of yours?"

At that moment, the Steksis let out a huge burp, making them both jump. But there was a huge smile on its face.

"I think we're going to be okay, Nom," Nay said. "We'll live to see another day."

— CHAPTER TEN —

Into the Cold Wide Open

[Quest Completed!]
[Separate the Marrow from the Steksis Completed!]
[Congratulations!]
[Reward: Truffle Marrow of the Steksis]
[You have been rewarded with Vigor Points]

    They had made the Steksis another sandwich, cutting the supply of their rations nearly in half but earning them an ally and allowing them to avoid being devoured by a monster. With its hunger satisfied, the Steksis wanted to show them gratitude for the meal and the newfound friendship. It had asked them how it could possibly help them after it had experienced such a special thing as a lovingly prepared meal.
    That's when Nay inquired about the glowing green growth on its back it kept concealed underneath its carapace.
    The segments of the carapace opened up like wings, revealing the pale white human torso of the Steksis. There were folds of aged skin, its exposed torso like a marble statue covered in a coat of melting candle wax. It turned, revealing the source of the glow on its back.
    It wasn't a deformed growth. It was a bioluminescent mushroom. It emitted a green aura. However, it didn't seem toxic like a poisonous gas cloud. There was something about it that felt safe and inviting, like finding a sacred plant that druids could use for miraculous medicinal purposes.
    She knew it was the Marrow that Piero had been hunting.
    The Steksis revealed that the mushroom was a source of discomfort for the creature. But even during a time it was around others, they had been too ashamed to ever ask for help.
    It had been so long that they had been alone, that all it could do was let the

mushroom grow. On the days when it couldn't ignore the itch caused by the fungus, it used maugrim bones like back scratchers to relieve itself.

The Steksis revealed that it would be a favor for them to remove it.

Nay used her dagger to slice the stem of the glowing mushroom, carefully severing it from the mound of skin on the Steksis's back. It instantly exhaled in relief when the stalk separated from its skin. Several notifications scrolled by in front of Nay.

[Marrow Detected]
[Marrow Acquired]
[Rewarded Truffle Marrow of The Steksis!]
[You have been rewarded with Vigor Points]

She took care to wrap the Marrow up in cloth. She set it on the flat stone for the time being. She wanted to research it more and possibly consume it, but it felt odd doing it in front of the Steksis. So, she set it here as they all settled in to drink more tea by the campfire.

The irony that they were able to share a meal and campfire with a monster when they couldn't even do it with a human didn't get by her. *What a strange world*, she thought, but maybe not so different from where she came from. There were only humans in her world, so the only de facto monsters there were other people. Yet, in both worlds, one couldn't just get by on judgments of appearance.

The Steksis told the tale of how it arrived here on this mountain as the caffeine from the tea got into its system, rendering it in quite a talkative mood.

"When I came through the Scar, I was just a youngling. My mother carried me on her stomach with the other siblings. Her job was to infiltrate the mountain and perform attacks on the city within, causing chaos amongst the small but vicious men who called this place home. Our kind is good for that in such a place because we're built for burrowing. We're built for the dark places others can't go. The Shrilling always commanded my kind. They promised my mother all the bones she would ever want if she did what they said. But she never got to enjoy it.

"The stout men here set off the bright light that took the breath out of everyone in that tomb. Even many of the Shrilling perished, causing the survivors to retreat back into the Scar. They promised me and my siblings they would return and that day would be cause for glory. We waited but now only I remain. And I continue to wait."

"You never wanted to leave this mountain?" Nay asked.

The Steksis shook its head. "It's not safe for me. The light that shines down from the sky burns me. In this mountain I am safe from that terrible burning."

Nay shook her head, knowing that it was talking about the sun. She wondered what the Scar was. Whatever it was, it was nearby, as Piero had mentioned it too. Had she and Nom also come through this Scar?

"Do people come into this mountain often?" Nay asked.

"Sometimes, I find bauble-pickers looking for shinies. They either leave here quickly or stay forever," the Steksis said.

"Stay forever?"

"They turn to bone before I visit them because they fear the cold and have no food. Or I help them along in their bone journey. Such lovely bones, either way."

Nay swallowed and was glad they were in this thing's good graces. It seemed like it was territorial and killed anyone that wandered in here, whether for shelter from the elements or for hunting for treasure in the ruins. She wondered how Piero had planned on dealing with the thing.

"Do you know if there are any settlements of people nearby?"

"People? I couldn't say. But sometimes I sense things, hungry things, dark things, passing by or lurking on the surface above."

Nay shared a look with Nom.

"Do you sense any of those things now?"

It stayed still and quiet for a moment. As if turning its ear to something far away. "The only howls I hear are of the air." Then it looked at Nay, its yellow eyes glinting. "But do not worry; you are broodling-safe down here with me."

It wanted another pot of tea and Nay obliged, making another kettle.

While the Steksis enjoyed more tea, talking to itself, Nay took Nom aside. "We don't have food to keep this thing fed. I'm not sure it's gonna stay happy if we run out."

Nom looked at their remaining rations, a grim look in his eye. "What are we gonna do?"

"When it falls asleep, we need to leave this place."

"Where will we go? Out into the storm?"

"We don't have much choice. I'd rather brave the elements than die to"—she nodded at the Steksis—"that."

"I don't know," Nom said, unsure. "I really don't do well in the cold."

"We can't stay in here forever. Not unless you want to become part of its nest."

Nom nodded. He still looked uncomfortable about the idea, but she knew he would follow her regardless. They had a bond now in their short time together, having survived two deadly encounters—well, three if they counted the riftway spider in the Korean church, and if anything, they were decent at keeping each other alive.

She would just have to trust they could survive the next thing that could kill them—the cold.

Nom watched the Steksis slumber, coiled up like a giant serpent, the tip of its pink tongue sticking out from between its sharp teeth as it gently snored. Nay gathered their belongings into a bedroll and packed as quietly as she could. As she was reaching for their cooking pot, the back of her hand brushed against the teakettle and knocked it over. The sound of ceramic tapping stone echoed through the chamber.

Nay immediately froze, wincing. Nom swiveled towards her, staring at her with a death glare.

Her eyes flew to the Steksis. It stopped snoring, rustling in its sleep. Its eyelids fluttered, the skin as delicate as Bible paper. She was pretty sure it was going to wake up, catch them trying to sneak away, and, well, that would be the story of them. Strangers in a strange land for not very long.

Cause of death? Clumsiness.

But it let out a wheezing exhale and started snoring again, its eyes never opening. She relaxed and she saw Nom do the same across from her. She quickly grabbed the kettle, wrapped it in cloth, and stuffed it into the leather pack. Then, heel to toe, she slowly walked towards the archway, and Nom followed.

At the archway, they both took one last look at the Steksis.

It looked peaceful and content, sleeping there with a full belly. Nay wondered if it always slept that well, but had a sneaking suspicion her food played a large part. Her mother always used to sigh in satisfaction whenever Nay made her favorite meal, shrimp and grits. The trick to that dish was using different amounts of butter and cream, depending on whether it was winter or summer. More for winter, less for summer. Her mother always said she took the best naps after eating Nay's food.

So, she knew her food improved the quality of life for people, so why wouldn't it be any different for monsters?

They stopped in the hot-spring chamber to fill the waterskins up with hot water. Nay wasn't sure if they would last long at all, but they could be some source of warmth until they grew cold. Something was better than nothing.

On their way to the cave entrance, Nay gathered up some fresh lichen for fresh torches. She had no idea how long they would provide light outside of the cave, or if at all, but it was worth trying.

The first thing that told them they were close to the exit was the creeping cold they walked into.

The condensation on the wall surfaces shifted to ice, and the winter wind whispered through the cave, nipping at their exposed skin. Soon, the light of the moon was visible, and the blue of the outside world was right in front of them.

Nay was happy to see there was some visibility. There was no white-out storm at the moment, and although it was cold, there was no more blizzard.

"You ready, friend?" Nay said to Nom.

"No, but it looks like this is happening anyways."

Nom slithered out of the cave first, and Nay followed after the tentacle.

The alpine pass glittered under the strange moon and stars like a blanket of crystals, covered in ice and snow. The evergreen trees rising up along the pass made Nay think of the winter wonderland of the Swiss Alps. But there was a gloom and darkness lurking here that put her on edge.

They were following the decline of the pass, as that seemed the most likely direction they would find anything. Only a madman would try to ascend the pass in these conditions. Either way, her mini-map didn't give her any clues upon settlements or camps where other people might be. From mountain peak to the valley and lake below, she was still too far away from either to scry any marks that might denote settlements. She wasn't even sure if her mini-map would mark any of that stuff. It just looked like a cartographer's map of a mountain range and a nearby gorge cutting through the rock.

"N-n-nay," Nom chattered. "I'm . . . starting . . . to feel . . . sluggish."

Oh, shit, Nay thought. *Was Nom coldblooded? Of course he was,* she thought. He's an invertebrate. Weren't all invertebrates coldblooded? It had been so long since middle school and earth science, anything that wasn't about cooking and food had been pushed out of her headspace.

Nom's normal purple skin changed to a bluish-white and a tiny icicle had begun to form on the end of his beak. Nay grabbed one of the waterskins. It still radiated warmth. She knelt and pulled the tentacle close, rubbing the warm waterskin over his body. It was like brushing a giant cucumber with a small heat blanket. "Here ya go buddy, let me help you get warm."

Nom pushed himself into her touch, absorbing the warmth. The color shifted from blue to orange and red where the waterskin touched his body. It was like he was one big infrared sensor. She knew he was pulling a limited source of heat from the waterskin and this might only work one more time before they needed to find a heat source or some shelter to start a fire.

"I really . . . really . . . hate the cold!" Nom said, teeth chattering.

"I know, buddy; I'm starting to dislike it too," Nay said.

"Is your world . . . a cold one?"

"Parts of it. Where I come from, it's beach weather year-round."

"What's beach weather?"

"It's not too hot, not too cold. I can wear shorts year-round."

"I don't know what shorts are, but you make it sound nice."

"They are." Nay put the wineskin back in their pack. "All right, let's keep moving."

They stumbled on. At one point, they slipped on a steep incline and slid down the icy path. Nay lay there and observed the strange stars and the strange moon above them.

The moon in this reality or world was bigger, probably closer to the planet. It had more of a green tint than a yellow one, and there was a ribbon of magenta gas swathed across the atmosphere near it. These celestial bodies felt a lot brighter and clearer here, probably because there was less pollution in this world. She wondered if it had to do with her location or was it the world itself. What were they going to find out here? Were there civilizations? What would they be like? She wondered so many things before she made herself move, sore and cold.

Nom was turning into a Popsicle. He moved so slow now that Nay had to pick him up. She wasn't moving very fast herself. They were going to have to build a fire.

Nay picked up Nom, "It's okay. I got you. You rest now."

"I'm . . . sorry," Nom said.

Nay wrapped him up in their bedroll and slung it over her back in a big sack. She spotted some shelter against a shelf of rock. It would keep the wind away. She set Nom down and got the kindling and flint rock out. It was then that she realized she was going to have to gather wood.

"Keep . . . moving . . ." she told herself.

She stumbled into the forest and searched for dry wood. All she could manage were a few branches. She carried them in a bundle and collapsed underneath the shelf of rock next to the frozen, blanket-wrapped tentacle. She cleared the snow away to set the kindling and build the fire. She lay there, striking the flint against the rock, praying for a spark.

Every time a spark shot out, it fizzled out before lighting the kindling.

"Please," she begged, her fingers raw with the cold. She kept striking the rock, curling her body around the kindling to protect the spark from the cold. "I'm sorry, Nom," she said, glancing at the frozen form of her only friend here.

Eventually, the cold defeated her.

She fell asleep, her face to the cold ground, her fingers raw and bleeding from striking the flint and rock.

The heat on her face woke her up. She opened her eyes to see a campfire blazing in front of her. She was hugging the bedroll that Nom was wrapped in like a burrito. The snow and ice around the fire had melted away.

There was a snort from the other side of the fire. She rubbed her eyes, clearing her vision, and that's when she saw a snout and a pair of dark eyes regarding her.

It leaned into the light, revealing a creature that looked like it had the face of a wolf and a mule smushed together. The alienness alarmed her, and her first reaction was to scream.

She shot up and scrambled away, screaming. Bells jingled as the creature moved. It was like a wolf, but it was the size of a mule. Nay drew her dagger and crouched.

"Whoa whoa whoa!" a male voice said. "That's no way to say hello!"

A young man stepped between the wolf-thing and Nay. He was wrapped in animal skins for an outer layer, and there was a brown robe visible underneath. Nay noticed a strange marking on his hand. It looked like a tattoo of an eye inside of a hexagon. He had short-cropped golden hair that reminded Nay of a Benedictine monk. "You can put the dagger away," he said. "Karka means no harm."

Nay turned to him with the dagger, then swiveled back to point it at the wolf-mule abomination. "What the fuck is that thing?"

"It's a fauglir. What else would it be?"

"I don't know . . . a goddamn werewolf."

He raised an eyebrow, indicating his mixture of confusion and intrigue. "I am not certain what that is, but it doesn't sound good, and I assure you Karka isn't one of those. He's my pack animal and friend."

It was Nay's turn to raise an eyebrow. "And who are you?"

"My name is Alric."

— CHAPTER ELEVEN —

The Silverbell's Leaf

Karka and I were coming down the trail when he started whining and pulling me towards the shelf. He sensed you before both of us even saw you. Fauglir have an excellent sense of smell and hearing, so he found you even though you were covered in snow. You were on the verge of turning blue, so I got the fire going. We mean you no harm. I'm with the Veritax."

"I don't know what the Veritax is," Nay said. She sat back down now that she established Alric and his animal had no ill intent. If they did, they could have harmed her while she was unconscious. So, it either meant he was telling the truth or he was a sadist. He didn't have the look of a sadist, but that haircut was kinda whack. So, she didn't completely lower her defenses.

"Truly?" Alric said, surprised to hear someone had never heard of the Veritax. "The church's reach covers the entire peninsula, from the tip to the furthest reaches of Stitchdale up here."

"Yeah, well, I'm from out of town," Nay said. With as much discretion as she could manage, she checked under the bedroll to see how Nom was doing. She wasn't sure whether or not she should reveal that her companion was a tentacle, because she wasn't sure how Alric or his pet would react. A talking tentacle wasn't really an everyday thing to see for her, and she wasn't sure if it would be for them, either.

There was some orange and red returning to his body; his outer surface had an orange aura. *Thank god*, she thought. He was getting warm, which hopefully meant his blood would start flowing again. She wanted him to be okay, and she hoped he retained no permanent damage from being turned into a tentaclesicle.

Alric noticed her looking down into the bedroll, and it seemed like he was about to ask her what she was looking at it when she spoke first. "What's that tattoo on your hand?" Nay said.

Alric looked down at the eye mark on his hand. "It's not a tattoo. That's my brand."

"Brand?"

"Yes. It's the Brand of the Veritax. It is a marking the church gives to all its monks."

"You're a priest?"

"More of a monk. I serve Lucerna's End and the Valley of Stitchdale. I was traveling from the abbey back to town when I found you. I rarely see travelers out here."

"So, there are other people nearby."

"It's a day's travel by fauglir, weather permitting." He looked at her with curiosity.

"Where are you from?"

"Not from around here, obviously."

"What is your business in Spineshard Pass, then?"

"My business?" she said. Other than survival and trying to get back to her world, she hadn't really considered anything else in between. What if no one knew how to help her get back to where she was from?

Her next words came slowly, like she was figuring it all out aloud. "I'm a cook. A chef looking for employment. Sure, I suppose that would be a good start." Then she looked back at him and said, "I'm looking for someone to employ me as a cook."

He stared at her as if he couldn't make heads and tails of her. "It doesn't seem like you're lying, so I'm only going to assume you're japing with me."

"Japing? No jape. Surely, this town . . . what did you call it?"

"Lucerna's End."

"Yes, Lucerna's End. Surely, this Lucerna's End could use someone with my skillset."

"Come to think of it, they could use someone who knows how to actually cook a tasty stew. Their goat stew is like chewing on *roch* leather. I'm sure there's nutrients in it, but it's torture to get down."

"Then that's where I'm going."

"But where are you coming from? Oblige a concerned stranger. I find you out here, high up on the mountain on a dangerous trail, almost frozen to death with no fire, no proper clothing or preparation. It's like you fell out of the sky with not even the bare essentials and, if not for my serendipitous arrival, you might not be alive to be having this conversation."

"You're not too far from the truth when you mention me falling out of the sky."

"Truly?"

"Look, it doesn't matter how I got here, because it doesn't even make sense to me. What matters is that I'm here now. I'm alive. And I'm grateful you found me to keep me that way."

He shook his head and then took out an honest-to-god wood pipe. It was polished and carved in stylish curves, like it was a big question mark. He opened a packet of tobacco and plucked a plug into the pipe. "Well, I suppose as long as you didn't come out of the Scar, then I have no reason to regret saving you from an icy death." He gave her a sideways glance to watch her reaction at the mention of the phrase *the Scar*.

"What exactly is this Scar?"

"You're really not from around here, are you?" He lit his pipe with the end of a wick he stuck in the fire, taking a few puffs. Once he got it going, he shook the wick until the ember fell off and tumbled into the snow, extinguishing.

"You're allowed to smoke?"

Alric gave her a funny look. "Why wouldn't I be?"

"Where I come from, the monks aren't allowed to do all sorts of things. I don't know; I assumed maybe your church had similar rules."

"The Veritax has no rules for keeping a monk away from the silverbell's leaf. If they did, I think they'd find they might have a problem recruiting followers."

"Good to know they don't separate people from their vices, then. A good vice is the best way to keep demons at bay."

The monk threw her another questionable look. Then he took a long puff and exhaled. The silverbell's-leaf smoke smelled pleasant, almost like spearmint chewing gum. "As to your question, on the other side of these mountains is a no-man's-land. There's a giant rent in the earth some say leads straight to the underworld. It stretches from one end of the horizon to the other. No cartographer has gotten close enough to measure its length, but it is considerable and dangerous. This is the Scar. The whole region is covered in smoke and hideous, noxious gases. Get close enough and it will boil skin. Some people believe this rent in the earth is the origin for some of the monster attacks that have befallen settlements and cities along this mountain range. It is why no one has interest in ever crossing these mountains. In fact, we're glad for the buffer."

"Part of you thinks I wandered out of the Scar?"

He shrugged. "Can't be too careful in Stitchdale. It can be amok with strange and beguiling creatures. It wouldn't be the first time a monster tried to trick me by wearing a human face."

"Are you fucking with me?"

"I swear by Verity's Truth. It disguised itself as a beautiful woman. I'd be skewered into the trees if it wasn't for the Gloom Rangers who saved me."

"Are you calling me a beautiful woman?"

At that, Alric was in mid-puff, and started coughing. He tried to clear his throat and started hitting his chest to clear his airways.

Nay enjoyed how uncomfortable he suddenly got, but then she let him off the hook by asking him another question. "Gloom Rangers?"

Alric wiped the tears from his eyes and recovered from the coughing fit. "The men and women who patrol Stitchdale and the land on this side of the mountains. They have a fort not too far from the abbey. Fort Nixxiom, or Scarwatch as the locals call it. They hunt the monsters here and monitor any activity that they might suspect as Scar-related."

"So, they're like scouts who keep an eye out and then warn everyone else if there's something they perceive as a threat from the Scar."

"You got the idea."

It was then that Nay's blanket rose up as if there was a rod underneath it that suddenly went erect. The fabric slid off, exposing Nom to both Alric and his fauglir, Karka, who recoiled in surprise. Nom screamed at the sight of them. Alric nearly fell off of the log he was sitting on, and Karka was up, hackles rising, its form taking an aggressive stance towards Nom, barking at the tentacle.

Now it was Nay's turn to intervene and get Alric and Karka to calm down. "Relax! It's just Nom."

Alric clutched his staff in one hand and the talisman around his neck in the other. "What in the nether hells is that?!"

"I told you," Nay said. "It's Nom."

"What in the nether hells is a Nom?"

"You've never seen a tentacle before?"

"I know what a tentacle is, but what was one doing underneath your blanket, and oh my, it has an eye!"

Nom coiled up Nay's leg and wrapped around her torso, hiding much of his body behind her while poking his head out at Karka. "Nay, that thing is trying to kill us! Look at its teeth!"

"It speaks!" Alric cried, backing away, putting his staff between them.

"It's not trying to kill us," Nay said. "It looks mean but it's basically just Alric's horse." And she turned to Alric. "And Nom is harmless. He's my friend."

"What's a horse?" Alric said.

"I'm not harmless," Nom cried. "I can fuck things up!"

"You don't know what a horse is?" Nay said.

"Would I be asking what a horse is if I knew what one was?" Alric said.

"Good point," Nay said.

"Can somebody tell me what's going on?!" Nom cried. "Have I awoken into another nightmare?"

Nay sighed. "You're fine, Nom." Then she put her hands out to both Alric and Karka.

"It's fine! Nom, the tentacle, is with me. He's my sous-chef."

Alric shook his staff at them both. "How do I know he's not just your appendage of doom and you're beguiling us and your true form is actually some Scar monster that wants to tear us to shreds?"

Nay sighed. "Jesus Christ. I don't know how else to explain it. Can you just trust me? Can we all just calm down, sit down, and enjoy the warmth of this fire? I promise we're not monsters who want to hurt you. We're just a little lost and need some guidance on our way to your town. Besides, you saved us, and if anything, we owe you." Nay looked to Karka. The fauglir had stopped barking and was merely growling. "Yes, even you, Karka."

Karka whined and looked to Alric. His master nodded and Karka relaxed, slowly lowering himself in front of the fire again.

"Would you put down your stick?" Nay asked Alric. "You're gonna put someone's eye out."

"And I only have one of those!" Nom said.

Alric, suddenly self-conscious about the staff, put it vertical again and leaned it against the rock-shelf wall. He returned to his log, staring at Nom.

"Wha—" Alric began, then stopped himself, unsure of how to phrase whatever he was going to say.

"Nom," Nay said. "This is Alric. He's a monk. And Karka is, like, his horse or something."

"What's a horse?" Nom asked.

"Never mind," Nay said, exasperated. "Would you introduce yourself?"

Nom uncoiled from around Nay and slithered closer to the fire, wavering in front of it, basking in the heat. "My name is Nzxthommocus III, formerly the Third Whip of the Pain Lord Ormandius," he said, bowing before them. "At your service."

"Nom for short," Nay said.

"Wha . . . how do you two . . . how did you two meet?" Alric asked.

"Oh, well," Nay began, "we kind of just—"

Nom cut her off. "Yeah, it was an interdimensional spider attack that brought us together."

— CHAPTER TWELVE —

Do You Have the Paperwork for That?

Nom started to tell the story but Nay cut him off. "Yeah, it was one of those situations where it was beneficial for two species that you would normally think to be enemies to team up instead. And we've been best buds ever since."

The tentacle gave her an annoyed look and she gave him a look back. She wasn't sure how to convey that they shouldn't just tell people they're from other worlds, especially to people they just met, so she had interrupted him.

"Did you say 'interdimensional'?" Alric asked.

Nom was still looking at Nay, trying to read her. He rephrased his original statement. "Oh, did I?" he said. "Well, I just assumed, I'd never seen anything like the riftw—the weird . . . spider. You know how sometimes when you see something so weird, part of you thinks, *Wow, that thing looks it came from another dimension.*"

Alric frowned and shook his head. He had relit his pipe and was puffing away thoughtfully. "I'm used to seeing the strange and unusual, especially here in Stitchdale, so close to the Scar. The monsters found here tend to be more out of the ordinary."

"There's such a thing as ordinary monsters?" Nay asked.

"Down in the Peninsula, there are more common creatures."

He was talking about monsters like someone back in her world would talk about wildlife or nature. Were monsters just part of life here? She was getting a sense that life was more dangerous here. They had only been here a few days and had been fighting for their lives ever since. To make it worse, she for sure didn't have the skills to survive on her own. She was going to have to learn how to survive in this world, which not only meant she would have to learn how to defend herself, how to fight, but she had to get knowledge of this world here, the people, the skills to survive in the wilderness even.

She was hit with a wave of overwhelming thoughts.

Los Angeles could be a dangerous place, but there sure as hell weren't any monsters. The only monsters from her world were human. But here? Monsters weren't just humans. They were real. As real as cats and dogs.

"I'm hungry," Nom said. "Nothing awakens an appetite like being frozen."

"I have bread and cheese," Alric said. "I could also make us a vegetable stew."

Karka perked up at the talk of food. He didn't seem to be like Nom. Nay didn't think he could speak, and if he did, he hadn't revealed it yet. But she had the feeling he didn't. But he seemed to understand their words when the subject changed to food.

"I can cook for us. If you're kind enough to lend me your ingredients," Nay said.

Alric reached over and started pulling items out of his pack. A sack of vegetables, some bread and cheese. Little pouches of salt and spices. He laid them out for Nay. "All yours. I'll get you some water."

He took his own pot and started packing it with fresh snow, being careful to pick any leaves or twigs out of it. He set it by the fire to melt.

Nay examined the sack of vegetables. There were some potatoes and carrots. There was a yellow-white root vegetable that reminded her of pearl onions but weren't quite. She tasted the spices by dabbing her finger into each pouch and licking her finger. Her sense of taste was still messed up. Perhaps it only revived when she was eating a Delicacy.

"Nom, come here and taste these," she said. She dipped her finger in each pouch again and held it out for Nom to taste.

He tasted a yellow powder. "It's savory and sweet. I think there's clove in it."

That was probably a ginger-curry powder of sorts, Nay thought. Next was the spice that looked like crushed red pepper.

"Wow, that's spicy. This brings the heat!" Nom said.

So, that one was probably some kind of chili pepper. She was kind of impressed Alric was carrying around these spices. Salt, sure. But to carry around some variety? Either he was a man of taste, or spices were a thing here.

"Why did you have him taste those?" Alric asked. "You don't trust your own sense of taste?"

"My taste buds are shot."

"What?"

"They're gone. Where I come from, there was a disease that went through the population. It killed a lot of people. With others, it just left them with weird side effects. It took my taste buds away."

"A cook with no taste buds," Alric mused, puffing more smoke. "Now, that's something I've never heard of. There's a sense of twisted poetry to that."

She took out her dagger and started preparing potatoes. She peeled some, setting the peeled potatoes to one side. Some others she just gave a rough chop and set to the other side. She threw both of the differently prepared potatoes into the pot of water melted from the snow. Then she added a generous amount of salt.

Next, she chopped the carrots and peeled off the outer layer from the vegetables that resembled pearl onions. The stems of the roots were still attached, and she made sure to slice those off.

As she prepared the vegetables, the wind whistled around them, but the snowfall had stopped.

It was still technically night, for the stars were visible in the dark sky. Alric puffed on his pipe, Karka lay in front of the fire with eyes closed, and Nom swayed in front of the warmth. Nay had never really been camping before, but she imagined this was what winter camping must be like. Despite almost freezing to death, she was enjoying this moment, especially now that there was another human here.

"What does your church believe in? Do you worship a god or something?" Nay asked while she fished out some of the peeled, boiled potatoes with a spoon.

Alric was pulled out of whatever thoughts he was focused on. He was more than happy to talk about this subject by how he livened up. "The Veritax believes in the All-Seeing Truth, Verity."

"Is Verity a man or a woman?"

"The truth can appear as man or woman, person or beast. It chooses whichever manifestation it requires to communicate."

"And what is the truth?"

"The opposite of lies."

Nay looked up at him, smirking. "Well, no shit." She used the hilt of the dagger to mash the potatoes. She took the mash and started to form them into patties. "Where I come from, people have different ideas about the truth. One man's truth is another man's lies."

"That's why the world needs Verity. To truly decipher one from the other."

Nay drizzled some of the leftover olive oil into her own pot and set it on the fire. She regarded Alric with a skeptical look. "Churches telling people what to believe caused a lot of violence where I lived."

"Violence is necessary when dealing with those who have no conscience." Alric exhaled, forming the smoke into rings. "But I'm not man of violence. I mostly just keep the peace and help those who come to Verity for guidance. Monks of Veritax primarily just watch."

"Watch what?" Nay asked. As the pot heated, she set the mashed-potato patties inside. There was a sizzle as they began to fry in the oil. Their little camp filled with the aroma of vegetable stew and frying potatoes.

"Veritax's interests," he said. "Which is mostly giving people access to the truth wherever they may be. That smells delicious; what is that?"

Nay looked down at the potatoes. "Oh, these are like some hashbrown things I've whipped up. I figured we'd want something crunchy with the stew. Shame there's no meat. I'd be able to make a filling stock, then."

"What about the Marrow?" Nom asked. "Some mushroom could go well with your soup."

Alric's head turned sharply towards Nom. He took the pipe out of his mouth. "Did you say *Marrow?*"

"What of it?" Nom said.

Nay studied Alric. Was this some type of taboo topic?

He looked between them both. "You are Marrow Eaters?"

"I mean, bone marrow is pretty tasty if prepared correctly," Nay said. "It's like butter."

Alric addressed Nom. "Is that what you meant? Bone marrow?"

Before Nay could try and give an answer, Nom said, "No. The Marrow the Steksis gave to us. I have a feeling it will be delicious. Go on, Nay; show him."

So, it appeared there would be no hiding or skirting over this topic.

She sighed. She took the cloth out of her kit and unfolded it. A green glow radiated from the bio-mushroom in her hands. It had a truffle-like texture and scent.

The Truffle Marrow of the Steksis.

Alric stared at it in both fear and wonder. Even Karka opened his eyes and perked his head up to see.

"That is a Marrow!" Alric exclaimed. "Do you have the paperwork for that?"

"Paperwork?" Nay said.

"It's illegal to possess and handle Marrows unless you have a permit."

"Says who?"

"The DMA. The Delicatessa Marrow Authority. They control the acquiring, handling, and distribution of Marrow, and they are very strict."

"How strict?"

"They will execute any unauthorized or illegal Marrow Eaters. Are you registered with the DMA?"

Nay and Nom looked at each other. "Do we have to answer that?"

Alric stood up at that. "By the nether hells." He looked around, suddenly concerned if someone might be watching them. "Put that thing away before you get us all killed!"

"I seriously doubt anyone else is out here," Nay said. "Look at where we're at. We're in the middle of nowhere in the middle of the winter holocaust."

"We'll put it away," Nom said. "Put it away in our bellies."

Alric spun towards Nom. He stood there, mouth open, in shock. Finally, he shook his head and sat back down.

"If these things were so illegal to have, and someone was around to enforce it, I'm sure we would have already been slain," Nom said. He turned to Nay. "So, what do you think the best way to prepare this is? Something tells me if you fry it in some of that oil, sprinkled with some salt, it'll be delish."

Alric cursed and relit his pipe. He was muttering, "You are not privy to this; you are not privy to this."

"That's what I was thinking, too," Nay said. "Although I wish we had some butter instead of oil, but we gotta work with what we have."

She took the fried potato patties out of the pot and set them aside to cool. Then she rinsed the neon green mushroom with water from one of the skins and patted it dry. She gently set it in the oil that had some crispy fried-potato bits floating in the puddles. She sprinkled it with salt.

"It already looks tasty," Nom said. He swayed in front of the pot, wiggling his long tummy.

Green smoky light shined out of the pot, illuminating Nay and Nom's faces.

A rich smell wafted out with it, smelling of the earth. Nay was salivating a little. She could already imagine the slippery but tangible texture in her mouth, and if she still had the use of her taste buds, she was sure there would be that wonderful umami flavor. She thought she would do anything to have working taste buds again. She turned the mushroom with a spoon to make sure all sides were getting evenly cooked.

Alric said something about the nether hells again and then pulled what looked like a bottle of spirits out of his pack.

"Have you been holding out on us, monk man?" Nay teased. "Is that alcohol?"

"Frostbite Ale," he said. "Brewed by yours truly."

"You brew your own beer?"

"Many abbeys have their own distilleries. It's one of my jobs. How do you think Veritax raises funds? It's been a profitable venture for centuries."

"I guess monks do brew their own alcohol back where I'm from, too."

He popped the cap and took a swig.

"I want to try that," Nay said.

"Me too," said Nom. "But first, the Marrow. I want to see if it changes me like the Delicacy did."

Alric touched his talisman and took a big swig of Frostbite Ale.

Nay removed the mushroom from the pot to let it cool. She checked the vegetable stew. It was done. She ladled servings for the three of them, each with a side of fried hashbrown patties. She gave Alric his food. He took a bite of the patty and his face was overtaken with joy. "By Verity's sword! That is delicious! It's so crunchy and satisfying." He took another bite, amazed.

Nay took her dagger and carefully sliced the Truffle Marrow in half, releasing bright green juices that gleamed like a glow-in-the-dark Jell-O. She put Nom's half on top of his hashbrown patty.

She plopped her half in her mouth.

Her taste buds rejuvenated for the moment, almost knocking her over with the intensity of the flavor. It filled her sinuses and nostrils much like the effect of a fragrant and strong horseradish. It burned but in a good way. It was like dousing umami and wine together and then setting it on fire.

Her vision spun and she fell to a knee.

Alric looked up, alarmed. "Are you okay?"

Lights exploded across her vision and the magical text appeared.

[Marrow Consumed!]
[Truffle Marrow of the Steksis Consumed!]
[Would you like to unlock Marrow Ability for Tongue of the Hierophant Y/N?]
[Delicacy: Tongue of the Hierophant]
[Opening Delicacy Tree]
[Marrow Abilities: 0/12]

— CHAPTER THIRTEEN —

Whoa. I Can Make Magic Food.

Nay, with one knee planted in the snow, was trembling as she mentally chose *Y* for—

[Would you like to unlock Marrow Ability for Tongue of the Hierophant Y/N?]
[Opening Ability Tree for the Delicacy: Tongue of the Hierophant]

The tree looked like a 3-D holographic poster or chart of a human digestive system. From salivary glands and pharynx to the intestines and pancreas, it looked like all the organs were there. And each one glowed in a white aura with a cube next to it, signifying open Ability slots.

You have twelve open slots in this Ability Tree. You have consumed the Truffle Marrow of the Steksis. It has syncretized into the Chef's Delight Ability. Would you like to use a slot for Chef's Delight? [Y/N]

Before she decided, she mentally opened up the description for the Ability.

Chef's Delight. Through preparation and cooking, can imbue food and drink with basic Buffs and Debuffs for whoever eats and digests it. Grants you access to recipes straight from the spiritual database of Jezabelle Childe. Access to recipes and quality of food and Buffs will increase according to Rank.

"Whoa," she said.
"What is it?" both Nom and Alric asked. They were each staring at her with concern.

She selected *Y* and felt a warmth growing in her stomach, as if there was a cinder in her belly. The heat grew in intensity, and she thought she was either going to explode or give birth to an inferno. She tried to hold in her pain, but she started to groan. She staggered and fell forward, curling up into the fetal position.

Her vision went wild, like she was seeing in three hundred and sixty degrees all at once. It was disorienting and overwhelming. Not only did she see the forest in front of her, she also saw Nom and Alric to the side and the rock shelf behind her. She closed her eyes and the heat started to drift out of her, as if wisps of it were unfurling into the universe and connecting with something beyond her consciousness that was bigger than her. She felt tethered and connected to something, a presence or collective presence that appeared as a library full of cookbooks in her mind.

Then it disappeared.

[Ability Activation]
[Delicacy: Tongue of the Hierophant 1/12]
[Ability: Chef's Delight]
[Rank: Base]

The Rank text was blinking red.

She opened her eyes and her body tingled from consuming the Marrow. It reminded her of a heavy body high, which she would sometimes experience from some strains of indica or hitting a big dab. That was her closest frame of reference for it. She sat up.

Nom slithered up to her. "Are you okay?"

"I can make magic food," Nay said.

"Whoa," Nom said.

Seeing that she was okay, he went back to his food and immediately devoured his half of the mushroom. As he swallowed, his skin started to turn green. It started in his midsection and began to spread up and down his stalk. Soon, he was humming in happiness and emitting a green chartreuse glow like a neon art nouveau sign for absinthe.

"Is he going to be all right?" Alric said.

"He'll . . . be fine," Nay muttered. "He does that. Changes colors when he eats."

Nay opened up the Rank menu where she saw the odd marking and red blinking.

Rank is currently Base Level.
Error Message: There's been a Delicacy Activation without meeting appropriate Prerequisite. Delicacies require Prerequisite: Iron Rank.

Note: May experience errors or sense of dysphoria while using Marrow Abilities.
Diagnosis: Worldtripper Racial abilities seem to be creating Prerequisite Bypass. Please report to a DMA agent.

Alric helped her up and sat her down on the log.

Then he knelt in front of her. "Listen to me very carefully. You can't let anyone see or know what you can do. The Ligeia League doesn't look kindly upon unregistered Marrow Eaters."

She still trembled from the aftereffects of eating the Marrow. She looked up at him, meeting his eyes. "What's the Ligeia League?"

"The alliance of cities on the Ligeia Peninsula. Their government controls anything having to do with Delicatessa and Marrow. They like to control who is able to become a Marrow Eater. As you can imagine, Marrow Eaters have access to . . . resources others do not have. They represent power and wealth. Any Marrow Eater who has somehow bypassed their system is considered a threat."

Nay figured that made sense. Why wouldn't the government try to control magic-users and the resources that made them magic-users? It was power. Humans would always try to control and hold on to power. It was the one resource that people would go to any length to always try to control. Craving power was human nature.

"Got it, so keep a low profile with this stuff," Nay said. "Shouldn't be too hard, right?"

"Stitchdale and anywhere near the Spineshards is considered the wilds compared to the Peninsula. This is the world's edge. It's less tame out here, and there's less law. DMA agents or those associated with them may be passing through, but they are rare. Still, it is better to err on the side of caution. You never know who may be watching or listening."

He sat down next to her and passed her the bottle of Frostbite Ale.

She took a swig. Her sense of taste was gone again. Seemed like Delicacies and Marrow were the only foods strong enough to get through her numbed sense of taste. The ale was just cold to her, but when it went down, there was a nice, crisp feeling, like the liquid was burning away phlegm in her throat. She handed him the bottle back. "Do you know any Marrow Eaters?"

"You mean besides you?" Alric said. "I've encountered my fair share, usually when I'm in one of the cities performing duties for the Veritax. Many of the important family lines in each city are comprised of Marrow Eaters."

"Does the Veritax employ Marrow Eaters?"

"We do. Specific positions and posts require different needs. All of the higher-ups are Marrow Eaters."

"But not you?"

"I do not possess the affinity required for Marrow. My body would just digest a Delicacy or a Marrow as normal food. My Vigor is still Base Rank."

"What does that mean? *Base Rank*?"

"You truly don't know?"

Nay shook her head. "I assure you I have no reason to lie about it."

Alric finally started slurping up his vegetable stew. "Hey, your soup is pretty good, too, you know."

"Give me more time, some animal fat, and flour, and I'll show you a suitable stew."

On the other side of the campfire, Nom's skin had shifted towards purple again, but there was still a faint green aura around him. He was completely focused on a fried potato patty, eating slowly and with total concentration, like he didn't want to miss a second of getting to enjoy the experience.

After Alric got down a few bites, he began to explain the concept of Vigor to Nay. "Okay, so, where do I even begin? Vigor is like, that thing inside of us, a measure of our souls."

"Like our spirit?"

"It's the . . . energy our spirit generates. Vigor is the breath of life. It flows through everything."

"Okay, I get it. What did you mean when you said 'Base Rank'?"

"There are ways to make one's Vigor stronger, more powerful, more voluminous. Everyone, well, most people, is born with the Base foundation of Vigor. It's the bare minimum one needs to live. But there are those who wish to go beyond that Base level and build upon that foundation. Some people dedicate their whole lives to cultivating their Vigor. There are schools and guilds and organizations devoted to this."

"It sounds intense."

"It is. But to measure the different Vigor levels, there's a ranking system. The first step after Base is Iron. You have to be an Iron to be a Marrow Eater. That's where most stay. But if one were to advance past Iron, the next Rank is Bronze, followed by Silver, Gold, and Diamond. But honestly, anything past Bronze is pretty rare. At least that I know of. But like I said, most people aren't cultivators and are just satisfied with their Base-level Vigor."

"Why though? Why wouldn't you want to try and climb the ranks? Wouldn't that essentially mean more power?"

"Sure," Alric said. He munched on a fried potato patty and washed the bites down with more Frostbite Ale. "But it's not exactly easy."

"My mama would always say nothing easy was worth doing."

"It's not exactly cheap, either. Instructors, training, the right food, the right tonics, the right herbs . . . all that stuff. That stuff costs serious coin. Then there's the DMA and their monopoly on it all. If a Marrow Eater wants to climb ranks, they need DMA approval, so there's also politics involved. They'll hunt down anyone who tries to skirt the system. So, it can also be quite dangerous."

"Sounds almost as bad as the federal government from where I'm from and their old Prohibition policies on alcohol or their current policies on marijuana."

"What's marijuana?"

"It's a type of leaf you can smoke out of a pipe. It can have a relaxing effect."

"I would like to try this . . . what did you call it?"

"Marijuana."

"Marijuana."

He burped and said, "Excuse me." He patted his belly. "That was a fine meal." He had saved half of his fried potato patty.

He tossed it at Karka, and the fauglir snapped it out of the air and began chewing happily. The large animal looked content, eating Nay's cooking while stretched in front of the campfire.

"So, now are you going to tell me where you're really from?" Alric said.

Nay looked up at him. The high of consuming the Marrow was still lingering. She held out a hand and nodded at his pipe. "Can I try?"

He grabbed it and tamped out the old contents. "I just answered a bunch of your questions. So, maybe now you can answer mine." He put in a fresh plug of silverbell's leaf, lit his wick in the fire, and got the pipe going. He handed it to her.

She took a hit of the silverbell's leaf and coughed. She was sure her lack of taste buds muted the flavor, but a rush of spearmint tickled her sinuses. It was odd, taking in the smoke and getting both a warm and tingly cold feeling. It was nice. She took another puff and exhaled. She wondered if the silverbell contained nicotine or its analogue on this world.

"I'm fairly certain I'm from another world," she said.

He didn't seem surprised by this. He just nodded, watching her, as if she confirmed his suspicions.

She continued. "Because I'm pretty sure me, here with you now . . . this isn't my world. And the things I've seen and done here already don't exist or are not possible where I'm from. So, I don't know if this is like . . . another planet . . . or another reality . . . or an alternate universe. I have no idea. I just know it's a different place than where I'm from."

"As implausible and as fantastic as it sounds," Alric said, taking another sip of ale, "it does kind of make sense. It at least explains why you don't know anything about how things operate here. It also explains why someone as clueless as you is wandering up in the Spineshard Pass with no equipment or proper clothing. And it kind of explains why you have a tentacle as a traveling companion."

"The tentacle has a name, buddy," Nom said, coming up for air from his bowl of soup.

"Have you ever heard of or met people from other worlds here?" Nay asked. "Is this like a normal occurrence for you guys here?"

"I've never heard," Alric said. "It is not an occurrence I've heard of. Although we do get strange new breeds of monsters every now and then. But that's usually attributed to the Scar. But never people."

"So, this must be as strange for you as it is for us," Nay said.

"It is most strange," he said.

He held out the bottle of ale to Nay but she declined. Then he held it out to Nom. The tentacle moved so fast, he may as well have teleported over. He hugged the bottle with his protuberances and poured the rest of the ale down his beak.

Nom burped loudly, loud enough for his burp to echo throughout the mountain pass.

"Excuse me," he said.

In the distance, there was an answer. But not an echoing burp.

A howl.

— CHAPTER FOURTEEN —

Lucerna's End

After it was established that it was a local Spineshard wolf answering Nom's burp of satiety and not some creature that would hunt and kill them, they all retired and slept for the remainder of the night.

A quick breakfast of leftover soup and a few pulls of silverleaf later, Nay, Nom, Alric, and Karka set off down the mountain path.

They traveled a winding path of switchbacks, the gray sky above them and Frostbite Gorge to their east, a winding chasm of arctic-blue water full of ice floes. The water was slush for the most part, but it cut a ribbon of blue through the mountain pass. There was a gentle snowfall and the slight whisper of wind, but it was a nice reprieve from the battering blizzard Nay and Nom had first encountered here.

Karka carried their packs and gear, the silver bells jangling on his harness. Alric walked by his side, using his staff as a walking stick. Nay had found a stick of her own and followed close behind the pair, and Nom was behind her, using his protuberances and traveling close to the ground like a lizard.

By midday, he had decided to coil around Nay's waist and rest his head on her shoulder, and she didn't complain. He didn't weigh that much, and carrying him like this wasn't much different from using a backpack.

As the alpine trees became sparser, the world opened up below them. Alric and Karka stopped so Nay and Nom could take in the view.

"Stitchdale, my friends," Alric said.

The snow-scoured land below them was tundra-like, and parts of it were covered in ice. Frostbite Gorge branched into two rivers, one flowing east, the other flowing west. And they each found their way into separate valleys. There were herds of elk-like creatures and what looked like reindeer near both of the lakes that were in the valleys.

There was a settlement on the border of the eastern lake, which was Lucerna's End, their destination. It seemed to be a large frontier town that bordered the lake, and part of it followed along the eastern river in sporadic dots of civilization. They could see smoke rising from chimneys and lights coming from the wood and stone buildings. There were fishing boats in the lake, and Nay wondered if fish was this place's main export.

Overall, there was little sunlight and this looked like a harsh landscape to live in. Nay suspected that the people eking out lives here were hardened frontiersmen and perhaps even barbarians. No wonder Alric referred to Stitchdale as the end of the world.

"If we keep the pace, we should make Lucerna's End before nightfall," Alric said.

As they entered the outskirts of Lucerna's End, Alric suggested that Nom should tuck in underneath Nay's blanket, which she was huddled in like a cloak. There was no telling how civilization might react to a talking tentacle, and being both outsiders and Marrow Eaters, it was best to keep a low profile as is. Alric was mounted on Karka, letting the animal carry him now that they were on flat ground.

Nay got her first look at the inhabitants of the town, as there were gaggles of people on the muddy roads, tending to their trades or working outside the buildings. They looked human but also like something else. They were shorter than most humans, just around five feet, and their bodies were more stout, more muscular. They were a sturdy stock. A few of the men were unloading timber from a wagon hitched to a pack of *fauglir*, and the beasts regarded Karka with knowing looks as they passed.

Nay whispered to Alric, "Why is everyone so short?"

"They're stitchmen, the descendants of the maugrim that used to live inside of the Spineshard mountains and the clans of men who lived along the shores of Lac Coineascar. The maugrim were a stout folk of the mountains, short in stature. But both races were hardy, rough-and-tumble folk. It takes a certain kind of toughness to live off the land here, and there's not much tougher than the Spineshard clans here and the maugrim. Combine them and you have the stitchmen."

The vibe here reminded Nay of a frontier Western town during the gold rush in California, except more fantastic and strange. And cold. She couldn't shake the cold. They passed warehouses and a sawmill, a fishery, stables for fauglir and reindeer, a blacksmith working his forge outside, a general goods store and various shops for different trades and goods, tailors and furriers and carpenters and tanners.

Nay saw some human men coming out of an establishment in good spirits. They wore sword scabbards and were dressed in a mixture of furs and leathers.

There were female stitchgals on the wide wraparound porch, wearing hardly anything at all. One of them spotted Alric and smirked at him, "Why, hello again, Alric."

Alric muttered something under his breath and touched the talisman at his neck. He tried to tuck his head into his cloak, and he looked straight ahead.

"You can only run from Rosina for so long, monk boy!" She blew a kiss at him, and all the other women on the porch laughed, their painted faces and lips expressing mirth and pleasure.

"Is that your girlfriend, Alric?" Nay asked.

He stammered. "Absolutely not! She's a stitchgal of the Lucerna House of Saccharine Delights! I would never be seen with the likes of her."

"Oh, come on," Nay teased, "she seems like fun."

"She just wants my coin."

"I think she wants more than that."

Alric turned red with embarrassment. "I have nothing to offer her except Veritax's ear."

"Relax, lover boy," Nay said. "I'm just messing with you."

They walked on with the giggles of the stitchgals behind them.

"In my world," Nay said, "monks and priests are usually celibate. Is it the same here?"

"It is the same here," Alric said. "In the eyes of the Veritax, there's nothing inherently wrong with carnality, but it can be a distraction for Men and Women of the Veritable Truth."

"Hey, that's good! In my world, people have all sorts of funny issues and hang-ups about sex because how strict religion can be on the matter. They'll shame even non-clergy men for thinking about it or being tempted by it outside of marriage. What happens if you have a slip-up? Say you have too much Frostbite Ale one night and accidentally fall for Rosina's charms? Would the Veritax kick you out of the church or something?"

"No, if it got out, I would get a stern talking-to to make sure it didn't become a regular occurrence. In that case, they might replace me and demote me to some other assignment where I would not be subject to carnal temptations. Mostly, I would just have to live with my own shame."

"Hey, that's not so bad. That's why you brew Frostbite Ale, huh? Nothing like drowning shame in drink, I say."

"Remind me not to take any kind of spiritual advice from you."

"Aww, come on, Alric," Nay said. "I think you might find yourself pleasantly surprised."

"I want to visit this House of Saccharine Delights," Nom whispered. "Perhaps we should look into lodging there."

"He raises a good point," Nay said. "Maybe the stitchgals need a pair of chefs to oversee their kitchen. Should we inquire, Alric?"

"That's a staunch no from me," Alric said. "I will deliver you to Quincy's Lodge as we discussed, but where you choose to go after that is up to you."

"You're not going to stay with us?" Nay asked.

"I have to report to the church after we eat together at Quincy's."

"That's kind of a bummer."

"Don't worry; when I'm not at the church, I have a room at Quincy's. I'll be in town for a bit until I have to return to the abbey."

"Fair enough."

The main street ended at a large, three-storied tavern sitting on a cliff above the waters of Lac Coineascar. Quincy's Lodge was where most travelers in Lucerna's End were staying. "The original structure was the mead hall for the clan that lived here," Alric said. "It's using the original foundation."

Smoke puffed out of the two huge stone chimneys, and they could hear music, laughter, and chatter coming from inside. A huge sign hung above the porch with the logo carved into the wood. It was of a barrel-chested man who looked like he should be holding a war axe in his hands. Instead, he was holding a huge meat pie in one hand and a drinking horn in the other. And the runic letters translated to *Quincy's Lodge*.

Alric led Karka to the stablemaster, a gray-haired stitchman with a gob of something pressed between his gums and lower lip. He wore a short-sleeve tunic, and although he was older, he still moved with a muscular spryness. Karka nuzzled his forehead against the stitchman's chest. "Lo there, Karka. That's a good lad. I've got some fish bites for you."

He took Karka's reins from Alric and nodded. "Alric." He looked Nay up and down and winked at the monk. "Finally find some company on the edge of the world, did ya?"

"A humble servant of Verity is always willing to lend an ear to those who are lost, Bruennig," Alric said and handed the stablemaster a coin.

Nay caught a glimpse of the silver but didn't get a good-enough look to see the image embossed on the currency.

They walked up the stairs and opened the doors of Quincy's Lodge.

They entered a lantern-lit common room, where a pair of saloon doors marked the way into the tavern. Alric nodded at the young stitchgal who was stationed here, refilling the lanterns with oil.

Then they were through the saloon doors and Nay was blasted in the face with pipe smoke, the aromas of baked fish, and the music of a troupe of stitchmen and gals who were performing on a small stage. There was a fiddle and a flute and what she thought was a lyre and lots of stomping, dancing, and singing.

There was a giant hearth on one end and massive skulls and heads of creatures on the walls, the likes of which she couldn't identify. It looked like the trophy wall of some strange and barbaric bestiary. There were wooden staircases on each side of the tavern leading up to the second and third floors, which had open balconies so lodgers could see down into the tavern. Lanterns hung from the walls and candelabras hung from the ceilings, and there was a bar where the likeness of the huge barrel-chested man on the sign was pouring beer into horns and flagons while barking orders at one of the stitchgal servers, who was loading up a wooden tray with drinks.

Another stitchgal server passed them and said, "Coming through. Watch ye backs," as she weaved in between the tables, carrying a tray that had plates full of baked whole fish and roasted potatoes. Nay looked at the steaming food as it passed by her, and she thought it smelled all right and that the presentation was average. It looked a bit like bland bar food, to be honest.

Alric led them to a table near the hearth and they sat down. Nay looked around, and although the current diners were raucous, more than half the tables were still empty. The chairs were filled with mostly stitchmen, but she noticed a few humans in the crowd.

"Most of these lot are miners, fishermen, and lumberjacks," Alric said. "Iron-ore veins run thick in the rock here, and the best lumber is harvested off the side of the Spineshard mountains. Most of the Peninsula's iron and winterwood comes from Stitchdale. As for fish? Lac Coineascar and Maer Scathan have plentiful slivermoon trout."

"Does this place ever fill to capacity?" Nay asked. "It's only half full in here."

"Ever since the Two-Headed Trout Inn opened up on the other side of town, Quincy lost half his business there," Alric said. "Don't mention it to Quincy or you'll sour his mood. But the inn is closer to some people's day-to-day business. Staying there on that side of town saves them some travel. There's always been talk of someone setting up shop there for just that reason, but no one's gone and done it till now."

A stitchgal server approached them. "Lo, Alric."

She nodded at Nay, not recognizing her but acknowledging her as a new customer. "Welcome to Quincy's Lodge. What will ye be having today? Can I start ye off with some pints of Quincy's Icemarrow Ale?"

— CHAPTER FIFTEEN —

The Dinner

The stitchgal server's name was Hilde and her nose and ears were pierced with metallic hoops. Her hair hung in black braids, and she had enough skin exposed that Nay thought she was immune to the cold.

She returned to the table with two pints of Icemarrow Ale served in horns affixed with a metal ring that could be hung on stands on the table. "What it'll be, then, Alric? You and your friend want the dinner?"

"What's the dinner?" Nay asked.

Hilde answered without looking at her, her eyes drawn to the group of miners snickering at one of the other tables over. "Baked slivermoon trout with the baked potatoes. Same as always."

"You always offer the same dinner?" Nay asked. "Every day?"

"Since Ol' Pat's dropped off this mortal coil, yes," she said. "What of it?"

She looked at Nay then, defensive, almost daring her to have a problem with it.

"Two dinners will be fine, Hilde," Alric said.

Nay felt a sharp jab on her torso. Nom had pecked her with his beak. "Make that three," she said. "I've got an appetite for two today."

Hilde looked Nay over, then shrugged as if to examine if she was a big eater, but Nay's frame and her oversized clothes from Piero betrayed nothing about her capacity to eat. The server headed for the kitchen but cursed at the table of miners as she passed them, shutting them up.

Although the third dinner was for Nom, Nay felt like she could eat a horse after all the traveling they had done.

The descent down the mountain into Lucerna's End had left her sore, hungry, and exhausted. Her leg muscles were burning from all the walking, and the cold had sapped her of energy. As an Angeleno, her body was accustomed to walking but nothing like she had experienced here.

She wasn't sure if she was built for this kind of terrain and life, but she would have to adapt fast if she wanted to survive life in Stitchdale.

She took a sip of the Icemarrow Ale and was surprised to find it smooth and crisp, like a good cider. She couldn't discern the flavor, which she found frustrating. "Nom," she said. "Describe this to me."

She tilted the top of the horn underneath the blanket she had draped over her shoulders to hide the tentacle. He leaned forward and placed his beak over the opening. His thin tongue unrolled and slipped into the horn, and he began slurping. "Easy!" she whispered. "You're splashing it all over me!"

He slowed down his drinking and then stopped, releasing a burp that rippled the edges of the blanket. Some of the miners looked over at the sound, and Nay said, "Excuse me," and tapped her chest with her fist, pretending to burp again.

"Well?" Nay asked.

"It's smooth," Nom said. "But there's a cold bite to it, like an icicle poking at the back of my mouth. And instead of a warmth that you sometimes get from alcohol, there's a frigidness to it that spread throughout my body and made me shiver. I like it."

He drank some more.

"Save some for me, dammit!" Nay said.

"Why don't you get another horn?" Nom said between slurps.

Alric took a long guzzle from his horn and smacked his lips. "It's Quincy's own personal brew. It's what the Lodge is known for."

Hilde returned and set down a bowl of what appeared to be a mix of nuts and seeds and a plate of sliced cucumbers soaking in some type of dressing or vinegar. Then she was off again and, as usual, cursed at the group of miners as she passed them.

Nay picked up one of the cucumbers. "Oh, what's this?"

Alric grabbed two cucumber slices and tossed them into his mouth. As he chewed, he said, "Cucasalat."

Nay bit into the cucumber. It was crunchy and refreshing and she suspected it had a tang. "These are fermented. Nice."

"It's one of Quincy's starters," Alric said. "Probably the last of Ol' Pat's batch before she passed. A shame. Maybe she wrote down the recipe and instructions for Quincy. Because the Lodge just won't be the same without them."

Nay fed a few to Nom underneath her blanket, and she felt the tentacle squirming with joy as he crunched on the little treats. "Oh, these are good!" Nom said. "Salty, cool, and addictive. I bet you can't eat just one!"

Next, Nay rifled through the bowl of seed and nuts with a finger. The main nut seemed to be pecan-like. She plopped one into her mouth. It had a satisfying crunch but she couldn't pick up the taste. She fed one to Nom.

"This tastes of the forest," Nom said. "But it's fatty. Like a good butter. Oh, and it crumbles like when I bite into some cookies! Very delightful!"

Alric took a handful of nuts and seeds and poured them into his mouth and chewed away. "A nice bit of something salty to go with the Icemarrow Ale. Just a bit of a chew to keep you slavering while you wait for the meal. It's got pumpkin seeds and starflower seeds. The nuts are pistachios and spinecrackers. I think the mixture is designed to keep you drinking ale. At least, that's what it seems like to me."

Nay followed his lead and took a handful and chewed. He was right. It had a nice preoccupying mouthfeel. She scattered the mixture on the table in front of her. One of Nom's protuberances quickly swiped the nuts and seeds towards his beak. The sound of crunching came from inside the blanket.

"Yes, we're definitely going to need more ale," Nom said through a mouthful of the nut mix.

As they ate the snacks that were a prelude to the dinner, Alric gave Nay some history on Quincy. "He was an adventurer from the Peninsula, one of the more well-known ones, too."

"An adventurer?" she said.

"Yes, it can be quite profitable for the skilled ones," Alric said. "There's a fortune to be made from finding and acquiring cultivation boons, the ingredients for the special elixirs, the herbs, any relic or item that may help one strengthen and rank up their *Vigor*. Many do contract work for the different schools or guilds, even certain powerful families. Even the DMA commissions freelancers for acquiring Delicacies and Marrow. A lot of that stuff comes from monsters, and sometimes, taking down a monster is not easy. Even for skilled Marrow Eaters who work in an official capacity for the authorities. Some adventurers may not even be interested in that stuff, but they just like to travel and accept quests from towns and cities. These adventurers do anything from pest control to investigating disappearances or strange happenings. Still, some just do it for the thrill of adventure. There's even an Adventurer's Guild where they compete with each other for standing and notoriety."

The idea of adventuring and being an adventurer got Nay's imagination racing. It sounded exciting. "That sounds dangerous."

"It's highly dangerous," Alric said. "The tale of the adventurer perishing while trying to make a name for themselves is a tale as old as time. That's why when there's someone like Quincy, who survives into old age and actually retires, it's somewhat of a big deal. Someone like him is considered a legend for a reason."

"Why retire in Stitchdale, though?" Nay said. "Seems like there would be less-stressful places to retire."

Alric tossed more nuts into his mouth. "You'll have to ask him that yourself. I've never gotten him to explain it to me. Only thing I could figure is that he did a lot of adventuring in this region and developed an affinity for it. Or maybe he just doesn't like Peninsula life. Don't know why, though; it's certainly a lot cushier compared to this. The weather doesn't try to kill you."

Hilde arrived and set three plates onto the table before them. "Here's the dinner and I brought ye more ale." She pulled more horns of ale that were wedged into slots along the edge of her tray and hooked the rings on the table stand.

Nay felt Nom wriggling with excitement against her. She nudged him to calm down and be patient, but he didn't really get the message. The last thing she needed was for him to burst out into view because he couldn't control his enthusiasm for food. She didn't want to think what that situation would cause. She suspected that these people might draw steel and try to attack him, which was pretty much the worst-case scenario.

Hilde took their empty horns and moved to her next stop, which was slapping one of the miners in the back of the head as he was trying to drink, making him spray ale all over his mates. "What was that for?" he exclaimed. "I didn't even try to grab ya that time!" But she was already checking on the next table along her route.

Steam rose off the baked slivermoon trout. It was so long, its tail and head were hanging off the edge of the plate. It had been baked with its skin still on. It was the color of tuna, and it even looked like there was a glow coming off the fish, reminiscent of the light of the moon. Its eyes were milky white, probably some development to inhabiting near-freezing water all the time.

"Interesting choice," Nay said, "not to descale the fish. They really do need help."

At least it smelled good, and Nay saw flaky salt and a batch of herbs wrapped and stuffed in its mouth.

There were lemon wedges and a lump of white sauce along the edge of the plate. She dabbed a finger in and tried it. It had the lumpy and creamy texture of tartar sauce.

Across from her, Alric began digging in with his bare hands. He quickly plucked off flakes of the white meat, plopping it into his mouth before the heat burned his fingers. The fish was still hot, and he blew a few times so he didn't burn his mouth too badly.

Nay positioned Nom's plate in front of her and his tongue whipped out, tearing bits of the meat and smearing it in the sauce. She looked down and saw him turn a rosy color denoting that he was pleased.

She carefully peeled off some of the flaky white flesh and followed Alric's lead, blowing on it before sticking it into her mouth.

The meat was delicate and melted on her tongue. The texture was great, reminding her of trout from back home. The last time she had it was at a Fourth of July celebration with her friends. They had gone camping out at Big Bear Lake, and back then, she still had her sense of taste. The memory of fresh, hot fish sprinkled in lemon juice and dipped in tartar sauce made the pleasure areas of her brain tingle.

She squeezed some of the lemon wedges on the fish and dipped it in the sauce. Her tongue tingled a little and she got the faint hint of the flaky salt's taste. She wished she could experience all the flavors, but swallowing the food satisfied the ravenous hunger in her stomach.

The bones of the fish had a silver hue; it looked almost as if it had a metallic skeleton in the light of the hearth.

"This is damn good fish," Nom said, between bites. He had almost stripped his fish clean. "The sauce is all right, too. But I can't shake the feeling that it's missing something. Like it needs more salt or more seasoning or something."

Nay sliced through her baked potato. The skin was slightly charred, and she was surprised to find there were no fixings, not even butter to put on it. So, she grabbed a bunch on her fork and dipped it in the sauce.

"The potato's kind of bland," Nom said. "But the food is making me less hungry. Someone should really tell Quincy that they need to dress the potatoes up more. It wouldn't take much. Even some salt and butter would make a difference."

Nay watched Quincy, who was behind the bar, regaling the stitchmen sitting on the stools there with a story. She finished her fish and potato and guzzled down her ale. She stood.

"Where are you going?" Alric said.

"I think I'll tell him myself. I think it's time I make my introduction to the proprietor."

— CHAPTER SIXTEEN —

Owlsquatch Reins and Tapioca Pudding

And that's when I came back to the doors of the keep that actually ended up being a Scarsister bordello. I entered with the reins of an owlsquatch in one hand and a bucket of tapioca pudding in the other—"

Quincy cut himself off when he saw Nay take a stool at the bar, making her the only girl in the crowd listening to his raucous tale.

"And then?" The lumberjack stitchman leaned forward, needing to know what happened next.

"And then I let the owlsquatch loose and drew Samuel here," Quincy bellowed, gesturing at the massive and cruel-looking crossbow hanging on the wall behind him. "He was already locked and loaded and ready to administer some justice. I let him fly and impaled two of the sisters of the night with one bolt. They did not like that. They transformed then, showing me and my party behind me their true forms. They ripped the bolt out with their poison-dripped talons and let loose shrieks that would turn your blood to curdled milk!"

He was animated while he talked, and there was a charisma about him that reminded Nay of her favorite volleyball coach during high school.

Up close, she could see that his forearms were covered in scars. That was probably a good indication that the rest of his skin was similar. He sported a salt-and-pepper mustache that would have certainly attracted attention back in Los Angeles. It was the type of facial hair that wins awards or is endemic to certain types of adult films. He had a prominent scar running from the corner of his left eye down past his lips and down his chin.

He had a bar towel over one shoulder, and he started cleaning some flagons as he turned his attention to Nay. "I see you could use a top-off." He put his hand out for the horn.

She gave it to him and he flipped a spigot on a barrel and filled it to the top. He handed it back. "I assume this is going on Alric's tab."

Nay nodded. "I heard you lost a cook. My condolences."

Quincy poured a little ale out onto the ground. "Ol' Pat, may Verity rest her soul. She kept this kitchen running and these mouths fed. I reckon I've lost some customers since she passed too. Gracie has taken over. She's a good lass, doing the best she can, but Ol' Pat's shoes are big shoes to fill." He nodded at a server, who almost tripped and dropped a whole tray of food. Some diners helped her stabilize. "She works hard and hasn't missed a day, so I guess that's something. The lads like her well enough."

"Well, not everyone can be like Ol' Pat around a pot," Nay said.

"That's the honest truth," Quincy said. "None of the other servers have been interested in the position. We're getting along, but I am on the hunt for an experienced cook."

"You know, Quincy," Nay said. "It's funny you say that. I happen to be a cook."

As he shined a glass, he turned to her to examine her directly. As he studied her, she felt like she was being scrutinized. A prompt appeared.

[Aura Detected]
[Scryer's Eye Aura Detected]
[Rank: Bronze]

Nay realized Quincy was a Marrow Eater. And he was Bronze-level. Hadn't Alric said anything above Iron was kind of out of the ordinary? Or was it Bronze? She couldn't remember. Either way, no wonder he was able to survive a life of adventuring. Now he was using an Ability on her. She wondered what kind of information it showed him.

"Odd," Quincy muttered. "Where have you been traveling from?"

She tried not to let on that she knew he was using magic on her. "I came down from the mountain, near the abbey, with Alric."

"But you're not with the church?"

"Nope."

"What were you doing in the mountains?"

"Mostly trying to survive the storm."

Quincy prepared an order of ales and beers for one of the server tickets. His eyes were focused on the drinks, but Nay could tell he was regarding her.

"Where are you from? Which city on the Peninsula?"

Nay thought about lying. But she was basically applying for a job here. She thought it would be bad luck to start things off by lying to a potential employer.

"I'm not from any of the cities on the Peninsula," Nay said. "I'm from a place called Los Angeles."

He nodded, not as if he knew what Los Angeles was, but as if she just passed the first part of a test. "It's good you didn't lie to me. I know you're a Traveler. It's very obvious. Written all over you."

"It is?" Nay said. "I guess I just did tell you I basically traveled all of yesterday."

He got closer to her then and leaned so he could whisper. "That's not what I mean. I know you're a Worldtripper."

Nay tried not to freak out. It would not be good to have attention focused on them while they talked. She swallowed. "You do?"

"Aye. Those who have eyes can see. If they have the right eyes."

Nay knew his Scryer's Eye Ability tipped him off that she was an outsider here. What an interesting and useful spell to have, especially when one was working in the food industry. She wished she could have had access to an Ability like that in all of the kitchens she worked in back home. That would have been especially useful to a front-of-the-house worker.

"So, you were a cook in Los Angeles?" Quincy asked. He placed a bowl of the nut-and-seed mixture in front of her.

She took a handful. "I was a chef, yes."

"So, you have experience serving people food in a fast-paced establishment?"

"It's all I've ever known, since I was a kid."

"Is the Lodge why you came to Lucerna's End?"

"Honestly? I was just trying to find other people so I could have a chance at surviving. Then Alric found me and he told me about this place. And after eating the food, I thought to offer you my help. Since I have the skillset."

"So, you think there's something wrong with my food?"

"There's nothing wrong with the food. The fish and potatoes are solid. The ingredients are simple and fresh, and in my experience, that's what you want. I just think it would help to offer your patrons some variety. It's clear you already offer them passion. Also, did you know you've been serving the fish without descaling them?"

"A little bit of scales stuck between the teeth never hurt anyone."

"Also, it would have been nice, as a customer, to have had a choice. Another option for dinner instead of the fish."

"But that's what we had ready. The fish here is always plentiful and fresh."

"Yes, that's the nice thing about being next to big lakes and rivers. But surely there's gotta be other proteins that are just as plentiful and fresh."

"Proteins?"

"Meat."

"Oh, right. The problem with that is that Ol' Pat would handle all of our stock. The Two-Headed Trout Inn swooped in and took advantage of her passing. Since then, it's been hard to make a deal with the vendors, and I haven't had time to go out personally to convince them. There's already enough to do around here as is."

"Let me handle the vendors. I'll make sure your kitchen is properly stocked so you can offer your diners both passion and variety. If you give me a chance, I'll show you the possibilities."

Quincy grew silent and looked out over his half-packed house. The light of the hearth cast a warm glow on his face. He looked towards the stage, where the stitchmen troupe of bards was performing. The music hadn't been enough of a draw to keep the place packed. Seemed like he was imagining what it would be like to have all the seats filled again.

After a moment he spoke again. "Okay, Renee Favreau of Los Angeles. This is how this is going to work. I know you need a place to live, a means to survive while you learn how my world works."

She stammered, but he held up a hand.

"I'll give you lodging. You have a week trial where you run the kitchen for Quincy's Lodge."

"And after the week?"

"If my customers like your food, then we'll talk about more permanent arrangements and the matter of pay. Until then, it's a test. It's sink-or-swim time. For both you and your pet."

Nay stiffened and she felt Nom go rigid. He knew about Nom.

Nom spoke from inside the blanket. "I'm not her pet, sir."

Quincy raised an eyebrow.

"He's definitely his own . . . person," Nay said.

"He's not a nuisance or a threat, is he?"

"He's a bit odd-looking and has a goofy personality, but no."

"Odd-looking?" Nom said. "Who's odd-looking?"

"Good," Quincy said. "This is a drama-free establishment. For my staff, at least. We get enough from the diners and lodgers. I don't need it from my own team."

"I don't like drama either," Nay said. "Nom is actually my sous-chef."

"Really?" Quincy smiled, his bushy mustache bristling like a hairy caterpillar. "So, I'm getting two cooks for the price of one."

"Oh, we shall talk about the matter of pay after our first week!" Nom said.

Quincy chuckled. "That we will, strange one. And I'll warn you now. If you get monstrous with any of my customers, I'll be the first to show you the edge of my axe."

He nodded at the massive, wicked-looking battle-axe that hung over the hearth and gleamed in the firelight. "Gertrude hasn't seen any action in a few years, but she was my secret weapon when I took down the Laugher in the Lac.

Lots of tentacles, that one had. Gertrude just loves tentacles. Loves 'em. She loves the way they feel when her edge cuts through them."

Nay felt Nom swallow. His eye peeked out from the blanket to look at the axe named Gertrude hanging over the hearth. "The Laugher in the Lac?" Nom asked. "Why was it called that?"

"Because of the way it laughed as it devoured men."

"Sounds like a pleasant fellow," Nom said. "Don't worry, boss man; you'll have no problems from me. I don't eat people. I prefer pizza."

"After you finish your meal," Quincy said, "Hilde can show you to your room. You start tomorrow, before first light. Breakfast right now is more of a self-serve arrangement we have set up. Lunch isn't too busy, because most of our clientele are in the forest or in the mines. Dinner is the big draw and that's when we'll be the busiest."

"Wait," Nay said. "You guys do a complimentary continental breakfast?"

"I don't know what that means," Quincy said. "But the breakfast is oats and bread and fruit people help themselves to."

Nay chuckled to herself. "Where I'm from, that's called a continental breakfast."

"Why is it called *continental*?"

"So, it was coined on this island called Britain. It was a meal that resembled what a breakfast would look like on the continent closest to them. As most of the travelers staying in their hotels were from that continent, that's the type of breakfast they were used to."

Quincy grunted, a bit indifferent to the linguistics lesson. He scooted close to her again. "One last thing. And I'm sure you already realize this. Don't let people know you're a Traveler. If anyone asks, tell them you're from across the Vancian Sea. And then be extremely vague."

"What's across the Vancian Sea?"

"A kingdom called Reith. Just mention the harbor city of Emphyrio. You traveled here because with the recent developments in changes within the Voreheim royal family, things have become too dangerous for your kind."

"And what's my kind?"

"Women with a bit of color in their skin tone."

— CHAPTER SEVENTEEN —

Market Tactics

Nay and Nom's room was on the second floor.
There was a single bed, an oak chest at the foot of it. A mirror and a sink with a washbasin.

There was plumbing, and Alric mentioned Quincy had some amenities installed by a gnomish artisan Marrow Eater, so some stuff was operating off magic. Not a lot, but enough that people didn't have to use chamber pots and each room had a heat source, and supposedly the bulk of the amenities were in the kitchen and within the foundation of the structure.

Alric had given her a set of new clothes he had purchased from Igby's, the local tailor shop.

"You didn't have to do this," Nay had told him.

"You're wearing oversized bloodstained clothes, whose origin I would rather know nothing about," he had said. "If you're going to be making and serving food for the people of Lucerna's End, you could start with a fresh and clean set."

She had hugged him before he retired to his room. She had thought he blushed when she did so, but he had turned around and excused himself so quickly, she couldn't exactly tell.

There was a fresh tunic, dyed black, with some string to close the chest and collar. A green cloak that she could use outside to shield her against the wind and snow. A pair of leather pants that were form-fitting, comfortable, and probably the most durable piece of clothing she had ever put on in her life.

And best of all, a pair of gray boots that seemed to be made out of some water-resistant material. It made her think of otter skin. He had called them "nagaskin boots." He said they were also good against slipping, which he thought would be perfect for a kitchen.

She didn't have any heavy hides or furs or anything if she had to travel in the snow, but that was okay.

She figured she could start building a wardrobe when she got paid. She would be spending most of her time in the kitchen, anyways.

Nom was happy not to be attached to her and was exploring the room. Quincy made sure the tentacle had a goose-feather-stuffed mat to sleep on.

"I'm still offended Alric didn't get me anything," Nom said. "What am I? Chopped liver?"

"What's he supposed to get a tentacle?" Nay said as she washed her face in the water basin. There were two agate-like stones on the rim. One was red and black, and the other was blue and black.

When she tapped the reddish agate, the bowl grew warm, heating the water. She tapped the blue stone and the bowl chilled, cooling the water.

"It's more the gesture that counts, not so much the gift," Nom said, spinning in circles on his bed, getting the mat trampled just right, before finally lying down.

Nay stripped down to her skivvies and crawled underneath the wool blanket on her bed.

"Get some sleep, Nom. We have an early morning."

Gracie was the young stitchgal who had filled in for Ol' Pat when she passed.

She was barely out of her teens and more interested in boys than she was in cooking, although Nay recognized the gal had an affinity for baking in the way she handled the duties for the production of bread.

When Nay examined the dough, she knew it was of a pretty low quality. It looked to be comprised of legumes and bran. Baking wasn't her strong suit, but she knew enough methods to improve what the Lodge was currently serving.

"After these rolls are done," Gracie said, "I set them out in the dining room for the breakfast with the oats, hot water, and milk. We also serve a nice pepper tea that gets the blood flowing in these early morning hours. In fact, I have some now. I always drink a few cups as I'm baking. I need it to wake up."

"I'll have a cup or two," Nay said. "I need coffee to function. Especially before the sun is up."

"What's coffee?" Gracie said.

"It's like tea, but it comes from a bean. A harsher drink but addictive. I'll see if I can get some soon so you can try it." *If it's even a thing in this world*, Nay thought.

Nay set down the basket Quincy had left in front of her door. He left her a note saying it was for Nom, for his transport from their room to the kitchen so no one would see him.

As Gracie turned to pour Nay tea, Nom slipped out of the basket and slinked into the shadows of the kitchen, exploring what Nay was beginning to think of as the "medieval line."

The kitchen was a huge arched chamber that had a firepit in the center and a spacious hearth against one wall. There were curved alcoves that served as ovens. The whole chamber was filled with a warm, amber glow from the candles hanging from the curved timber above. The floor seemed to be a mixture of stone and clay tiles, and the chimney was carved from big squares of stone. There was a buttery, a bottlery, a pantry, and several storerooms, one of which was a chamber for drying meat. The larder was stocked with containers of legumes, grains, and root vegetables.

There was a stove top adjacent to the hearth with iron surfaces, and Nay saw more of the temperature agate stones on the device.

There was whimsy to the design of the place, and Gracie explained that most everything was stitchmen-designed except for the special appliances that operated off magic, designed by a Marrow Eater gnomish tinkerer from the city of Mechalopolis.

Nay would have time to explore all the tools and devices later, but her first matter of business was taking inventory and then getting out to the market to meet the vendors of Lucerna's End.

She had told Nom, *"The key to ensuring this enterprise is a success is acquiring the best ingredients that are available in the town. We need to figure out who the suppliers are and make some deals. Fresh and simple ingredients is my philosophy."*

"You want me to go with you?" Nom had said. *"I'm perfectly happy exploring this kitchen and observing Gracie with her bread."*

"I need you with me because I need you to taste the product of these vendors," Nay had said.

Gracie handed her a wooden cup of pepper tea. Nay took a sip. There was a kick to it. She knew because she could feel a burning at the back of her throat. She was sure this was loaded with caffeine.

"So, you're the new cook, eh?" Gracie said, observing her.

"Not yet," Nay said. "I'm the new trial."

"Well, I'm grateful to have the help. Only so much I've been able to do. I'd rather go back to serving. I like talking and meeting with people. But Quincy said I was the only gal that didn't burn the breakfast bread and if I wanted a job, then I best be comfortable in the kitchen."

Nay nodded and got her first good look at Gracie. She was young and pretty with rosy cheeks. She kept her long blond hair in braids and kind of looked like a young shepherdess and maiden. She was sure she got a lot of attention from the men in the Lodge, which was probably why she wanted to be working front of the house.

She was unusually chipper for being up this early in the morning, which was probably another reason Quincy had her getting up at baker's hours. It would be torture to someone who wasn't a morning person. Which meant Quincy cared about his employees. He could have just stuck anyone down here, but he chose the person who would be the most agreeable to the position.

"So, here's the deal for today, Gracie," Nay said. "You run things like you normally do every morning. I'm going to go meet with vendors and see about getting more product in this kitchen."

"I'm sorry, miss. Product?"

"You know, more vegetables and fruit. Different kinds of meat. We need to branch out from just fish."

"Sometimes, we do roast chickens and snowquail. But it has been a while since we've had any fowl to prepare for dinner."

"Exactly. So, you hold down the fort here and I'll be back in a few hours."

Nay set out towards the Wharf District of Lucerna's End, where she was told all the market vendors set up shop, with Nom coiled around her torso and shoulder underneath her cloak.

There was a cold drizzle that hit her sideways due to the wind, and the white of the sun was rising somewhere in the east. Dawn was blocked by a barrier of storm clouds in the dark, gray sky.

She shivered and she could feel Nom's body sapping her of some heat.

She carried a purse in a pocket on the inside of her cloak. It was filled with silver coins. It was some of the weekly kitchen budget for the Lodge, and Gracie had given it to her. She mentioned that it was more than usual because she rarely spent all of the allocated budget each week, so it had accumulated in savings.

The ground was muddy and cold, but the nagaskin boots kept her feet warm and firm on the icy street. There was a street crew of stitchmen wearing furs, who had shovels and carts of salt for keeping the roadways from being totally frozen over. They smoked tobacco cigarettes and hummed songs as they worked.

Lanterns hung from street poles, keeping the streets lit by gaslight, and already groups of stitchmen were up and on the way to their jobs. Still, two-thirds of the establishments and buildings were closed. Not everyone in Lucerna's End was an early riser.

"I don't think I'm ever gonna get used to this cold," Nom said.

"Well, we play our cards right," Nay said, "and we'll mostly be in the Lodge. But for now, we have to figure out how much of a stranglehold the Two-Headed Trout Inn has on the vendors here. And if we can manage, I'd like to check out their establishment sooner than later. I want to know what we're dealing with."

"Know thy enemy," Nom agreed.

Nay knew they were in the Wharf District when the smell of fish assaulted them. The whole town smelled like the Lac, but the distinct smell of sea creatures permeated the district. There were a few blocks of warehouses before they got a view of the shipyard and the boardwalk, which is where the Lucerna Market was located.

The Lucerna Market was a street before the boardwalk where vendors had set up shop on each side. They mostly dealt in fish and freshwater crab, but Nay spotted the fruit and vegetable vendors, and there were sellers hawking meat that clearly wasn't seafood.

"We're interested in anything that isn't seafood," Nay said. "That's everything here; the rare stuff is the wild game brought in from the forests or even livestock meat. I want beef, poultry, and pork."

[Quest Detected]
[Quest: Make Deal with Moonglum Farms]
[Accept Quest Y/N?]

She accepted the quest, and a middle-aged stitchman handling a crate full of eggs in front of a wagon seemed to shimmer with a yellow aura. A dot appeared on her mini-map, designating him. Sure enough, as they got closer, they saw the brand on the side of his wagon. Moonglum Farms.

He had cages of chickens, and he had various cuts of beef and pork wrapped in butcher paper and sticking out of barrels. His tables displayed different vegetables, stuff she recognized like potatoes and squash and other stuff like "icebite cilantro" and "tundra peppers." Green, lettuce-like vegetables that somehow flourished in the cold soil here in Stitchdale.

Nay picked up a cut of beef loin and unwrapped the butcher paper a little to get a peek at the meat.

"The finest beef you'll find in all of Stitchdale," the Moonglum farmer said.

"That's what every farmer and cattleman here says," Nay said.

"Who said that?" the farmer said. "Was it Bill from Snowdew Farms? You should know he's a liar."

"Didn't sound like he was lying when he offered me a wholesale deal on what he described was grade A beef even better than Japanese wagyu."

The farmer blinked, only half-comprehending what she said. But he had definitely picked up on her tone. And her tone said she got a better deal from a rival farmer who though his cattle was superior.

"He's lying. You're making a big mistake if you make a deal with him."

Nay took out her pouch and idly tossed it up and down in her hands, jingling the silver coins. "I don't know. He offered to throw in some poultry and pork as well. It's a deal that's hard to beat."

The farmer's eyes lit up with greed. "Before you make a decision, why don't you do a taste test so you can see for yourself?"

He produced a plate and pulled the cover off it, revealing some roasted beef rib. It was covered in some type of brown sauce. He offered it to her. She grabbed it and took a bite. The farmer leaned in to watch her. She took her time chewing and showed no reaction.

"That's pretty good," Nay said. "I'll tell you what. I'll pay point five percent less per pound than what the Two-Headed Trout is paying you for a week's supply of beef. And I'll pay you more than whatever they're paying for poultry and pork if I get here first at the beginning of each week."

"How much more?"

"What sounds good to you?"

[Quest Complete!]
[Make Deal with Moonglum Farms Quest Completed!]
[Congratulations!]
[You have been rewarded with Vigor Points]

— CHAPTER EIGHTEEN —

Kinky Martha Stewart

Nay and Nom had returned to Quincy's Lodge at midmorning with a hand cart full of produce.

The Moonglum Farms vendor, whose name ended up being Don, met her shortly after with a wagon haul of meat near the kitchen exit that would serve as a loading dock.

Quincy had wandered outside to watch the exchange as Don and Gracie rolled barrels of beef, poultry, and pork into the kitchen.

"You spent *how* much on *how* many pounds of meat?" Quincy said, concerned.

"Before you worry about the numbers," Nay said, "just know that this is the best-quality meat we're going to find in town. I had to make a deal with Don if we wanted to start with the best ingredients."

"You spent a nearly half a month's budget on, if you're lucky, a week's worth of meat!" Quincy couldn't hide his worry. "I say *lucky* because most of it might rot! We are not getting that many customers who can justify this purchase!"

Nay winced and turned towards him. "Trust me. Give me two days, two dinner services before you start worrying. If I have leftovers, I can dry-age and freeze it to make it last. So, either way, it will be put to use."

"This is a bold move, Renee Favreau," Quincy said. "For your sake, you better hope it pays off."

"Fortune favors the bold, sir," she said.

Quincy walked back inside, shaking his head.

[Quest Detected]
[Quest: Prove Quincy Wrong and Sell All the Product]
[Accept Quest Y/N?]

Nay accepted the quest and the opened the menu for *Vigor Points*.

Collect Vigor Points to cultivate your Vigor! Collect enough Vigor Points and you will ascend in Rank!
Current Rank: Base
Progress: 5%

Don reappeared and shook her hand. "That's everything. Glad to be in business with the Lodge. It's about time Quincy got someone sensible to make a deal with me. Same time and amount next week?"

Nay smiled. "You bet."

He climbed back into his wagon, which was pulled by actual reindeer. He waved as the animals pulled the wagon back onto the street.

Gracie emerged and sidled up next to her. "What did Quincy say to you?"

"He has doubts about handing me the reins of the kitchen for a week."

"Aye," Gracie said, "he does get nervous about the budget. Can I let you in on something?"

Nay nodded.

"He's been a bit of a mess since Ol' Pat passed."

"How did she pass?"

"The Thief of Time finally caught up with her. She's been running the kitchen since the beginning."

"And she didn't prepare a successor? She didn't have a sous-chef or second-in-command?"

"No, can't say that many people were ever interested, and she liked to do things by herself. She never liked people in her space when she was cooking. She was always shooing gals away."

"What about recipes? Did she write them down? Keep a record of them somewhere?"

"Aye, I'll show ya."

Once back in the kitchen, Nom had slunk away into the shadows when Gracie wasn't paying attention. Nay had given him instructions to start prep on the vegetables for dinner service. She gave him the tasks of peeling the garlic and washing and cutting the blue-hued tundra peppers and the icebite cilantro and the other stuff on the list.

Nay only knew it was a matter of time before Gracie stumbled upon him. There was just no way to have him perform sous-chef duties in the kitchen while also hiding from another member of the kitchen staff. But she would deal with that as it happened. Best to give Nom a head start before the inevitable occurred.

Gracie led Nay to one of the storerooms, and there was a stool and table hidden in one of the corners behind some stacks of crates. There was a candleholder on the table. She opened the drawer revealing a small battered notebook bound in leather. There were pencil nubs and Ol' Pat's last hand-rolled cigarettes and some wicks. "That's it there," Gracie said.

Nay picked up and opened the small cookbook. Ol' Pat's handwriting was best described as a runic scrawl, but Nay was able to read thanks to her Rosetta Stone Passive Ability. There were recipes for various appetizers, including the cucasalat she had last night. There were different recipes for bread and methods to prepare roast chicken and winterquail. Also, various tarts. It was hearty peasant-like cooking, and Nay was sure she had seen variations of some of these recipes in highfalutin' French cookbooks. All those dishes were based on simple farmland meals. She closed the book and would come back to it later to read in more detail.

Nay put Gracie in charge of the lunch service, which was just dried fish, a bit of cheese, and more bread. Gracie's lunch station was on the end of the kitchen closest to the doors that led into what Nay called the expo room, a small anteroom where there was a table to set the dishes and trays for the servers. It was a buffer between the kitchen and the tavern, and Nay was glad to see it because it would mean less front-of-the-house staff wandering into her kitchen. She was a stickler for only having back-of-the-house staff in her kitchens, and she wasn't going to break the tradition and standards just because she was in a different world.

So, the stitchgal stayed on this side of the kitchen, transporting her premade lunches into the expo room.

Nom was on the opposite end of the kitchen, closer to the pantry and the cool storeroom where they stored produce. This room had one of the magic amenities Alric had mentioned. The walls were constructed by the gnomish Marrow Eater and they had designed the room to keep a cool climate, which was perfect for keeping goods that needed to be chilled.

Nay thought of it as her walk-in fridge.

Nom had blown out some of the candles on this end so there was more darkness here, so he could go about his tasks without calling too much attention to himself. If someone did wander into the kitchen, there was enough shadow to give him a few moments to retreat into the pantry or larder. Or even hide under a table if need be. Nay wondered if she could eventually get the Lodge to warm up to the idea of a sous-chef tentacle. Maybe one day the town would accept him. *But baby steps*, she reminded herself.

One couldn't rush tentacle acceptance.

Nay had taken a blank page out of the back of Ol' Pat's cookbook and one of the pencil nubs. As she began writing down ingredients, a magic prompt appeared in her vision. Tabs appeared, marked with the words:

[Chef's Delight Recipes]
[Nay's Garlic Knots] [Base Rank Recipe]
[Goatkick Tacos] [Base Rank Recipe]

Her Chef's Delight Ability seemed to be naturally combining with the ideas she already had for tonight's dinner. As her eyes scanned over the ingredients like garlic and tundra peppers, they pulsed, indicating they were ingredients in these recipes. She opened the menus for each one.

Nay's Garlic Knots are tasty treats for those carb-loaders who love fluffy, buttery bread. These will both satisfy and stimulate the appetite for more. The more they eat, the more ravenous they'll become. The perfect appetizer for preparing a customer for the main course to come!
Imbues the eater with a Hunger Debuff.
Goatkick Tacos are the perfect bite for the man or woman who has come to dinner with a major appetite. The goat is stewed to a melt-in-your-mouth tenderness in a salty and sweet consommé of broth and peppers. Will leave each eater feeling renewed. The only thing they'll want afterwards is to wash it down with a hearty brew.
Imbues the eater with a Strength Buff and a Thirst Debuff.

She automatically knew every ingredient she needed, and she could combine that with her knowledge on cooking techniques.

"Magic food recipes," she said in awe. If these recipes meant what she thought it meant, then she could use her Chef's Delight Ability to manipulate the sense of hunger and thirst in a customer with these particular Debuffs. Which meant she could essentially create addicts. She would be able to get them to eat and drink more. Hopefully, that would also mean, if it really worked, that word of mouth about how good the food was would spread. All she had to do was figure out some sort of dessert, and she had her menu for tonight's service.

The first thing Nay got started on was making and preparing the dough for the garlic knots. She had two ways to do it, and for this first batch, she was going to have to use dough that Gracie had previously made. It would take a day or so for the yeast to rise, so she would make her personal recipe today and leave it to sit overnight to rise. But for tonight, she was just gonna take some of Gracie's premade dough so she could just shape it, cover it in the garlic butter and oil, and bake it.

For the batch she would use tomorrow, she used the flour she picked up from the market that a vendor had imported from the Peninsula, which was where most of the wheat in Stitchdale came from. Wheat grew abundantly on the Peninsula because of the soil and conducive climate. She combined it with sugar, yeast, salt, and water. She covered the dough in olive oil and then covered the pans with towels so the dough could rise overnight.

Nay showed Nom how to prepare the pans of garlic and olive oil so they could make the garlic-infused oil they would use on the garlic knots. They set the pans filled with garlic soaking in olive oil over the fire.

As Nay prepped and cooked, she was aware of an aura around her. Although others couldn't see it, it appeared in her vision and the tab to a menu appeared.

[Marrow Ability Log]

She opened it up, and text scrolled by in her sight HUD.

Chef's Delight [Base Rank] in use.
Nay's Garlic Knots being created.

The next time-sensitive thing they had to prepare was the consommé for the Goatkick Tacos. This was essentially the stew the goat meat would boil in. Nom had already chopped the onions and tundra peppers, so these they roasted with snowdew seeds and tomatoes Ol' Pat had stored in the walk-in. Like wheat, all the tomatoes came from the Peninsula, as it was too cold for them to grow in Stitchdale.

After they were done roasting in the pans, Nay had found some tins that turned out to be magic-operated gnomish blenders. They reminded her of the handheld bullet blenders from back home. They took the roasted veggies and seeds, and they blended these with some of the spices Nom had identified as having some heat to make a purée. They poured all batches of the purée into a big cauldron. Nay added water and a clay jug of snowapple cider vinegar she found in one of the pantries.

Chef's Delight [Base Rank] in use.
Goatkick Tacos being created.

She seasoned the goat meat heavily with salt, pepper, cumin, and dried tundra pepper and then added it to the cauldron. She hung it over the firepit in the center of the kitchen, and it would boil there all day and afternoon until customers started trickling in for dinner. By then, the meat would be falling apart in a velvety sauce.

They then found what appeared to be cornmeal on one of the shelves. As Nay ran it through her fingers, she tasted it, and the texture was much like corn or something wilder like maize. She combined this with globs of lard and salt and water to make the tortilla batter. She showed Nom how to roll the batter into balls, which could then be smashed with the bottom of an ale bottle and fried on a pan to turn into a tortilla. When Nom tasted the first one, he turned a reddish color, indicating delight.

She showed him the ingredients for the pico de gallo, which they made out of chopped tomatoes, onions, and some of the icebite cilantro. The garnish would add some winter chill to the spicy tacos.

With the appetizer and main dishes either cooking or ready to be cooked, and with Nom busy prepping all the ingredients, next on deck was figuring out a dessert. She looked through the pantry again and when she scanned over the sugar another menu prompt appeared for her.

[Chef's Delight Recipes]
[Sinsucker Blondies] [Base Rank Recipe]

Sinsucker Blondies are the divine dessert for those with a sweet tooth. The combination of brown sugar and white chocolate is strong enough to make an ogre weak in the knees.
Imbues the eater with a Stamina Buff and a Dexterity Buff.

Nay chuckled to herself. "Eat your heart out, kinky Martha Stewart."

She wasn't sure if she should make it, though. It sounded like the baked-good version of Viagra, and she wasn't sure if she wanted to fill the Lodge with randy customers.

Although, on the other hand, it could fill rooms on the second floor, and it would mean more business overall for Quincy. It might make for a night to remember at the old Lodge.

She had started to collect the ingredients, white chocolate from Delicatessa City and brown sugar from the island of Amoa, when a shrill scream came from the kitchen.

"Help! It's a monster!" Gracie said. "Quick, grab the cleaver!"

She hurried out there to see Gracie holding a wooden spoon, waving it at Nom, who stood there with tortilla batter covering his protuberances.

— CHAPTER NINETEEN —

If A Faun Eats a Goatkick Taco, Is It Cannibalism?

Nay inserted herself between Gracie and Nom.

"Careful!" Gracie cried. "It's right behind you! It's a tentacle—thing! Watch out!"

"Gracie," Nay said. "Take a breath."

Gracie looked at her with confusion. Nay put a hand on the tentacle's head, totally relaxed.

When Nom didn't make any sudden moves, just stood there and shrugged, Gracie's eyes widened. This tableau did not compute for her. She was trembling, ready to flee.

"Say hello to our sous-chef," Nay said. "This is my second-in-command. His name is Nom."

Nom waved a protuberance. "Hello, Gracie," he said. "It's a pleasure to officially meet you. I look forward to manning the line with you."

He went back to flattening the balls of tortilla batter and storing them between layers of wax paper.

Gracie's bottom lip quivered. She looked like she was about to burst into tears. As she spoke, she stammered: "What—what do you mean? That thing is working with us? It's a cook?"

"I'm also a tentacle," Nom said, not looking at her, focused on his task. "Best get used to me now, as we're going to be spending a lot of time in the trenches together."

"A . . . tentacle?"

"Yep."

As Gracie tried to process this, her eyes began to roll into the back of her head. She passed out and slid down the wall, and there she was, unconscious on the floor.

"Great," Nay said. She bunched up a towel and propped it up under Gracie's head.

"Well, that went better than expected," Nom said. "I think she handled my presence quite well. I do make quite a bold introduction, don't I?"

Nay revived Gracie from her fainting spell by holding some crushed tundra pepper seed under her nose.

The stitchgal came to, saw Nom, and started screaming again. But Nay got her to relax and gave her a cup of water. She let her cool off in the walk-in freezer and made sure Nom was working in her line of vision so she could accept the reality that one of her new coworkers was a sentient tentacle. When she became more conscious and seemed okay, Nay gave her the task of writing the new dinner items in chalk on the menu boards.

She went to check on Gracie's station to see how much fish she had prepared to bake. She also had her potatoes ready to bake. These were for backup. But if all went according to plan, they would have more orders of the goatkick tacos than the fish.

With both Nom and Gracie busy, and some time to kill before dinner service, Nay stepped outside to drink more pepper tea and gather herself.

It was the calm before the storm, and she wanted to have a clear head before the chaos arrived.

Outside the back exit of the kitchen, she had a great view of Lac Coineascar. It was a gray-and-silver body of water, and it seemed to carry out to the horizon, where there were mountains demarking the next valley over. There was a mist over the water, and it was quite the sight with the banks and trees covered in ice and snow.

There were fishing boats in the mist. The air smelled crisp and fresh, and the cold actually felt good against her skin since she had spent most of the day working near the kitchen fires. She exhaled and took a sip of her tea. There was a savage beauty to the harsh landscape, and she thought that this was quite the contrast to sunny Los Angeles.

Movement on the shore below caught her attention.

Quincy was down there, shirtless, barefoot in a pair of breeches, performing what looked like stretching or tai chi. As suspected, he was covered in scars from his life of adventuring. He was fluid in his movement, and Nay had no doubt that he had trained and honed his body into a weapon. She could tell by the way he moved. He had the body of not just an athlete but a fighter. This was probably his way of grounding himself before the busy night.

He finished his dynamic routine and then walked into the frigid lake.

He kept walking until he was completely submerged. Nay had heard of cold therapy before, but she had never done it herself or witnessed it in person. But it obviously had some benefit to blood flow and musculature and overall health, because she couldn't imagine someone torturing themselves if there was no benefit to it. He sat there in the icy water, eyes closed, probably meditating. She wondered if this was also some cultivation process.

It seemed like Quincy was a man with a lot of mystery to him, as she had a lot of questions and she was sure he had a lot of tales. She was intrigued. This stuck in her mind as she finished her tea and then walked back inside the kitchen.

The Lodge's serving staff gathered in the kitchen in front of Nay. She had sent Gracie to fetch them for a pre-service meeting. Nom was in one of the darkened storerooms, wolfing down family dinner.

Nay could tell this wasn't a common practice, as they waited impatiently, wondering what they were doing back here in the kitchen.

The three servers were stitchgals, and in addition to Hilde, whose face was pierced with iron rings, there was also Ullabella and Bryja. Ullabella was another stitchgal, that hybrid of maugrim and human who populated this valley, but Bryja was something else entirely.

She had two ram's horns curving off her skull, one on each side of her blue-haired head. From her head to her waist she had a human body, but her legs were those of a goat or a ram. They were hooved, and there was an extra joint a foot below her knee that slanted the lower half of her legs forward. They were covered in a blue pelt of fur.

Gracie had explained that she was a chillwind faun and not to be surprised with her appearance, as she could be quite sensitive. They were endemic to Stitchdale, especially near the Spineshard mountains.

The servers looked young, but they had all worked here for a few years and were staples of the tavern experience at the Lodge. Nay wasn't sure how stitchmen and chillwind faun aged. Did they age slower than humans? She didn't know, so she would make sure to ask Gracie when she got a chance.

On the table before them she had four plates prepared. Each plate had a couple of garlic knots, a serving of goatkick tacos, and, to the side of each plate, one sinsucker blondie each.

"What's this?" Bryja said, her stomach audibly growling. She leaned forward to inspect the food, nearly salivating. "Whatever it is, it smells good." Bryja's blue hair was shaved on one side. It looked like she could wrestle most of the men who frequented the Lodge into submission.

"Nether hells," Hilde said, "have you not had anything to eat today? Your stomach sounds like there's a goblin moaning in pain." Her hair looked like it was bleached white but she had explained it was natural.

That hair color was a thing here up in this cold climate. There was a constant air of exasperation about her, like she was already tired of everyone's shit and the shift hadn't even started.

"Or pleasure," Ullabella said. Her lips were painted red and she had jet-black hair. Her whole vibe reminded Nay of goth chicks from back home. Her voice was wry and it seemed like her main mode of communication was sarcasm.

"This is family dinner," Nay explained. "I like to feed the staff before each shift so you all don't go hungry while you're working."

"See, this is what I've been talking about," Bryja said. "Some enterprising minds around here who think about us employees and our day-to-day work struggles. Quincy thinking outside the box for once."

"Also, we're going to have some new menu items tonight, and I want you all to know what they taste like so you can describe them to the customers," Nay said.

"Customers," Ullabella muttered in disdain.

"So, go ahead, eat up, and I'll describe what each one is," Nay said.

Bryja stuffed a garlic knot in her mouth. Her body seemed to react before her mind did. Her eyes widened and then rolled back into her head in ecstasy as she chewed. She let out a moan of delight and then opened her eyes, looking at Nay like *What is this diabolical mouth magic?*

"So, we're calling those Nay's garlic knots," Nay said. "It's a soft bread twisted into a knot. But it's brushed in an infused garlic oil and garlic butter. Also sprinkled with bits of this pecorino cheese you guys already had in the larder."

Bryja swallowed. "That's hammer-whacking delicious! My blood and marrow, that's the best bread I've ever put in my mouth." She grabbed her other garlic knot and took a bite, a feral and intense hunger on her face.

That must be the Hunger Debuff, Nay thought. *It seems to have an instant effect.*

Hilde and Ullabella were surprised by Bryja's reaction, and each grabbed a knot to inspect for themselves. They looked at each other before biting into their respective knots.

Again, that transformative look on their faces appeared like they were having a spiritual revelation.

Nay had seen similar reactions to her food before but never with this level of knee-jerk intensity. She could feel the waves of their pleasure and hunger radiating off them.

It was profound.

"Tomorrow, I think the knots should be even fluffier because I'll be using a different dough," Nay said. "But these should do for now."

Bryja was already looking around for more knots. "Are there more?"

"Well, the rest we want to save for the diners," Nay said. "But if there's some left over at the end of the shift, you're welcome to them. But go ahead and try the goatkick taco."

Nay cringed then, suddenly realizing that Bryja might be offended.

Were fauns related to goats? If she ate a goatkick taco, would it be like cannibalism? She had to say something. "Does it bother you that there's goat meat?"

Bryja looked at the birria taco. It was glistening with red moisture from the consommé. Nay had sprinkled the icebite cilantro pico and some shaved pecorino cheese on top. There was also a little dipping cup of the consommé.

"So, the idea is you can eat the taco as is," Nay said, "but if you want it to have a little more kick, you can dip it in the consommé. It's a sauce that's full of flavor. But if the goat-meat thing bothers you, you don't have to—"

Bryja picked up the taco and bit into one end. At the first bite, she did a double take at the taco in her hands, swallowed, and then took another bite. As she chewed, she hummed a little. "I don't know what a taco is, but that is another bit of magic. You said that's goat?"

Nay nodded.

"That's not like any goat I've ever tasted," Bryja said. "When I've had goat before, I always thought it would be better to chew on a fauglir saddle. It would be softer. But this!"

So, fauns didn't have a problem eating goat.

Nay exhaled in relief.

Bryja took another bite, devouring most of it. "It melts on the tongue! But the spices kick you in the back of the throat! But in a good way, of course. Boy, I'm thirsty now." She grabbed a cup and slammed some water down.

Hilde and Ullabella moved from the garlic knots to the tacos. Ullabella's wry look was now one of curiosity and wonder. She actually tasted the consommé first, taking a sip of it. She whistled. "That's a spicy soup. Has a tang to it."

Hilde bit into her taco and did the same double-take reaction Bryja did. As she chewed, she looked at Nay. "Are ye some kind of sorceress? Where are you from?"

Nay said as Quincy instructed her. "I'm from across the ocean. Reith."

"Is all food from the Kingdom of Reith this good?" Hilde said. She continued to work on her taco.

"No," Nay said. "It all depends on the skills of the cook."

"What in the underrealm are you doing here?" Ullabella said. "You belong in Delicatessa, cooking for one of the Promenades. This food is straight witchcraft."

"I appreciate the compliment, ladies," Nay said, "but let's see how the patrons react to the food tonight."

"Whatever Quincy is paying you," Ullabella said, "it's not enough. Word is gonna spread. Lucerna's End has never had food this posh."

"Or delicious," Bryja said.

Gracie gave Nay a reaffirming look. Her kitchen assistant had already finished her family meal and looked like she was floating on a cloud.

The serving staff guzzled water and remarked how they felt refreshed and excited to work tonight's shift. Nay thought that must be the Strength Buff from the goatkick tacos. She was beginning to think that maybe giving them the sineater brownies was a mistake. It might not be a good idea to give it to the stitchgal waitresses, because of its particular love-potion-like effects. But it was hard to deny the benefits of a Stamina and Dexterity Buff.

The brownies would keep them limber on their feet and give them the resolve to last through a busy shift and be in a good mood.

The girls all but squealed in delight as they ate the brownies, singing Nay's praises down to the last bite.

— CHAPTER TWENTY —

FOMO

As the stitchfolk made their way back into town from the forests, mines, and water of Lac Coineascar, thirsty and famished from a hard day's work cutting down trees, mining iron, and catching slivermoon trout, they headed towards the Lodge for a night of music and food.

Nay, Nom, and Gracie waited in the kitchen for the first orders to begin trickling in.

Nay had placed Gracie in the buffer room between the tavern and kitchen, where she had her in charge of expediting the orders brought in by the trio of servers.

"So, you don't want me in the kitchen, baking the fish and potatoes?" Gracie asked, unsure.

"Not tonight, Gracie," Nay said. "Tonight, you're in charge of expo."

"Expo?" Gracie said.

"You're in charge of expediting every food order that the servers bring in. It's your job to keep the tickets in order. You'll call them out to us so we can cook and prepare them. You're the one who makes sure that the first orders that come in are the first orders that go out."

"I don't know; I feel like baking the fish is more important."

"Let us handle the fish. The fish is easy. Your job is super important."

"It is?"

"You're the one who makes sure everything is running smoothly. You're the glue between the kitchen and the tavern, the cooks and the customers. You make sure we're not only getting everything out in the proper order, but you're the one making sure we're getting the food out in a reasonable time."

Gracie nodded, suddenly understanding. Confidence appeared on her face. She flipped one of her milkmaid braids over her shoulder and set her jaw. Nay knew she was ready to take to the task now that she knew her role wasn't a downgrade.

It wasn't long before they could hear the voices and laughter on the other side of the double doors in the tavern. Dinner service had begun.

Nay waited impatiently, a ball of nerves and energy ready to be released. Feeling nervous before a shift was about to begin, especially a dinner service, was a normal thing for Nay. It was just part of the process. She was anxious to get her food out onto the tables.

So, she didn't hide her disappointment when the first table's order came in and it was for the baked fish and potatoes. Gracie called it out and Nay almost deflated.

Nom shrugged. "People like the familiar."

Gracie peeked out into the tavern. "That's Old Man Finchley and his crew from the lumber mill. He always gets fish, even when Ol' Pat made other options. Won't be changing his ways."

Nay reluctantly threw the seasoned fish in one of the alcove ovens with the potatoes.

Another ticket came in.

Again, it was the fish.

In fact, the next ten orders were for the baked fish. As Nay and Nom put the plates of the fish dinners on Gracie's table to be organized by her and taken out by the servers, Nay had an idea.

"Nom, fire up three baskets of garlic knots," Nay said.

Nom didn't question her. He got right to it. When they were ready, Nay set them on Gracie's expo table.

"No one ordered these," Gracie said.

"I know."

Hilde entered and she saw the garlic knots. "Oh, our first orders of knots! Those must be for Ulla and Bryja's tables. None of mine ordered them yet."

"One of those baskets is for one of your tables," Nay said. "Choose one with the most people. Say they're complimentary, on the house as loyal customers to the Lodge. Or however you want to say it."

Hilde understood. She smiled and grabbed the basket. "Oh, this is a good idea." She practically skipped back into the tavern.

Nay told Bryja and Ulla the same thing. "Choose the table with the most people and give them the basket of garlic knots."

Nay knew the curiosity would eventually get the best of at least one person at each table. All she needed was for people to try it and she knew people would start ordering the new food.

But she couldn't have predicted the speed and the fervor that orders for garlic knots started rolling in.

"They loved 'em!" Hilde said as she burst back through the door. "That basket never stood a chance, they ate them so fast. They want two more baskets, but I told them these ones they have to pay for."

"Good girl," Nay said. "That's how you start any addiction. The first taste is always free." As she was talking, Bryja and Ulla came in with more orders for knots.

"They practically inhaled them," Ulla said.

It didn't take long for word to spread throughout the tables. Gracie was peeking outside when she said, "The other tables are noticing the garlic knots! They're inquiring about them!"

"Nothing motivates a buyer like FOMO," Nay said.

"FOMO?" Gracie said.

"Yep," Nay said. "The Fear of Missing Out. People always want what their neighbor has. If they think they might not get it, it drives them wild. Makes them impulsive."

Gracie processed this. "How do you know this stuff?"

"From a lifetime of trying to get people to eat my food."

Soon, the alcove ovens were filled with baking garlic knots. The kitchen was filled with the intoxicating aroma of garlic, olive oil, and butter. And it wasn't long before the whole tavern was filled with the smell.

The volume outside grew louder as more people entered the Lodge. Between the Hunger Debuff spreading amongst the eaters of the garlic knots and the people at the new tables wanting to try the new starter, Nay began to wonder if they had enough dough to get them through the rest of the night.

Between trips, Ulla said, "Are you going to give people a free taste of the goatkick tacos as well?"

"Shouldn't be necessary," Nay said. "People are already loving the knots. They'll be ready to try the new entrée as well. Just give it another ten minutes."

As the knots started turning the diners ravenous, more orders for baked fish came in.

And sure enough, orders for the goatkick tacos finally started as the hunger began to make people more adventurous with their food choices.

The expo table was now mostly orders of garlic knots and the goatkick tacos.

The trio came in and then walked out with the first order of the tacos. Nay couldn't help herself. She peeked through the crack of the double doors to watch the first diners try them out.

Bryja pulled plates of the tacos off a tray and placed them in front of a group of stitchfolk miners, who looked at the arrival of food with greed. Although she was putting on charm, *thank you, sineater brownies*, they were mostly ignoring her for the food.

Dinner service was in full swing, and the doors to the kitchen might as well have been a set of rotating doors, as empty plates were coming in as fresh orders of knots and tacos were going out. No one seemed to be interested in the fish anymore. In fact, people were ordering seconds and thirds of the tacos, and compared to the past couple of months, sales were going through the roof for Quincy and his Lodge.

Quincy was behind the bar, having trouble keeping up with all the drink orders as the Thirst Debuff worked its way through the raucous crowd.

Their thirst couldn't be easily quenched, and entire barrels of Icemarrow Ale were being emptied with that goal in mind.

Nay accessed her Chef's Delight HUD overlay and could see the food Buffs and Debuffs on everyone.

Every single diner at each table had the Hunger Debuff, visualized as a red square with the image of an empty plate in the center, crossed with fork and knife, as well as the Strength Buff and Thirst Debuff. These appeared as more squares, but the strength one had the image of an arm flexing a muscular bicep and the thirst was of an empty flagon.

All these squares hung over the heads of each diner.

"I'm almost beginning to wonder if we have enough food," Nom said. "We're less than halfway out of the goat-meat consommé for the tacos, and we have even less of the garlic-knot dough."

"We're lucky the tavern is only half full," Nay said. "We would run out for sure if all the seats were full. Each table is ordering seconds and even thirds."

Bryja scampered in, sweat beading on her forehead. She was harried but excited. "It's a madhouse out there! But everyone is raving about the food. They want to know who the cook is!"

Nay was taken aback.

She was supposed to be keeping a low profile. Now she was attracting unwanted attention. *Was it unwanted, though?* she thought. She wanted people to like her food. And she wanted people to recognize her skill as a cook, and back in Los Angeles, she would have craved the attention and the recognition.

But now attention was dangerous. Would it be worth it? It wasn't a question she could answer now, but the thought was rattling around in her brain.

She glimpsed a large figure moving through the half-packed tavern.

As it got closer to the double doors, Nay saw that it was Quincy, pushing his way through the crowd and turning sideways to scoot past tables.

Some of the rowdier customers were demanding where their ale refills were.

"You all can wait on your ale for a few more minutes!" Quincy said. "Keep in mind I'll be back, and if I catch one of you trying to sneak behind the bar, then me and Samuel are going to have a few words with you!"

Diners, rambunctious and in good spirits, cowered as the massive Lodge owner passed them.

He shoved his way through the double doors and strode into the threshold between the expo area and the kitchen. He pointed a thick finger at Nay.

"You . . ."

His eyes seemed to shimmer. He looked her up and down and grunted. There was a realization appearing on his face. His eyes widened. Surprise flickered in his pupils before he composed himself, becoming stoic.

[Aura Detected]
[Scryer's Eye Aura Detected]
[Rank: Bronze]

He knew she was a Marrow Eater.

He had used his own Marrow Eater Ability to see that she was radiating with her Chef's Delight Ability, which must have appeared as some type of signature to him.

That quick knowledge that passed over his face meant he knew why the costumers were reacting to her food so passionately.

"Fix me a plate," Quincy said. "I want to try your food now. Before you run out and these people riot."

Nay swallowed and nodded.

She broke eye contact with him and silently prepared the food under his watchful eye.

She handed him the plate. He stared at it and then looked up at her. Then he looked back down to the food.

He shoved a whole garlic knot in his mouth and chewed. His stoic face softened with joy. Amazement and shock broke his composure. He ate another knot and closed his eyes, enjoying the experience. After he swallowed, he half-frowned.

He opened his eyes and studied Nay.

She watched the Hunger Debuff icon appear over his head.

But then he grabbed a goatkick taco, dipped it in the consommé, and took a large bite.

"My Celestia," he said, a soft exclamation of reverence. As he chewed, his eyelids fluttered and he slammed a fist into the table as if the action was an expletive. The gesture seemed to say, *This is ridiculously good.*

After he swallowed, he tilted his head, as if he was feeling out the effect.

Nay saw the Strength Buff and Thirst Debuff icons appear over him.

He looked at her and smiled slyly.

Then he sighed.

"When dinner is over," Quincy said, "me and you are going to have a long talk. For now, though, you are not to leave this kitchen."

He exited and disappeared back into the tavern.

The servers followed him, carrying new trays out with them.

"So, I think he likes your cooking better than mine," Gracie said. "I've never seen him act like that before."

Nay smiled grimly. "I'm not sure if that's a good thing."

Nom tossed a sineater brownie down his beaked gullet and turned pink. The Dexterity Icon, an image of two feet sprinting, and the Stamina Icon, a red heart, appeared over his head.

Then he burped.

"We're in so much trouble, aren't we?"

— CHAPTER TWENTY-ONE —

An Epicurist?

They had gone through a few barrels of Icemarrow Ale, easily half a week's supply in one night. They ran out of garlic-knot dough halfway through the shift, and the cauldrons of goatkick taco meat and consommé were gone just as the real drinking was just beginning. The clientele had to settle for the fish, and so many of them still had an appetite from the Hunger Debuff that they went through two nights' worth of fish in a couple hours. Nay had been hit with the familiar ding of a completed quest once all the sineater brownies were devoured.

[Quest Complete!]
[Prove Quincy Wrong and Sell all The Product Quest Completed!]
[Congratulations!]
[You have been rewarded with Vigor Points]

Quincy all but had to kick people out or send them up to their rooms after both the bar and the kitchen were off duty.

As the trio of servers sat at a table in front of the tavern hearth, counting through the massive amount of tips they had received that seemingly flowed out of happy diners' fingers, Nay, Nom and Gracie sat out back outside of the kitchen, decompressing in the chill night air, sharing a hand-rolled cigarette of iceflint tobacco the stitchgal had made for them. They passed it between each other after a few puffs, never breaking the order of rotation.

Nay inhaled the crystal-cold smoke into her lungs and exhaled the smoke that looked and felt like frost. It was perfect for winding down from a busy and chaotic shift. She enjoyed the post-dopamine rush and adrenaline crash of pure calm that came with surviving a busy dinner service. She looked at the cigarette in her hands and thought that something like iceflint tobacco would be a major hit back home. As dangerous as this new world was, its simple pleasures were the stuff of whimsy and wonder. She passed it to Nom.

"I've never seen the Lodge like this before," Gracie said, sighing. "And I don't think I've ever been this tired before."

Nom blew frost smoke and passed the cigarette to her. She took a hit and gazed out at Lac Coineascar. The moon was reflected in the dark water that rippled with the wind coming down out of the Spineshards. From one of the streets they could hear drunken singing from someone who was surely a Quincy's Lodge patron a few hours ago.

"I keep thinking what it might be like when we're a full house," Gracie said.

"We're gonna need more product," Nay said. "Maybe an extra server or two if we're dealing with a packed house."

"Your food absolutely bewitched everyone," Gracie said. "What are you cooking tomorrow? They're going to demand the garlic knots and tacos."

"I have a variation of the garlic knots, but I'm thinking of a poultry dish," Nay said. "I want to use the product we have first while it's still fresh."

"Well," Gracie said, "I can't wait to see what you come up with."

The kitchen exit opened and Quincy came through. He had a clay jug in one hand that he raised to his mouth and took a swig from. He stood next to the three of them, who were sitting with their backs to the building's wall. He looked out over the Lac.

"We made as much coin tonight as we did during the Three Moons celebration," Quincy said. Without looking, he handed the jug to Nay. She took a sip. It burned the back of her throat like a good whiskey. She passed it to Nom.

"And I suspect we're going to make more tomorrow night," he said.

"You do?" Nay said.

Quincy nodded. "The folk of Lucerna's End are always hungry. Word of your food will spread."

Nay sat there, a little dumbfounded. *If it were only this easy to please foodies in Los Angeles*, she thought. "So, does this mean I'm no longer a trial?" Nay said.

He walked back towards the kitchen and said over his shoulder, "Let's go discuss in my office."

He disappeared inside. Nay looked at Nom and Gracie, who gave her excited looks, gesturing for her to hurry and go inside. Nay pushed herself up and entered the Lodge.

Quincy's office was a small room behind the bar that seemed even smaller with his massive form squished behind his desk. It looked like a big-game hunter's trophy room showing off his most coveted kills and relics from his world travels. Except, instead of wild game, everything seemed to be from a monster, and the relics weren't so much exotic as fantastical.

The walls were adorned with strange horns, claws, and tails of what were presumably monsters. There was even the head of something that looked like a giant man-bat that had red eyes and was off-putting to stare at. It was right behind Quincy's desk on his wall, so it was like it was looking down at Nay. One of the more curious trophies was what looked like a fairy creature inside of a glass bell jar hanging from the ceiling. Upon closer inspection, the supposedly cute creature had a face only a mother could love. Its face was contorted in rage, and it had nasty sharp teeth and no nose. Nay had shuddered when she had observed it up close.

Even more curious to Nay was a sepia-toned map covering one of the walls that seemed to depict the Ligeia Peninsula and, above it, Stitchdale. She didn't have much time to study it in detail, even though she wanted to, because Quincy started talking to her in a serious tone.

"So, you are a Marrow Eater whose specialty is cooking," Quincy said.

"I'm gonna be honest with you," Nay said. "I didn't know what Marrow Eaters were until the other day."

"*Be honest* with me? That suggests you haven't been honest with me."

"Sorry, it's a phrase from my world. It doesn't mean I've been lying to you. It just emphasizes I'm being earnest with you. I promise I've been telling the truth."

He studied her and again she could feel his Scryer's Eye aura scanning her. He seemed perplexed. "Are there Marrow Eaters in your world?"

"Boss, there's not even magic in my world."

"Yet your food was imbued with magic. So, I have to assume you've been lying to me and are a Delicatessa Chef, trained and sanctioned and authorized by the Culinary Guild. Because such cooking is only possible by members of the Culinary Guild. It is impossible for a Marrow Eater cook to exist otherwise. It is highly illegal."

"I don't know what any of that is. All I know is that I came to this world as a chef, and ever since I got here, I could see magical . . . prompts and information. And after I consumed a Delicacy and some Marrow, I could not only see magic stuff, I could do it. I only know the term *Marrow Eater* because Alric explained it to me."

"Delicacy?" Quincy said, flabbergasted. "And Marrow . . . and Alric . . ." He shook his head, sorting through his thoughts. "Okay. Tell me everything that has happened to you since you got here. Start from the beginning."

Nay shrugged. "All right, sure."

So, she told him about everything, starting with the events in the Korean Church back in Los Angeles to her arrival here in the middle of a blizzard and all the events inside the mountain cave and Paleforge. She told him about Piero and the Delicacy she found on him, and the Steksis and its Marrow. He listened to it all in rapt attention, leaning forward, only stopping her every now and then to ask her questions to clarify details. She suspected it was his way of reading her to see if she was lying. After she was done, he sat back, amazed.

"I don't know if it's a blessing or a curse that you've found your way to the Lodge," he said.

"Can't it just be neither? Maybe you just ended up with a skilled cook with exotic recipes for the folk of Lucerna's End."

He snickered at that. "You aren't just some normal girl, though. You are a Marrow Eater–enhanced cook. An Epicurist."

"An Epicurist?"

"It's what someone like you is called. You can cook Delicacies and Marrow. You're a Marrow Eater Chef. Epicurists are needed by all Marrow Eaters for the preparation, serving, and rituals of acquiring and harnessing abilities. Do you know how rare that is? Epicurists are kept on a leash and are only allowed to exist if you're working for the Culinary Guild and the DMA. They are usually chosen from birth and trained in the role until they become of age. One existing outside of the carefully and painstakingly curated system is the equivalent of heresy."

"So, what you're saying is that if someone realizes I'm out in the wild cooking and someone important finds me, I could get in trouble?"

"They will either take you and make you submit to the will of the Culinary Guild or they will have you killed. Those are the only two options. And anyone associated with you would probably be tortured and killed."

"That's crazy. I understand people want to control magic, but this is madness."

"Think of it this way. Epicurists are like high priests who enable and connect people to a god or gods. You're the stepping-stone between someone and their ability to transcend. Gaining power isn't possible without what you can do."

"I'm just getting used to the idea that magic is real and that I can do it."

"Through fortune and fate, you've become a Marrow Eater. One with a rare and important role. I'm not sure if that's happenstance or good or bad luck. But it happened and here you are."

"So, now what? You want me to move on? Get out of Lucerna's End?"

"No, I don't think that's the answer. Lucerna's End is as far from the rest of the world as you can get. And except for the Gloom Rangers, it's rare for other Marrow Eaters to live or even pass through here. Although it does happen every now and then. A Marrow Eater would be the only type of person who would have the senses to know what you can do, and not all of them at that. Not all Marrow Eaters can read auras or are sensitive to the abilities of another. But still, if someone were to scry you and your food . . ."

"What if I just don't use my abilities to imbue the food with magic? I think my food is good enough that people would love it on its own."

Quincy mused over this, frowning. "Here's the thing. I know everyone who lives here. I think it's safe for you to enhance the food when it's just the regulars. But it would be when strangers wander through that I would worry about."

"You want the food enhanced?"

"I want the customers back that Wint stole from me when he opened the Two-Headed Trout."

Now, this was something Nay could understand. Wanting to destroy the competition. Everyone had that somewhere in their heart. Especially if it's someone one has a feud with.

"If we keep serving food like the stuff you made tonight," Quincy said, "then he doesn't stand a chance in the nether hells. I want him out of business."

"Even if it puts you at risk?"

"Anything worth doing in this life requires risk. We just have to decide how much we're willing to risk. This Lodge is my life, and I'm willing to risk everything on it."

Nay nodded. "Maybe I can do it without making magic food."

"No. I want you to make magic food. I don't want there to be any question of his establishment's survival."

"What if Marrow Eaters come through? Ones who can scry?"

"There's none in town at the moment. And if they do happen to arrive, then we cease making magic food until they leave. Just to be safe."

"You're the boss. So, does this mean I'm hired on in an actual position?"

— CHAPTER TWENTY-TWO —

A Tale of Two Lodges

Nay had accepted two more quests from her magical quest-giver, who was somewhere in the sky or was invisible, guiding Nay through this alternate reality like it was her own personal video game she was playing.

[Quests Accepted]
[Entice Lost Customers Back]
[Destroy the Two-Headed Trout]

She wondered if the magic quest-giver was a person, an AI, or some kind of system guiding her. Something was writing the text in her prompts and menu system. But who? Or what? She wondered if there was anyone in this world who could answer such questions. She had asked Quincy, but he just stared at her like she was crazy. He didn't interface with the magic like her, and from his reaction, it didn't sound like anyone else did, either.

As she and Nom drank pepper tea in the kitchen, slowly waking up, Nay wondered if there was a Marrow Ability that could help her clean quickly. Her least favorite part of being a chef was cleaning the kitchen after service. Her and Nom had spent almost two hours scrubbing the ovens and tables and sweeping the floors. She would have to find more Marrows. She wondered how to go about doing that, other than just wandering around aimlessly. Her thoughts went to what a fully powered Epicurist looked like. What Delicacies and Marrows were used? What was their full array of abilities? Maybe there was someone else in Stitchdale who was like Quincy and had personal knowledge of Marrow Eaters and the operations on the Peninsula. But someone who had more knowledge in different areas from him.

Nom slurped on his pepper tea. "This stuff is all right, but I'd do anything for a good xloodhawpoer."

"What the hell is that?" Nay said.

"So, it's like pepper tea. In that you take it in the morning to help wake up. But you don't drink it."

"It's not a drink?"

"No."

"So, it's a food?"

"You can eat it, but it's not recommended. Some like to rub it all over their gums inside their mouth suckers."

Nay looked at him. "You rub it on your gums? So, it's like a cream?"

"No, it's more of a powder. I think the most common way is snorting it."

"Are you talking about cocaine?"

"What's cocaine?"

Nay shook her head. They had never had a chance to have a full-on discussion about his world, but she suspected they would be covering that ground soon.

"Do you snort cocaine?" Nom said. "And when you do it, do you suddenly feel great, like you can do a million things at once and succeed at every single one of them? I guess if we drank ten entire kettles of pepper tea, it might have the same effect, but you would have to pee like crazy."

"I would be fine settling for some hot coffee."

Gracie wandered in and sat at the table with them. It looked like she just woke up. She poured herself some pepper tea and held the cup between her hands, sipping on it while closing her eyes. "That's the deepest sleep I've had in a long time."

"Nothing like hard work to make you sleep like a baby," Nay said.

They all grew quiet for a moment as they drank their tea and slowly awakened, letting the caffeine filter through their bloodstreams. That's when Nay thought she heard something coming from the dish room. They all heard the rhythmic noise and looked at each other.

It was someone snoring.

Nay got up and walked to the dish room. There was a sink in here magically connected to the lake. It was fashioned by the same Marrow Eater gnome that Quincy had design and outfit the Lodge. There was a stitchman-shaped figure passed out on the floor underneath the sink. It was Pwent, the teenage stitchguy dishwasher. He was snoring away, his head rested on some straw, and he had a hide pulled over him.

"Is this normal?" Nay said.

Gracie shook her head. "Nope. Guess he was worn out."

Nay had made sure to feed Pwent during the middle of his shift last night so he wouldn't starve and would be able to keep up with the dishes. She had made him wolf down the food because she knew sometimes dishwashers got so busy, they forgot to eat until it was too late. In Nay's experience, she liked to keep the dishwashers well fed and taken care of because not only was it the right thing to do, it made them feel appreciated. Which was important because being a dishwasher was usually the lowest rung on the ladder of kitchen jobs. Take care of them and they'd do the work, and sometimes, today's dishwasher was tomorrow's sous-chef. Everyone usually started as a dishwasher in the kitchens back home, and if they worked hard, they could actually ascend the ladder.

"We might have to find another dishwasher to help him, then," Nay said. "We're only going to get busier."

"Want me to put the word out?" Gracie said.

"Yes, let people know we're hiring."

Nay brought Gracie to the Wharf District with her on the morning trip to the market. They needed more product for dinner again, and she wanted the Lodge to be prepared when the place filled all its seats. Plus, the more she purchased, the more she proved to the vendors that they could push their wares and turn it into profit, so the more willing they would be to partner up with her and cut her deals. The more business they did, she'd establish more of a foothold over the vendors compared to the Two-Headed Trout. And then when it came time, they could truly put the squeeze to their competition.

In Lucerna's End, aside from the street hawkers selling quick bites to eat and snacks, usually consisting of skewers or kabobs, although there were a few that sold bowls of stew and bread, the only dining establishments that were housed in buildings were Quincy's, the House of Saccharine Delights and the Two-Headed Trout.

Quincy didn't really view the bordello as competition, since the main thing they sold was carnal pleasure of flesh. That was their main draw, and there really was no way to compete with that unless one opened up another pleasure house. Which would be a form of chaotic suicide in Lucerna's End. If someone built another bordello in direct competition to Madam Snowstroke and the House of Saccharine Delights, there would be an all-out turf war and its violence would spill out onto the streets. At least, that's how Quincy explained it to Nay.

Which left Wint the fishmonger and the Two-Headed Trout. Wint mainly worked as a fisherman and fishmonger, and he was smart in that he had used his money to purchase a fishing boat he named the Silvertail. As captain of the Silvertail, Wint was ruthless in his control of good fishing spots in Lac Coineascar, often bullying and threatening the other boats, at times even sabotaging if need be. Wint had two children, a brute of a son named Krill and a right bitch of a daughter named Mishell. They weren't afraid to get their hands dirty, and there was a rumor going around they had something to do with the disappearance of Captain Skorr, one of Wint's competitors on the Lac.

A year ago, Wint had used some of the fortune he had been acquiring through his control of the fish market to build and open the Two-Headed Trout. While Quincy's Lodge was on the edge of the Lac, the Two-Headed Trout was on the edge of the Frostfroth River that flowed from the lake into the rich forest where the lumberjacks worked. The mines were also located nearby. Its location gave Wint access to a lot of the town's workforce that traveled to these locations each day for work.

The Two-Headed Trout essentially ripped away half of Quincy's customers. It might have been more honorable if the food and drink was good, but in Quincy's mind, it wasn't a suitable alternative for the townsfolk. The fish and fowl were overcooked, the ale was diluted with water, and whatever swill they were using for alcohol left its drinkers with incredible and mind-ripping hangovers. Quincy suspected that Wint was using embalming fluid he was getting from either the taxidermist or the undertaker, he wasn't sure which, but he was sure one of them had worked out a deal with the bastard. And to further heap insult upon injury was that it was grossly overpriced. Its patrons were sacrificing quality for convenience, and in Quincy's mind that was a damn shame.

All of these offenses were enough for Quincy to take action, but they paled in comparison to the true reason the retired adventurer and Marrow Eater wanted to put Wint out of business.

Quincy simply didn't like the man and thought his presence in Lucerna's End was an infection upon the community. The man was a criminal and had left a trail of violence and graft in his wake all in the name of greed. The man's nature was an offense to Quincy for simply existing. He didn't like bullies, especially ones that profited off their victims.

All this he had expressed to Nay so she could understand why he was willing to take the risk of using her as an Epicurist. She was willing to take on the Two-Headed Trout because her chef's sense of ego liked the competition, but the more she learned about Wint, his family, and his business, the more she thought she might like to be a thorn in his side. Plus, her new spin on cooking was exhilarating, and she was just getting started with exploring the possibilities. The threat of discovery by the Culinary Guild wasn't something that scared her at the moment, because the idea seemed so foreign to her and she was, geographically, far away from the influence of their reach.

Gracie had them take Quincy's fauglir, an old and silver-haired boy named Al.

The fauglir had yawned and stretched languidly upon fetching him, but once he was up and moving, his tongue lolled out of a mouth that seemed to be pulled back in a goofy grin. The creature was happy for the excursion. They hooked Al to a cart that he pulled behind him now. They had already half-filled it with more beef, as Nay suspected they would need more for the rest of the week.

She wanted Gracie to see how business was done and what to look for when it came to product. Also, she wanted the vendors themselves to associate Gracie with Nay and Quincy's Lodge. The stitchgal was a hard worker and took to knowledge quickly, which made her a good protégé to have for the operations and business of the kitchen. Part of being a chef was teaching and passing on to one's staff knowledge and methodologies, because someone like Gracie could help make Nay's life easier in the kitchen.

But Nay also found that Gracie had some things to teach her.

"These are called moon melons," Gracie said, holding up a blue-tinged melon the size of a cantaloupe. But instead of a brown rind, the rind was different shades of blue in a tie-dye pattern. It looked like someone had spilled all sorts of different blue paints on the rind.

"What does it taste like?" Nay asked.

"It's a bit sour. But some kids love them and eat them like candy."

"And what's this called?" Nay said, pointing at a cluster of berries that looked like they were sculpted from ice.

"Crystal berries. They burst in your mouth with a pop."

"Sounds like Pop Rocks."

"What's that?"

"These candies that crackle and pop on your tongue."

"Oh, sounds similar. Those are common in Reith?"

"Yep." Nay didn't like lying to her, but there were things she had to keep secret.

An obnoxious voice rose in volume over the crowd in front of them.

"How dare you try to pawn off wilted crystal berries to me!" it said. "Perhaps I should go see if the proprietor of Icerend Orchards has superior product. I hear he's meticulous in his pruning and light management when it comes to his berries. Which you clearly have been neglecting!"

Nay pushed her way through the crowd to see a round stitchguy dressed in the clothing of a dandy. The clothes were ostentatious, new, and expensive. He had a ridiculous mustache that dropped below his chin on each side, and the hair on his head was pulled back in a shiny ponytail. In one hand he had a cane, which he used to whack the vendor on the knee.

"I know who that is, don't I?" Nay said.

Gracie nodded. "Wint the Fishmonger, before your very eyes."

— CHAPTER TWENTY-THREE —

Wint the Fishmonger

There was an object pushed up around the rim of Wint's captain hat that was a cross between a monocle and jeweler's loupe. He pushed it down over his right eye and examined the crystal berries in the palm of his hand. "Just as I suspected," he said in a shrewd voice that was raspy from a lifetime of harsh tobacco use. "The skin of these berries hasn't received enough sunlight."

Then, to the shock of the vendor and the onlookers nearby, Wint spat on the berries and smashed them into the vendor's shirt. "That should make you think twice about selling me inferior fruit," Wint said, staring down at the thin farmer through the lens of his odd monocle. Then he took a crate and shoved it into his manservant's arms. "For your inattention to detail, I'll be taking today's order of berries as compensation on this matter."

"Imagine being so cheap, you can't afford to pay a farmer for their product or labor," Nay said in a loud voice so everyone in the vicinity could hear.

Mortified, Gracie grabbed her arm and whispered, "What are you doing?"

Nay didn't know why she said it other than that she'd never liked bullies. Even in Los Angeles, she was never afraid to run her mouth at one or become vindictive. She didn't like to see people slighted when they didn't deserve it. And personally, she never liked to be slighted at all. This had caused her plenty of problems in the past, and it didn't look like being in a different world would change that.

Wint froze, and his manservant, a stitchguy who wasn't used to seeing his boss verbally chastised, whipped his head towards Nay in shocked curiosity as he loaded the crate of crystal berries onto their cart.

"Who said that?" Wint said. He slowly turned to look into the crowd.

Nay stepped forward like she was about to confront a shrill Karen. "Looks like he spent all his money at the tailor and doesn't have any left over to pay a man for his honest work. Some would say that's stealing."

Wint gazed at her in shock. Even though he was half maugrim, he was still a bit taller than Nay, as she was more petite for her size. And he was much wider and much more muscular than her. "Are you accusing me of stealing, lass?"

"Are you hard of hearing or are you just slow at comprehension?" Nay said. "You took that farmer's crate of fruit and you didn't pay him. In fact, I saw you threaten and assault him. Which means you wanted the berries but you didn't have the money to pay for them."

By now, everyone in the market had stopped their own conversations and business to watch the confrontation between Wint and this human girl who was new to town, embarrassing Wint the Fishmonger in public.

It was a sight no one had ever conceived possible.

Gracie tried to hide her face as she clutched Nay's arm. "Oh, Celestia, somehow spare us," she muttered under her breath.

Wint took a step forward, and everyone around Nay and Gracie backed away from the duo.

"Maybe you missed part of the conversation, girl," Wint said. "But me and Unloc have an arrangement. He supplies—"

"Unloc and I."

Wint flinched. He wasn't used to being interrupted and didn't know how to deal with it. The points of his mustachio trembled in irritation. "What?"

"You said 'me and Unloc.' It's *Unloc and I*. But I guess you stumble over the rules of grammar after you've been caught stealing."

Wint lost his composure at that and his face rippled with anger. He lifted his cane and pointed it at Nay, flinging mud between them, which Nay leaned out of the way of. He spat. "We have an arrangement! I've paid plenty of coin to Unloc, and one may consider my dealings with him generous. It is our business and no one else's if we should amend our arrangement to compensate for lackluster product. I demand precise performance from my farmers, and if one week the product is questionable, then we find ways to work around it. And it concerns no one but us, as it's a private affair."

"Then forgive me for mistaking a private matter as a public one. You might consider my confusion, as you seemed to make this private matter loud enough for all of us in public to hear."

At that, a few people in the crowd guffawed and snickered but then quickly covered their mouths, turned their heads, or disappeared into the crowd when Wint glared at the offenders.

Nay continued twisting the dagger, prolonging the fishmonger's humiliation. "It also looked like a one-sided conversation and arrangement. I hope you also pay for Unloc's dry cleaning bill."

"Dry cleaning?"

How things got easily lost in translation when one was from another world, Nay thought. She corrected herself. "Excuse me. *Cleaning* bill."

"Who are you?"

"Someone who doesn't like Karens."

Wint scrunched up his face in utter confusion. "Karen?"

"It's a type who like to abuse and belittle and take advantage of people doing their jobs. Whenever I see it, *Karen*, I make it my duty to bring attention to the behavior so you can be publicly humiliated. I don't know if that will change you or prevent you from doing it again, but on my end I gain satisfaction. And I will have my satisfaction."

Wint stood there, his face going through many emotions as he processed her words. He glanced and saw the crowd talking excitedly amongst themselves and smiling.

He grabbed his walking stick with his other hand and pulled a long blade from the stick, revealing that the cane was also a sheath. The walking stick was in actuality a type of cane sword.

Everyone gasped and Gracie pulled Nay back in fright.

As Wint took a menacing step forward, two stitchmen appeared between them.

They were identical twins, with the same hardened faces and the same red hair that fell in braids from beneath skullcaps. They wore a mixture of leather armor and ring mail, and crossbows hung from their backs. In their hands they held what looked like steel billy clubs. Their left fists were covered in studded gauntlets. On their collars they wore badges marked with a crest that resembled the town of Lucerna's End. They looked like medieval riot police in a way, and Nay did not want to anger them.

"Stop!" one of the sheriffs yelled. "Sheathe your blade and call it a day, Wint."

"But," Wint stammered, "she has offended me! I am a person of high status in Lucerna's End, and I will not stand for this treatment. I demand you arrest her and flog her in the square!"

"Should we arrest every pretty girl who gives you a verbal lashing now?" the other sheriff asked. "Leave the administration of arrests and punishments to us."

Wint looked between the twin sheriffs and Nay. Then he looked to the crowd watching.

He sheathed his cane sword. "What are you lot looking at? Have you nothing better to gawk at today?"

His eyes settled back on Nay. His lip curled underneath his trembling mustachio.

"Perhaps we'll run into each other again soon. But I hope you'll be wise enough to mind your own business. Because the Brothers Bouldershield don't run everything in this town. Some affairs are left to more influential elements."

He spun on his heel, once again using his cane as a walking stick. The crowd scrambled out of his way as he stabbed at the ground with each step of the stick, striking his way through the dirt and back onto the cobblestone street, loping with a lumbering stride, joining his manservant and cart.

Although it was satisfying to humiliate Wint in front of everyone at the market, Nay was aware she had foolishly put her and Gracie's life at risk. If it wasn't for the Bouldershield Brother sheriffs, they might have been skewered like kabobs in front of a crowd. There was also the thought at the back of her mind that she would come to regret humiliating the fishmonger, but it was too late to dwell on it now.

"What in the nether hells were you thinking?" Alric ran up to them. Gracie grabbed him for support and buried her head in his shoulder. "Provoking Wint in public?"

Nay shrugged. "Not my fault if he can dish it out but can't take it."

"I take it no one has told you about him!" Alric said, patting Gracie on the shoulder, comforting her.

"I know all about him," Nay said. "And I can say with absolute certainty the man deserves any misfortune that befalls him. In fact, I believe that would be karma. Or justice long overdue."

Alric shook his head. "Verity isn't about justice but pulling people close to the truth."

"Sounds vague and a little boring."

One of the Brothers Bouldershield had retracted and holstered his strange billy club. He walked over to them and addressed Nay. "Are you all right, lass?"

"My heart's pumping a little fast from all the excitement, but I feel safe now, thanks," Nay said. "I'm sorry, what was your name again?"

"I'm Rolf," the sheriff said. He cocked his thumb over his shoulder towards his twin brother. "That's Jolf. We're the sheriffs of Lucerna's End."

Nay put out a hand. "I'm Nay. Thanks for halting my inevitable impalement."

Rolf angled his head and made a face, trying to figure out her accent and manner of speech. "You're new to Lucerna's End?"

Gracie spoke up then. "She's the new cook at Quincy's."

Then she turned away, blushing.

Nay caught the exchange. She smiled to herself. Seemed like her kitchen manager had a crush on the Bouldershield twins.

The sheriff seemed impressed by Nay. "Oh, I love Quincy's. I hope you're not changing too much! I'm a stickler for the baked trout. The bit of citrus sprinkled on top? It does my belly good."

"Don't you worry, sheriff. We're still keeping the fish."

"That's a lass!" He went to knock her on the shoulder with his meaty fist but then realized she was a human and not a stitchgal, and he stopped himself mid-movement and then settled for patting her awkwardly on the shoulder.

"Watch your back for that one," Jolf said, gesturing down the street where Wint went off to. "You won't want to be walking around the streets and alleys at night alone. Wint has associations with the town's more . . . unsavory elements."

"Message received," Nay saluted.

"We've been looking for a reason to take him off the streets, either in a cell or by a good whack of the ol' shillelagh, but he's a slippery old bastard," Rolf said. "Nothing ever sticks to him."

"Verity will reveal the truth and shed the darkness with light," Alric said. "Then you can administer justice."

"Yeah," Jolf said, "if you could do anything to help Verity along with that process, that would be mighty fantastic."

"Verity's timing is a mystery that sometimes baffles all," Alric said.

"Do you think?" Rolf said. The sheriff rolled his eyes. Then he shouted at the crowd, "The show's over, folks! Go back to your business. The rest of the day beckons."

The crowd dispersed and the market settled back into its usual business.

Rolf turned back to Nay. "I like your gumption, but the next time you decide to provoke Wint, make sure me or my brother are nearby. The next time we meet, I'd rather you not be on the end of a skewer."

"You and me both," Nay said.

He tipped his skullcap at her, and he and Jolf strode back onto the street.

"They're so . . . handsome," Gracie said, watching after him, a dreamy look in her eyes. "How did you stay so calm while talking to him? I forget where or who I am if I look into his eyes for so long. It's like staring into a magical Lac."

Nay and Alric glanced at Gracie and then looked at each other and smiled.

"So, Alric," Nay said, "what are you about today?"

— CHAPTER TWENTY-FOUR —

Nay's Naughty Nachos

Alric accompanied Nay and Gracie as they purchased product. Gracie had made them buy something called rock cakes from a sweets vendor. They were made of flaky dough and had a marzipan-like crème filling in the center that came in different flavors. Shaved stone nuts that were similar to almonds were sprinkled on top.

Nay desperately wished her sense of taste was present for moments like this. She adored good pastries. When she took a bite, the dough flaked and crumbled to give way to a soft and pillowy mouthfeel. There was crunch with the stone nuts, and the filling had a sweet, nutty aroma. She suspected this was the kind of thing Quincy's Lodge should have available for their continental breakfasts.

She and Gracie worked out a deal with Nisse, the baker and sweets vendor, and bought a few dozen of the pastries for the Lodge.

Nay would have to make sure Nom didn't make too large of a dent when he was trying them out. His enthusiasm sometimes had a way of getting away from him.

As they munched on their second portion of rock cakes and strolled, Alric explained he had several appointments in town throughout the day. "I'm meeting with one of the foremen at the lumber mill, then with the Stitchgals' Anti-Temperance Movement—"

"Anti-temperance?" Nay said.

"Yes," Alric said. "They are alcohol enjoyers and believe that imbibing spirits and liquor and things that have been fermented can help one be more truthful. There's a sect of monks in the Veritax who believe the same thing and always include ale and wine in their rituals."

"I guess people tend to be more honest when they're drunk," Nay said. "Filters seem to disappear, anyways."

Alric nodded. "Verity is in it, no doubt. Now, whether it's the effects of the alcohol or that the person is more willing to align their soul with the truth, who knows. I think I lean more towards the latter."

"I don't think I've ever bothered to try and concoct elaborate lies while I've been three sheets to the wind," Nay said. "But then again, there's a reason why my mind is always hazy trying to remember those moments."

"Listen," Alric said, "it wasn't happenstance that I ran into you at the market."

Gracie perked up at that and gave Nay a look as she bit into what was left of her rock cake.

"Are you following me now, Alric?" Nay said.

"Am I following you?" Alric said. "No, no. It's not like that. I was gonna stop by the Lodge and was passing through the market when I saw your scene with Wint. The sheriffs are right; don't go looking for that man. Best to avoid altogether."

"So everyone keeps telling me," Nay said.

"I received word from Fort Nixxiom that they expect heightened monster activity in Stitchdale over the coming weeks," Alric said.

"Why?" Nay said.

"Every now and then, more monsters come out of the Scar. I'm not privy to why it happens. It's just something that does."

"So, what does that mean for me? And the townsfolk? We stay inside more?"

"Especially at night. Mostly at night. You should be fine during the day unless the monsters decide to get bold. But there will most likely be a Gloom Ranger presence in the town, but it's always a good idea to stay indoors, keep a low profile. Do you know what I mean?"

"Loud and clear."

"I was going to stop by the Lodge to tell Quincy, but I can see now that Verity wanted me to tell you myself."

"How come you didn't tell the sheriffs?"

"They most likely already know. Fort Nixx sends their own messages to them. As Veritax's representative to Lucerna's End, it's part of my duty to keep a log of all happenings in the town and in the valley. For the church's records, you see."

"The church likes to keep tabs on current events, huh?"

"It's what they've been doing for centuries, tracing and tracking the footprints of Verity."

"Thanks for the heads-up. I'll try and stay out of trouble."

"Sorry I didn't get a chance to try your food last night. I was at the chapel. But I'll try and stop by tonight so I can try your cooking."

Alric excused himself and headed off in a different direction to conduct his Veritax business. Nay watched the earnest monk round a corner and vanish into the street traffic.

"Forgive me, chef," Gracie said, "but I think he likes you."

Nay laughed. "He's cute in an innocent way. Too bad he's a man of the cloth."

"Man of the cloth?"

"He's a monk. He's more interested in his precious Verity than girls."

Gracie giggled. "What an eventful morning! Life has certainly gotten more interesting with you around."

"It's only been a day. You'll be bored of me soon enough. Come on, let's get back to the Lodge, and I'll go over tonight's menu with you and Nom."

Word of Nay's cooking had spread.

Or it had at least reached enough ears and expectant stomachs that Quincy's Lodge was filling up. A third of the tables were still empty, but there were more diners at more tables compared to the previous night.

Service was in full swing.

Nay had taught Nom and Gracie how to make tortilla chips out of a tweaked recipe of the winter corn batter they had used the previous night to make tortillas. Nom had been in charge of frying the batter in oil and drying the chips out on racks. They were being used in tonight's appetizer if people wanted something else other than the garlic knots.

[Chef's Delight Recipes]
[Nay's Naughty Nachos] [Base Rank]

**Nay's Naughty Nachos are the snack of choice for those who love a good chip 'n dip. A pleasing plate of heaping tortilla chips loaded with ice tundra peppers, seasoned ground beef, and an ooey-gooey melted blend of cheese, this appetizer will hit eaters with a kick while also stimulating their appetite for more.
Imbues the eater with a Stamina Buff and a Hunger Debuff.**

Turned out that Nay's Naughty Nachos were being ordered in addition to the garlic knots. The combination was priming bellies for more food, which resulted in even more orders of appetizers in addition to the main course.

[Chef's Delight Recipes]
[Mother's Monster Meatloaf] [Base Rank]
[Robochun's Mashed Potatoes] [Base Rank]

Mother's Monster Meatloaf is made with prime beef that was raised with love on Moonglum Farms. Now here it is, prepared and cooked with a touch of magic, and you can tell your hungry audience it's traditional farm-to-table eating. Mixed with a proprietary blend of spices and seasonings, there's never been a meat cake that gets straight to the spirit of things. It's meatloaf like Ma used to make with a little extra love. Topped with a brown sugar glaze.
Imbues the eater with a Spirit Buff.

The protein was, of course, accompanied by a side of starches. Creamy, buttery starches, that is.

Robochun's Mashed Potatoes is made with enough salt and butter to clog your arteries and send you to the undertaker's with a heart congealed in cream and fat. But don't worry; the ride's not over, as you're revived with a new ticker and a renewed sense of purpose, feeling better than ever. These are so creamy, you'll never settle for regular potatoes again. Perfect to dip a nice braised short rib or a finger into.
Imbues the eater with a Stamina Buff.

Nay had racks of the personal loaves of meat ready to go, and a cauldron full of the mashed potatoes. She made sure to overcompensate their servings because, again, she was scared of running out of food.

Nom had his protuberances full handling the app stations. He was constantly moving, preparing and cooking both the nachos and garlic knots. "These babies are flying off the racks. These people love their apps."

Nay knew that probably half of the reason they had more customers tonight was because of the curious townsfolk that wanted to try the knots.

She thought she could probably open a side business selling prepackaged ones for people's hearths at home. It was something to think about, if she could figure out a way to package them and have them keep for a decent amount of time.

"No one is ordering the fish tonight," Gracie said. She was working the expo table, arranging all the plates for the serving team.

Bryja skipped in and grabbed two trays. "Minekeeper's Daughter is singing a song about the nachos!"

Nay looked up. "Really?"

Minekeeper's Daughter was the name of the group of stitchfolk bards who performed as a band.

Nay hadn't had a chance to listen to their lyrics, but it had sounded like they were singing of legendary deeds and bloody battles and lost loves, the typical bardic fare. But as she listened now, she picked out a few of the lyrics:

*Nay's naughty nachos
they leave ye wanting more
one plate, two plates, three plates, four!
best watch yer belly
when you're hungry like a whore
Quincy's got the wheelbarrow
to roll ye out the door!*

Nay chuckled. "It's randy but not as raunchy as some rap songs I've heard."

"Rap songs?" Gracie said. "What's rap? Is that the music in Reith?"

"Yep."

Nom looked at Nay and Nay shrugged.

She pulled a bunch of piping-hot meatloaf trays out of one of the alcove ovens. Steam rose off the meatloaves, and their tops glistened with the dark brown glaze. After they cooled a little, she popped them out of the molds and plated them. She scooped out some of the mashed potatoes on each plate, and she sprinkled them with a little pecorino cheese and a garnish of fresh parsley.

This type of homestyle cooking was one of her specialties, as opposed to some of the fine-dining places she had trained in. There was pressure to perform here, but none of the crazy abuse and toxicity that would happen in some of those kitchens she used to work in.

All in all, cooking in Quincy's Lodge was pretty cozy.

For dessert tonight, Nay had prepped a few dozen pies her Chef's Delight Ability had shown her when she was staring at the crystal berries.

[Chef's Delight Recipes]
[Moonsliver Pie] [Base Rank]

Moonsliver Pie is just the thing you want in your belly on a frigid night. Made from a crystal-berry pie filling and a special Stitchdale pie dough, a bite of this will keep the belly warm like a pleasant flame. Sweet, fruity, and with a warm, gooey mouthfeel.
Imbues eater with a Satiated Buff.

Although Nay wanted the diners to eat more, she wanted them to feel satisfied by the end of their experience. She didn't want them to leave hungry, so she needed a dessert that would help the diners feel full when it was time for them to retire for the night.

Hilde came through the double doors and put a ticket in. She gestured at Nay. "Alric wanted you to know he is here. He got one of everything and says he can't wait to try your food."

Gracie's eyes sparkled at Nay. "I told you the boy likes you."

"They do say the quickest way to a man's heart is through his stomach," Hilde said, winking.

"Very funny, ladies," Nay said. "The last thing I need is more complications in my life, and the last time, I checked a Veritax monk with a crush is on the list of complications."

Ullabella strode in, catching this bit of the conversation. "At least you would know he would always tell you the truth. Which is a lot more than most men will do here in town. This place is full of liars and scoundrels. He's the only honest one in the bunch."

"*Liars and scoundrels* is more my speed," Nay said.

"It's just something for you to think about," Bryja said.

"He's a monk, Bryja," Nay said.

"He might not be after he eats your food."

The girls laughed.

— CHAPTER TWENTY-FIVE —

The Gloom Ranger

The first stitchchild went missing a week later, well after word of the new cook at Quincy's Lodge had made its way through the town, resulting in its tavern being packed to capacity for several nights in a row with no sign of slowing down. She introduced the townsfolk to a variety of starters that were not just a novelty to them, but the food had that special quality, flavor, and satisfaction that made one crave more.

From fried potato skins loaded with skyr, melted cheese, and bits of pork belly to an onion fried in oil and served with a magical tangy sauce which everyone thought was a staple in the Reith royal court thanks to a bit of gossip that spread amongst the townsfolk, the bar food at Quincy's became a topic of conversation at every street corner and shop counter.

On the same night the stitchchild went missing, the Two-Headed Trout tavern across town started to lose its first batch of loyal customers to Quincy's Lodge.

Like all of the patrons that had made the tavern by the Frostfroth River their new "home away from home," they had originally been patrons at Quincy's until convenience won out over quality.

It wasn't ideal, but concessions could be made because it meant a shorter commute. And in the minds of these stitchfolk, if they really wanted a better meal, they could always eat at Quincy's on weekends, when they didn't have to wake up early the next morning and trek to their shifts at the mine or in the forests.

But all the glowing talk of the food was genuine news to people, and those bored with the bland and overpriced food and watered-down ale at the Two-Headed Trout got curious.

Nay knew the exact moment these return customers showed up, because she got a Quest Complete prompt.

[Quest Complete!]
[Entice Lost Customers Back Completed!]
[Congratulations!]
[You have been rewarded with Vigor Points]

After the Bouldershield Brothers had established *something* took the child from his bed in his family's home, and by *something* they meant something *not human*, which they had surmised through a bit of evidence they had found they weren't publicly discussing, word spread that there was a monster visiting Lucerna's End.

Nay and Quincy were sitting in the empty tavern midmorning in one of the empty corners, going through numbers while drinking pepper tea and eating rock cakes, when the Gloom Ranger strolled in, his entrance bringing with him a cold wind and flurry of snow.

The scant and hungover breakfast crowd glanced up from their continental breakfast munchies and from their cups of tea, and did a double take at the human man cloaked in what appeared to be crow or raven feathers.

To make his appearance more unsettling, there were actual bird heads poking out of the cluster of feathers on his shoulders. Two black hand crossbows hung on either side of his waist, and there was a smallsword hilt poking up out of a scabbard strapped to his back. His hair was the color of the feathers he wore, and his skin was as pale as the freshly fallen snow.

Quincy rose from his chair and greeted him. "Martygan! Get bored of shooting at birds in Scarwatch?"

Martygan smiled a wicked grin and marched up to Quincy, clasped his hand, and beat a tattoo on his back. "I figured visiting civilized folk could do me some good. But I decided to stop here and warm myself in front of your hearth first!"

The men laughed and unclasped each other.

Martygan moved in front of the hearth and warmed himself before its glow, sighing.

"I'm so accustomed to the cold, sometimes it's the heat that truly hurts."

"When you took your vow at Scarwatch, you became a child of the frost. But that doesn't mean you should deprive yourself of a good hearth every now and then. You're still a man, after all."

Martygan grunted. "The man part of me is trying. You don't happen to have any of that hot cider that you had last time?"

"Indeed, I do," Quincy said.

He went behind the bar and took a tin pot off the burner. He poured the hot cider into a wooden mug and walked back and put it in Martygan's hands.

The man took a sip and closed his eyes, enjoying the hot drink on his throat. Nay thought she saw some color return to his cheeks. There was a feral intensity about the man.

"Let me introduce you to Nay," Quincy said. "The Lodge's new cook."

Nay wasn't sure if she should stand and try and shake this man's hand—this man who came in from the wilderness looking like he communed with animals—or stand and do a curtsy. She wasn't sure what protocol was for greetings here, and she was thrown off by the man's good looks and primal presence.

So, she settled for a polite smile and curt nod.

"Because of her food," Quincy said, "the Lodge has had its most profitable week in a very long time." He handed Martygan a rock cake. "This goes great with the cider."

Martygan took the rock cake and glanced at it like it was some foreign luxury whose purpose confused him. But he bit into it and washed it down with more of the cider. "How quick the sweet tooth comes back. No matter how long I deny it, it always finds ways to remind me that part of me will always enjoy a good sweet."

"A man can't live off raw wild game and water trickling off a leaf alone, my friend," Quincy said. "These excursions back to civilized society are good for you."

Martygan's eyes found Nay, and for some reason, she felt like she was under a lens.

There was something about his gaze that made her self-conscious. She felt out of place but did her best to look comfortable. "Did you bake these cakes? It's very good."

She must have stared at him wide-eyed without saying a word.

Quincy brought her out of her reverie. "Nay? Did you hear that? He asked you –"

"I'm sorry, no," Nay said. *Dammit, was she blushing?* "I wish I could say I did. These are from a baker and sweets vendor in town we're quite fond of. Her name's Nisse. I worked out a deal with her to supply us pastries for our breakfasts here."

He considered this, finishing his rock cake. "You have a mind for enterprise, then. Smart of you."

"You think these are good?" Quincy said. "Come by at dinner and try the food. I just might have to stop you from whisking her away to Fort Nixxiom to cook for the Rangers."

"I will if my duties permit," Martygan said. He turned back to the hearth and nursed his cider.

Nay couldn't believe she was acting like this. She was usually composed, cool, and collected. Men rarely caught her off guard and made her feel this way. She found herself intrigued and intimidated by this man. She was usually so focused on her work, she never had time to date back in Los Angeles, aside from the random hookups that would happen, but those usually never meant anything, involved a lot of alcohol, and were often a mistake at worst and a blip on the radar at best.

She felt weird to even be thinking about this stuff. But there was a mystique about Martygan. He didn't seem real. But here he was, real as the rock cake in her hand.

"The business with this missing child," Quincy said.

Martygan nodded. "There are more tracks and monster activity than usual along the range. Our scouts say there was another outpouring from the Scar."

Quincy cursed under his breath. "Last time that happened, you and your brothers and sisters kept the trouble away from the town and settlements."

"That's the plan this time as well, but it seems like something slipped past our guard," Martygan said. He lowered his voice then. "I tracked it here. And I will finish it here."

"What is it?" Quincy said.

"That's what I intend on finding out," Martygan said. "The signs it's leaving behind don't point to anything I recognize. All I know is it's somewhere it's not welcome and I must stop it before more people suffer."

"Scarwatch must not be taking any chances if they've sent you," Quincy said. "Considering how much you're needed up there."

"It weighs heavy on the conscience on everyone at Fort Nixxiom that we've let something from the Scar slip into Lucerna's End. Our whole presence along the Spineshards is to prevent that very thing from happening. Yet it's happening."

"Don't blame yourself, lad," Quincy said. "You lot have it hard enough as it is. We've had no warning something was here lurking in the shadows. The sheriffs and the town watch have seen nothing."

"Which is why I want you to keep your eyes open for me here," Martygan said. "Something might be blended in with the men and the stitchfolk."

"Something taking the form of man?" Quincy said.

"Maybe," Martygan said. "I mustn't rule anything out."

"That kind of monster is at least a Tier Four," Quincy said. A disturbed look dawned on his face. His eyes went to his battle-axe, Gertrude, hanging over the fire. Then he turned towards Samuel, the massive and scuffed crossbow, hanging over the bar. "Maybe Gertrude and Samuel should come out of retirement for a little while."

"It's been a time of peace for you," Martygan said. "I don't see that changing, but it never hurts to know that your old friends are within easy reach."

Quincy looked around the tavern, making note of the faces in here. Putting them to memory. "I can maybe hire a town watchman to be in the tavern when it's busy tonight. It could help to have one of them around, watching for anything out of the ordinary."

"How often do these outpourings happen?" Nay said.

"The last one was four years and three months ago," Martygan said with no hesitation. "They don't come at regular intervals where we can predict them. Usually, we deter the creatures from wandering too far on our side of the Spineshards."

"Where are they coming from in the Scar?"

"That's the great mystery," Martygan said. "Our records go back almost a century, and all we have are theories. Some think it's another world or plane of existence. Some think it leads to the center of our world. Still others think it goes straight to the Nether Realm. But the men of Scarwatch are men of the arrow and claw, not so much men of lore. We are too busy tracking, hunting, and slaying to have our noses buried in books and scrolls. Although some of my ilk have a ken for knowledge."

"I'll tell you who has deep lore and records that go back," Quincy said. "The Veritax. They have churches and outposts and men all over the world. It's always been that way. Making their logs, recording. They've had eyes everywhere longer than anyone. There's men and women in the Veritax that know more than they let on."

"I don't doubt it," Martygan said. "I find *that* religion . . . incompatible with my own beliefs and way of life." He finished his cider then and set it on the bar. "Thank you, Quincy. When I return, I hope it's just to have more drink and a meal."

"Me too, friend," Quincy said. "Me too." He patted the Ranger on the shoulder as the man of the wilds headed towards the exit.

The Ranger turned to say one last thing.

"May this hunt come to its conclusion."

As his eyes passed over Nay, she felt that charge again, as if a fuse had been lit inside her.

He disappeared through the doors, and she shivered as a chill blew into the tavern.

She exhaled, glad for the chance to bask in cool air.

— CHAPTER TWENTY-SIX —

Cruel Folk

Another week passed and there weren't any more abductions. Yet the anticipation of another occurrence hung in the air like a heavy fog. News of a monster from the Scar hunting in Lucerna's End was the topic everyone whispered about, but people could find some relief from the fear by enjoying lively company and good food at Quincy's Lodge. The people needed some form of release from the tension, and they naturally gravitated towards the place that lit up the dark nights with light and laughter.

Although the Bouldershield Brothers had issued a curfew that went into effect once the sky got dark, many of the town folk ignored it to get to Quincy's Lodge. Everyone was on heightened alert, including the town watchmen, whose numbers were boosted with concerned volunteers, mostly other parents who wanted to protect their children, too wound up to sit around and wait for something to happen. They wanted to do something, so patrolling the town became an outlet for their nervous energy.

And while most of the town was shuttered up and quiet, most of the after-dark activity was coming from the Lodge and the House of Saccharine Delights. Laughter and mirth traveled through the air from these establishments.

Meanwhile, across town, the Two-Headed Trout was having its worst night of all time.

Everyone knew that the real party was happening at the Lodge, and people always eventually followed the current of social flow, so the servers at the Trout found themselves mostly standing around, wondering where all the customers were at.

When its owner, Wint, entered the common room of Quincy's, perched on his cane in the threshold of the entrance, the whistling wind fluttering the ends of his fine coat, no one took notice of his presence because the place was so busy.

Nay and Nom were in the kitchen in the midst of the dinner rush, arguing about chicken wings. She had created a recipe for a Stitchdale-inspired spin on wings.

[Chef's Delight Recipe]
[Frostfire Wings] [Base Rank]

"Take it from a fried-food connoisseur," Nom was saying. "The best chicken wings are fried chicken wings."

"Look, no one is not on your side here," Nay said. "Fried wings are best. Everyone knows that. But it's good to have a baked-wing option for those customers who might want to make sensible choices."

"How is not ordering wings fried a sensible choice?" Nom said. "It's the only choice if they have any damn sense about them!"

"Some people might want a healthier option," Nay said. "Am I right, Gracie? Help me out here."

"No one here usually has much of a choice on their food," Gracie said. "Sorry that I can't help you out, but this is the first time they've probably been presented with such a choice."

"See?" Nom said. "Life is hard here. Their daily activities make them strong and keep them in shape! And it's so damn cold, they could use a few extra calories!"

Bryja came through the double doors in a hop on her faun legs, which Nay had never seen her do before. She had been in a hurry to get back here. "Wint the Fishmonger is here!" she said.

Gracie looked out into the tavern, alarmed. Nay made sure her new Kickin' Chicken Pot Pies weren't burning the alcoves and then made her way to the anteroom. "What?"

Bryja hissed, picking up a tray. "The owner of the Two-Headed Trout. In here! Can you believe it? He hasn't been in here since he opened the inn."

"Gracie," Nay said. "Watch the pies for a few minutes, will you?"

Bryja went back out into the tavern with her tray, and Nay grabbed a tray of her own, following her. "Bryja!" she said, under her breath. "Where's this order going?"

The chillwind faun nodded her head at a table full of stitchguy lumberjacks near the hearth. Which also happened to be near where Wint was sitting. A basket of stripped wings was on the table, and he was currently digging into the Kickin' Chicken Pot Pie entrée.

Quincy was standing in front of him, holding a horn of ale, looking not all too pleased to see the Fishmonger in his establishment.

As Nay started putting the plates in front of the lumberjacks, one of them said, "What an honor! Served by the cook herself!" She smiled politely but turned her attention to Quincy and Wint.

"Don't think I haven't noticed that you're screwing me over with the stunt you're pulling on the vendors," Wint was saying between mouthfuls of pie. He was doing something Nay couldn't stand, which was talking with his mouth open, full of food. Chicken juice dribbled down his chin.

"What? A man isn't allowed to do business in the market anymore?" Quincy said.

Wint didn't say anything to that. He continued attacking the pie with his fork, plucking chunks of it into his mouth like a man at a buffet on a mission.

"It's not my fault that they like the deal they have with me," Quincy said. "We just gave them an offer they couldn't refuse."

"You edged me out," Wint said, and burped loudly. "Doesn't that put your finances in the hole?"

"Does it look like it puts my finances in the hole?" Quincy said.

Wint froze mid-bite and looked around him. The place was doing business hand over fist. Then he looked down at the food and set his fork down. "That girl from the market. She's your new cook, isn't she? I knew there was something fishy about her. These Reith girls, you can never trust them."

Quincy stared Wint down. "I'd be careful about giving attention to a Reith girl. I hear they can also be quite devious."

"Where is she?" Wint asked. "She's in the back now, isn't she? In the kitchen, whipping up all this exciting and delicious new food. How lucky you are! To snag a cook like that. Tell me, can you make an introduction? I want to confirm it's who I'm thinking of."

"I'm afraid the kitchen staff is quite busy now and can't be bothered by visitors," Quincy said. "They must focus on their work."

Nay put her head down and held the tray up near her face, hiding behind it as she made her way back to the kitchen through the crowd.

Nay and Gracie were decompressing behind the Lodge after another busy dinner shift, smoking iceflint cigarettes the stitchgal had rolled, sharing a bottle of Icemarrow Ale between them.

"Didn't expect Wint to show up here," Gracie said. "I reckon that's not a good sign."

"You really think he's bold enough to start some shit with someone like Quincy?" Nay said.

"There's whispers he's the one who put Captain Skorr at the bottom of the Lac," Gracie said.

"Yeah, but Quincy is a retired adventurer," Nay said. "He's one of those . . . Alric called them cultivators. He can do things normal people can't, right?"

"Aye, if he can," Gracie said, "he's been good at hiding it. I've always just known him as the bartender and owner of the Lodge. The charming old man with lots of wild stories. I figure he exaggerates them, ya know? To make them more entertaining."

"No," Nay said, "that old man has seen and done things. If Wint is going to try something, it's not going to be straightforward. He'll try and hurt him another way. I've seen his kind before."

"Him and his family, they're cruel folk," Gracie agreed. She took a swig from the bottle of ale and discovered it was empty. "Ah, damn. I'll get us another one." She got up and went back inside the Lodge.

Nay looked up at the green-tinted moon above and the swath of magenta in its vicinity. She figured that was probably gas of some kind. She wondered where this world, where this planet was in relation to Earth. Was it in the same galaxy? Or even the same universe or reality? She wondered if anyone here had such knowledge.

"So, you're the new cook everyone is talking about."

Nay took a drag of her iceflint cigarette and squinted at the figure emerging up from the shore of the Lac. It was a stitchgal as tall as her. She moved with a litheness that didn't seem so common for her kind. As she stepped into the lantern light, Nay saw the runic-style tattoos on her neck and along the side of her head where her hair was shaved. Her hair on the other side was long and gray and down to her waist. Her nose was pierced with what looked like a bone fishhook. Her coat was lined with dark bear fur. It was open at the collar, exposing her runic-decorated chest and midriff.

She got an instinctive feeling that the stitchgal was bad news, and she climbed to her feet.

"I'd love to stay and chat, but I have a kitchen to clean," Nay said. She turned to go back inside, but there was a tall stitchguy standing in front of the door.

His wide frame completely blocked it. His face was scrawled with runic tattoos, and a thick beard covered the lower half of his face. His lips protruded out of the hair. They were etched with runes. His nose was as big as a tuber and was riddled with blackheads that poked out of the craters like the bulbous tips of maggots.

"Excuse me," Nay said. She went to move around him, but he moved with her, blocking the door.

"You don't happen to have another one of those?" the stitchgal said. She was looking at the iceflint cigarette in Nay's hand. "Would be nice to have a smoke while we chat."

Nay knew these two were trouble. And now she was stuck in between them. If she tried to run, they would just grab her. And there was no shoving her way back into the Lodge with the stitchguy blocking her. She could cry for help, but she didn't want to give them the satisfaction.

So, she remained calm and produced another hand-rolled iceflint cigarette and held out to the stitchgal. "You must be Mishell."

The stitchgal smiled and accepted the cigarette. "My reputation must precede me." She struck a match and lit the cigarette, then exhaled frost into the air between them. "Iceflint? I would have taken you for an elderleaf gal."

"Why's that?" Nay said.

"Because don't all humans from Reith love elderleaf?" Mishell said. "Or am I mistaken?"

"So, you know where I'm from?" Nay said, deflecting the question with her own question. If Mishell was trying to trick her to see if she was really from Reith, it was best to not even engage in the game. "I guess my reputation precedes me."

Mishell smiled at that and chuckled to herself, pulling another drag of iceflint. Her pale blue eyes gleamed in the lantern light. "You're a pretty little thing, aren't you?"

"I appreciate the compliment," Nay said. "But I don't think you're here to talk about my looks, are you?"

The stitchgal was amused by that and made contact with the stitchguy behind Nay blocking the door. He shook his head and snickered.

"And you must be Krill," Nay said, turning to him.

As he regarded her, he stopped snickering. He didn't say anything, just looked at her like she was a curious specimen.

"Don't talk to him," Mishell said. "You're talking to me. In fact, don't even look at him; look at me."

Nay put up her hands. "Chill out; we're all friends here, right? So, what is it you wanted? You wanted to have a word with the cook who made your dinner?"

"Sure, we're friends," Mishell said. "Except the thing is, you're the type of friend my father doesn't exactly approve of. In fact, he's not very happy with you."

"He's not?" Nay said.

"He says you accused him of things in the market last week," Mishell said. "Embarrassed him in front of some people."

Nay played dumb. "He's a big boy. Shouldn't he be telling me this and not his children?"

At that moment, the back door budged open, nudging Krill in the back. He turned around in surprise and Gracie looked out through the crack, confused. "Nay?"

"Gracie, go back inside—" Nay started to say, but Krill grabbed her by the arm and yanked her outside.

Gracie started to scream, but Krill put a hand over her mouth and pinned her against the side of the Lodge.

"You don't need to hurt her," Nay said. "Your beef is with me, right?"

Mishell walked over to her brother and exhaled iceflint frost into Gracie's face, then put the cigarette out on her cheek. Gracie screamed into Krill's hand and tears ran down her face. She thrashed against Krill, but he held her tighter against the wall.

Nay couldn't believe her eyes. She watched this in shock and then found herself swinging at Mishell. But it was a clumsy punch. The stitchgal caught her fist in her hand and then twisted it behind Nay's back. Searing pain shot up her elbow and upper arm, and Mishell forced her onto the ground.

The stitchgal planted a knee on Nay's back and pressed one of her hands into the back of Nay's skull, holding her cheek against the cold cobblestone. "Our problem is with Quincy and his Lodge and everyone who works for him."

Nay whimpered in pain; the weight of the stitchgal was killing her spine. "Your problem is my cooking; leave her alone," Nay said through gritted teeth.

"Consider this a warning," Mishell said. "If we have to come back, then it will be the back of your skull next time."

Mishell reached in her coat and pulled out something tucked into the back of her breeches. Nay saw the moonlight reflect off silver metal. She glimpsed a shaft ending in a flanged head.

The stitchgal was holding a compact mace.

Krill pushed Gracie to the ground and then grabbed Nay's arm and stretched it out, pinning it on the ground to expose her hand.

"No," Nay said, panicking. "No, wait—"

Mishell brought the mace down on Nay's hand, shattering bone. Her vision went red and she screamed.

— CHAPTER TWENTY-SEVEN —

The Hue & the Cry

Nay woke up to a world of pain.

Her head was pounding, her throat was dry, and her entire right arm throbbed with a sharp ache that radiated from her ruined hand to her shoulder.

Her eyes cracked open and dim lantern light stung her sensitive eyes. She moaned and looked at the hand that was the center of her agony. It had been set with splints and at the moment, it was covered in bandages.

The image of Mishell's flanged mace smashing her hand against the cobblestones flashed through her head, and she whimpered.

Alric appeared above her and gingerly held a tin cup to her lips, wetting the cracked and dry skin with water. "You're all right," Alric said in a soft voice. "You're safe now."

She sipped the water, and the coolness moistened her parched throat. She began to gulp with greed, and water spilled down her chin. "Easy, easy."

After he had poured her another cup of water and she drank it down, Nay managed to push herself up against the bed's backboard with her good hand. "How long have I been out?"

"Two days," Alric said. "You woke up some when Quincy set and bandaged your hand, but after you drank a bottle of dreamwine, you passed out again."

"Gracie?" Nay said, looking around. "Where is Gracie? Is she okay?"

"Gracie is fine," Alric said. "A little shaken up, but she's okay. She told us who did this to you."

"Her face," Nay said. "They burnt her face. I couldn't do anything. They were too strong. I should have done something. Something more . . ."

"The important thing is that you survived," Alric said. "They caught you by surprise; it's not your fault."

Nay wasn't so sure about that. None of this would have happened if it wasn't for her. She had welcomed, hell, she had invited this danger into her life. And she did so without being able to protect herself or her friends. A sense of shame and guilt began to weigh her down. "I should have been able to stop them."

"These people," Alric said, "are savage. While their father is a cruel and greedy man, his kids have embraced the barbaric nature of some of their predecessors. While you grew up making people happy with your cooking, they grew up fighting and hurting others. Even if you had wanted to stop them, they come from a different world. It's not your fault."

That still didn't sit well with Nay. "Being helpless is no excuse."

She tried to push herself up but got dizzy. A jolt of pain ran up her arm and she grimaced.

"What are you doing?" Alric said. "You need to rest."

"But the kitchen—"

"Nom and Gracie have it under control."

A wave of weakness came over her and she settled into the bed again, not fighting the drowsiness. "Is there medicine . . . for the pain?"

Alric uncorked a green bottle that contained a red liquid. The label on the side indicated it was dreamwine. "This is from Quincy's own personal stash," Alric said. "Dreamwine is hard to find in Stitchdale. You have to get it from one of the cities on the Peninsula."

Then he emptied a packet of white powder into a flagon. He poured a generous amount of dreamwine on top of it and swirled it around. "This is some medicine derived from crushed herbs and the leaf of a plant that grows on the Spineshards that can fight off infection."

He handed her the flagon and she gulped the wine. She sloshed it around some, but her lack of taste buds just interpreted it as watered-down juice.

As she lost consciousness again, she did so while wishing that her sense of taste would return.

Nay was dreaming about her taco truck back in Los Angeles, Taco the Town, going out of business. They weren't getting enough customers, the engine broke down, and bills piled up where she had to sell the truck. When she was selling the truck, the Steksis appeared and offered her an eternal spot in its Bone Dolmen, and when she opened her eyes, Nom was in her room, munching on pumpkin seeds.

"You're awake!" His stalk lit up a pinkish-yellow color, and he waved his protuberances and slithered closer to the edge of her bed.

She wiped sweat off her brow with the back of her good hand. Then she reached over for the tin cup of water and drank. "Who is running the kitchen?" Nay said.

"Oh, dinner service finished a few hours ago," Nom said. "It's the middle of the night now."

"You ran dinner service . . . by yourself?" Nay said.

"Gracie helped," Nom said. "Though the servers had to be introduced to me. There was no way I could run the kitchen and remain hidden at the same time. Hilde and Ulla took it surprisingly well. Funnily enough, it was the faun who had the most trouble accepting that a tentacle could talk and cook. Go figure."

"And it went well?" Nay said.

"There were some hiccups," Nom said, "but a lot of that stuff got worked out the first night. The next three nights went smoothly, considering how busy we were."

"You ran the kitchen for three nights?" Nay said, surprised.

"Four, actually." Nom recounted the shifts in his head and then nodded. "Yep. Used all your recipes, of course."

Nay didn't know if she should be relieved or worried if Nom started to gun for her job.

"How's your hand?" Nom said, looking at the bandages.

"A throbbing nexus of pain and agony," Nay said. She was scared that it might not work properly again. She wondered what it looked like underneath all the splints and bandages. Right now it was stiff and it throbbed.

"I should have been outside with you," Nom said, regret in his voice. "They jumped you when you were outnumbered. Bunch of cowards."

"No," Nay said. "You were cleaning while I was taking a breather. You couldn't have known."

"Is it true that it was the owners of the Two-Headed Trout?"

"Pretty much."

"They're not happy people prefer our food more."

Nay reached for more of the dreamwine and took a swig.

Nom watched her drink for a moment and reached one of his protuberances into the bowl of nuts and seeds. He munched away, seemingly deep in thought.

When he broke the silence, she was already losing consciousness again. But she heard him say, "So, what are we going to do for revenge?"

When Nay gained consciousness again, the pounding in her head was finally gone and she felt like she was no longer floating between the real world and the dream world.

Quincy was sitting in a chair next to the bed, reading from a leather-bound book. His oversized frame looked almost comical. He made the chair look small, and his hands made the book seem tiny. When he glanced up and saw her eyes open, he closed the book and said, "There's my star cook. Finally returned back to the world of the living."

Nay groaned. "I'm starving."

Quincy got up and grabbed the tray from the table, walked over, and set it on Nay's lap. There were rock cakes, boiled eggs, fresh moon melon, and a kettle of pepper tea. She went for the boiled eggs first, grabbing a pinch of salt from the small bowl and sprinkling it over the protein. She bit into one and spent the next minute eating.

"I set your hand as best as I could," Quincy said. "I have some experience handling broken bones and other wounds. That type of knowledge is useful for adventurers, but usually a group has a designated healer. And I'm no healer."

"How bad is it?"

"It wasn't pretty to look at," Quincy said. "I can tell you that. But I spoke to Martygan and put in a request for one of the Scarwatch healers to pay a visit to Lucerna's End. They should be here today or tomorrow. When you're able to use your hand again, it will be because of them and not me. But I set it so they won't have to break your hand before properly treating you. So, I've mostly minimized the amount of pain you will experience."

"That's better than nothing," Nay said. She poured herself some tea and sipped on it. "Sorry to inconvenience you like this."

Quincy sighed and looked at her as a father would to a daughter full of shame. His face softened. "Why would you blame yourself for this? I'm the one who put you in danger."

"Yeah, but, at the market—"

"I know about you and Wint at the market."

"You do?"

"Not much happens around my staff without me knowing."

Nay realized Gracie probably told him. Which made sense. He had to keep eyes on her somehow.

"Look," Quincy said. "It was only a matter of time before Wint would have struck at us. I just didn't expect it to be so soon, and I didn't expect him to hurt you. This whole time, I thought he would come after me. That's what I wanted. I've been looking for ways to give him a reason to come after me. If he did, then I would be able to defend myself without facing consequences from the law. So, I'm afraid this is all my fault. I was shortsighted and should have foreseen something like this. I should have done more to protect you. Do you forgive me?"

He had been using her in a way. Sure, he had given her a place to live and a job in this strange world, but he also had ulterior motives. And now he was expressing his guilt about it. Nay wasn't sure how to feel.

But she nodded anyways. "What's my recourse against them? Does Lucerna's End abide by laws or have a justice system or whatever? Like do the twin sheriffs know what happened to me?"

"Well," Quincy said, "that's what we need to discuss. I haven't reported the attack on you because I wanted to tell you what would happen first. I didn't want to set anything in motion that you wouldn't want."

Nay nibbled on another boiled egg. Her body craved the protein after almost a week of withering away, caught between moments of consciousness and unconsciousness. "That makes sense. Okay. Lay it on me."

"Lucerna's End operates on a system that's kind of a bastardized combination of maugrim military law and the tribal justice of the human clans that lived along Lac Coineascar and Maer Scathan. There's a Justicar who hears cases and administers justice. Your case, in which you've been assaulted, falls under something called Hue and Cry."

"What does that mean?"

"It means you bring attention to Mishell and Krill by telling the sheriffs they attacked you. It's basically you demanding justice. I and others who are willing to back you up will support you in this claim. Public pressure and outcry will require the Bouldiershield Brothers to arrest Wint's children. It's then that one of two things happen."

"And what are those two things?"

"The Justicar will give you two options. As punishment for the attack, he will either fine them, and they will have to pay the fine. Which, Wint has considerable funds, so this will be nothing more than a slap on the wrist for them."

"And what's the other option?"

"You can choose to duel one of them to the death."

Nay just stared at him. "What?"

"They'll put you in a ring with either Mishell or Krill, and a crowd will watch as you settle your dispute by violence."

Nay's head spun. *What the fuck?* That felt downright medieval and brutal. And although it seemed a fine option for a fighter, there was no way she could beat one of them in combat.

"I don't think I like either of those options," Nay said.

Quincy nodded. "Which is why I wanted to present you with a third option."

"A third option?"

"We bypass the Hue and the Cry. We don't tell the sheriffs. And we administer our own brand of justice."

"I'm listening."

— CHAPTER TWENTY-EIGHT —

Pine Sap & Orange Rinds

The next morning, Nay felt well enough to be back on her feet and back in the kitchen. Quincy gave her a sling so she could keep her bandaged hand close to her body. "Take it easy," Quincy said as he helped her into it. "No one is expecting you working again. The healer from Fort Nixx should be here today. Until then, make sure you don't overexert yourself."

"The kitchen isn't going to run itself," Nay said.

"You're right," Quincy said. "That's why you have Nom and Gracie."

"Only a matter of time before Nom sets the Lodge on fire," Nay said. "I can at least be down there working on recipes and the inventory."

Quincy made sure the sling was on proper, then backed away and nodded. "I was thinking. You think you could have a chat with Alric? Maybe work out a deal with the abbey to provide the Lodge with a cask of Frostbite Ale? I think it would be good to have more varieties of beer for the customers. Some have been complaining I only give them my Icemarrow."

"The next time I see him, I'll bring it up."

After noticing how Gracie was cutting onions, Nay had to intervene. "Ol' Pat never taught you any knife skills?" Nay said.

"Ol' Pat never really liked anyone in her space," Gracie said. "I think having to train someone would have interrupted with her own routine too much. She was a bit of a curmudgeon."

Nay, with her one good hand, took the knife and showed her where to cut the onion in half. "See, if you cut it here, it still leaves a bit of the root on the end."

"I thought we were supposed to cut the root off."

"Not until you can use it to help you dice up the rest of the onion."

Next, she showed her where to make vertical cuts on the onion. She handed the knife to Gracie and watched her.

"Okay, now you cut horizontally in. But only halfway," Nay said. She pointed where to cut.

"Like this?" Gracie said.

"Yep," Nay said. "Now you can start dicing."

Nay showed her how to hold the onion and how to tuck her fingers in so she could guide the knife along her knuckles. "Do it like this, and you won't accidentally nick a finger."

Gracie followed her instructions and was delighted that she was actually properly dicing an onion. "That's so much better!"

"One more thing," Nay said. "Instead of pushing straight down, which is kind of making you saw at the onion, let gravity do the work for you."

She took the knife back and showed her to move the knife forward as she cut, letting gravity carry the edge down. "This is also easier on the blade and you won't have to sharpen it as much. The more you saw away at something, the rougher it is on the blade. It dulls it. This way, you're being kinder to both the blade and yourself."

Nay looked at the cigarette burn Mishell had left on Gracie's cheek. The girl had been rubbing ointment on it to accelerate the healing.

"I'm sorry."

"Chef?"

"I'm sorry you got hurt the other night. That should have never happened."

Gracie stopped cutting and looked up at Nay. "I should be the one apologizing. It's just a small burn. I've burnt myself worse taking food out of the ovens. If I wasn't so weak, maybe I could have . . ." Her eyes went to Nay's bandaged hand in the sling.

"They won't hurt you again. I promise."

Gracie nodded. Her face seemed to darken at the prospect of what that meant. But then Nay thought she saw a hint of a smile form on her face.

Nay showed her how to julienne peppers and how to quickly chop carrots and celery. Wouldn't hurt Gracie to know how to properly dice the trinity of vegetables.

"Nom," Nay said, "help her out if you ever see her doing something that needs instruction."

He was holding a fried drumstick in one of his protuberances. He stuck it in his mouth and stripped it clean and tossed the bone in a stock pan.

Nay was mortified. "Is that how you've been making the stock?"

"What?" Nom said, all innocent.

"Oh, hell, no," Nay said. "That's I think the most unsanitary thing I've seen!"

"I'll have you know that nothing is cleaner than my mouth," Nom said. "If it's good enough to feed my young, it's more than fine to feed our customers."

Nay felt herself gagging. She took the pan and dumped the bones into the trash barrel.

"I haven't heard anyone complain about it yet!"

"The bones that go in your mouth go in the trash! The bones from the oven that are left over go in the stock!"

"How do we not know that my method is responsible for the flavor, though?"

Nay threw a winter eggplant at him.

The healer from Scarwatch arrived just after lunch and was brought up to Nay's room. Her name was Lain and she was originally from the city-state of San Violeta on the Ligeia Peninsula. She had the same aura of wildness about her that Martygan had on him, but instead of a cloak of feathers, she wore white fur that had streaks of blue. It looked like it could have come from a chillwind wolf or bear, one of those species native to the Spineshards.

Her hair was golden and there were alpine twigs with clusters of red berries decorating her head. She wore ivory bracelets hewn from some type of horn or bone, and she spoke in a soft whisper, as if whenever she spoke, she didn't want to scare any delicate animals that had ventured to be close to her presence. Nay glimpsed what looked like razor-sharp golden rings strapped to her back, poking up out of her fur vest.

"I'm sorry this happened to you," Lain said as she sat in a chair next to Nay's bed, inspecting her bandaged hand. Her touch was soft and her presence was calm. Nay instantly felt relaxed and peaceful with the woman next to her.

[Aura Detected]
[Peaceful Presence]

So, it was a Marrow Eater Passive that was putting her at ease. Nay suspected Lain would have the same effect on people even without the Passive Ability. The healer smelled like pine sap and orange rinds, and Nay found herself craving hot chocolate with cinnamon or, hell, even a goddamn pumpkin spice latte. It was a little ridiculous how much this woman smelled of autumn and winter, and Nay wished she would become friends with her.

Lain undid Nay's sling and stretched out her arm. She examined the bandaged hand and her forearm. "All of the bones in your hand have been shattered. There's dozens of breaks here. The metacarpal bones might as well be dust. There are stress fractures even traveling up your ulna and radius."

Nay felt sick to her stomach hearing that. She was struck with the thought that she would have to cook with one hand. Mishell had not only maimed and disfigured her body, but she had legitimately handicapped her and affected her ability to do what she loved: cook.

"Can you help her?" Quincy said.

Lain stood up and took off her cloak, placing it on the knob on the wall. She rolled up the sleeves of her tunic. "Of course I can. I was the one who restored Frazetta's skeleton after his fight with the Njorbane."

"Who's Frazetta?" Nay said.

"He's a captain with the Scarwatch," Quincy said. "One of their most skilled monster-slayers."

"The Njorbane was a Tier Four monster that awoke from its deep slumber in its lair in the Spineshards during the last outpouring," Lain said. "It is native to the Spineshards but for some reason made itself a chieftain over the creatures that came out of the Scar. They had gone on a rampage, killing chillwind shepherds, and they slaughtered an entire village of chillwind fauns on the Onyx Strait. Captain Frazetta slew Njorbane after a battle that raged three days and three nights. Although Frazetta survived the fight, he was a broken man. Literally. His spine looked like your metacarpals." She pantomimed blowing dust off of her palm. "Powder."

"His fight with the Njorbane is the stuff of legends," Quincy said.

"From what he says, you've had a few of those yourself," Lain said.

Quincy played it off. "The tales of my deeds are greatly exaggerated."

"Your boss is a humble man," Lain said to Nay. "Now, as unpleasant as it may be, I have to remove your bandage."

Nay nodded, steeling herself. "Let's get it over with, then."

Lain opened a kit, taking out a pair of scissors. She held Nay's hand in her lap and began cutting through the bandage. The dressing fell away, revealing Nay's mangled hand. It was a grotesque sight. The skin had turned black and purple with bruising and crushed blood vessels, and it was misshapen, the shape distorted from the bones shattered into splinters. There was torn flesh from the edges of the flange of Mishell's mace, the cuts held together with some kind of unguent and tape. With the splints holding the fingers outstretched, the extremity looked like fruit that had burst.

Nay felt weak at the sight of it and had to look away.

Lain looked at her then, making eye contact. "The damage that physical violence does to our bodies is a horrible sight to behold. Flesh can be repaired, though. It's the emotional and spiritual, the psychic damage that burrows in deep and is sometimes impossible to repair. That's the damage we have to worry about. We have to make sure the trauma done to our spirits, to our Vigor, doesn't take root, lest our souls turn black."

She cocked her head, regarding Nay, as if noticing something. She looked at Quincy. "She has increased Vigor; I can see it." She turned to Nay. "Are you a cultivator?"

She wasn't sure how to answer, so she told the truth. "Sometimes, when I'm doing certain things, or have . . . completed a goal I had that was hard to accomplish . . . I feel like I'm becoming . . . more. Does that make sense?"

"It does," Lain said. She looked back at Quincy. "If she were in one of the city-states, she could train and ascend."

"What does that mean?" Nay said.

"You could increase in Rank if you had the proper guidance and structure," Lain said. "Which is possible on the Peninsula. Or, if you ever wanted to become a Gloom Ranger like me, you could do so at Scarwatch."

Quincy spoke up at that. "I think the girl just mostly wants to cook."

Lain looked at Nay then. "Well, if you ever become interested in trying to increase your Vigor Rank, it's something to think about. It appears to be happening regardless of structured training. In fact, I'd say that's why there's still blood flow in your hand. Your strong Vigor helped preserve your hand, along with Quincy's first aid treatment. You could have lost it before I got here."

"Thank goodness for small miracles, then," Nay said.

"Now let's get to restoring your hand," Lain said.

She carefully cut through the tape holding the splints in place. Every little movement or nudge sent a sharp, blinding pain up Nay's arm. She gritted her teeth as Lain removed the splints.

"Don't be alarmed with the light," Lain said. "It's just a manifestation of my healing. I'm going to be using a combo of my Bone Mend and Lifeblossom spells."

She laid Nay's hand on her thighs, in the cradle she had created between the bed and her lap. She raised a hand in the air, and a globe of gold light flared up around her hand. The room instantly grew warm with this new heat source, and it sounded like a gas burner's flame getting higher as the globe grew in size.

It lifted off Lain's hand and was floating in the air, spinning, filling the room with sparkling gold light. Another shape formed from the globe. It looked like a flower bud that was starting to blossom. The petals opened up and it flew towards Nay. She flinched and it hit her hand in a flash. In an instant, the light flower exploded into vapors as the healing magic splashed into her ruined hand.

As her flesh, blood, and bone absorbed the vapors, she immediately felt the pain fade and then disappear. While this was happening, another image floating off the globe formed into a shape. This time, it was of an antlered creature, what Nay thought was a majestic elk, and it ran through the air and crashed into her hand and arm, exploding into golden-white motes that fluttered around the room before entering her hand.

Nay could see her bones highlighted underneath her skin as they glowed, the hundreds of broken bits and splinters mending back together and forming back into the recognizable structure of a hand. She gasped as it felt like her hand and lower half of her arm had been dipped into cool water. It was a refreshing sensation that moved in, pushing out any remnant of ache or pain.

The lights faded and she could see her hand now.

It was whole again with a normal color, except for two scars that ran from between her knuckles to her wrist. The lines where the flange split open her skin. She held up her hand in amazement and opened and closed her fingers. There was no pain at all.

"The scars remain so you don't forget," Lain said. "For some memories could be folly to lose."

— CHAPTER TWENTY-NINE —

Knife Work

With her restored hand, Nay made Lain a private meal. It was the best way she knew how to say thank you. As Nom and Gracie ran the dinner service, Nay commandeered herself some table space and used of one of the oven alcoves.

Nom had done a double take at her freshly healed hand sans bandage. "What . . ."

"Long story short," Nay said, "I got healed."

She told him and Gracie about the healer from Scarwatch as she slowly cooked down the onions and butter for her rendition of French onion soup. "So, to say thanks, I'm making her dinner."

"That's the right thing to do," Gracie said. "She'll love it."

"Make enough so I can have leftovers," Nom said as he seared a pork chop.

Nay looked at one of the chalk signs and read the menu item, *Nom's Chops*. She looked again at the pork chop he was cooking, and she saw a Food Buff icon cube glowing inside of it. The icon was of the flexing bicep. She looked at the prompt log ticking by on her HUD.

Chef's Delight [Base Rank] in use.
Nom's Chops being created.
Imbuing Strength Buff.

Nom had gained access to the Chef's Delight Ability when he had consumed the Marrow of the Steksis with her a few weeks ago.

She got next to him. "Nom," she said.

"Mm, yes?" Nom said.

"Have you been putting Buffs in the food every night since I've been recovering?"

"Yep."

Nay nodded, of course he had. "If you see Gloom Rangers in the tavern, or if Quincy says not to, you are to listen to him? Okay?"

"Yeah, yeah. Don't worry. I know we're trying to keep a low profile with the fact that we can make magical food."

"Okay, I just want to make sure we're on the same page. So, no more Buffed food at the moment, all right? There's a Ranger inside the Lodge."

"Can you go back to your station? You're kinda cramping my mise en place."

Nay carried the tray of food out to Lain, who was sitting in the corner near the hearth. She was rolling what looked like dice on the table. When she saw Nay approaching, she scooped the dice off the table, making them disappear.

Nay set down all the food in front of Lain and put the tray on an empty table next to them. Then she sat across from the healer.

"All this is for me?" Lain said.

"As thanks for giving me my hand back," Nay said. "I wish I could do more, but I don't have much, and cooking is what I'm good at."

"Nay," Lain said, eyes sparkling, touched by the act of service, "you didn't have to do anything. It's my duty to heal people."

"Still, it just felt appropriate," Nay said. "You took a long journey to get here; the least I could do is make sure you're well fed while you're here."

She gestured at the wooden bowl of greens. "That's a winter salad, there's kale, sliced Moonglum apples, starflower seeds and goat cheese. I put my version of green goddess dressing on the side."

Lain's eyes grew wide as she examined the salad and dressing. It was simple, but she was impressed. Which made Nay wonder about the quality of the food at Fort Nixxiom.

"Then the soup," Nay said, "is French onion soup."

"French?" Lain said.

Shit.

"Yes, it's a type of soup in Reith."

"Oh, of course," Lain said. "Sorry, I'm ignorant about the Kingdom of Reith. You're the first person I've ever met from that side of the Vancian Sea."

Then Nay pointed at the entrée. "And the main course is braised beef short ribs. They were cooked with carrots, onion, shallots, sprigs of rosemary, and blue stitchleaf and braised in Quincy's personal brew, his Icemarrow Ale. I also used some of my diced garlic knots."

"Wow," Lain said. "I don't know what to say. But it smells wonderful and now I'm hungrier than before."

"Don't say anything," Nay said. "Just eat."

Lain tucked in and Nay took satisfaction in watching the show of emotions play across the healer's face. She tried the French onion soup first, and she was blown away by the taste, her eyes widening.

Nay hadn't imbued the food with any Buffs or Debuffs, as she didn't want Lain to know that she was a Marrow Eater. Quincy wasn't sure how the Gloom Rangers would react to an unregistered Marrow Eater in Lucerna's End. There was the small chance they might report her, and he didn't want to take that chance. It was one thing to have the capacity to rank up in Vigor Ranks, but Marrow Eating was a different business. A person could have the natural latent capacity to improve their Vigor. At some point, they would have to be documented, but it was normal for latent Vigor to manifest spontaneously in people or reveal itself as they matured.

As Lain made her way through trying the winter salad and the braised short ribs, the symphony of emotions and surprise continued to light up her countenance. Nay got a ding in her HUD.

[Reputation Menu]
[Factions]
[Gloom Rangers: Friendly]

The friendly bar filled with green light and then was replaced with a new bar as her reputation with Scarwatch leveled up.

[Gloom Rangers: Honored!]

Quincy had woken up Nay early, and when he had brought her to the rowboat tied to the Lodge's dock, she protested. "I really should be getting to the kitchen to get a head start on everything."

"The kitchen can wait," Quincy said. "Let your staff get things started." He climbed into the rowboat and held out a hand. She looked around. It was still so early, it felt like night. There was a thick fog hanging over Lac Coineascar. Then she reluctantly took his hand and climbed into the rowboat.

He rowed them across the surface of the Lac and she shivered in her cloak. The green-tinted moon still reflected off the surface of the water, still visible even through all the fog. She looked into the water and saw schools of slivermoon trout glistening as they swam by below, like seeing minerals glint in a creek bed. It was eerie being out on the water at this hour, and every now and then she saw the silhouette of a fishing boat deep in the mist.

"Where are we going?" Nay asked.

"You'll see," Quincy said.

That was something her father would say to her when she was just a kid, whenever he would take her on car drives to the park to play or even a gas station so she could get candy, packs of Nerds and Fun Dip. It was his little way of surprising her. One time, he even said that when he took her on a trip to Disney World. He had died before she had entered high school.

After a bit, Quincy rowed them to a secluded shore where the snow-covered evergreens came right up to the water. There was a little pocket between the root structure where he parked the boat and tied it to one of the trees. They got out, and he led Nay to a snow-covered glade that had a view of the Lac through the trees.

In the center was a dead tree. It looked like it had been cut in half by lightning, the top half sheared off, and its trunk ended in jagged shards of wood. Its branches had no leaves. On one side, up to about Quincy's head level, all the bark was gone and it was smooth as a wooden dummy. There were scratches, furrows, and even what looked like a circular target on part of it.

"What is this?" Nay said.

"This is where you're going to spend the first part of your mornings," Quincy said. "Even before you go to the kitchen."

"What do you mean?" Nay said. "Why?"

"So what happened to your hand doesn't happen again."

Nay looked at her healed hand, at the dual vertical-line scars on her flesh. She opened and closed it, still in awe that it was healed. Then she looked back at Quincy. "How are we going to do that?"

He pulled a box-shaped wooden case out of his pack and walked over to her. He traced the engraved cover with his hands. There was a name on the top.

Quella.

"My older sister," Quincy said.

He opened the case and there was a knife with a thick blade, with a short white handle that was curved like a talon. There was a wide bolster, and the butt of the handle ended in what looked like a short thorn. On the blade itself there was a swoosh that looked a lot like an ocean wave. There was a glyph stamped into the center of the blade at the bottom towards the bolster.

"This was her knife," Quincy said. "She called it Thorn."

That's what the glyph translated to. It was the name of the weapon.

Quincy gestured for her to take it. "Go ahead, pick it up."

Nay grabbed it, wrapping her scarred hand around the handle. It had arcs on the underside to accommodate the fit of her fingers, allowing her to take a strong grip. This wasn't a kitchen knife.

It was a combat dagger.

"I figured since the knife is your most-used tool in the kitchen, you would have a natural affinity for it as a weapon," Quincy said. "It was made by the famed bladesmith, Drixt Taglieri of Crescentia. The handle is hewn from the bonewood of the Cenotaph trees that grow in the Boneyard of Crescentia, where the ground is filled with the skeletons of the monsters that were defeated in the Battle of Scythes. The blade is steel blasted from the iron ore of Paleforge."

He reached out and pointed at the thorn on the butt of the bonewood handle. "That's a skullcrusher. Most knives, if you're holding it in the icepick grip, you want to keep your thumb on the cap so if you plunge down, your hand doesn't slip off the handle onto the blade. But since there are curved grips, the cap can be used as another weapon."

He pantomimed bringing the skullcrusher down on someone's head. "It's a good move if someone's head is exposed to you like that."

Nay stared in wonder at the weapon, a little terrified of it. "That's nasty."

"All knife fights are nasty," Quincy said.

"And you want me to learn how to knife-fight?"

"I want you to learn how to defend yourself when running or talking your way out of a situation is not an option. Dueling for the sake of dueling is foolish, especially with knives. No one walks away without bleeding. Most of the time, especially at Base Rank, both participants will die, either on the spot or if they walk away, then slowly from blood loss while someone is trying to treat them."

"But not Marrow Eaters?"

"Marrow Eater fights are a different thing entirely. But we're going to pretend you're not a Marrow Eater, so you can learn the basics. A good foundation will separate even Marrow Eaters. Sometimes, technique edges out pure power."

"I'm not sure I could have stopped Mishell and Krill from doing what they did, even if I knew how to use a knife."

"Maybe, but maybe you would have left them with injuries of their own and made them think twice about attacking you. Street fights are often instigated by reputation. They sensed weakness, so they weren't afraid to engage, even though it was foolish on their part. If an assailant senses strength, then that makes them hesitate and reassess. I'm going to help you be strong."

Nay didn't argue with his logic. If there were people out there like Mishell and Krill, she better mitigate her odds. Then she was struck with a thought. What if they had been Marrow Eaters? Then she'd really be paste. There would have been no chance of defending herself.

"Maybe I should work on getting out of Base Rank," Nay said. "Like Lain said, maybe it's possible for me to . . . level up."

Quincy didn't say no. In fact, he wasn't opposed to the idea at all. "That's why I want to get you started on the basics. Consider all of the time you remain at Base Rank your tutorial."

Nay felt a surge of blood and adrenaline rush through her. She was bolstered by the prospect of harnessing and strengthening her Vigor. She knew something had been missing in her life, and it wasn't just ending up in this world and being adrift. She had her cooking and her job with Quincy, but this felt like the missing piece of the puzzle that had been nagging at her during her rare periods of downtime.

Quincy took Thorn and taught her the two grips: the more-standard grip where she grasped it in a more natural position like she was shaking someone's hand, and the icepick grip or the ghiaccio grip, as those on the Peninsula called it. "I'm no expert with knives," Quincy said. "That was Quella. But I know the basics."

"Where is Quella now?" Nay said, venturing to ask. She wasn't sure if his sister was a sore subject, but since she was inheriting her weapon, she thought it was okay to ask.

"She's moved on to the Celestial Realm," Quincy said. "She's been gone for fifteen years now."

Nay wasn't sure how to reply to that. Was she supposed to say she was sorry? But he sounded okay with it, his tone indicating she had moved on to a better place. It was awkward, so she just nodded, pretending she understood what he meant.

"So, there are three basic methods of attack," Quincy said. "There's the slash, the thrust, and the jab." He demonstrated each one.

For the slash, he raised the knife and brought it down in a diagonal direction.

For the thrust, he punched forward with the tip.

For the jab, he flicked his wrist, using the blade like a short whip, an extension of his hand.

"And there are three invisible strings for the directions you choose for each attack," Quincy said. As he spoke, he showed her what they looked like. "There's diagonal . . . there's horizontal . . . and there's vertical. You see?"

"Seems pretty simple," Nay said.

"I'm glad you think so." Quincy handed her Thorn. "Now show me." He backed away to give her space in the snow.

"Slash!"

She slashed.

"Thrust!"

She thrusted.

"Jab!"

She jabbed, whipping her arm out and flicking her wrist.

"Slash diagonally!"

She exhaled with each slash, inhaled with each retraction of the blade.

"Slash horizontally!"

She shifted her axis of attack, instinctually letting her arm adjust to the movement.

"Slash vertically!"

She was beginning to understand the flow, realizing that the blade could be an extension of not just her body but her will. These ideas began to form in her head, and a whole world opened up before her. A world that showed her the possibility of a new kind of dance.

In the secluded glade by the Lac, underneath the dead tree that was struck by lightning, underneath the protective snow-covered boughs, and underneath the watchful green-tinted moon, Nay worked through her routine of slashing, thrusting, and jabbing. Quincy called out the attacks and the directions, and she would shift from one attack to another, from one direction to a different direction, performing at the pace of his commands.

— CHAPTER THIRTY —

Mind Meld

Nay's mornings began while the moon was still hanging in the night sky. Quincy had hired town watchmen to stand guard at the Lodge through all hours of the day and night, so she only felt a little nervous getting in the rowboat by herself and rowing to the training glade.

She always found herself checking behind her, constantly concerned Krill or Mishell were out there, watching her, waiting to fulfill their dark promise to her. But they must have been keeping a low profile during these few weeks, staying in the shadows until they surely showed their faces again. Word of mouth indicated that the Two-Headed Trout had all but been gutted of business.

They knew Wint was out there fuming, planning something, yet Quincy didn't seem worried. He seemed excited to put their plan in action. Like he wanted Wint to make a move. But he was making all the staff operate under cautious protocol to ensure no one was attacked again.

There were two watchmen outside at all times, front and back entrances. And there were two more watchmen inside the tavern itself, ready to take action if Wint or his children or anyone suspicious was lurking around or on the premises.

Once in the glade, Nay found peace in the quiet and the isolation and the winter beauty. She spent a few minutes doing the stretches Quincy had shown her, and then she drew Thorn out of the sheath at the small of her back and began her practice.

After Nay finished her knife routine, which Quincy called her "knife dailies," she was to do her "fitness dailies."

"Training your body is important to surviving here," Quincy had said. He had stacked stones on top of a sled and tied two ropes to it. Part of her fitness daily was to pull and drag the sled around the perimeter of the glade as many rounds as she could for an hour. When he explained it to her, she got the prompt.

[Quest Detected]
[Quest: Pull Sled for an Hour, No Stopping]
[Accept Quest Y/N?]

Of course she had complied.

[Quest Accepted!]
[Pull Sled for an Hour, No Stopping]

Her boosted Vigor gave her extra stamina and grit to make it twenty minutes before collapsing in exhaustion. This morning, her hands were rubbed raw from gripping the ropes.

The rest of her dailies consisted of push-ups for her upper body and leg raises for her core. Afterwards, she would lie in the snow next to the ice-cold stream, drinking up the chill water and groaning in pain. It was a grueling workout, especially for someone whose sense of fitness in a previous life was walking from the couch to the fridge to retrieve the leftover takeout boxes from the night before.

The first week of doing these dailies, she had never felt more frustrated or weak in her life. Her heart felt like it was going to burst out of her chest, and her lungs were constantly tight and on fire.

But each day, she had managed to pull the sled for a little longer or do a few extra push-ups and leg raises.

By the time she had rowed back to the Lodge that morning, her body felt broken and she was light-headed and starving. She stumbled into the kitchen, dripping ice and snow. She collapsed into one of the tables, fatigued.

"You know," Nom said, appearing with a flagon full of some thick, green concoction in one of his protuberances, "I should have a nutritionist fee written into my contract with Quincy."

He set the flagon in front of her. "This is Nom's Nutritional Post-Workout Smoothie," he said. "There's wintergreens, star seeds, green tea, and the powdered whey we made from the cow's milk we purchased this week."

Nay grabbed the flagon with both hands and started guzzling the thick smoothie. She couldn't taste the intricacies of Nom's shake, but she felt the Strength and Stamina and Spirit Buffs coursing through her. It really was the perfect recovery concoction. Already her fatigue was fading and she was beginning to feel renewed.

She reached the bottom of the flagon. "Is there more?"

Nom retrieved the leftover smoothie from the little gnomish blender, and before he could fill her flagon, she grabbed the container out of his hands and started chugging.

"*You know*," Nom said, "you might want to go easy on that. If you're not burning enough calories, it might make you grow . . . big."

Nay, mid-chug, punched him in the equivalent of his shoulder.

"I'm not kidding! All this working out and slamming protein is going to make you put on muscle! You'll have to get new breeches! Your quads are going to get huge!"

"And that would be my prerogative!" Nay said, wiping her mouth with the back of her hand. "It's rude to talk about a woman's body, Nom."

"Why?" Nom said, genuinely confused. "I'm just talking in practicalities."

"But you're doing so when it may be uninvited," Nay said. "You have to read the emotional temperature of the room. How do you know I'm not self-conscious? Maybe I'm sensitive about my body. Maybe it's none of your business."

Nom blinked.

"You could hurt someone's feelings," Nay said.

"I've done something bad," Nom said.

"Relax, I know you're still learning about social etiquette and manners. Hell, we all are here."

"No, I'm not talking about that. I understand what you're saying and I'll think twice next time I comment on someone's body. But I'm talking about something else. I've been up to . . . *mischief.*"

"Mischief?" Nay frowned, a bit confused by the topic change.

"I've been sneaking out at night," Nom said. He said it like an altar boy in confessional with a priest.

"You have?"

Nom nodded. "Before I made your smoothie, I just got back in."

"From where?"

Nom didn't answer.

"From where, Nom?"

"First, promise me you won't get angry."

"Nom. *From where?*"

"The House of Saccharine Delights."

"Mother of God," Nay said. "You went to the whorehouse?"

"They don't really like to be called whores," Nom said.

Nay couldn't believe what she was hearing. She stared at Nom in shock and dismay, wondering what his desires or moment of weakness had brought upon them. Did the girls of the House of Saccharine Delights know that a sentient tentacle was the sous-chef at Quincy's Lodge? Wait, did he . . .

"Did you sleep with one of the ladies?" Nay said. "Did you have relations with a woman of the House of Saccharine Delights?"

"No!" Nom said. "You got it all wrong. I was just watching from underneath the bed, from the rafters. I took care not to be seen. I was just curious. I just had to know, Nay. *I had to know!*"

"Jesus, Nom!" Nay said. "Had to know what? You can't just use your imagination? You had to go and be a voyeur!"

"Don't get judgmental with me!" Nom said. "A tentacle is allowed to watch! *We're allowed to watch!*"

"Ew!" Nay said. "No! Ew! You're not allowed to watch! Not unless you're invited to watch! That's just creepy!"

"Don't look at me like that!" Nom said. He went and hid under the table in shame. "*Don't look at me!*"

Nay sat down and put her head in her hands. Her sous-chef was a total perv. Well, it wasn't so uncommon. She had heard worse stories from every other sous-chef she had had. Hell, tales from line cooks could downright make one want ear bleach.

"That's not the worst part."

Nay looked under the table at him. "What do you mean?"

Nom didn't say anything, but he was shaking.

"Nom. What do you mean that's not the worst part?"

"I couldn't help myself," Nom said. "He was hurting her, so I had to do something . . . but he deserved it for . . . for what he did, *he deserved it . . .*"

"Who was hurting who? Back up for a second, who is 'he'?"

"You know they have food there . . . for the clientele. There's a kitchen and they'll make food all hours of the day. Nothing as good as we make, but the men can request food whenever they're hungry, and I . . . well . . ."

"Nom what did you do?"

"I think it will be easier if I just show you."

"Show me?"

He came out from underneath the table and leaned forward towards her. She flinched and backed away. But he grabbed her hand with his protuberances. "No, put your forehead against me. I'm going to use my Mind Meld spell."

"Mind Meld?"

"It will let you see what I saw," he said. He bent his head forward. Nay obliged and leaned forward as well, so her forehead touched the point of the tentacle.

Upon contact, she saw sparks and everything went white.

There was a rush of visual distortion and a sound and a fury like Nay was a charge of chemicals traveling through Nom's synapses, finally reaching his visual cortex. Then the blur crystallized into a clear image.

She was high in the shadows of the rafters, looking down into one of the rooms in the House of Saccharine Delights. The general vibe for Nay was like the French Nouveau as filtered through a maugrim escort who really liked the color burgundy.

For some reason, there was a lot of use of the color burgundy. Burgundy bedsheets. Burgundy bedcover and blankets. Also, there seemed to be strategically placed mirrors in the room, so that from no matter where one was, even in the rafters, one could catch their own reflection in a mirror. It was like being inside of a jewel.

There was a stitchgal touching up her makeup at a vanity mirror when a large stitchguy entered the room. He cut a wide and familiar silhouette.

The stitchgal froze at the sight of him. Her face was stricken with disgust and fear. "You again," she said. "I told Madam Snowstroke that one of the other girls would be a better match for you."

"I'm not interested in any of the other girls, mot skljef," he said in a low voice, more of a sinister whisper.

It was Krill.

Nay felt both fright and anger at the sight of him as he stepped into the candlelight. The feeling of wanting to recoil but also lunge at him was a weird one, made even more so that she wasn't in her own body but was rather experiencing one of Nom's memories from his point of view. Still, the urge to both run and fight surged through her, and that must have been the adrenaline releasing back in her own body.

She wanted to close her eyes at what happened next but found that she couldn't because Nom had watched everything.

When it was over, Krill had lain against the headboard and demanded that the stitchgal put in his order of food. It didn't matter that she was weeping into a pillow, smearing the fabric with her makeup, blood, and tears.

"I said order my mot skafjerik's pie!" Krill said, shoving her off the bed.

That son of a bitch, Nay thought, as the stitchgal scampered off, covering herself in her robe and sobbing.

At that moment, Nom took off down the length of the rafter and slithered down the opposite wall on the dark side of the room. Then there was a rushing blur as he squeezed through a crack in the wall and raced through the inner architecture of the House of Saccharine Delights, through the spaces between the walls, emerging into a dark corner of the kitchen.

The cook was an old stitchguy, smoking a pipe with one hand and preparing the mince of a shepherd's pie with another. He stirred at the mince with a wooden spoon, then set it down and sprinkled seasonings into it.

He coughed and went to pull on his pipe, but the tobacco had burned out. He stepped away from the bowl of mince to go refill his pipe with a fresh plug of tobacco.

That's when Nom rushed to the bowl and deposited a dropper of some type of liquid into the bowl of mince. As he did it, Nay's HUD came to life, coming from her vision but overlaid over Nom's memory.

Poisoner's Gambit [Base Rank] in use.
Lamprey's Spit.
Lamprey's Spit is a poison derived from a surfeit of Lac lampreys, by extracting bile from their venom sac glands and mixing with a bit of fermented crystal-berry juice.

Nay was somehow using her HUD to interpret the Marrow Ability Nom had used to create and deploy the poison. Somehow, Nom had developed the Marrow Ability to create poisons. She wondered if it came from the Marrow of the Steksis, that it had somehow combined with one of his latent skill trees or something. When this memory was over, she was going to have so many questions for her sous-chef.

Nom disappeared back through the walls, and soon they were back in the rafters, watching Krill from the dark ceiling. The stitchgal was staying away from him, sitting at her vanity and covering her bruises with makeup.

There was a knock at the door and a stitchgal entered, depositing the tray of food with the shepherd's pie on the bed for Krill. He guzzled a goblet of wine and then started digging in to the shepherd's pie with his bare hands, shoving a scoop into his mouth.

The stitchgal saw him choking through the reflection in the mirror. At first, he coughed, irritated. But when his throat wouldn't clear, he hit his chest, as if to dislodge something in his throat. Except there wasn't a foreign object blocking his airway. His throat was swelling and closing up.

He stood, panicked. He was wheezing and clutching his throat with one hand, and pointing at it with the other. The stitchgal stared at him through the reflection, realizing what was happening.

But she did nothing to help him.

He staggered and fell to his knees, clutching at his throat. The veins protruded on his face and the vessels in his eyes burst. He collapsed to the ground, foam bubbling out of his mouth.

Then he grew still.

Dead.

Nom, the son of a bitch, had poisoned Wint's only son.

— CHAPTER THIRTY-ONE —

Madam Snowstroke

When Nom leaned away from Nay's forehead, it was like pulling the plug on the Mind Meld connection.

There was the chaotic blur again as if Nay was being ripped out of one world and teleported into another. When she blinked, she was suddenly back in the present, seeing the world with her own eyes again.

She gasped and had to sit down, shaken by the entire experience. Her arms and legs felt weak and she was dizzy. It was akin to the feeling of having low blood pressure. She bent over, taking deep breaths as she got used to her own point of view and body again.

"Before you say anything," Nom said, "I don't regret poisoning him. He helped pulverize your hand and was probably planning on killing you. But also, you called me a pervert. To which I say it takes one to know one!"

Nay waited a moment so that when she spoke, she would be calm.

"Okay, first off," Nay said, "when were you going to tell me that you know how to make poisons?"

"I don't know," Nom said. "It just happened after we ate the Marrow of the Steksis. You got Abilities and spells because of it, too!"

"Yeah, but I never got a poison option. How come you got that and I didn't?"

"I don't know. How come you can see magical text and prompts and maps and I can't? We're two different beings with different skills. The Delicacies and Marrows probably react differently to each person's Vigor."

It wasn't a bad thought. For all she knew, his guess was as good as any.

"Also, you killed Krill!" Nay said. "Without telling me first! This really messed up our plans. What were you thinking?"

"I was thinking that someone should do something about him. He hurt you; he hurt that girl. It just seemed like the right thing to do."

"Quincy had it all worked out. We just had to be patient. Now . . . now it's screwed up."

"No one told me," Nom said. "Maybe if I had known about these plans, I wouldn't have killed him. But come on; I know you wanted him dead too."

Nay got up and started pacing.

"There will be fallout because of this when Wint and Mishell discover that he's dead," Nay said. "We'll have to expect the worst."

"They will probably blame the poor stitchgal at the brothel," Nom said. "Maybe I *should* have thought twice about poisoning him. I don't want her to get punished."

"You're right," Nay said. "Wint will come after the House of Saccharine Delights and the stitchgals there. I guess the question for us is, do we intervene? I personally don't feel comfortable letting them deal with the blowback of your actions."

"If I'm honest with myself," Nom said, "I don't either." He sighed. "I knew I did something bad. Even though it feels so right!"

"So, they're probably in the process of telling the Bouldershields, reporting his death. If they're doing that, then the clock is ticking on when Wint finds out his son is dead."

Nay started putting on her cloak.

"Where are you going?" Nom said.

"To go see what's going on at the House of Saccharine Delights."

Nay made her way through the cobblestone streets as the sun was starting to appear through the gray clouds. She felt renewed from Nom's magical smoothie, and she walked with an extra bounce in her step, her pace almost at a jog.

The brothel sat on the street, the house of ill repute overlooking the intersection and towering over the buildings around it. Like Quincy's Lodge, it was three stories with a wraparound porch. The windows on the second and third stories were covered with red curtains. Baroque ironwork decorated the rails, and the lattices framing the windows were flamboyant, all meant to draw the eye.

There was a tall human woman on the porch, smoking a cigarillo via a glass cigarette holder. She wore white gloves on her hands, her torso wrapped in a burlesque corset. Her red hair fell onto her shoulders in ringlets. Her skin was alabaster pale and there was a wry smile on her candy-apple-red lips. There was no mistake who this was.

It was Madam Snowstroke.

There was no sense of urgency or worry about her. And there seemed to be no commotion about the bordello. If Nay didn't know any better, it would seem like nothing of note had happened here at all lately.

"You're Quincy's new cook, aren't you?" Madam Snowstroke said, leaning on the railing, the cigarillo dangling off her cigarette holder in her hand.

Nay crossed the street and walked up the stairs onto the porch. "That's me. How do you know?"

"Your cooking is a nightly topic of conversation in my establishment," Madam Snowstroke said. "There's not any way I could convince you to come run my kitchen, is there?"

Nay was taken aback by her offer. It seemed like a plush gig, probably akin to being a private chef. "It's tempting, but . . ."

"Your loyalties lie with Quincy."

Nay nodded.

"I understand," the madam said. "That makes me respect you more. I like a loyal girl. I'll have to give Quincy a visit sometime so I can try this food everyone has been raving about. I'm familiar with Reith cuisine, and I must admit I do miss it."

Nay stiffened at that. Here was a person in Lucerna's End who had actually been to Reith. So, she was acquainted with the land, its people, its customs. Nay would have to be careful around her lest she be discovered to be an imposter.

"I'm just so busy around here, I rarely get to leave for extended periods of time," Madam Snowstroke said.

"Maybe I'll have a meal delivered to you," Nay said.

"Now, that would be delightful," Madam Snowstroke said. "Maybe you can make those buns . . . what are they called . . . they're fluffy white buns with this filling . . ."

Nay couldn't tell if she was really searching for the words or if this was a way of seeing if Nay was really from Reith.

"Pork," Nay said, daring to bluff and take a guess. But she said it with a confidence that covered her uncertainty. "Pork and scallions."

"Is that what it is?" the brothel owner said. But her eyes lit up and she turned. "You know, I think you're right! I'm remembering the taste now! Of course it was pork. What were those called, again?"

Nay could feel Madam Snowstroke's gaze. She was looking at her, unblinking. It was unsettling.

"Most people will call those bao," Nay said, bluffing again. "Steamed pork buns. Though you can use different meat for the fillings. Some people like lamb."

Madam Snowstroke ashed her cigarette and then smiled. She looked away from Nay.

"Bao," she said. "That's right. How could I forget?"

"I can make you those. Easy."

"You know, I have a feeling me and you are going to be good friends."

Nay wasn't sure what information the madam had just extracted from her, but she did suddenly feel at ease. For some reason, she had the impression that even if she knew Nay was lying, she wasn't going to rat her out.

"Are you always up this early?" Nay said. "I always figured brothel owners were late risers because of all the late nights."

"Didn't you know?" she said. "A madam never sleeps. A brothel is practically a rotating door all hours of the day and night. There's rarely a moment where my girls let me rest."

"Sounds bad on the beauty sleep but good on the pockets," Nay said. "A busy business is never a bad thing."

"No, it's not. I like it this way." She took a drag of her cigarette and watched the morning townsfolk go about their business. "What brings you to this side of town this morning?"

"I was on my way to the sheriff's," Nay said.

Madam Snowstroke looked at her with concern. "I hope it's not because you've been the victim of a crime."

"Oh, no, nothing like that," Nay said. "Rolf had helped me with an incident a few weeks ago, and I wanted to stop by and thank him." She produced a growler of Icemarrow Ale from inside her cloak. "He's a fan of Quincy's ale."

"I had heard you had a run-in with that cretin of a fishmonger," the madam said. "I understand he was quite uncouth towards you."

"I guess that story got around, huh?" Nay said.

"Not much happens in this town without me knowing," the madam said. "That's part of running a brothel. People that come see my girls, they talk a lot. They're like my little birds who hear everything. And they tell me everything."

"So, you must know the fishmonger has it out for Quincy because he thinks we're stealing his business," Nay said.

"You don't have to have the ears of whores to know that," she said. "Everyone knows. Of course he blames you all. You're offering people a better product, a better experience."

"So, should I be worried about him?" Nay said. "I'm not going to stop cooking good food just because a rival tavern owner doesn't like it."

Madam Snowstroke smiled. "I have a feeling the fishmonger will be preoccupied in the near future with some bad business decisions he's made. The Two-Headed Trout will be the least of his worries."

That's when Nay understood.

There wasn't a commotion here this morning because the House of Saccharine Delights hadn't alerted the sheriff when Krill died in their establishment.

Madam Snowstroke had it taken care of. She had hidden all evidence of his body and was covering up his death.

Wint would be preoccupied with the disappearance of his son.

* * *

When the second child was taken, Nay was spooning garlic-infused butter onto a piece of filet mignon cooking in an iron pan when she got the alert.

[Tongue of the Hierophant Delicacy Trait]
[Detect Marrow]
[Status: In Use]

Nay kept bathing the meat, which was offered as Nay & Nom's Prime-Cut Steak on tonight's menu, as she accessed her mini-map. There was the blinking green dot that signified the Marrow in the northeast part of town.

It blipped, streaking out of range, and was gone.

She looked up and saw Nom looking towards the northeast, then he looked at her, his eye wider than usual.

"You saw it too?" Nay said.

"There's a Marrow in Lucerna's End," Nom said. "What do we do?"

They were in the middle of dinner service. They couldn't ditch their job and leave Quincy high and dry to go and investigate. It would be too much for Gracie to run if both of them left. It was a packed house, and either Nay or Nom had to be there for things to run smoothly.

"You go," Nay said. "I'll handle the apps."

"You sure? You're having to babysit steaks."

"Please, I can run a grill station and a fry station at the same time. Ask me about the time I had to run both sauté and pantry one night when a bunch of people quit in the middle of a shift. I was so far in the weeds, I needed a machete to hack my way out."

"Okay," Nom said. "What should I do if I find it? Should I try and retrieve it?"

"No," Nay said. "The last Marrow was attached to a monster. It's not worth the risk."

He tilted his head. "It's a Marrow. It's definitely worth the risk."

Nay knew he wasn't wrong. Still, she didn't want him putting himself in danger. Sous-chefs could do stupid shit from time to time, but getting killed trying to go after a Marrow by oneself would be on a different level. Especially when it was avoidable.

"Doesn't mean we can't be smart about it," Nay said. "The most important thing is to stay out of danger. The second most important thing is not to be seen. Just get some intel and scope it out, and then come back. And then we'll figure out what to do."

"But what if we can't find it again?"

"Them's the breaks. I'd rather lose a Marrow than my sous-chef."

Nom nodded, handed her the fry ladle, and headed for the exit.

"Wait," Nay said. She tossed him Strength- and Dexterity-imbued biscuits she had made and stored in the pantry. "Stack these."

He caught them in his protuberances and began stuffing them into his mouth as he disappeared out the door.

Nay set to the task of running the stations, but she kept her mini-map open, in case the green dot appeared again.

― CHAPTER THIRTY-TWO ―

The Doom That Came to Lucerna's End

If the green dot appearing on Nay's mini-map was the first sign that doom had come to visit Lucerna's End that night, the town at the edge of the world, then the watchman bursting through the tavern doors and jumping up on the stage to interrupt the band to proclaim there was a monster running through the town, carrying a stolen child, was surely the second.

Nay heard the commotion of dinner eaters and drinkers and partiers rising from their tables in alarm and the shouts and questions that started to fill the air. She stepped through the double doors to see what was going on.

At first, she was stricken with the thought that maybe Nom was responsible for this public disturbance. Had someone seen him and assumed him to be a monster? But there's no way he would be doing anything with a child.

"Everyone get to their families!" the watchman cried. "Protect your wives and your children!"

"What is it?!" a lumberjack shouted.

"Did you get a glimpse of the monster?" another voice shouted.

The watchman trembled and he seemed to struggle with how much he should say. Finally, he said, "Aye I saw it and it's not anything you want to see! Get back to your homes and stay indoors! There's a Gloom Ranger in pursuit!"

There was a buzz of chatter as people made exclamations about said Gloom Ranger, excitement and fear working their way through the crowd.

"Let the Gloom Ranger, the sheriffs, and the night watchmen handle this!" the man on the stage reiterated. "We don't need any casualties tonight!"

"I'll not stand by twiddling my thumbs and plucking my arse hairs while some monster has taken one of our own!" a miner said.

"Whose child did it take?!" a voice rose up, demanding an answer.

There was more tittering among the mass of people as speculation spread. The watchman shifted nervously.

"Tell us!"

The watchman licked his lips. All eyes were on him. "'Twas young Finch, Mawrella's son!"

There was a cry of anguish and a clattering as a tray full of dishes and cutlery hit the ground.

Nay's head swiveled towards the sound and crash and she saw Bryja, her chillwind server, collapse into the arms of a group of a stitchguys next to her. Tears began to pour from her face as she howled.

"Oh, no," Gracie said next to Nay. "That's Bryja's family. The monster took her little brother."

"Jesus Christ," Nay said, disturbed.

Quincy shoved his way through the crowd and took Bryja out of the stitchguy's arms. He comforted her as she passed out in grief and emotional shock.

A table of stitchguys headed for the door, bloody murder on their faces. As they exited the Lodge, their leader stayed behind for a moment and looked up at the watchman. "I'll not leave it to the watchmen nor the sheriffs to get back that young faun alone. We will find the monster and make it pay for setting foot in our town, and we will return the boy to his family."

And that's when the mass in the Lodge started emptying into the streets. Nay watched with conflicted feelings of dread and exhilaration as the crowd exited and went their separate directions, following their separate missions. The energy of the mob was contagious and spread like an airborne virus.

It would be a mixture of women and children hiding in cellars, attics, and barns and men taking to the streets with pitchforks and battle-hammers. It had been a while since the citizens of Lucerna's End had dealt with a monster that was bold enough to prey on their town.

Within a minute, Nay was looking across the tavern at Quincy, who was comforting Bryja. They made eye contact. Nay wasn't sure what was being said in that look, but the moment was interrupted when Bryja gained consciousness and started trying to get up.

The only diners left in the tavern were the older stitchguys nursing their ale and their buzzes, and they couldn't be bothered to do much other than sip on their ale and stare into the hearth.

One of them, playing with a set of rune dice and smoking a pipe, said, "Might as well bunker down next to the fire with your drinks, lads; it's going to be a long night."

"Gracie, hold down the kitchen," Nay said, putting on her cloak. She checked to make sure *Thorn* was still strapped in the scabbard she had at the small of her back.

"But what if we get busy?" Gracie said. "I can't run it by myself!"

Nay put a hand on the stitchgal's shoulder. "You'll be fine. Most of the diners have left, and I don't expect them coming back anytime soon. It's not going to be busy, but I need you here to hold it down for the customers we do have."

"Where are you going?" the stitchgal asked. "And where did Nom go?"

"I'm going to go find him."

Nay headed for the exit but Gracie grabbed her. "Be careful. Don't do anything stupid. I can't run this place by myself."

"I'll be fine," Nay said. She had wanted to add, *I've already survived this long, haven't I?*

But Gracie wouldn't have understood.

If Nay had any questions about which direction to head in, the inhuman shriek piercing the night sky and the flashes of light that followed, tendrils of energy crackling over the roofs of the buildings, were a good giveaway.

Each shriek was followed by a noise that sounded both like the crack of lightning and the unfurling of chains, a man's voice shouting something unintelligible. Nay thought of a cowboy barking orders at a group of cattle.

As she hurried in that direction, stuffing her face with imbued Strength and Dexterity biscuits, the blinking green dot appeared on her mini-map.

The Marrow.

Her sinking feeling was confirmed. The Marrow, like with the Steksis, was probably attached to the monster that had taken Bryja's little brother. The monster that was responsible for the shrieking and snarling she heard in the center of the town.

There were angry voices up ahead, and she saw the flare of torches and lantern light creating shadows on the walls of the buildings.

The closer she got to the Marrow, the more likely she would be to find Nom, who was also probably following the Marrow with his own version of the Detect Marrow Ability.

She was only a couple of blocks away from the Lodge when she turned into an alley because it provided a direct line to the center of the commotion, and was confronted by a figure in silhouette blocking the other end.

"You must be incredibly brave or incredibly stupid to wander away from the safety of the Lodge," a familiar voice said. "Or perhaps I'm just incredibly fortunate."

A flare of violet light crackled over their heads—something having to do with the monster—and illuminated Mishell's face for a moment. The half-maugrim, half-human girl stepped into the lantern light.

Her face looked haggard, and Nay caught a strong whiff of ale and piss in the air. The fishmonger's daughter had been drinking. She was a live wire looking for a puddle of water.

Nay took a step back, her hand going to the small of her back. "I owe you a ruined hand. But I'm willing to take a rain check on that tonight if you are. With current events and all."

"Let me see your hand," Mishell said.

Nay let go of Thorn's handle and moved her hand back in front of her and held it up. Mishell stared at Nay's healed hand and frowned.

"That's not how I remembered leaving it," Mishell said.

"Well, you are drunk," Nay said. "Maybe you're not perceiving events as you should right now."

Mishell put her head down. Her hair hung in front of her face on one side. Her shoulders were shaking. Then Nay heard her laughter. It was a laugh undercut with a healthy dose of bitterness. "Where's my brother, *kitchen wench*?"

"Is that supposed to be an insult or something?"

"I know it's you and your boss that have something to do with it. I can feel it."

"I don't know. Have you checked all the gutters? What about outhouses? He's the type that's probably passed out in public, probably pissed and shit all over himself, too."

Mishell bellowed and charged Nay. She drew her compact mace and swung it backhanded. Nay almost tripped over the cobblestone as she backpedaled.

She felt the rush of air kiss her face as the flange swept by her, millimeters away from caving in her cheek. The head of the mace continued into the wall of the building, hitting the stone with a crunch. It dented in the wall, and flakes of plaster and dust sprinkled the ground below.

Nay turned and ran as Mishell swiped at her again. The clang of the flange hitting the other wall echoed down the alleyway.

"Run, coward!" Mishell said. "It's a game I know well. The running, the hiding . . . the finding, the bashing!"

But Nay was already turning onto the street. She was taking Quincy's advice and running away from the duel. True, she had a weapon now and she had been training, but she was still no match for someone as strong and experienced as Mishell. No amount of leg raises or push-ups in the past few weeks would have closed that skill gap.

She heard Mishell's heavy footsteps and shouts as she pursued May through the streets and alleyways. More crackles of light and monster squeals filled the night air a few blocks away. She ran towards the cavalcade, hoping she could find the crowd of people.

But as she emerged out of an alleyway onto another street, she realized she still had blocks to go. She looked around and saw a wagon. The back of it was filled with bundles of pine needles. Across from the wagon were barrels of half-frozen rainwater.

Mishell's footsteps were pounding the cobblestone nearby.

Nay chose her hiding place just as Mishell came out of the alleyway.

She stopped running, slowing to a walk, her mace in her hand. She saw the wagon and the back filled with pine needles. She smiled.

As she casually passed the back of the wagon, she suddenly raised the mace over her head and swung it down into the back of the wagon. The flange crushed through the pine needles and embedded in the bottom of the cargo bed. Wood splintered outwards.

One of the barrels across from her tipped over, spilling a torrent of rainwater slush onto the street. It splashed towards Mishell and she jumped away, but the water rushed underneath her feet.

It froze just enough upon contact with the cold cobblestones to slicken the ground in a thin layer of ice.

Nay emerged from behind the cluster of barrels and darted away from Mishell. The fishmonger's daughter yanked the flange out of the bed of the wagon, tearing wood. She took a step towards Nay and slipped in the slush.

She fell to one knee and hooked an elbow over the back of the wagon, catching herself. Her boots slipped around as she struggled to stand and get to a dry surface. She screeched at Nay, "After I kill you, I'm going to kill all the other kitchen wenches who work with you!"

Nay took another alleyway, and another, zigzagging her way towards the center of the town. When she emerged into the town square of Lucerna's End, she froze and gaped wide-eyed at the spectacle.

Martygan, the Gloom Ranger, held dual crossbows in his hands and was advancing towards his target. There was a giant creature backed against the shops on one side of the square.

To Nay, the thing looked like a hulking bidepal toad. Its gelatinous eyes bulged, amber Jell-O shots the size of lanterns. It had the biggest distended belly Nay had ever seen on a being, pale and yellowed like a fish belly but covered in warts and some kind of slime. Its drooping chin was the same color as its belly, and every swollen lump on the thing seemed to be pulsating. A long, slavering tongue the color of raw liver hung out of its wide mouth. Square, uneven teeth filled its mouth like football cleats.

It had a potato sack tossed over its back; something was squiggling and squirming inside. That was presumably Bryja's little brother, young Finch. The fact that there was movement was a good sign. It meant he was still alive.

Something was pouring out from underneath the belly hang of the beast, a mass of soup filled with algae spilling from its groin region. It looked like a deluge of boba tea falling out of it in clumps and forming mounds on the ground. The tapioca balls inside were embryos the size of basketballs.

The embryos expanded and burst.

Little tadpole monstrosities erupted forth, growing quickly.

The gelatin-like mounds of afterbirth rolled, a mass of slime, and creatures growing in real time were separating from it and bursting out of amniotic sacs and shaking fluid off themselves. They stumbled onto the street. Their uneven first steps became a run.

They were tadpole monstrosities enlarging to the size of dogs.

The street was roiling with these things.

They charged the Gloom Ranger and were exploding into bursts of bile, slime, and blood against the volley that was pouring out of his crossbows.

A barrage of glowing bolts was streaking, arcing out of the dual crossbows and exploding upon contact with the wall of tadpole dogs. Streaks of Vigor bolts were also flying from Martygan's crossbows, creating a violet-and-crimson lightshow against the fog.

With each volley there was a crack of lightning.

The Gloom Ranger's hands were glowing white, and tendrils of Vigor essence were crawling up his arms, a spirit aura encasing his appendages. The outpouring of Vigor was causing a reaction with his magical crossbows, transforming them into the equivalent of rapid-fire machine guns that churned out magical bolts.

The volley was melting the tadpole dogs, filling the street with fish-bait-like gore.

Lain was crouched on top of a building, her boots planted in the tiled roof, sending out bursts and pulses of golden healing light at Martygan with her hands. It looked like she was chucking darts or shuriken of healing Vigor at him.

There was a golden, razor-sharp hoop spinning in the air next to her, shooting out a concentrated beam of Vigor and frying any tadpole dog that scaled the walls of the house and got close to her. It was like a motion-sensor buzzsaw of golden light.

Her halo protectors.

As she did this, her face was calm and composed.

Nay was so caught up in watching the Gloom Rangers in action that she didn't notice the tadpole dog half-wriggling and half-running towards her until it was too late. It was somehow churning up flecks of cobblestone as it torpedoed at her.

As she dived out of the way, three things happened.

One, she crashed into a spit trough that the townsfolk used to spit their chewing tobacco in, dousing herself in the juice equivalent of dozens of dip cups.

Two, the tadpole dog flew over her, passing by close enough that Nay caught a glimpse of its needle-like piranha teeth.

Three, Mishell's mace clobbered the tad-pole dog in the side of its bulbous head—a blow meant for Nay, which she had managed to avoid by diving—splattering both her and Nay in weird gore that smelled like rancid fish guts that was left to rot in the sun for several days.

Mishell stood over Nay, mace in hand, as the tadpole beast flopped and spun in circles on the cobblestones, spraying ichor in a pinwheel pattern.

"I'll give you one last chance to tell me where my brother is before I smash your brains in. Just like I did that thing."

— CHAPTER THIRTY-THREE —

Lament for the Fishmonger's Daughter

"I don't know where your brother is!" Nay said. She was telling the truth. Kind of. She had no idea what the women at the House of Saccharine Delights did with his body.

There were cries of terror all around them as the townsfolk who formed the mob dispersed, barricading themselves in buildings or running for places to hide, trying to get away from the tadpole monsters.

It was chaos.

There would be no one to help Nay against Mishell. And the fishmonger's daughter knew that. She looked around and smiled. She was going to kill Nay, and when the townspeople found her body, it would be blamed on the monsters.

"My father doesn't take kindly to competition," Mishell said. "This didn't have to be personal. It was just business."

"You made it pretty goddamned personal."

Mishell swung the mace down. Nay rolled out of the way. The flange struck the cobblestone where her head was just at, cracking the stone.

Nay managed to push herself to her feet. The half-maugrim girl threw out a front kick that was more of a horizontal stomp.

It was like getting kicked by a mule.

Her boot hit Nay's midsection so hard, she was pretty sure a rib or two cracked. The momentum threw her into the wall of a building, and she felt the back of her skull bounce off the surface.

Dazed, and with adrenaline coursing through her, Nay grabbed Thorn's handle and drew the dagger. She operated purely off some inner instinct, a biological directive that told her she better act or die.

As Mishell closed the distance, raising the mace over her head, Nay jabbed with Thorn, flicking her wrist and whipping the tip of the blade into the half-human's face. Nay felt the steel scrape across her orbital socket. There was a scream of pain and the mace fell out of Mishell's hand.

It tumbled to the ground with a clang.

The fishmonger's daughter's hands flew to her face and cupped her eye. Blood trickled from between her hands as she howled.

Nay stood there, the half-maugrim girl's blood dripping off the point of Thorn, in shock. She was so taken with what she just did and Mishell's reaction that she stared at her opponent in horror.

"My eye!" Mishell screamed.

She lowered her hands, revealing the wound. Nay had cut her across the eye. The flesh was perforated at each corner. The cuts oozed blood, winking like little kisses.

Nay couldn't see how bad the wound was on the eye itself because the socket had filled with blood.

It trickled down Mishell's face, red tears.

Consumed with rage, Mishell charged Nay. She had more mass and more muscle than Nay. They were opponents of two entirely different weight classes.

Nay raised Thorn and delivered a diagonal slash. But she would have had better luck trying to stab a charging bull. Mishell backhanded the dagger out of Nay's hand and crashed into her.

The fishmonger's daughter wrapped both hands around Nay's throat and squeezed, lifting her into the air. The muscles in the half-maugrim's arms went taut. Nay's airway was suddenly cut off. It felt like her neck was caught in a vise between Mishell's strong hands.

Nay scratched at the girl's fingers, trying to loosen her clamp-like grip. But she was too weak, and Mishell was consumed with blind rage. Her feet were hovering over the street, heels kicking against the wall.

Nay couldn't breathe. She couldn't even cough. She opened her mouth to shout, but no sound came out. Her face was turning red and she was beginning to lose consciousness.

Something purple whipped out of the darkness, coiling around Mishell's thick neck.

Green protuberances covered the half-maugrim's mouth and nose, blocking her airways.

"You want to know where your brother is?" Nom said. *"Here, I can show you."*

He pressed the tip of his stalk against Mishell's forehead, and her one good eye glazed over as she was thrust into the tentacle's Mind Meld connection. As he tightened around her throat, Nay knew he was showing her the poisoning of her brother.

It happened in a flash.

Nay watched Mishell's good eye widen in terrible comprehension.

Her hands released Nay.

The cook dropped to the ground, choking. She crawled on her hands and knees, hacking, clearing her airways, and her fingers found Thorn.

Mishell fell to her knees. Her hands tried to rip Nom off her, but he was too thick, too rubbery, and too slick. She couldn't get a grip on him.

"Now that you've seen where he's gone," Nom said, "it's time to schedule a reunion."

When Nay pushed herself to her feet, that's when the river of tadpole dogs hit them.

One clipped her at the knees, and she flew up into the air and landed on the backs of the pack.

The same thing happened to Mishell and Nom, and the stream of monsters carried them off in different directions.

"Nom!" Nay cried.

He uncoiled off Mishell. Nay's last glimpse of him was the tentacle bouncing in the air across the backs of the mutant tadpoles as the flow carried him onto a different street.

Nay crashed into a fountain and fell into the cold water. She groaned, scrambling so that she was right-side up. Two of the tadpole monsters had broken off from the main roil and were in the fountain with her, righting themselves.

Before the one nearest could get its grounding and attack her, she grasped Thorn in an icepick grip and drove the dagger down into the top of the thing's head. The amphibian's flesh was soft, and there was a crunch as the combat dagger punctured its skull, finding its brain.

It immediately went still and fell limp, almost pulling Thorn out of her hand. She jerked up and a glop of pink-and-blue ichor apexed into the air, then fell into the water.

"Why does everything that tries to kill me here have to be so gross?"

Then that's when the other tadpole dog spun towards her. Instead of running at her on its legs, it dropped into the water and propelled itself at her with its undulating tail.

She didn't have time to jump out of the fountain, so she braced herself, getting ready to thrust. As she was about to strike, fearing that the thing would missile into her and tear at her flesh with its piranha teeth, the thin spike of a poleax pierced its head, pinning it.

The poleax lifted into the air, taking the mutant tadpole monstrosity with it.

Rolf Bouldershield swung the poleax, flinging the corpse out of the fountain.

More tadpole dogs poured into the fountain, and Rolf and his brother Jolf jumped in with Nay, water splashing all over their armor.

They positioned themselves between the monsters and the cook.

"Do we need to ask why you're out here and not in the kitchen?" Rolf said.

"Don't you think that's a little sexist?" Nay said.

"Huh?" Rolf said.

"Shut up," Jolf said. "Here they come!"

The first wave of tadpoles rocketed towards them, and the Bouldershield Brothers demonstrated their namesake.

While Rolf was swinging the poleax, slicing and thrusting at the tadpole dogs from afar, Jolf wielded a battle-hammer, swinging it like a baseball bat, hammering tadpoles into the sky as he dealt with the creatures that managed to slip through his brother's defenses.

"Bring it, ye ugly shits!" Jolf said.

The Brothers were brutal, dealing with the first wave like a pair of machetes hacking through a jungle.

But by the time the second wave came, the Brothers were a bit gassed. One of the tadpoles got past both of them only to meet the tip of Thorn in its brain. Its razor teeth posthumously snapped at the air.

Nay had to jump back to avoid the nip, the movement a manifestation of last nerve signals being sent from the brain.

Then the third and fourth waves arrived together, spilling over each other to get into the fountain.

They had to get out of there.

The Brothers hitched Nay up over the fountain. She leaned over the side and put out a hand and grabbed Jolf. Jolf threw his hammer over the side.

His brother pushed him up as Nay pulled him. Not an easy task for her, as half-maugrims had a lot of body mass and the man was wearing some ring mail. But he hooked a hand over the side and scrambled out of the fountain.

Rolf leaned his poleax against the side and had to jump to grab his brother's hand.

But as he did so, the tadpoles crashed into him, smashing him against the inner wall of the fountain. The sheriff pounded on their heads with his gauntlet, shattering their faces.

There was a horrible sound of claws and teeth scraping against plate mail.

"No!" Jolf shouted. He was about to jump back into the fountain full of tadpole dogs with his battle-hammer to save his brother when a volley of exploding crossbow bolts arced into the fountain, hitting the tadpole mutants and turning them into a pink-and-blue mist.

Nay looked up and saw Martygan perched on the lip of the fountain, sweeping his crossbows back and forth, spraying bolts and Vigor projectiles into the pool, mowing the tadpoles down.

Rolf was half-buried in the creatures, punching them with his gauntleted fist and bellowing.

Their teeth punctured his armor, peeling it open like it was a soda can. He screamed as they started to rip at the exposed flesh of his arms and torso. He disappeared under their numbers, his gauntlet reaching out from underneath the mass.

The aura encasing Martygan's arms and hands changed colors from violet to orange as he reloaded the crossbows with different cartridges, an array of bolts that looked like glass.

He fired, and the glass bolts tumbled through the air, trailing tendrils of orange light, before they landed in the fountain, causing a chain reaction of bursting tadpoles as they succumbed to a magical napalm.

A fountain of tadpole gore bubbled into the air, revealing Rolf, bloodied and half his armor torn off, covered in puncture wounds, lying in the mixture of water and gore.

Lain landed on the side of the fountain, jumping down from one of the roofs.

Jolf hopped back into the fountain. "Rolf!"

He picked his unconscious brother up and handed him up to Lain. Nay helped her pull the unconscious sheriff out.

The flesh on his arm and torso looked like raw hamburger. Nay had to look away.

"Brother . . ." Jolf put his forehead against his brother's face.

Lain whispered over him, "Mend Flesh."

Wisps of gold light blew out of her mouth like dandelion fluff and settled over the sheriff. As each feather of gold touched him, there was a burst of light.

When the lights faded, his damaged flesh had been healed. It was smooth and pink, like the new skin underneath a scab.

The healer looked at the amazed Jolf. "He's going to be okay, but he's going to be asleep for a bit. Trauma still takes its toll, even when its physical manifestation has been erased."

Martygan continued firing globs of the napalm into the streets, exterminating the tadpole dogs.

He was making his way to where the giant bipedal toad was thrashing, one of its legs pinned to a stone building with a large crossbow bolt that had gone through the flap of skin on its massive toad leg.

A night watchman, keeping his distance, tried to jab it in the face with a long pike.

But its brown-pink tongue shot out of its mouth, the blossoming tip thwacking the man in the face. The sucker on the end of the tongue wrapped around his head.

In the blink of an eye, the tongue retracted, ripping the watchman's head off.

It flung back, disappearing back into its mouth, swallowing the man's head with a gulp.

"What the fuck!" Nay said.

The young faun's bleating cries could be heard coming from the sack slung over its back.

The humanoid toad grabbed at the bolt with its hands and began to pull. It ripped the bolt out of the stone, bringing the wall down with it.

"No, you don't," Martygan said. He loaded a different set of bolt cartridges into his crossbows. These looked like coiled discs of chain and a rack of eyebolts.

As he pointed the crossbows at the bipedal toad, he shouted, "Chains of Harrow!"

He pulled the trigger on one crossbow, and multiple barbed hooks shot towards the creature, trailing chains.

The toad let out a strange bleating and hacking sound as the barbed hooks impaled its flesh.

Then Martygan pointed his other crossbow at the cobblestone street and fired.

Eyebolt anchors quivered into the ground. He anchored the Chains of Harrow to the eyebolts studded into the street.

The toad tried to hop away but it was leashed to the ground. It pulled on the chains. They grew taut but didn't give.

"Martygan!" Lain said.

He glanced away from the toad and saw more tadpoles coming at them in a half-crescent.

He reloaded another set of cartridges into the crossbows.

There was a moment where he closed his eyes in concentration, the Vigor aura around him encasing his whole body. Then he blurred, vaulting into the crescent of tadpole dogs. He spun through them like a literal whirlwind, arms outstretched with the crossbows, bolts firing in three hundred and sixty degrees, melting the clusters of monsters.

Martygan appeared out of the blur, Vigor smoke rising off him, standing in the remains of the monster tadpoles.

He checked his bandolier. He was out of bolts and cartridges.

He slung the crossbows to his belt holsters and drew his smallsword. He pointed it at the chained bipedal toad.

"Now we finish this."

CHAPTER THIRTY-FOUR

Mini-Boss Battle

Although Nay couldn't take her eyes off the weird amphibian monstrosity, she couldn't ignore the sack on the ground next to it. It was moving as Young Finch inside floundered.

And it wasn't just any child. It was Bryja's little brother.

She was hit with a series of prompts that scrolled down her vision. With each one there was a ding and a chime. The text-and-audio burst was disorienting.

[Marrow Detected!]
[Frog Leg Marrow of the Mewlipped Tode]

Surely, the Marrow wasn't one of the thing's fucking legs.

She looked at the monster's oversized toad leg. It was the off-color chickenshit yellow of gator belly. And it was riddled with pulsating wart sacs and purple lesions. She gagged, thinking about consuming it. There was no way in hell any chef could take that ingredient and make it appetizing.

[Quest Detected]
[Quest: Separate the Marrow from the Mewlipped Tode]
[Reward: Frog Leg Marrow of the Mewlipped Tode]
[Accept Quest Y/N?]
[Quest Detected]
[Quest: Help the Gloom Rangers Slay the Mewlipped Tode]
[Accept Quest Y/N?]

She quickly accepted the quests so they would no longer interfere with her vision.

"We need to be careful," Lain said. "Many of my major heals are on cooldown."

Martygan grunted. "It's not going anywhere. Not when it's hooked with the Harrow Chains."

"Still," Lain said. "It's not a catalogued creature. We don't know what else it can do."

"It can die."

Martygan held his smallsword up to the sky. Vigor vapors coiled off his arm and swirled around the sword. He shouted, "Blade of the Ranger!"

Crackles of electricity and spinning shards of metal seemed to materialize out of the air. The shards of metal flew to the smallsword, snapping in place and adding to its mass, reforging the small sword into a huge blade. There were cracks in the surface of the newly forged blade, giving it a crude but intimidating nature. Within these fissures, green light ran up and down the cracks, signifying the power of Martygan's Vigor.

His form blinked and reappeared in front of the Mewlipped Tode, emitting a blast of Vigor energy that dazed the monster.

The Gloom Ranger grabbed the sack with the child and threw it over his head.

The sack flew through the air and Lain caught the child. She gently set the sack down.

She pulled the fabric down, revealing the blue face of the terrified faun toddler inside. He was shrieking in fear.

"Calm, my handsome one," Lain said. She touched the boy's forehead with a finger. There was a blink of her golden Vigor, and a shimmering translucent golden blanket fashioned of interlinked autumn leaves rippled around him, calming him. He fell asleep and she set him back down.

As Martygan lunged forward with his sword, about to deliver a combo, the Harrow Chains ripped out of the street.

The tode twisted, whipping the chains around the Gloom Ranger. They pulled his arms close to his side, and though he still held on to his sword, he was trapped in his own chains.

At that moment, an obnoxious prompt splashed across Nay's vision in an ostentatious battle-royale-style font.

[Mini-Boss Battle Engaged!]
[Nay & The Gloom Rangers & The Bouldershield Brother]
VERSUS
[The Mewlipped Tode!]

"Shit," Nay said. She gripped Thorn. There was no question of whether she wanted to accept the mini-boss battle or not. Which she thought was rude of whoever or whatever the quest-giver was. It was happening whether she wanted it to or not.

Next to her Jolf stood up, leaving his brother next to the child they were rescuing. He grabbed the pike and shouted, "To the nether fooking hells with ye!"

He hurled the pike at the tode.

It flew through the belly of it like a spear piercing through tissue paper. It bleated in pain and ichor squirted out of the wound, spraying Martygan.

The Gloom Ranger let out a cry of agony as the skin on his face began to melt.

The ichor appeared to be acidic.

At that, Lain simultaneously jumped to her feet and pulled one of the golden hoops strapped to the small of her back.

It hummed and started to spin, growing in gold light. But instead of emitting a harmful beam, it blasted Martygan with a healing stream.

The spinning halo appeared to have different modes.

One, like the first mode Nay saw, was pure damage. This second mode was pure healing.

The healing stream hit Martygan in the face. His melting skin began to mend.

Watching it was like observing a crazy optical illusion. Squint just right, and his skin was bubbling and melting. But if Nay opened her eyes wider or tilted her head in a certain way, she saw the skin regrowing.

There was a push and pull to it, but the healing stream seemed to be winning.

Lain drew another hoop and jumped in an arc; as she descended, she brought the razor edge of the hoop through the Harrow Chains restraining Martygan. All the while, the other hoop followed her, hovering near like a halo, healing her Gloom Ranger companion.

Martygan burst out of the severed chains and blinked into the tode, delivering a combo of lunging and slashing.

The strikes were so fast, Nay's vision could barely register their delivery. She just saw visual distortion.

The sword wounds opened on the tode, the skin on its chest and belly opening up, spilling more of that ichor. Its guts slipped out of its belly and one of its arms slid off its shoulder.

The ichor hit Martygan and steamed, burning him, but the heals negated the damage.

The tode bleated, its mouth distending.

Its gecko-like tongue shot out of its mouth and hit Lain's halo hoop spinning over her.

Its sucker tip grabbed it and the tongue flung back into its mouth, swallowing Lain's hoop.

Taking away Martygan's heals.

The Gloom Ranger's blinking movement ability seemed to be on cooldown, so he merely dove away from the ichor squirting out of the tode.

The tode shot its tongue out again. This time, it attached to Martygan's blade.

The tongue tried to retract and rip the sword away, but the Gloom Ranger held on tight. Brute physics pulled him forward, dragging him towards the tode and its leaking acidic ichor.

The liquid was melting the cobblestone. Noxious steam rose into the air.

And Martygan was being pulled straight to it.

Lain held out a fist, and her gold Vigor aura turned crimson. She turned her wrist, pointing her thumb out.

Red light glowed inside of the tode, lighting up the inside of its belly like a Christmas bulb. Red light shot out of its open wounds.

The healer had toggled the hoop's settings, turning on the damage mode.

The disc was spinning inside the tode, churning its innards and filling it with a buzz-sawing beam of damage.

As the tode trembled violently, being devoured from the inside, its tongue still dragged Martygan closer to the acid.

But the Ranger would not let go of his sword.

So, Nay ran forward and slashed vertically, severing the tode's long tongue with Thorn.

One half fell to the cobblestone and retracted back towards the tode like a limp spool of measuring tape. The other half fell to the ground, an organ separated from its host.

More beams of light shot out of the tode and it exploded.

Pieces of it flew in all directions, leaving Lain's spinning hoop hovering in the air where its stomach used to be. A shower of gore rained down on them.

Lain gestured, and an Autumn Shield glowed around all of them, protecting them from the rain of acidic ichor.

[Quest Complete!]
[Help the Gloom Rangers Slay the Mewlipped Tode Completed!]
[Congratulations!]
[You have been rewarded with Loot]
[You have been rewarded with Vigor Points]

Nay's inventory was blinking.

She opened it to see that she had received one of the gelatinous eyes of the tode, except it was encased in a metal frame and was connected to a chain, like it was a lantern or morning star.

It was labeled *Mirkwood's Eye*.

Mirkwood's Eye. Activating the Eye will let you see into the Nether Realm for thirty seconds. Three uses.

[Mini-Boss Battle Over!]
[Mini-Boss Defeated!]
[You have received Boon]

Nay's inventory was blinking again. She quickly looked at it to see an item in her inventory.

Boon of the Mewlipped Tadpole. Consuming this Boon will accelerate your current Vigor Rank up by 25 percent. Side effects may result in turning into a toad for a day and being compelled to catch and eat nothing but flies. Will be in all the danger that toad form is susceptible to while a toad.

Nay was surprised by both of these items.

She was about to explore how to pull an item out of her magical inventory when new text made her freeze.

[Boss Battle Detected]
[Boss: Nether Sister]

She looked around but didn't see any huge boss nearby.

Martygan jumped to his feet. His reforged sword had returned to its normal form. "Do you sense that?"

Lain retrieved her hoop and scanned the area.

Martygan closed his eyes for a moment.

When he opened them, the whites had turned to a red glow. He was looking around, half-frantic.

That's when Nay saw the blinking red light in the corner of her HUD on her mini-map.

It was to the north, where most of the tode gore had landed.

"It's an Eidolon," Martygan said.

"It was smart and waited till we had run through most of our Vigor reserves," Lain said. "Everything important is on cooldown."

"Show yourself!" Martygan said.

He spun in circles, brandishing his sword.

"It's that way," Nay said.

Lain looked at her, suspicious. "How do you know?"

"*Look.*"

They looked at where she pointed. There was something emerging out of the gore.

It was a human hand emerging out of the puddle of tode remains, slicked in the ichor and gore. The fingers were pointed at the sky, and then the palm slammed down on the ground and pushed against the earth.

Violet flames rose out of the puddle.

It was a crown of supernatural fire.

A head emerged out of the puddle.

The dark hair was framing the angular face in wet strands.

As the blood and ichor dripped off it, they got a glimpse of its true form.

Its body was a mixture of the corporeal and the incorporeal. Its torso seemed to be composed of spirit, translucent and wavering. Yet its arms and legs were corporeal, having a material presence.

To Nay it was monochrome like television static, as if the woman had crawled out of an old box television.

But its black-and-purple armor, a leather cloak, vest, and breeches were as vivid as the night was dark.

The supernatural crown of fire could probably burn flesh or set aflame anything that touched it.

Lain cursed. "It's from the Nether Realm."

Martygan sneered and brandished his smallsword, angling his body at her.

"A Nether Sister," Nay said, whispering it under her breath. But Lain heard her. The healer glanced at the cook, surprised that Nay might know what it was called.

"My poor familiar," the Nether Sister said. She looked around at the remains of the tode, sorrow on her face. "He was just doing as he was told. Yet this is how you treated him."

"Don't worry," Martygan said. "You'll be joining it soon."

The Nether Sister focused her purple eyes on the Gloom Ranger. The fiery pupils swirled, flaring as she spoke. "The underworld is my domain. I see the spirits of the dead whenever I please."

"So, tell me," Martygan said, "what happens to the spirit of a mistress of the Nether Realm when she is slain? Does she return to her domain but as spirit?"

"That's knowledge you will never be privy to know."

Her crown of violet fire flared.

"Now. I'll be taking the child."

— CHAPTER THIRTY-FIVE —

Boss Battle

[Boss Battle Engaged!]
[Nay & the Gloom Rangers & the Bouldershield Brother]
VERSUS
[The Nether Sister]

"You know," Nay said, speaking to the invisible quest-giver and game master in the sky, "you need to learn about this thing called consent."

The Nether Sister touched her crown of violet flame. A bit of the fire spread to her hand. The flame grew, lengthening into a blazing whip the color of blood.

She flicked her arm, cracking the whip at Martygan. He held up his sword in a defensive stance. The cord of flames wrapped around his sword. She yanked, tearing the sword out of his hands. It spun through the air off to the side.

The Nether Sister reared her arm back and crouched, winding up to deliver another whip crack.

As the flaming whip lashed out, Martygan dove.

In midair, Vigor vapors swirled around him and his form shifted as he transformed.

A white wolf landed on the ground and ran for the sword, dodging the unfurling scourges of the whip.

The white wolf leapt and shifted midair again, returning to the form of Martygan. The Ranger landed, grabbed his sword, and rolled across the ground. He leapt to his feet and charged the Nether Sister from a different angle.

She pivoted and the whip flew out again.

Lain moved in tandem with her companion, throwing up an Autumn Shield for him.

The flame whip cracked against the shield. Flames spread across the surface, weakening it.

Martygan delivered a reverse slash, cutting off the Nether Sister's hand at the wrist. Her hand holding the whip separated from her body.

Coils of shadow spilled out of her fresh stump.

He continued his sword sequence with a lunge, pushing his sword through her armored tunic.

It went through her incorporeal torso, but the tip of the blade did not protrude from her back.

The monochrome substance underneath her armor absorbed his blade.

The sword was somewhere inside of her, inside the incorporeal void. Perhaps that part of the sword had entered the Nether Realm itself.

The coils of shadow battered against the Autumn Shield, finally cracking through it in a dissipation of Vigor.

The healer cried out in surprise. "Martygan!"

The shadow coils wrapped around his other arm, winding up his torso and neck, restraining him.

One of the coils shoved its way through his lips, hammering past his clenched teeth and down into his throat. The veins in his neck and face turned blue, then black as the nether witch invaded his body.

The nether witch smiled at her captive Gloom Ranger. Martygan was in too much shock and pain to return the look with defiance.

The man was suffering.

Then the Nether Sister said something cryptic. "I do need a new familiar."

Lain shouted and was already running towards the Nether Sister.

As a healer, she had been trained to heal her companions no matter what. One moment of distraction could get someone killed. She had never failed in her duties as a healer, so to see this now was a new experience for her. She reacted as many perfectionists might do when they realized something wrong, something that defied the plan, was happening.

She reacted blindly, without thinking, in desperation and anger.

She, too, leapt and shifted.

But her mobile shifting form was that of a majestic elk. She had eight bronze-tipped points to each antler, a monarch elk.

She lowered her head and hit the Nether Sister in the knees. She jerked her antlers up and tossed the witch into the air, tearing the shadow coils away from Martygan. Upon disconnection, he collapsed to the ground, in the throes of a seizure.

The monarch elk shifted back into Lain. She pulled out her hoops.

Lain used the last of her Vigor reserves to toss one into the air and focus a damaging beam blast into the Nether Sister, shooting her into the ground.

The healer threw her other hoop like a Frisbee. It razored through the air and hit the witch in the incorporeal midsection. The weapon disappeared into her like into a cloud.

Jolf picked up his unconscious brother's battle-hammer. He looked at Nay. "We have to help them."

Nay swallowed. "How?"

Lain knelt next to Martygan, comforting him as he was seizing, but out of Vigor reserves and with all her big spells on cooldown, the most she could do was comfort him with her presence and touch. "Come back to us."

The Nether Sister smiled at the Gloom Rangers. "It's been too long since I've had capable thralls on this material plane."

She approached them, her back to the other two in their party.

Jolf gestured at the witch, and Nay nodded; they each gripped tight their weapons and held their breath, creeping up behind the Nether Sister.

Nay imagined herself making no noise, footsteps silent and nonexistent. Just like when she was a child and she would play hide-and-seek with the neighborhood children.

But instead of hiding, she was backstabbing.

Shadow coils extended out of the Nether Sister's wrist stump, wriggling in the air towards Lain. Her purple eyes flashed in anticipation.

Nay peeked at the incorporeal torso underneath the witch's armored tunic.

She had seen what had happened to the Gloom Ranger weapons. They had disappeared within the spirit matter of the Nether Sister. Is that where the weapons had gone? Some kind of spirit realm where she had originated from?

Regardless, she chose a more tangible target.

So, she drove Thorn into the side of the witch's neck.

That was corporeal enough.

The blade plunged into the flesh and bone with a crunch. The Nether Sister spun, her hand flying to her neck, only to see Jolf swinging the battle-hammer into Thorn's handle. It tapped the skullcrusher with a sharp clang and buried the entire weapon through the creature's neck and spinal column.

The witch clamped down her teeth. Blood from her throat bubbled up, coating them. She stared down her surprise attackers, red-tinged slobber dripping down her chin.

She staggered and collapsed to the ground, blood squirting out of her wound. She started hacking as breath hitched in her ruined throat. But she managed to dig Thorn's handle out of her neck. She grimaced, pulling out the combat dagger.

Blood sprayed out of the wound. She put her hand up to her violet-flame crown, grabbing a handful of fire. She shoved it onto her neck, cauterizing the entry and exit wound.

She started to push herself up.

Lain saw that the Nether Sister wasn't dead. It was recovering.

The healer addressed them. "We have to get out back to the Fort and tell the rest of the Rangers that there's a Nether Being here."

"You'll just leave the town?" Jolf said. "Leave us to fend for ourselves against this thing?"

"No one stands a chance if Scarwatch isn't alerted," Lain said. "I'm sorry."

She stood, lifting Martygan in her arms. "I'll get us to safety, but then I must leave and get us to Fort Nixxiom. Two Rangers, one unconscious, most of our spells on cooldown or not strong enough—it's not enough to defeat her! Come with me!"

Vigor fog surrounded her, and she shifted into her elk form, Martygan atop her back.

"By Voreheim's arse," Jolf said. "I will stay in town with my brother. I have to organize the watchmen and convince the townsfolk to stay hidden."

He put a hand on Nay's shoulder. "You should get to Quincy back at the Lodge. You'll be better off with him."

Nay gently picked up Bryja's brother. He was still asleep, still under Lain's calming sleep spell.

Lain knelt on her foreleg so Nay could mount her. Martygan was draped over the elk in front of her.

The elk sprinted off, away from the rising Nether Sister.

The witch saw the elk darting off with Nay and the fallen Ranger.

A black cloud swirled into existence in front of the Nether Sister. She walked into it, disappearing.

Nay looked back, seeing no trace of the witch.

But then a black cloud formed in front of them.

The Nether Sister stepped out of it, blocking their way. She extended her wrist stump and the scourge of shadow coils undulated out, oscillating and extending.

Before Lain could change directions, the shadow coils wrapped around her antlers. They yanked the elk to the side, and its forward momentum whipped them around, spinning Lain's mobile form in a skidding one-eighty, her elk head caught on the tendrils of shadow.

Nay and Martygan flew off the elk.

Midair, the cook held Bryja's sleeping brother tight, wrapping herself around him as she landed on her back. The crash knocked the wind out of her.

The tendrils held the elk's mouth open, and they flickered, poising to travel into Lain's throat.

Something buzz-sawed out of the sky, slicing through the Nether Sister's foot and impaling it to the earth.

Vapors of Vigor rose off the spirit weapon in the form of a massive and cruel-looking battle-axe bisecting the witch's foot.

There was a bellowing battle shout, and everyone looked up to see Quincy descending out of the sky like a comet. Nom was draped across his shoulders, making what sounded like a trilling scream. The tentacle didn't have a weapon, but he was flailing and amped up to join the fight regardless.

Ostentatious text overtook Nay's vision, flashing in synthetic, eighties-style Battle Royale font.

[New Contenders Have Entered the Boss Battle!]
[Quincy the Doomhearted and Nzxthommocus III, Third Whip of the Pain Lord]
VERSUS
[Nether Sister]

Gertrude, the battle-axe, was spinning in Quincy's hand, and more spirit axes were flying from it. They whipsawed straight for the Nether Sister.

The spinning spirit axes sliced through the shadow coils, freeing the elk from the witch.

The Nether Sister managed to lean and dodge the other spirit axes.

Quincy landed, swinging the axe down like a guillotine at the witch. Gertrude dug into her shoulder, going a foot into her chest. Smoking green Vigor began bubbling off the edge of the blade embedded inside the witch.

Her shoulder started to swell, veins turning black from an infection. Boils began to form and burst from the plague-ridden flesh.

Quincy ripped Gertrude out in a spattering of blood and sickness. He watched the witch stumble.

Nom flew at her, straight as a javelin and disappeared into the incorporeal gray matter of her torso.

Nom floated through the Nether Space.

He seemed to still be in Lucerna's End, except it was the town floating through a monochromatic wasteland. Color and sound save for a distant wind were void from the place.

The cobblestone streets and buildings were drifting through space, everything in black and white. Between the objects Nom glimpsed a gray void whirling in the negative spaces.

And there was a creeping darkness always on the edge of his peripheral vision. He got the sense it was a different realm underneath the reality he was used to occupying.

In front of him he saw a sword and a golden hoop floating in the air. He wiggled his body towards them, swimming like a sea snake.

The Nether Sister, severely injured, conjured another black cloud and escaped into it right as Quincy swung at her with another guillotine combo. Gertrude swung through empty air.

Quincy and Nay looked at each other, then looked around, searching for the witch.

That's when Nay got an idea.

She accessed her inventory and mentally clicked on Mirkwood's Eye. The object automatically appeared in her hand. She held a handle connected to a chain, and the eye itself, in its triangular metal frame, dangled on the end of the chain.

She clicked the button on the handle, activating the eye. A cone of light shined from it, highlighting the realm underneath the material plane they were in.

Within the cone she and Quincy could glimpse the Nether Realm.

The monochrome gray realm underneath their material plane. It was like peering into a shadow realm.

They spotted the Nether Sister crouching in the Nether Realm, observing them from this different plane. She snarled as the cone of the Mirkwood Eye exposed her.

Quincy swiped Gertrude through the air as if it were a hook, creating a rush of wind that pulled the witch towards him.

With his other hand, he pulled the massive crossbow, Samuel, from his back. There was a glowing bolt already loaded.

Nay caught a flowing script carved in a corkscrew pattern around the bolt.

The Nether Sister was pulled back into the material plane by Quincy's distance-closing Ability. Then he used his crossbow for some intimate, up-close wet work. He pulled Samuel's trigger, releasing the bolt into the witch's face.

It was like a pumpkin exploding. A flaming pumpkin.

The Nether Sister's head separated into its component atoms as the glowing bolt pierced her forehead, its special energy causing a chain reaction with the Nether Being's matter.

The flaming violet crown extinguished. The disintegrating head and its body fell back into the Nether Realm, disappearing as the duration of the Mirkwood Eye ended.

Nay, Quincy, and Lain, back in her human form, stood there in stunned silence.

"Has anyone seen Nom?" Nay said.

And as if on cue, Nom flew out of the dark, dissipating cloud where the witch just was, his protuberances wielding Martygan's smallsword and Lain's missing gold hoop. He crashed onto the street, sliding, the weapons clanging across the stone. He stopped.

"What did I miss?"

CHAPTER THIRTY-SIX

The Place Beyond the Ice

Jolf charged Nom, swinging at him with his battle-hammer.

The tentacle's middle section sucked itself in, evading the swing.

The sheriff took another swing, and Nom dodged it in the same way, just bending his body in the other direction.

"Stop!" Quincy shouted. "He's with us."

Jolf stopped swinging and looked at him, dumbfounded. "*What?*"

"That's Nom, my sous-chef," Nay said.

"Sous-chef?" Jolf said. "But . . . but it's a monster."

"He's also on our side," Quincy said. "Now, lower your weapon."

The sheriff complied, still just as confused, though.

"You swing like a blindfolded child trying to hit a piñata," Nom said.

"How do you know what a piñata is?" Nay said.

"I saw it in some of your memories during our Mind Meld."

"You can see *my* memories when we do that?"

"Why, sure, there's always some cross-contamination that happens during the spell."

"Just how much of my life have you seen?"

Quincy cleared his throat, interrupting them.

Nay gave Nom a look. *We'll talk about this later.*

Quincy walked over to Nay to examine the Mirkwood Eye. "Where did you get that?"

"It was loot from killing that thing," Nay said, pointing to the remains of the tode. "It still has two more uses."

Quincy grunted, touching the chain connected to it. The object looked like it was fashioned from the eye of the monster. It seemed weird it would be carrying around the eye of another one of its kind. "You said this was loot?"

Nay nodded.

Seemed like maybe she received loot in a different way than others here. She felt uncomfortable under his scrutiny and changed the subject.

"What was that arrow you shot her with?" Nay asked Quincy.

"A bolt," Quincy said. "Crossbows shoot bolts, girl. Not arrows."

"My bad," Nay said. She corrected herself. "Bolt."

"It was a Celestial Bolt," Quincy said. "Very effective against beings from the Nether Realm."

Lain, cradling Martygan's head, processed this in wonderment. "Where did you get a Celestial Bolt from?"

"An Arbiter gave it to me as a reward for helping destroy a netherspawn nest in Amethyst Fields," Quincy said.

Lain was taken aback. "An Arbiter? In our plane?"

"It's a long story," Quincy said. "Anyways, it's the only one I had. I never thought I was gonna have to use it. It was one of my prized trophies."

"You saved our asses with it," Nay said.

Nom cleared his throat. "I helped."

Nay walked over to Nom. "I was afraid I might not see you again."

"What can I say?" Nom said. "If I'm anything, I'm a survivor."

"What happened to Mishell?" Nay said.

"I couldn't say," Nom said. "Things got a little too chaotic. We were both being swept away on a tide of polliwog spawn—"

"*Polliwog spawn?*"

"That's what they looked like to me," Nom said. "What exactly would you call them?"

"I guess it doesn't matter," Nay said. "But you didn't see what happened to her? You don't know if she died or not?"

Nom shook his head *no*. "Like I said, I was just too busy trying to stay alive myself."

"How did you hook up with Quincy?"

"Here, it's easier if I just show you—"

But Quincy interrupted them. "We need to get all the injured to shelter."

"And the child back to his family," Nay said.

"We can do that," Jolf said.

There was the sound of clanking metal, and they all turned to see the Bouldershield Brothers approaching them.

Jolf was helping support his brother.

Rolf was conscious again. He was taking in all the destruction in amazement. Not only was there considerable property damage, it looked like the sky took a shit and rained down mutant tadpoles onto the town. "Oy, this is gonna be a job to clean up."

Lain's eyes went to the sleeping child. "What did that witch want with the child? Why did she want children from this plane?"

Quincy shrugged. "Dark ritual. A toy. A remedy. Who knows. Could have been any number of things."

Lain shook her head. "I don't like it. There's something else to it that I'm going to figure out."

Nay looked down at Martygan. He looked like a beautiful marble statue while he was unconscious. He was paler than usual, but that was no surprise, considering everything that had happened to him tonight. "Is he going to be okay?"

"My bigger spells will be off cooldown soon," Lain said, "so I hope so. He seems stable now, and I think he'll be even better when he's safe in the Lodge."

"What about getting back to Fort Nixxiom?" Nay said.

"Since the witch is defeated, it's not as urgent," Lain said. "But they need to know sooner than later. And we need to send word out for more healers."

She looked around. "The townsfolk who were victims tonight will need it."

"We can send a snow raven," Jolf said.

"You'd see to it?" Lain said.

"Aye," both of the Bouldershield Brothers said.

Jolf picked up the sleeping faun child. "Now let's get this wee one back in the arms of his mother."

As Quincy went to fetch a wagon to help Lain with Martygan, Nay couldn't ignore the blinking green light in the corner of her HUD.

The Marrow.

Nom grabbed her and started pulling her towards it. "It's this way. What do you think it is? Another yummy mushroom? Or maybe something interesting, maybe some type of rich and delicious tadpole caviar?"

Nay almost gagged. "I know what it is and I am not excited about it."

Nom grabbed her again. "What is it? Tell me."

"You'll see soon enough."

As they walked to the remains of the tode, Nom asked, "Why can't the Gloom Rangers sense it?"

"The Marrow?" Nay said. "Because they're not trained to. Their abilities seem to be more martial. They're monster-slayers, so it seems like all their Delicacy Trees have to do with combat and stuff. Only Marrow Eaters trained to Detect Marrow can sense it."

"Like Epicurists," Nom said.

"Yep."

They found the severed tode leg inside a shop display in the general store. It had crashed through the window and landed in a display of candies. It looked like a giant yellow-green ham hock sticking out of a barrel of licorice.

Nom saw the warts and lesions on the thing. "That's it? There must be some type of mistake."

"I wish you were right."

"Well, maybe the meat inside isn't as bad as the skin looks."

They both stood in front of the general store, staring at the disgusting *tode* leg.

"How are we going to carry this thing back?" Nom said. "We're going to need a wagon."

"I don't know about you," Nay said, "but I'm not going to eat that whole thing. That might be close to a hundred pounds of meat. Technically, we only need a bite of Marrow to get a new Ability, right?"

"I don't know," Nom said. "Probably. Wouldn't make sense to have to down all that. That would be sadistic. Could you imagine being in a food-eating contest where you had to speed-eat that thing?"

"I wish you hadn't put that image in my head."

Nay stepped through the broken window and drew Thorn. She pulled her tunic up to cover her mouth and nose and made an incision in the tough, warty skin of the tode. She tucked the blade between the skin and the meat and started slicing the membrane that connected the skin away.

To her surprise, some of the meat underneath was unblemished and looked untainted. It looked edible. The leg was big enough where she could cut out perfectly round filet medallions. She took out six filets and wrapped them in some paper she found that was meant to wrap up candy sticks.

[Quest Completed!]
[Separate the Marrow from the Mewlipped Tode Completed!]
[Congratulations!]
[Reward: Frog Leg Marrow of the Mewlipped Tode]

"All right, the deed's done," Nay said. "Let's get out of here. I'm going to sleep for forever."

When all was said and done, when all the bodies had been accounted for, it was discovered that sixteen people, sixteen townsfolk of Lucerna's End, had lost their lives during the night of the attack. Countless more had been injured, either directly by the tadpole dogs or the tode, or in the collateral damage as a result of the skirmish.

Two more Gloom Ranger healers and a captain from Fort Nixxiom had arrived to help heal the wounded and investigate the aftermath of the attack, the captain dead set on looking for clues that would lead to the why of these brazen child abductions.

But two days after the attack, the townsfolk were gathered on the edge of the river for the funeral ceremony that was done according to the customs of the human tribes that dwelt in the valley.

Alric was on a podium that had been set up in front of the river. The monk was overseeing the service and delivered the speech for the fallen, not so much because it was a duty as a representative of Veritax but that it was the right thing to do for a grieving town. He respected the customs of the stitchpeople and did not overstep his bounds as a clergyman.

"The men and women that fell two nights ago were not victims," Alric said. "They were heroes trying to save an innocent boy who were looking out to protect the people who call Lucerna's End home. That's the truth, as confirmed by Veritax.

"Today, we gather here to see that their souls depart on the river to their destination in the next life. The Place Beyond the Ice, as your ancestors called it, a place free of pain and sadness and suffering. A place where they will be waiting for you at the threshold when it is your turn for your soul to travel the river.

"Remember them, and their love, and their valor. You all carry it with you in your hearts, in your minds. These souls aren't forgotten but remembered. And honored.

"May they smile under a warm sun, and may you see them in your dreams. Na marie."

The mourners nodded and repeated, "Na marie."

Nay and her crew, minus Nom, were operating a food table courtesy of Quincy's Lodge. She had battered and fried up enough slivermoon trout to feed the people attending this goodbye to the fallen. She had also made french fries sprinkled in sea salt from the Vancian Sea. They were serving what she was calling Quincy's Fish 'n Chips and Nay's Snowslaw Sliders.

The Snowslaw was made from cabbage and shredded beets, carrots, and icefield scallions. It was mixed in a mayo-based sauce for which the secret ingredient was a touch of winter cider and vinegar. This was added to the grilled burgers made from the meat from Moonglum Farms.

Food that people could eat with their hands without getting too messy. She served the food in butcher paper so people could walk around and eat at the same time.

She had been tempted to imbue the recipes with buffs, maybe something to boost the spirits or give people extra strength, but she had decided against it for two reasons.

One was what she had previously discussed with Quincy. There were more Marrow Eaters in town because of the Gloom Ranger presence.

Two, adding buffs to the food to numb someone's pain or grief wasn't doing them any favors. It would be best to let the townsfolk process their pain.

But Bryja, Ulla, and Hilde were all at the table, helping hand out food. Bryja was in renewed spirits because her brother had been rescued, yet Nay could tell she was struggling with guilt that so many townsfolk had died or been injured.

It wasn't Bryja's fault or her brother's fault, but she was sensitive to people's anger. She was afraid they might blame her family for what befell the town.

It was impossible for Quincy to work, as townsfolk kept coming up to him to hug him and give thanks for rescuing the town. The tale of his coming out of retirement to take up Samuel and Gertrude to slay the nether demon that had terrorized the town was being told by everybody. He was not just viewed as the proprietor of the Lodge and the town's favorite bartender, but he was being referred to as the town's protector.

One by one, the fallen were placed into small boats hewn from winterwood, their material vessels decorated with vines, flowers, jewelry, and keepsakes from family members.

And one by one, the boats were released into the icy currents of the river, where they traveled through the winding currents that led out to the Caraxe Sea, where they would drift into the setting sun, in the Place Beyond the Ice.

— CHAPTER THIRTY-SEVEN —

'T'wasn't Any Heroics

As the townsfolk were gathered at the Helcharaes River, saying farewell to their fallen loved ones traveling to the Place Beyond the Ice, no one noticed that the Silvertail, Wint the Fishmonger's fishing vessel, had been anchored at the harbor and shuttered up.

In the following weeks, people would learn that the crew had been let go and would be working on different boats. Hunt one down, and the consensus was that they didn't know why Wint had shuttered the enterprise, only that they were given no notice.

There wasn't even the courtesy of a parting fee for their broken contracts.

At the same time the Silvertail was put out of commission, all the remaining staff at the Two-Headed Trout were let go. Again, no notice. Curious townsfolk would learn that the lien on the property had expired and that it was now under the control of the Winterfist Bank, which operated solely in Stitchdale.

Nay was probably the first person in Lucerna's End to know what was happening. After all, she had received a prompt.

[Quest Complete!]
[Destroy the Two-Headed Trout Completed!]
[Congratulations!]
[You have been rewarded with Vigor Points]

No one noticed the black carriage pulled by half a dozen mangy fauglir leave the edge of town under the cover of night, and no one had the misfortune of sharing unpleasantries with Wint or either of his children again.

For Lucerna's End, it was as if a boil had been lanced. And once the boil was gone, people were happy to forget about it as well as the inconvenience and discomfort it had caused.

* * *

Nay took it upon herself to deliver tea to the Gloom Rangers who had gathered in Martygan's room. She rolled the cart in, and Lain turned from the window and smiled at her arrival.

"Nay," Lain said. "What a pleasant surprise! And you've brought tea! What kind is it this time?"

"We have a few options," Nay said. "As per usual, there's some pepper tea if you need some extra perk. But there's also some rimefrost tea, if you want to feel hydrated and refreshed, and then there's bristlecone pine, which I'm told has even more of an edge than the pepper tea."

"Rimefrost for me," Lain said.

The other two Gloom Rangers with her were the other healers sent from Fort Nixx. They wore similar garb to Lain, the same mixture of leather armor with fashion flourishes that bespoke the wilderness.

There was Jacob, a younger Ranger who made Nay think of a kid in high school who had just attained Eagle Scout. He had a mane of yellow hair and a dimple on his chin. Nay kept thinking he had sort of a blond Travolta vibe. He was like the eager conservative medic in a platoon of Vietnam soldiers.

"I'll have the bristlecone pine," Jacob said. He smiled at Nay. "I like things that have an edge."

Then there was Gull, an older woman with silver hair. Her face had creased lines, probably from constantly frowning. Though she was a healer, she exuded a coldness and an adherence to the letter of things rather than the spirit. Like everything must absolutely be done by the book.

Gull declined tea.

"How's he doing?" Nay asked.

"He's stable," Lain said, "but—"

"But his condition defies us," Gull said, cutting her off. "Which is why we need to get him back to the Fort, where we can conduct further studies on him under observation."

"Nothing stops us from doing that here," Lain said.

"Except none of us are versed in the type of curses or wounds or ailments that can be inflicted by a being from the Nether Realm upon a person," Gull said. "At the Fort we can consult with the Loremaster Avery. It's what would be best for Martygan."

Lain acquiesced. She couldn't really argue with her. The older healer was right even if her delivery rubbed people the wrong way.

"Whatever ails him stays hidden from my sight," Lain said. Nay suspected she was referring to her abilities that allowed her to see illnesses and wounds and be able to get a magically extracted diagnosis, a magical scan of what ailed a person's biology.

Gull stood. "I will inform Captain Cassius that we must transport Martygan back to Fort Nixxiom."

She exited the room.

When she was gone, Jacob remarked on her manner. "Well. There we have it, I suppose."

"I don't envy you having to have her as a travel companion," Lain said.

"She's not so bad," Jacob said. "What she lacks in social graces she makes up for in wisdom."

"That's what I find so frustrating," Lain said, under her breath.

Nay couldn't help but observe Martygan. His chest slowly rose and fell, and the look on his pale face was utter calm, like a wild prince who had fallen under a sleeping spell.

"The way you two fought," Nay said.

Lain smiled. "We're Marrow Eaters. It's what we've been trained to do as Gloom Rangers."

"It was something to see," Nay said.

"They're Bronze Rank Marrow Eaters," Jacob said, correcting Lain. "They can do things that look like they defy the laws of nature. That's what cultivators do. Defy and transcend." At that last bit, he articulated with his hands and almost knocked over his tea. "Whoops."

"The offer still stands," Lain said. "You have naturally increasing Vigor. You could train to become a Marrow Eater and a Gloom Ranger if you wanted to."

Nay was intrigued by the idea. Could she too fight like that if she consumed a Delicacy that opened up a combat-skill tree? Part of her was excited by it, but she didn't see herself as a magically enhanced monster-slayer. Although, admittedly, it could be useful to at least have some combat abilities so some psychopath wouldn't crush her hand again.

"A Gloom Ranger?" Nay said. "That's a little intense for me. I prefer cooking."

"The world needs good cooks," Jacob said. "I still can't get over that meat pie the other night. What was it called again?"

"Shepherd's pie," Nay said.

"Absolutely satisfying, that," Jacob said. He took a sip of his tea and exhaled, whistling. "This bristlecone pine is good stuff."

"Well, I should be getting back to the kitchen," Nay said. "Just wanted to stop by for the update and to give you some afternoon tea."

"Here, I'll see you out," Lain said.

Before Nay exited, Jacob stammered, finally spitting out, "If you ever get a chance, you should come to the Fort and cook for us Rangers. As militaristic as it might sound, the Fort is actually a beautiful place. Best view in the Spineshards. And we always have fresh wild game."

"If I ever visit the Fort," Nay said, "I will call on you specifically to give me a tour."

Jacob smiled at that and leaned back, cradling his tea. "Then I shall look forward to your visit."

In the hallway, Lain shut the door so Jacob couldn't hear. She stood close to Nay and whispered, "You should be careful, Nay."

"Of course," Nay said. "Always."

"No, I mean . . . I don't think any of this is over. I can feel it. There's something happening in the Nether Realm, and I don't think that it's done with Stitchdale."

Nay stared at her. She could feel it too. A sense of dread deep down in her stomach. A lingering worry in the back of her mind.

She accessed her quest log and gasped.

[Boss Battle]
[Nether Sister]

Why was the quest still there? It wasn't completed.

"What is it?" Lain said. "What's wrong?"

"Do you think it's possible the witch is still alive?" Nay said.

"It would be hard to survive a Celestial Bolt . . . but there's always a possibility, I suppose."

Lain reached into her cloak and pulled out a seashell the color of a glacier. She put it in Nay's hands. "If trouble comes again, use this."

"What is it?"

"Something that will call me to your side," Lain said. "But it can only be used once. So, make sure you absolutely need my aid before you use it. If you're absolutely sure, then do not hesitate."

Later that day, Nay had pulled the seashell Lain gifted her out of her inventory. As she stared at it, she accessed the gift's description.

Nautilus of Teleportation. The cephalopod shell of a cerulean mollusk. It has been imbued with Vigor by a Marrow Eater Trinket Maker. Whisper the name of the person the Trinket Maker recorded inside the shell and it will teleport them to the location of the caller. This nautilus has the recorded name of one Lainya Elkstar.

"Well, that's fucking neat," Nay said.

She put it back into her inventory with the other loot she had categorized as *cool and crazy shit*.

* * *

Nay was out back behind the Lodge, drinking a hot cider, working on some recipes in her notebook, when Bryja came through the back door.

"Got a minute to talk, chef?"

In mid-scribble, Nay said, "Sure, what's up?"

The chillwind faun shifted from hoof to hoof, exuding awkwardness. "All right, I don't know how to say it, so I'm just going to say it."

Nay put down her pencil.

"Thank you for helping save my brother," Bryja said. "I heard you were part of the group that took down those monsters."

Nay was a little surprised to hear this. She had left the Lodge that night to look for Nom and the Marrow. Everything that happened after was just happenstance.

"I was there," Nay said, "but I didn't really do anything that someone else wouldn't have done if they were there. It was the Gloom Rangers and Quincy that did most of the fighting."

"That's not what I heard," Bryja said. "But still, you were there. You put yourself in danger and risked your life to save my brother."

"Wait. Back up for a minute. What did you hear, exactly?"

"Folks be saying you had some magical trinket that helped Quincy find the she-demon hiding in the Nether Realm. That you were the one that used it and shined a light into the darkness."

She remembered the Mirkwood Eye. That was what she was talking about. But how did she know? Who had been spreading the story? She couldn't see Quincy or Lain or even Nom telling anyone about that night. It was still too raw, too fresh. They had all almost died.

Which had left Jolf, one of the town's sheriffs.

It was definitely him who had recounted the skirmish, the battle, whatever one would call that whole encounter, to the captivated townsfolk.

"We were all just trying to stay alive that night," Nay said. "It wasn't any heroics. Except for the Rangers and Quincy. Heck, even Nom. I was just a scared girl."

"I also heard you stabbed the she-demon in the neck."

"Bitch deserved it."

Bryja started laughing. It was contagious. Nay started laughing too.

Then Bryja's laughter turned into tears and she hugged Nay. She whispered in her ear, "Thank you."

Nay had trouble sleeping, so she had taken the boat and rowed to the glade. She had wound the ropes around her wrists and hands and she was dragging the sled through the snow.

Memories of the terror that night flashed through her head as she pulled the sled around the glade. The tadpole things. The tode. The woman from the Nether Realm.

And Mishell.

The crew tasked with locating and retrieving bodies in the aftermath of the monster attack hadn't found Mishell.

Which either meant she was dead and hidden somewhere, or she had been devoured by the tadpole dogs and her body was digested in the bellies of a pack of monsters.

Or neither of those things happened and she had survived.

This possibility was one of the things that kept Nay from sleeping. If Mishell had survived, then it was apparent she had probably left Lucerna's End.

Nay collapsed from exhaustion, her heart racing, her lungs on fire. She had managed to pull the sled for thirty minutes this time, beating her old time by ten minutes.

Nay wanted to be ready for the day Mishell returned to Lucerna's End.

And should they meet again, she wasn't going to run this time.

She would fight.

— CHAPTER THIRTY-EIGHT —

Chef's Thermometer

Nay pulled two of the medallions filleted out of the tode's severed leg from the ice bucket, leaving the other four filets untouched.

The Marrow was still wrapped in butcher's paper. She carried the medallions out of the walk-in and into the kitchen. Nom waited eagerly in the kitchen as Nay set them down on the cutting board.

She sprinkled the medallions with flaky salt. That was when the medallions started to twitch. The twitches quickly turned to full-blown movement. They wobbled from side to side like a coin just coming out of a spin, threatening to careen off the table.

Nom fell off the stool when one jumped at him, leaping off the cutting board.

"It's still alive!" Nom said, twisting backwards and slithering across the floor and disappearing into the pantry. His voice came from inside. "It's trying to get me!"

Nay had backed away and had grabbed a rolling pin, ready to play whack-a-mole with the possessed tode flesh. She raised the rolling pin and was preparing to tenderize them into submission when she remembered something.

Of course, she thought. When you salt frog legs, the salt has a reaction with the nerves, triggering the muscles to move. When meat was this fresh, there was still stored energy in the muscles.

"Nom," Nay said. "You can come back out."

Nom peeked out of the pantry.

"When you salt frog legs, they twitch," Nay said.

"What?"

"It's the same principle for fish or eels that are being prepared as sushi. Sometimes, for presentation and spectacle, a chef will pour soy sauce or sprinkle salt on the flesh to make the dead animal move."

Nay felt ashamed she hadn't thought of it sooner. Nom had run, but she was ready to do battle. Both normal reactions when the meat you're about to cook seems to come alive and dance around the kitchen.

She picked up both medallions of the Marrow and slapped them inside of a bowl. She held them down until the reaction stopped.

Next, she got out a jar of cow milk, and she poured a little winter-apple cider vinegar into the jar and stirred.

"What does that do?" Nom said.

"It creates buttermilk," Nay said. She poured the fresh buttermilk into the bowl with the Marrow. "We need to use it as a marinade for this flesh. Milk is sweet, and by nature, frog legs pick up a brackish flavor from living in creeks and swamps. This is a way to pull out that unpleasant flavor."

"That thing wasn't a frog, though," Nom said.

"It was an amphibian monster. So, I'm guessing same principle, right? And I'm sure it had exposed itself to more disgusting things than muddy bodies of water. I'd rather not taste what it was up to; you know what I mean?"

She crumbled up bread from some leftover garlic knots and breakfast bread with her bare hands and scattered them into a roasting pan. She threw it into one of the alcove ovens. Soon enough, they'd come out as panko bread crumbs.

"I wonder if it's going to taste like chicken or fish," Nom said.

"If it tastes like either of those things, I think we'll be lucky," Nay said. "I figure while we let these marinate for a bit, you can show me how Quincy found you the other night."

"Show you?"

"Yeah, your Mind Meld spell thingy."

She reached for him so they could link, but he pulled away.

"Excuse you," Nom said. "You can't just demand that I use Mind Meld. I'm . . . not a piece of telepathic meat."

Nay froze and realized she'd tried to get him to Mind Meld with her without consent.

"You're right. I apologize. I should have asked you."

Nom crossed two of his protuberances like he was crossing his arms and nodded. "You're right; you should have asked me. I can't just go touching foreheads all willy-nilly and sharing memories like I'm someone who would just do it with anyone. I'm not that kind of tentacle."

"Jesus," Nay said. "You don't have to make it weird. I'm sorry, okay? Now can you just hurry up and show me your side of the story from that night?"

Nay was watching herself bounce across the back of a pack of mutant tadpole dog parasite thingies. The spawn of the Mewlipped Tode.

She was jacked into Nom's memory thanks to his Mind Meld Ability.

"Nom!" she saw and heard herself cry out, reaching towards herself.

Then she disappeared as the river of tadpole dogs carrying Nom flowed into a different street.

She could hear Mishell nearby, cursing and screaming. Nom looked over at her then, and there was a view of Wint's daughter whaling on the monsters with her compact mace before they were separated.

His last glimpse of Mishell, she was being overwhelmed by the things, and soon he was fighting for his own life.

Watching through his point of view was like watching a found-footage sequence filmed with a chaotic shaky cam. He was slipping and squirming through the mass of tadpoles, dodging their piranha teeth.

But there were just too many of them. Two of the creatures had seized him, one from each end, and through Nom's grunting, Nay surmised the tadpole dogs were playing tug-of-war with him.

"If I had a spine, I might hire you for chiropractic services," Nom said. "But I don't, and this is getting old fast!"

They thrashed their heads side to side, trying to rip him apart.

Nay felt dizzy from all the movement, and she thought when this Mind Meld was over, she would have whiplash.

The thrashing stopped when the first tadpole dog's head dissolved. Nom looked up at and he saw the thing's jaw fall off in a mass of green pus and exploding boils. It fell over, its body hemorrhaging blood and the flesh smoking off it in a noxious cloud.

Then the same thing happened to the creature that was holding his other end. Nom rolled away, suddenly free, and saw Quincy step by him.

The Vigor aura radiating off his hands and arms was green, the color of a toxic cloud. His axe, Gertrude, had the same sickly color on its edge. He swung it into a tadpole, and the green putrid Vigor infected the thing.

It stumbled into the pack and the poison began spreading through all the tadpole dogs here, like a mini-plague.

Quincy didn't even have to engage them anymore with his axe. He just watched the exploding boils and malady spread through the creatures. The fast-motion plague spread through them, and it was like watching one of those time-lapse videos of animal decay.

Soon, they were all twitching on the ground, the green Vigor rising off them.

Quincy looked over at Nom. "How come you're not in the kitchen?"

Nay was back in the kitchen, slightly disoriented. "Hey! It wasn't finished."

"But the panko is done roasting," Nom said. "I'll show you the rest later. I'm hungry."

"Fine," Nay grumbled, taking a moment to get adjusted to her body again.

Nay pulled out the pan of panko bread crumbs and poured them into a separate bowl.

She sprinkled the crumbs with garlic powder and a little salt and pepper.

"Would you get a sauté pan going with some oil?" Nay said. "Just a little; not too much. Just enough to coat the bottom of the pan. We're not deep-frying these things."

"You're not going to use butter?"

"In my experience, oil always works better with amphibian meat. Plus, we already have some dairy with the buttermilk, which should also help it be soft and juicy after we sauté it."

Nay used tongs to lift one of the Marrow tode medallions out of the bowl of buttermilk. As she transferred it to the dry station, which was the bowl of panko bread crumbs, some glowing orange motes floated out of the Marrow and sparkled in the air.

This was some effect of her latent Epicurist Ability, the capability to prepare and cook Delicacies and Marrow, activating and interacting with the Marrow as she handled it for cooking. Something about touch and her handling of the ingredients triggered the magical process.

Maybe one day she could get a technical explanation from someone versed in the ways of Epicurists, but that would probably involve someone from the Culinary Guild, and right now, her mere existence would be an affront to them. Surely, there had to be more renegade Marrow Users and Epicurists like her out there somewhere, right? That was what she hoped.

She tossed the Marrow in the panko-seasoning mixture.

"How's that pan looking?" Nay said.

"Ready, chef," Nom said.

"Thank you, chef," Nay said.

She set the breaded Marrow into the warm oil in the frying pan. It immediately started to sizzle upon contact. She repeated the steps with the other medallion and set it next to the first.

Soon, an orange glow was coming out of the pan. The motes floated out and stirred around the kitchen like fireflies on a summer night.

Nay wasn't sure what to expect smell-wise when the meat started to cook, but she was pleasantly surprised to discover the aroma was pleasing. In fact, it was more than pleasing. It smelled downright delicious, like the smell of frying soft-shell crabs with Old Bay seasoning. There was a hint of spice in the air that tickled her nose.

"Oh, my," Nom said, his little beak twitching. "This was definitely the right way to cook it, I can already tell."

After the medallions had browned, Nay moved them out of the pan and set them on a frying rack to cool. Next, she lowered the heat and poured some white ice wine into the pan and began deglazing the bits of fried goodness caramelized to the bottom. She used a wooden spoon to scrape and stir at the deglaze.

She quickly cubed a tomato and added it to the wine and fond and let it reduce.

She and Nom watched in rapt silence as all the mixture in the pan concentrated itself into a sauce full of nothing but flavor. While they waited, Nay moved the Marrow medallions to plates.

Then she took the pan and poured the sauce over the fried medallions. As the sauce came into contact with the meat, the orange motes started to burst like fireworks, filling the kitchen with beautiful, magical light.

The medallions sat seductively on the plates, the sauce glistening, the bits of tomato sparkling in the light.

Nay realized her mouth was watering.

She grabbed two forks and handed Nom one. "Bon appétit."

They both ran their forks through the tender, lightly fried tode medallions and plopped them into their mouths.

She was never ready for the explosion of flavor that Marrow and Delicacies brought to her mouth as they rejuvenated her taste buds each time she consumed them.

Each time, she was brought to her knees because of the pure intensity. The experience was spiritual. There was a soft *pop* as she bit into the medallion, a crunch from the breading. The meat was sweet, and the flavor confirmed the initial aroma.

It didn't taste like either chicken or fish.

It tasted like soft-shell crab more than anything.

But like the best soft-shell crab she ever had in her life, and that included the soft-shell crab burger her father used to make when she was a kid. The batter had Old Bay seasoning in it, and he served it with a garlic aioli and thin slices of pickled yellow squash.

She was transported to one of those moments of eating that meal with her father as she ate the Marrow. It lasted for only a few seconds, but they were impactful seconds, before her body and its Vigor began to process the Marrow.

Bursts of light and magical text danced across her vision.

[Marrow Consumed!]
[Frog Leg Marrow of the Mewlipped Tode]
[Would you like to unlock Marrow Ability for Tongue of the Hierophant Y/N?]
[Delicacy: Tongue of the Hierophant]

[Opening Delicacy Tree]
[Marrow Abilities: 2/12]

She mentally clicked on the *Y*.

Opening Ability Tree for the Delicacy: Tongue of the Hierophant.

Like with the Marrow of the Steksis, she was met with a diorama of a human digestive system, all the organs surrounded in a white aura with cubes rotating next to them, indicating open Ability slots.

You have eleven open slots in this Ability Tree. You have consumed the Frog Leg Marrow of the Mewlipped Tode. It has syncretized into the Chef's Thermometer Ability. Would you like to use a slot for Chef's Thermometer?
[Y/N?]

She accessed the description for the Ability.

Chef's Thermometer. To give you further control and command over your cooking, this Ability will allow you to channel heat and channel cold purely through Vigor. Can create circles of heat or cold down to the exact temperature for more accurate cooking. These channeling circles can be cast over a greater distance according to Rank. There's a five-second cooldown between each use.

This was a no-brainer. She didn't even have to think and couldn't have hit *Y* any faster. Her stomach started to burn, her body temperature flaring hot. She felt feverish and ungrounded, as if her consciousness was separating from her physical brain.

Her vision expanded into a three-hundred-and-sixty-degree view. She stumbled and sat down on the kitchen floor.

Just like the first time consuming a Marrow, there was that feeling of being tethered to a presence that was greater than her. Like she had an invisible umbilical cord that was connected to something significant.

Then it was gone.

[Ability Activation]
[Delicacy: Tongue of the Hierophant 3/12]
[Ability: Chef's Thermometer]
[Rank: Base]

The Rank section on her menu was blinking red, just like after she consumed the Truffle Marrow of The Steksis.

Rank is currently Base Level.
Error Message: There's been a Delicacy Activation without meeting appropriate Prerequisite. Delicacies require Prerequisite: Iron Rank.
Note: May experience errors or sense of dysphoria while using Marrow Abilities.
Diagnosis: Worldtripper Racial abilities seem to be creating Prerequisite Bypass. Please report to a DMA agent.

When she opened her eyes again, Nom was looking down at her. Two of his green protuberances were shifting to a bluish hue, and she could see a mist of frost blowing at her.

Her forehead felt cool, and it was as if a nice breeze was whispering across her skin. She felt her body temperature going down.

"It's going to be so easy to make ice cubes for drinks now," Nom said. "And think of the possibilities with making crème brûlée or melting cheese toppings. And we don't have to worry about freezing to death anymore! We can generate heat at will. We need to get more Marrow, Nay. Marrow can solve all our problems!"

— CHAPTER THIRTY-NINE —

Vigor Sickness

Or Marrow can cause all sorts of problems, Nay thought, as she remembered what Nom said after they consumed the Frog Leg Marrow of the Mew-lipped Tode.

They were in the middle of dinner service when Nay collapsed, almost smashing her head against the edge of a table. She lay there, dizzy and lethargic, as a blinking red light filled her vision.

[Error Message]
[Error: Marrow Ability Detected at Base Rank]
[All Marrow Abilities Require Minimum of Iron Rank]
[Not Enough Vigor to Sustain Abilities]
[Please report to a DMA Agent]

Nay swiped the error message away and another replaced it.

[Error Message]
[Worldtripper Anomaly Detected]
[Please report to a DMA Agent]

She closed her eyes, and the imprint of the flashing red light and text prompts lingered on the inside of her eyelids. It was making her head pound.

"Fuck," Nay said, groaning. She turned onto her side and curled up in the fetal position. "Make it stop." She directed that at the mysterious quest-giver who communicated to her through the HUD, whoever or whatever it may be. It was a plea. *"Please make it stop."*

There was commotion around her and she cracked her eyes open to see Nom looking down at her, holding a raw cut of tomahawk steak in one of his protuberances. "Chef down! Chef down!" Nom said. "Little help over here! Are you okay? What happened?"

"I . . . fell . . ." Nay said.

"I can see that. Did you trip or something?"

Nay ground her teeth. She felt nauseous. She didn't have the strength to explain that she had been using her new Chef's Thermometer Ability to cook half a dozen tomahawk steaks to rare perfection when everything felt wrong all of a sudden and she felt light-headed. At first, she thought she was having a stroke, because her head didn't feel right. But that's when her HUD went haywire and she collapsed.

She finally managed to say, "*Get . . . Quincy.*"

She glanced at Nom, who was gesturing at Gracie. She took one look at Nay and heard her request, and she disappeared through the double doors.

"I'll be fine," Nay said. Her voice a whisper. "Just . . . my blood pressure . . . take over . . . the kitchen . . . "

And she lost consciousness.

When Nay woke up, she was in her room and Quincy was in there, studying a map he had rolled out on a table. When he saw that she was awake, he rolled up the map. He walked over to her and picked up a cup of water from her nightstand. "Drink."

She drank some of the water. It was still cool and refreshing.

Next, he handed her the other cup there. This one was full of some kind of juice. "This will help you pep up."

She drank the juice. From the taste and coloration she knew it was citrine juice, which came from a citrus fruit that grew in the cold climate. It was like the cross between an orange and a lemon. The sugar would be good for her blood. "Thanks, I don't know what came over me. One second I was fine, the next—"

"You consumed another Marrow, didn't you?"

Nay was quiet for a moment. She looked at him, not denying it. "How did you know?"

"You collapsed from Vigor Sickness. I can tell."

"What's Vigor Sickness?"

"It's when you exhaust your Vigor because you're pushing yourself beyond your limits. You have all the signs."

Nay processed this. "Remember how I told you about the magical words I see?"

Quincy nodded.

"Well." She sat up in the bed. "It was warning me that something was wrong. It said I was supposed to be Iron Rank to be able to use Marrow Abilities. That there would be side effects if I kept using them."

Quincy pulled on one end of his mustache. He murmured something, staring into the distance. Then his eyes refocused. He had just decided something.

"We have to cultivate your Vigor," Quincy said.

"What?"

"You have to get your Vigor to Iron Rank. Especially if you want to keep using your abilities. If you keep consuming Marrows without advancing your rank, you're going to kill yourself."

"And how am I supposed to do that?"

"Quickly."

Nay had instructed Nom through everything. He was to be in charge of the kitchen while she was gone, and Bryja was going to be de facto bartender in Quincy's place.

"Where are you going that requires you being away for several days?" Nom said.

"I'm not sure where exactly," Nay said. "He says we're going to meet someone who can help me cultivate to Iron Rank."

Nom's eye glinted in excitement. "Cultivation . . . I see!"

"There were cultivators on your world?"

"Many. I served one; well, my host served one who had attained godhood. He was supposedly immortal and had surpassed Diamond Rank eons before I was even spawned."

"Diamond Rank?"

"There were a lot of old and powerful beings in my world. I suspect there's no peak of cultivation. Just your own personal limits."

He seemed to be more exuberant than usual.

"Why are you so happy?"

"Two reasons. One, it was only a matter of time before you became a cultivator. Two, I can visit the House of Saccharine Delights and you won't be here to judge me."

Before they left the Lodge, they met Bruennig at the stable. The stablemaster procured Al, Quincy's old fauglir, and for Nay he had retrieved a young female fauglir.

"I don't know how to ride these things!" Nay said.

"Then you better learn, because we sure as nether hell ain't walking," Quincy said. "Also, she's not a thing. She's a fauglir and her name is Juniper."

Juniper nuzzled her large snout against Nay's shoulder. Her nostrils flared as she took in her scent, then she licked Nay's face with a sandpaper tongue. The animal smelled of clove and fresh pine. "All right, all right there," Nay said. "*Juniper* it is."

Before they left Lucerna's End, Quincy gave Nay a quick lesson in fauglir riding in front of the Lodge. This included showing Nay how to put on Juniper's saddle.

"Now lay the skirt across her back," Quincy said. "See this underneath the seat? That's called the skirt. Yep, lay it across her back just like that."

Then he pointed at a strap. "That's the billet."

Nay grabbed it. "This?"

"Yep. Now bring it underneath her and slide the end of it through that buckle on the other side. Make it snug but not too snug. There you go."

Nay examined the saddle on the fauglir. "Now what?"

"Now you grab the horn in the front, put your foot in the stirrup, and pull yourself up."

"You make it sound so easy."

"It is once you get used to it."

He demonstrated for her on Al. Even though Quincy was a large man, he swung onto the fauglir with grace.

Nay, unsure, grabbed the horn with both hands and put her foot in the stirrup. Then she yanked herself up, swinging onto the saddle belly-first. Juniper let out an annoyed yip.

There was a clumsy moment where Nay had to pull herself up by the horn and off her belly to properly straddle the beast. Juniper snorted, finally content.

"Now grab the reins," Quincy said. "Pull back on them when you want her to slow down. To make her go faster, give her a little tap with your feet."

"That doesn't hurt her?"

"Not unless you're looking to hurt her. Believe me, a fauglir will let you know when you're hurting them. Now, here's the key. Relax your body. The more uptight you feel, the more she's going to pick up on that. So, take a few deep breaths and clear your mind. Be relaxed, and she'll be relaxed. Got it?"

"You say that like I wasn't on anti-anxiety meds half my life."

"Just, whatever you do, don't panic. The last thing you want is a panicked fauglir. Your mood is her mood."

He tapped Al with his heel, and the fauglir started walking down the road. Nay did the same with Juniper, and she had to steady herself when her fauglir followed Al.

She got used to her gait. It was like being atop a wolf the size of a mule, and somehow it had the stride of both. It moved with the loping stride of a wolf and the steadfastness of a mule. She carried Nay through the mud at a steady trot.

"I'm doing it," Nay said. "I'm riding a giant wolf thing!"

"Fauglir," Quincy said.

"I'm riding a fauglir!"

* * *

They headed north out of the valley and followed a wagon road Quincy said was called Twelve Trail, because it once led to Twelve Stones, a town near an ancient meeting place of Stitchdale's frost giants.

The town itself had sunk into the mud during the Nether Thaw, an event where several clans did battle with a Nether Being and their under-realm horde. The Nether Being had summoned nether fire, which resulted in the permafrost melting on the battlefield, flooding the area.

Quincy mentioned this was all a long time ago, before the clans of men and the survivors of Paleforge had joined and produced the stitchmen.

Twelve Trail was built as a trading route between Lucerna's End and Twelve Stones, but now it was rarely used except for the few travelers who headed north each year, which was few.

Even further beyond the sunken town of Twelve Stones was the icy wasteland of the Caraxe Strait, a shifting mass of broken ice that led to the Norwaith Sea.

"Are you going to tell me whom we're headed to?" Nay said.

"We're going to find Caer Ilyawraith."

"Who's that?"

"The Wraith of the Moving Ice, former leader of the Banshee Sect. I believe she has a cultivation technique that will help boost you to Iron Rank in a short amount of time."

"Is that cheating?"

"No. It would take you a while to advance your Vigor the way you have been. Which is semi-blindly. There are certain sects who have developed effective techniques for rapidly accelerating the process without loss of purity. It's not cheating; it's more that they're secrets. Each sect protects their own knowledge. Of course, some techniques can be quicker but sacrifice purity of Vigor. Meaning the cultivator's abilities aren't as strong as they could be."

"Sounds like sacrificing quality for quantity, in a way."

"Quality for speed, perhaps."

"What makes you think this person is going to help us?"

"Because she owes me a favor."

At midday, they had stopped by a frozen stream to feed and water the fauglir and also themselves. Quincy cracked the sheet of ice over the stream so Al and Juniper could drink.

Nay had brought some carnitas burritos she had made earlier. Since she and Nom came up with the recipe together, they called them Nay & Nom's Carnitas Bombs.

They were imbued with Strength, Stamina, and Dexterity Buffs to aid with the traveling. She shared half of hers with Juniper, and she watched as the Buff

Icons appeared over Juniper's head. The fauglir had curled up at Nay's feet and was happily eating.

She gave a whole one both to Quincy and Al, since she figured Quincy would want a burrito all to himself. She was right, as he ate the whole thing and fed the separate one to Al.

The Buffs would perhaps double their speed of travel, at least make traveling through the cold and harsh land more bearable.

"Is it wise for us to leave Lucerna's End?" Nay said.

"Why wouldn't it be?" Quincy said.

"What if, I dunno, there's another attack?"

"Then let's hope it doesn't happen until we get back."

Nay frowned.

Quincy picked up on her mood. "You're not telling me something."

"I have reason to believe that the Nether Sister isn't dead."

"Oh? And what reason would that be?"

"Magical text again," Nay pointed at her head. "It's still in my log of quests."

"Doesn't change our plans. We still need to get you to Iron."

"But—"

"If she's still alive, she's going to attack you and I. Not just the town. She'll want revenge. So, more reason for you to be Iron."

The ground beneath them shook and snow fell off the branches of the nearby trees.

The fauglir stood up, alarmed, but Quincy was unfazed, chewing on his burrito.

"Easy, easy," Quincy said. "It's just a frost giant. Far away at that."

"Frost giant?" Nay said.

Quincy produced a retractable bronze spyglass and extended it. He stood and thumbed one of those gnomish agate stones on the side and peered through it. He turned in an arc, slowly sweeping the spyglass across the landscape until finally pausing. "Aha!" he said.

He handed her the spyglass. When she looked through it, in the direction he pointed, she was surprised by two things.

One, the visual clarity was like viewing a high-quality camera feed. The spyglass was enhanced in some way by the agate stone. Quincy would later explain these were aptly named Vigor Stones since they were imbued with Vigor.

Two, the blue-hued giant humanoid loping across the landscape in the distance. A monolith in motion. The wind was blowing through its mangy white beard. She zoomed in and could see shards of ice and frozen birds stuck in the hair. The eyes of the frost giant were an ocean blue and seemed full of sentience.

"Should we be concerned?"

"No, we're downwind of it. Plus, it's really far away. Now, if we were upwind and it was hungry? Different story."

Nay watched the giant disappear into the frost and mist, a dark, enormous shadow fading into the horizon.

— CHAPTER FORTY —

Things Worth Fighting For

As nightfall approached, the snow started to come down heavy, and it was accompanied by a powerful wind.

Nay leaned down, wrapped in her cloak, pressing her face against the back of Juniper's neck. The fauglir's pelt provided extra warmth. Juniper was strong. She pushed forward through the wind and snow, her powerful legs carrying them through the storm.

Quincy was ahead of them, positioned in the same way, protecting himself against the blizzard's force.

They were headed for a structure before them, a crooked, violet-hued, crystalline finger pointing up at the sky. Besides its pellucid surface, it fit right in with the craggy ice formations and snow.

By the time they reached it, night had arrived and the green-tinged moon was visible through the clouds and the flurry of snowfall.

They entered the formation through a cracked entrance. It was like being at the bottom of a tower, a silo-shaped geode that pointed at the heavens.

The walls were made of amethyst, and the wind hitting the outside of the structure sent an eerie chime and whistle through the ruin.

Silver moonlight entered through cracks in the purple surface, slanting across the chasm above them.

"What is this place?" Nay said.

"The Last Spire of Amethain. Some say it fell from the sky, part of a cultivator's floating fortress that was passing over our world. Whatever its origin, it should provide good shelter from the snow."

Nay was leading Juniper to their prospective camp, a circle of crystalline growths that were chair-high with a divot in the center to build a fire, when the fauglir growled, going tense.

Nay froze. "What is it, girl?"

There was a wet, chittering sound, and then an anaconda-sized white worm rose from behind the juts of amethyst. It had a circular mouth rimmed with teeth.

There was a red glow in its core, as if it was revving up with heat.

Quincy pushed Nay to the ground as the white polar worm spewed a red, magma-like secretion. It sprayed between them, the droplets sizzling as they hit the ground, melting the amethyst.

The Lodge owner rolled across the floor, closing the distance, and when he came up, Gertrude slashed horizontally, severing the worm's head. More of that magma spewed from the severed worm.

It flopped and fell over.

The secretion smoked and sizzled and burned a hole into the floor.

Quincy picked up the thing's head and held it over the divot, pouring the magma-like secretion out of it.

A small fire blazed to life.

"Didn't even have to break out the flint," he said.

They sat in front of the fire created by the polar worm's saliva.

Nay had qualms about heating up their Succulent Stew in a fire made from the weird fluid of a weird monster, so she used her Chef's Thermometer Ability to heat up the tin thermoses.

All she had to do was picture a ring of heat around the containers—she could even adjust the radius and size along with the temperature—and with a gesture of her finger, it would become reality.

"What are you doing?" Quincy said. "Do you want to get Vigor Sickness again?"

"Relax," Nay said. "I'm only using it for a moment. I won't overexert myself."

When the thermoses were heated, she handed Quincy his thermos and a spoon.

The Succulent Stew was a beef stew made with red wine imported from San Violeta, winter squash, ice peas, carrots, and potatoes. It was imbued with a Spirit Buff and a Recovery Buff, which were the perfect Buffs for resting.

They would sleep well and wake up renewed.

Nay poured some in the lid of her thermos and set it in front of Juniper. The fauglir went to slurping.

When they were done eating, the fauglir closed their eyes, but Quincy and Nay were still gazing into the fire.

"Nom said you scared him when he saw you fight," Nay said.

"I'm not pleasant when Gertrude or Samuel is in my hands," Quincy said.

"It wasn't that. He said . . . he told me you used evil powers."

Quincy grew quiet for a moment, as if he was carefully figuring out how to phrase his next words. "Good and evil are sometimes not always clear-cut."

Nay thought she knew what he meant, but she asked anyways. "What do you mean?"

"For example," Quincy said. "Stealing is bad. We can all agree on that, right?"

Nay shrugged. "Sure."

"But what about stealing a loaf of bread for your child who is hungry? You have no money and he must be fed. Is stealing still evil? Or is there some nuance required there?"

"Hey, if you're talking about gray morality, you're preaching to the choir. I think circumstances and context and specifics can paint a better picture for deciding what's right and what's wrong."

"It's good to know you have an open mind."

"If I didn't have an open mind, I would have lost it the first day I got here."

Quincy chuckled. "You remind me of my sister."

"Quella?"

He nodded. "You two have a similar sense of humor. I think you would have gotten along."

Nay wondered if that's why he gave her a chance all those weeks ago, because she reminded him of his sister. She wanted to know more about her, but she felt this wasn't the right time to ask.

"Nom saw me use Marrow Abilities from my Bile of the Plaguemonger tree," Quincy said. "It's not the prettiest thing to see, and I can see why he would mistake it for evil. But I was using those because when I choose violence against monsters, I don't settle for degrees. I prefer overkill."

"Degrees?"

"I believe in avoiding violence when necessary. I don't believe in small-scale escalation of violence. On a scale of one to one hundred, it's either zero or a hundred."

"I'm not sure I follow."

"Say I'm in a situation. Naturally, I opt for nonviolence. That's what I prefer. I believe nonviolent solutions are the best solutions. Until they're not. Now, say, this theoretical situation I'm in. If it becomes violent, and I choose to respond in a violent manner, but I choose to do so by, say, a three on a scale of ten, well, if the other person responds to me with a four, or anything above a three, then I'm probably a dead man."

Nay understood. "Once the violence switch gets flipped, you commit all the way, to minimize the danger against yourself."

"Half-measures can get you killed. If you're going to choose violence, then make sure the other guy, or monster, doesn't have a chance to counterattack. That's why I used my Death and Decay Abilities in that situation. We were outnumbered, and I didn't want Nom or I to come out the losers."

"What's a tree?" Nay said.

"Pardon?"

"You called it your *Bile of the Plaguemonger tree*," Nay said. "The tree I use for cooking is called *The Tongue of the Hierophant*."

Quincy realized she didn't know the fundamentals of Marrow Eater magic. "Sometimes, I forget that you're not from here."

"Sorry."

"It's not your fault. No one taught you the basics."

"It's true."

"So, all Marrow Eaters have the capacity to unlock three different skill trees. You open a skill tree by consuming specific Delicacies. The type of Delicacy establishes the type of skill tree it will be. All of my skill trees have to do with combat. Bile of the Plaguemonger are attacks, or amplifications of attacks, that use sickness, decay, and disease to deliver damage and death to an opponent."

"What are your two other skill trees?"

"Razor Tusk of the Elynine and Fang of Lillith. One's melee combat skills, the other is ranged respectively. Or think of it as one for Gertrude, my axe. The other's for Samuel, my crossbow."

"The Rangers, Martygan and Lain, I saw them change into animals."

Quincy nodded. "All of the Gloom Rangers have mobility skill trees. Those are so they can change into forms that can carry them through the wilds swiftly. And to blend in."

He continued explaining.

"In organizations like the Rangers, or even certain military, the members are provided with preplanned Delicacy and Marrow meals, all prepared according to the roles they are to become. So, say, someone is to become a Bow Sniper in the Crescentia Defense Force, then there's a multi-course meal for that."

Nay listened to this, flabbergasted. "So, someone can walk in as a blank slate and then eat a meal and come out with specialized skill trees designed to create a particular role?"

"It's usually more than one meal. These are multi-course feasts that last several days. And granted, this is only for big and well-funded organizations that can afford such a thing. Remember, Delicacies and Marrow usually come from monsters. These things are not cheap. There's one particular family in San Violeta that has a monster farm, and they can control whatever type of Marrow Eater they want to become."

Nay almost fell off her seat when she heard that. "A Monster Farm?!"

"Sure. It's where they breed monsters for their Delicacies and Marrows."

"What the fuck."

"They're not common, but they do exist. We're talking about a family with unlimited resources. They're the richest of the rich."

"Still, that is sick. How do they even capture the monsters? And multiple ones to breed?"

"Like I said, they're powerful people."

The more Nay learned about this world, the more amazed and terrified she was of it.

"I think you're going to want to unlock a combat skill tree soon," Quincy said.

"What makes you say that?"

"Trouble seems to have a way of finding you."

Nay thought about her time here. He wasn't wrong. From the moment she found herself in this world, she'd been fighting for her life in one way or another.

Hell, that was how she got here. She tried to think back to a time before she got attacked in the alleyway in Los Angeles when there was never a struggle. It was true everyone had their own battles and obstacles in life, but trouble had always had a way of finding her.

From when her father died, to hustling to survive when she was a teenager by working in kitchens and restaurants while attending school, to having to transfer various schools because of drama, to what happened with Chef Jean, it seemed like she had moved to Los Angeles to try and escape trouble.

But trouble found her there, too.

"Do you know if Epicurists usually diversify into a combat skill tree? Or do all their trees have to do with cooking?"

"You know, I'm not sure. The ones I've known or have run across have always been strictly kitchen types. There's a standard and uniformness to how they're trained. But you're not strictly an Epicurist, remember? The Culinary Guild knows nothing about you. You're living in a harsh land where you've been forced to defend yourself more than once. I think it would benefit you greatly to unlock a combat skill tree. Just purely in terms of survival."

Nay knew he was right.

"Also, we're caught in the crossfire of whatever is happening in Stitchdale and the Nether Realm. So, we need to prepare for the worst. There's a storm brewing. And Samuel and Gertrude are going to need companions."

"Are you talking about *Thorn*?"

"I am."

"Here, I was thinking that I'd get to do nothing but run a kitchen and cook food."

"Those are peacetime activities."

"You think we're going to be at war?"

"I don't know about war," Quincy said. "But I think we'll be fighting again. And like I said, we won't be using half-measures."

"I wish I could just cook. It's what I care about the most."

"I wish you could just cook too," he said. "But there are times we have to defend the things we care about. Like cooking. Or . . . the Lodge. Reading, fellowshipping, drinking, gardening, farming. All the great peacetime activities." His eyes sparkled in the light of the fire. "Those are all things worth fighting for."

— CHAPTER FORTY-ONE —

The Northern Wind

The Caraxe Strait looked like a shattered plain of frozen ice. But Nay could see the sea between the shifting plates of ice. From the cliff they could hear the screech and whine of slabs of ice sliding and shifting against each other, the rolling sea beneath pushing the puzzle pieces in different directions and causing haphazard differences in elevation.

"We're close now," Quincy said. "About half a day's travel."

"You're not telling me we're traveling out into that," Nay said.

"She's out there, somewhere."

"What do you mean, 'somewhere'?" Nay said. "Do you not know?"

"Caer Ilyawraith's the type of woman who likes to avoid straight answers. Do you know the type?"

"Unfortunately, I do."

That's what they call crazy bitches, Nay thought. But she kept it to herself.

She consulted her mini-map, but it gave her no clues. She wondered if there would ever be a way to upgrade the mini-map so it would have more useful features. Because right now, it seemed pretty basic and mostly useless.

As they descended down the trail leading to the strait, Nay hoped that if she increased in Rank that her Abilities would become more powerful. Or if she would learn or have access to more recipes. What she really fantasized about what was food that could imbue a Warmth Buff.

While Nay and Juniper followed Quincy and Al across the beach made out of snow instead of sand, she wondered if the cold affected Quincy as much since he was Bronze Rank.

She was interested in discovering the changes Iron Rank would bring compared to Base Rank. If she got there, of course.

At the moment, she wasn't sure if she was even going to make it to Caer Ilyawraith without freezing to death. Or if she did make it, Quincy hinted that the Ranking process could be dangerous. There was the possibility of dying while attempting to Rank so quickly.

By the time their fauglir were stepping off the beach and onto the thick layer of ice that covered the ocean at the edge of the world, Nay felt like she was going to pass out.

She was numb from the cold and tired from being battered by the wind.

It was like traveling across a low-level earthquake.

At one point, the plate of ice they were on rose and suddenly they were on a decline, sliding towards the frigid sea.

Quincy or Nay didn't have to instruct Al and Juniper what to do. The fauglir jumped to the nearest plate of ice on their own, the cold spray nipping at them as they leapt across the gap.

Nay shouted into the wind, snow, and sea spray. "Are you sure this is worth it?!"

Quincy's response surprised her. "No! No, I'm not!"

Well, that's a great vote of confidence in me, Nay thought. They continued across the shifting sea of ice.

Nay took out more of the Strength and Stamina biscuits she had in her cloak and started binge-eating them. In her experiments with this, she was sure the Buffs did stack a little, but it wasn't anything she could exploit.

There was the law of diminishing returns, the more biscuits she ate.

Time was skipping for her as she drifted out of alertness and into daydreaming.

So, when the mass of the iceberg rose up out of the whiteout mist, she didn't notice the skeleton of the great beast intertwined in the mountain of ice, half-exposed and half-embedded in the mass, until it was directly in front of them.

And even then, she thought it might be a figment of her imagination or an optical illusion, like a dragon or serpent that crashed into the frozen sea from the sky, becoming part of a glacier.

Its skull was like a cliff face in scope. Its cavernous eye sockets were above the sea, packed in the iceberg. But its maw was submerged below in the part of the berg they couldn't see. It was hard to tell how far down it went.

The bones of a god trapped in a glacial mass.

A haunting voice traveled to them with the wind. At first, Nay thought it was the cry of a weeping woman or someone trapped out here, doomed to sing a ghost song that would only be heard by travelers crazy enough to traverse this shattered landscape.

But then she could hear words forming out of the evocative banshee song.

"*Turn around . . . and leave this place . . .*" the singer sung.

Nay looked over at Quincy, a bit creeped out.

Quincy got off Al and stepped in front of the ice-encrusted god skull protruding out of the frozen sea.

He bellowed into the blizzard. His mustache was frozen on his face. "It's Quincy! Quincy the Doomhearted! I've come with a prospective pupil!"

"A pupil?" Nay said. "Is that what I am?"

He shushed her.

From the peak of the god skull, an eddy of snow flurries swirled, descending towards them. There was the form of a person atop it.

As it got close enough for them to discern details, Nay saw that there was a person riding the flurry of snow as if it were a cloud.

And the weirdest thing of all was that they were sitting atop the snow cloud cross-legged or in the lotus position. She wasn't sure which.

"Quincy?" the snow-flurry rider said. "With a prospect, you say?"

She hovered above, looking down her nose at them. Her white hair was braided with blue seaweed, and although there was something about her voice that reminded Nay of an old woman, she looked young, a gloss about her skin like she was preserved in time.

Her skin seemed to be encased in a thin layer of clear ice, and the armor she wore resembled silver fish scales. There were growths of pink coral on her shoulders that served as pauldrons.

Quincy gestured at Nay. "Aye, this is Renee Favreau. I thought you would be interested in meeting her. She has experienced Vigor Sickness while still at Base Rank."

"I can see that, of course," the woman said. "I'm not blind."

"Nay, this is Caer Ilyawraith," Quincy said.

Nay looked up at the floating woman of the snow and sea. Unsure, she waved at her awkwardly. "Hi."

She frowned at Nay, her expression cold. "What makes you think I will take a pupil these days? I haven't had a pupil in several generations."

"Because of the Night of the Seven Slaughters."

Ilyawraith's unsettling white eyes turned pink as she was reminded of the memory.

"Everyone would still think you were alive if it wasn't for me," Quincy said.

"How do you know no one followed you?"

"Because if they did, you would sense them."

Ilyawraith grumbled. Flurries of snow from her cloud blew onto them. She looked out across the landscape from which they came. "You can come in. But if you've brought trouble to my abode, you'll come to regret it, Night of the Seven Slaughters or not."

Her snow cloud circled around them and whisked her towards the frozen god skull. They followed her across the ice into her home.

* * *

The iceberg had been hollowed out into something of a palace inside.

Except *palace* wasn't really the right word. For Nay, it had a *Fortress of Solitude* vibe.

Some type of plush, blue moss was growing on the floor inside this portion of the skull. There was also a pool of melted snow they could drink from. They stabled the fauglir there, and Juniper immediately ran to the pool and started drinking.

There was a splash of water, and Nay saw something wriggling between Juniper's jaws. It was a green-scaled fish. The fauglir happily trotted to the bed of blue moss and began eating.

Their host was weird and standoffish, but she knew how to take care of their creature companions.

As they descended wide spiraling stairs that led to the inside of the iceberg below the ocean, Nay couldn't take her eyes off the bones of the behemoth that were frozen in the walls. It was like being inside the stomach of a serpent.

Nay caught up to Quincy, nudging him. She whispered, "Who is this person, again?"

"I," Ilyawraith said, "am the Northern Wind that brings the chill of the Caraxe into your heart when you think you're safe in the South. I am the one who speaks to the sea and controls the amount of fish in your people's nets. I am the one in the wind that brings the snow and the ice. I am also mostly the one who likes to be left alone."

Nay was shocked that she had heard her talking to Quincy.

The Lodge owner chuckled and said, "What's the matter? You've never been around a Silver Rank before?"

Nay almost fell down the rest of the stairs. She eyed Ilya, who was far ahead of them, walking down the stairs. "Silver? I thought Bronze was rare."

"Which is why you should use the floormats up ahead and make sure you don't track any muck into my dwelling. You wouldn't want to see a Silver Rank's wrath."

She wasn't kidding. They stood at the threshold of a chamber that contained a hearth where the fire was burning blue. And there was a mat of dried, woven seaweed and kelp at their feet.

Quincy shook the mud and ice off his boots and made sure to stomp on the mat. Nay followed suit.

They entered the chamber, following Ilyawraith. Nay looked around in wonder. The way the light was reflecting off the ice and bones made it look like it was the heart of the iceberg and maybe even the heart chamber of the long-dead serpent.

There were seats, couches, and benches carved out of ice and covered with the soft pelts of bear or some other animal with fur. There was a cooking table next to the hearth with the blue fire.

Ilyawraith went behind it and started picking out things on the table to cook.

"You really ought to let Nay cook for us," Quincy said.

Ilyawraith stopped and looked at him. "Why is that?"

"She runs the kitchen in my Lodge." She didn't look convinced. "Just trust me, all right?"

"The last time you told me just to trust you, I almost died."

"And look at us now! Still breathing and full of Vigor for multiple lives!"

"Very well," Ilyawraith said. She sat down in front of the hearth and started weaving dry seaweed together.

Nay went to the table and assessed the ingredients. There was a sack of flour. Butter. Vegetables.

She got to work.

She mixed together a pancake batter, then chopped scallions. She used her Chef's Thermometer Ability to heat up two pans.

When Quincy saw that, he glared at her. She shrugged.

Ilyawraith observed her, expressionless.

In one pan she began the scallion pancakes, and in the next she cracked what looked like quail eggs and started making crispy scallion omelets.

When they were finished cooking, she plated them and served Ilyawraith and Quincy.

Ilyawraith took a bite of the pancake. Her expressionless, stoic face didn't break as she chewed. But by the time she swallowed, she had started to tremble.

Finally, she gave in and took another bite, chewing in pleasure. In mid-bite, she said, "She's using Epicurist abilities."

Nay sat down at the hearth with her own plate of food. "Are you going to report me?"

"Oh, child. If you only knew. The DMA would want me dead if they still knew I was alive. You're around fellow rebels here."

Ilyawraith looked at Nay as if she was scanning her. Her eyes shined pink.

"Quincy, you haven't been forthright with me," she said. "I've never met an Elseworlder before."

Quincy ate his quail egg and scallion omelet and shrugged. "What's the point? You would have figured it out anyways."

"Her Vigor is almost halfway to Iron. Yes, the veins are strengthening and expanding. Fascinating."

That must have been the specialty of her Marrow Abilities. She could scan and read other cultivators and analyze their Vigor. She probably had a lot of experience in training cultivators. Which is why Quincy brought her here.

"So, you've been using Marrow abilities while at Base Rank. I have to say that's something else I've never seen before." She looked at Quincy. "You must let me see if I can train her. Even if it's just for knowledge's sake."

Quincy finished a pancake and waved his fork at her. "Why do you think I brought her here?"

— CHAPTER FORTY-TWO —

Elseworlder

Quincy was still snoring so loud, Nay thought the noise was going to crack the ice walls and bring them crashing into the sea when Ilyawraith got her out of bed.

The beds were upraised portions of ice with layers of what Nay thought was polar bear fur. It was so comfortable, she didn't even remember falling asleep.

Ilyawraith led her to a chamber towards the lower half of the iceberg. There was a pool where the cold seawater was coming up through the bottom. The spinal column of the beast was visible in the walls.

The cultivator led her to the edge of the pool, where she had set up seaweed mats.

There were a steaming kettle and a wood cup on one of the mats.

They sat down and Ilyawraith poured her tea.

Nay took the cup and took a sniff. The steam rising off the surface was crimson. There was an antiseptic and coppery smell to it. The strange odor wasn't entirely appealing.

"What is it?" Nay said.

"Coldblood tea," Ilywraith said. "Your veins absorb it and it helps me see the state of your Vigor."

"Like it gets into my bloodstream faster or something?" Nay said.

Ilyawraith shook her head. "Not those veins. Your spirit veins. It's the spiritual pathway on which your Vigor travels. The stronger and more extensive these pathways are, the stronger your Vigor usually is. Go ahead and drink."

Nay took a sip of the hot tea. Even through her ruined taste buds, the sourness still got to her. She puckered her lips. "Do I have to drink the whole thing?"

Ilyawraith nodded, reached out, and tilted the bottom of Nay's cup up so she would keep drinking. "It goes down easier, the quicker you drink it."

Nay grimaced and kept drinking.

It was like downing a hot bowl of sweet-and-sour soup, except there were no noodles and no sweetness. She reached the bottom of the cup, and she set it down.

Her stomach cramped up and she groaned. *What the hell?* She looked at Ilyawraith with an accusation on her face.

"No, I didn't poison you," Ilyawraith said. "Drawing out your Vigor veins can sometimes be painful. Especially if it's your first time."

Nay fell to her side and gasped. "Jesus Christ."

She curled up into a ball, wrapping her hands around her knees as the pain spread up and down the inside of her torso. It felt like her nervous system was set on fire.

"It will pass," Ilyawraith said. "This is necessary so I can do a proper scan."

Nay groaned. "Does everything that has to do with cultivation involve pain?"

"Pain is temporary, girl," Ilyawraith said. "Transcendence is eternal."

"I feel awfully mortal to concern myself with a concept like transcendence," Nay said. The pain started to fade, and her insides no longer felt like they were being crushed. She sat up.

"All of us start that way," Ilyawraith said. "It is the natural condition. But look around you. There is Vigor everywhere for the taking."

"I'm not sure I follow," Nay said.

"Quincy hasn't explained what Vigor is to you?"

"I mean, I get the general gist. It's like my spirit, right? My life force?"

At that, Ilyawraith floated into the air.

The chamber seemed to drop a few degrees, and the pool of seawater started to splash, spilling over the lip of the ice. Her hair seemed to blow in an invisible wind.

"Vigor is not just inside of you," she said, her voice deepening with import. "It is all around you. It dwells in the air you breathe, it waits in the ice you stand on, it's in the water of the sea, the birds in the sky, the worms in the ground, the trees in the field! Vigor is everywhere, not just giving you life, but it's an expression of the soul of everything around us! Everything beautiful and everything terrible. In the end, when we return to the dust, our Vigor remains."

Ilyawraith floated back down to the ice. The invisible wind died down. The temperature rose a few more degrees and the seawater in the pool calmed.

"I have some theories about your development," she said.

"You do?" Nay said. "Because I've been wondering myself about some of these . . . tools I've had ever since I got here. Did Quincy tell you about the magical word prompts I can see? And my mini-map and quest logs and all that?"

"Your Vigor has helped you adapt to this world, giving you abilities for simply being an Elseworlder," she said.

"Like a cheat," Nay said.

It was clear from Ilyawraith's expression that she didn't know what Nay meant.

"Like, in all fairness, I was dead to rights as soon as I got to this world," Nay said. "I shouldn't have survived at all when I first got here. And what you're saying is my Vigor helped me adapt and it gave me this tool set . . . *this interface* . . . because it knew I probably didn't stand a chance in this world without it."

"Tell me everything you can do," Ilyawraith said.

"Does it not show up in your scans?" Nay said.

"Oh, I can see it all clearly. I want you to describe it to me. In your own words."

Nay thought for a moment. "Okay, well, there's the mini-map, obviously. I'm not sure what the range is. But in the right corner of my vision, I can see the general layout of the area. Sometimes, when I get quests, I can see the locations. Oh, because I can Detect Marrow via my Hierophant skill tree, I'll see those show up on the map if I'm nearby. It would be nice if it could do other things, like adjust the range or track people at will. But it's still been helpful. I don't want you to think I'm complaining about it."

Ilyawraith nodded, observing her, like she was peering into her very soul.

"What else?" Nay said. "There's the fact that I can understand and speak the languages here when I shouldn't even know them at all. That includes written language, too. Sometimes, I get a prompt about auras. Like, I can detect certain auras from Marrow Eaters if I'm being affected by it. But I can't with you."

"I'm too high of a rank for you to detect my aura," Ilyawraith said.

"That makes sense. Let's see. I was able to detect and activate a Delicacy, Tongue of the Hierophant. It's how I got my Ability tree. I was told that this shouldn't have been possible, because only Epicurists have the Ability to prepare and activate Delicacies."

"You were told right," Ilyawraith said. "They need the Ability tree, which requires consuming a Delicacy. That's how the DMA controls Marrow Eaters. They control who can cook."

"I mean, if I was going to try and control who can become a Marrow Eater, I'd do the same thing, I guess."

"What would you do if an anomaly like you appeared?"

Nay felt the heaviness that came with this question. "I'd probably be very interested in this anomaly."

"It's good that you're self-aware."

Nay was reminded of something then. "Oh, so, here's the weirdest thing about my stuff, this interface or whatever. It feels like there's someone behind the scenes assigning these quests or describing abilities and objects to me. Because sometimes there's an odd sense of humor in the writings. Like this person is watching me in these situations and getting enjoyment out of guiding me along. I've been calling them the Quest-Giver in my head. Like I don't know if it's just another odd manifestation of my Vigor, but it feels like I'm connected to someone or something else in a way. I don't know; it's hard to describe."

For the first time since they were down here, Ilyawraith showed a sense of puzzlement on her face.

"I almost forgot," Nay said. "I feel like this Quest-Giver gave me loot after I helped the Gloom Rangers."

What looked like a green gummy candy appeared in her hand out of nowhere. It was about the size of an apple. And it was in the shape of a tadpole.

It was the Boon of the Mewlipped Tadpole.

In her other hand the Mirkwood Eye trinket appeared.

Ilyawraith's look of puzzlement turned to one of astonishment. She was one who wasn't easily surprised. "Where . . ."

"I forgot to mention my interface also has an inventory system. That's where these were stored. I can pull them out instantly, at will. Same thing goes for storing them."

The boon and the trinket both disappeared from her hands.

"Weird, right?" Nay said. "I'm not sure how much I can hold, like if there's a limit. But I stored so much food in the inventory for Quincy and me, we don't really have to worry about going hungry. Not for a long while."

A burrito appeared in her hand. She offered it to Ilyawraith.

The cultivator just looked at it in bewilderment.

Nay shrugged and took a bite of the burrito.

"I'm going to surmise that when some Elseworlders end up here," Ilyawraith said, "some of them develop Elseworlder abilities to help them survive."

"I mean, the theory makes sense to me," Nay said.

"But it's impossible to be sure, because Elseworlders are so rare. There's simply not enough of you to collect and compare knowledge."

"Quincy used the phrase *Worldtripper*."

"Again, there's so little of you, there's not an official phrase," Ilyawraith said. "Although I'm curious what the Veritax refers to your kind as."

"The Veritax?"

"In their vaulted library in Verudae City, I'm absolutely sure they have records of Travelers from other worlds. Their monks have been watching and recording events here for a millennium."

"You've never met someone like me? An Elseworlder?"

Ilyawraith shook her head. "Never met, but of course I've heard of your kind. The one I heard about was supposedly very powerful. Which doesn't surprise me. If you're able to come here from another world or plane of existence and survive, it requires the accumulation of power along the way. It requires the accumulation of Vigor."

Nay wondered if anyone from her world had ever ended up here.

"So," Ilyawraith said, "your spiritual veins are growing, hungry for more Vigor. That's a good sign. It means you have the pathways to obtain it. So, the next step is obtaining it and holding on to it, absorbing it into your veins."

"How do I do that?"

"The same way you have been doing it."

"Completing quests?"

"By breathing."

"Breathing?"

"Except I'm going to teach you a method for breathing in a more efficient way. Seeing as how Quincy hasn't even taught you that yet."

"He's never so much as mentioned breathing."

Ilyawraith smiled and her pink pupils flickered.

The ice floor shuddered beneath them, and a fracture appeared in the frozen surface. It moved around them, forming a ring, then the disc of ice started to descend through the iceberg.

The place rumbled as cubes of ice began to shift and move around them, as if they were descending through an intricate puzzle that kept forming and re-forming.

Ilyawraith seemed to be half-concentrating, manipulating the architecture of the berg.

Their descent slowed, and below, Nay saw a rectangle carved out of the ice.

It looked like a white open grave.

Soon, the lip of the open grave was at the same level as the disc.

"Climb in and then lie down," Ilyawraith said.

Nay looked between the ice grave and the strange cultivator. "Down there?"

Ilyawraith nodded and tilted her head to jump in.

Nay wasn't feeling it. "Nah, I think I'm good."

"Do you want to advance to Iron Rank or not?"

Nay bit her lip, uncomfortable. She was unsure. But Quincy trusted this woman with instructing her.

He wouldn't lead her into something he didn't approve of.

So, she lowered herself into the ice compartment.

She lay down as if it was her coffin.

She felt a cold wetness underneath her, nipping at her legs and back. There was seawater trickling through the ice below her and into the grave. She did a double take and realized the ocean was on the other side of the ice.

"Hey!" Nay said.

Ilyawraith continued to stare down at her, unconcerned, as ice crystals started to form in the air above Nay, spreading and interlinking and solidifying.

There was a tinkling sound as a roof of ice formed above her, closing her into the ice grave.

It was just a few inches from her face.

Nay pounded the underside of the ice with her fists. "Hey! What are you doing?! Hey!"

The seawater rose, half-immersing her.

But it didn't stop there. It kept rising, submerging her head, only stopping at the ice cover above her.

She was trapped in a tomb of ice.

Nay screamed bubbles.

CHAPTER FORTY-THREE

The First Trial: Spirit Song

Just as Nay was about to start chugging water into her lungs, enraged and terrified that this lady had tricked her so she could drown her, the water receded enough to create an air pocket for her mouth and nose.

She gasped and sputtered, spitting seawater.

Then she sucked in as much air as she could.

"Let me out!" she said. She thrashed against the ice lid, her teeth chattering. "Let me out!"

"Nay," Ilyawraith said, in an irritatingly calm voice. "Calm down."

"Don't tell me to be calm! You're trying to fucking kill me!"

The water rose again, taking away the air pocket. She was once again immersed and forced to hold her breath.

She focused all of her fear on Ilyawraith and channeled it into rage.

That's when she remembered her Chef's Thermometer Ability.

She focused on a part of the ice lid and conjured forth a ring of heat.

But before it started to melt, the ice started to harden even more.

Ilyawraith waggled a finger at her. *No, you don't.*

Then the air pocket was back, the water receding again.

"Focus on the rhythm of the water, Nay," Ilyawraith said. "Let your breathing fall in line with it, and you don't have to worry about drowning."

"What?!"

"Close your eyes and focus on your breathing, and you'll make it through this."

Before Nay could retort, the water rose again over her mouth and nose, and she had to hold her breath.

She tried to calm herself. She just had to make it until the water lowered again and she would be okay.

[Quest Detected]
[Quest: Learn Spirit Song Breathing Technique]
[Accept Quest Y/N?]

She accepted the quest and held in her breath and tried to remain still.
What the hell was the Spirit Song Breathing Technique?
Maybe counting would help.
She started to count, but by the time she got to the number five, it already felt like it was making this ordeal last longer. Seconds felt like minutes.
She wished she had bigger lungs. Or, hell, an extra lung.
The air pocket was back, and she sucked in big gulps of air as if she was a beached fish.
"That is an inefficient way of breathing, girl," Ilyawraith said.
Nay glared at her as she took shallow, panicked breaths.
It didn't feel like she could ever get enough in.
Then the water was back, tickling her mouth and nostrils, and she was underwater again.
She accessed her interface to see if she could find something that would help her. She looked at her inventory and saw the Boon of the Mewlipped Tode.
She scanned the text again.

Boon of the Mewlipped Tode. Consuming this Boon will accelerate your current Vigor Rank-up by 25 percent. Side effects may result in turning into a toad for a day and being compelled to catch and eat nothing but flies. Will be in all the danger that toad form is susceptible to while a toad.
Ribbit!

The green toad gummy appeared in her hand, and she shoved the whole thing into her mouth and started chewing.
Ilyawraith squinted through the ice to confirm what she was seeing. "No!"
A moment after Nay swallowed, she was seized with what felt like an adrenaline boost.
Something was surging through her and she couldn't stop shaking.
Please turn me into a toad please turn me into a toad please turn me
Her interface chimed and her HUD was blinking.
She clicked on the Vigor Rank Menu.
Dammit why am I not a toad yet come on did it not work please toad me oh well
The bar from Base Rank to Iron Rank was ticking up, getting closer to Iron. The bar filled rapidly and then stopped.

Vigor Points to Iron Rank: 57%

The trembling stopped, and Nay had never felt so strong in her life. She felt like something inside of her had grown. Like she had a stronger center.

She felt like she could punch through the ice and free herself.

She reared her fist back and punched.

And in mid-punch, her world expanded.

The seawater ice grave she was trapped in suddenly seemed massive, an ocean of its own.

Her fist had become a spade hand with four fingers. They looked like they should be webbed, but upon closer inspection, they weren't. They pulled at the water like a child grasping for a cookie.

And she was no longer holding her breath.

Nay had gotten her wish.

The side effect of the Boon had procced, turning her into a Mewlipped Tode.

Her lungs weren't flooding with water. Rather, the water ran over her gills.

thank god i have gills it's working mewlipped todes have gills!

The gills filtered the oxygen out of the water.

Above, Ilyawraith had cleared the ice and was looking down at her, hands flailing and shouting.

She was now gigantic. "What have you done?!"

Nay tried to speak, but the tip of her little tongue poked out of her mouth instead. She may have croaked. She felt a hunger for flies, but there were none in this iceberg.

Ilyawraith threw her hands up in exasperation and then floated into the air. "Quincy!"

She flew up into the iceberg, leaving Nay to herself.

Nay swam around her own personal sea, enjoying the sensation of her new amphibian legs, no longer having to worry about breathing.

When the metamorphosis effect wore off, she was sleeping. She was pulled out of the dream where she was floating through Jell-O, and she discovered she was her normal human self again, lying on the disc of ice.

Ilyawraith was hovering in the air above her in the lotus position.

Her eyes flicked open. "Is there anything else in that magical inventory of yours that I need to know about?"

Nay was back inside the pool, the ice lid re-formed above her.

She began to feel a sense of panic again. This time, she had no escape plan.

As the sea water trickled in, she mentally clicked on the Quest Log. There was an indicator next to the Spirit Song Breathing Technique Quest.

She selected it and a menu opened.

Spirit Song Breathing Technique. A basic but effective breathing technique used by Cultivators of the now-extinct Banshee Sect. It's used to strengthen your Vigor pathways and to extract Vigor from the atmosphere, fortifying your Core. A mastery of Spirit Song is a reward in its own right.

She held on to the little air she managed to gulp down. She wouldn't count, because that made the period of preserving her breath agonizing.

As she went under, she listened to the water around her. It was a dampening sound.

She could hear the hum of the water, and nearby she even felt she could hear the vastness of the ocean.

She felt small, just another infinitesimal creature in an infinite sea.

Just as she settled into it, the air pocket was back again.

Except this time when her mouth and lips were exposed to the air, she wasn't panicking.

She inhaled through her nostrils, accepting a slow but deep breath, she held it in momentarily, letting it feel natural, then she exhaled, pushing the air out as if it was wind leaving her body.

And then, the water rose and she let herself fall into it, yearning to float in its expanse.

The thought of holding her breath didn't even occur to her this time.

She was too entranced by the fuzzy motes of light drifting through the water. She felt like she could almost see the individual components of the water, and they all contained those ectoplasmic globs of spirit light.

She wanted to pull the Vigor into herself.

She could feel something happening with her, at her very center.

Her Vigor veins were stretching, reaching out to call for the ectoplasmic light wobbling there in the water like lava-lamp globules.

Then she could breathe again, the water sinking.

She imagined the Vigor veins within her contracting and expanding. On the contraction, she pulled at the air around her and imagined the pathways expanding with the air.

She envisioned the oxygen traveling along the pathways to her center, where it strengthened her.

Above her, Ilyawraith leaned forward.

As she watched Nay, a smile started to form on her face.

Then Nay was one with the sea again.

She could sense its song. While holding her breath, she sent a vein out, and she could feel the spirit tendril of her Core pathway connecting with the ocean.

She immediately felt enlivened and unafraid, and forgot that she even needed to breathe as she began to extract Vigor motes out of the ocean.

Her veins accepted them with a hunger, and she could feel her spirit soar with the sudden rush of Vigor.

When the water receded, a song filled the air pocket and vibrated the ice above her.

Above, Ilyawraith heard the muffled Spirit Song coming from the tomb of ice.

Nay was using the Spirit Song technique and was drawing Vigor out of the air.

She had never felt stronger in her life. The warmth and comfort and power of the Vigor was contained in her veins, in her spirit passageways.

Ilyawraith melted the ice lid and beckoned Nay to sit up.

Nay obeyed and was surprised to hear that the song that was filling the chamber was coming from herself.

She stopped and gasped, ending the song.

[Quest Complete!]
[Learn Spirit Song Breathing Technique Completed!]
[Congratulations!]
[You have been rewarded with Vigor Points]

Nay exhaled and put a hand to her chest. How could just breathing make her feel so much stronger?

She looked at her interface again and accessed her Vigor Points.

Vigor Rank: Base
Status to Iron: 67%

Did she just gain like ten percent by learning this new technique?

"You see," Ilyawraith said. "You can breathe in the Vigor around you and let your veins and Core process it into Vigor essence. It's important to master Spirit Song so you can acquire and obtain Vigor. Converting it to essence is essential for amplifying everything you do."

"How come Quincy never taught me this?" Nay said.

She was starting to get upset that she didn't know this technique sooner.

"He probably didn't want to make a mistake and sabotage your foundation,"

Ilyawraith said. "Or maybe he didn't want you to settle for an inferior technique. Either way, it seems maybe he wasn't confident in teaching you."

"Inferior how?"

"There's all kinds of techniques for breathing and harnessing Vigor. Not all are as effective as the Banshee Sect's way. It may be harder to learn, but the results are that much greater."

"Is that your Sect?"

"*Was.*"

"What happened to them?"

"I am all that remains."

Nay wanted to probe further, but she could tell that was the end of the discussion on the subject.

Perhaps the Spirit Song Breathing Technique would also help her be a better cook in some way.

If anything, the breathing would help her during those more-stressful moments in the kitchen. And it would help her get to Iron Rank so she could use her Marrow Abilities without conking out.

They had returned to Ilyawraith's hearth to find that Quincy was awake, warming himself in front of the fire. His mustache was in disarray from the way he slept, and there was something about his appearance that gave Nay a glimpse of what he must have been like when he was a child.

"She knows the technique now?" Quincy said.

"I'm still alive, so what do you think?" Nay said.

"Thank Celestia," Quincy said. "Pupils have perished during that teaching. I thought I was gonna have to fend for myself for breakfast. What a shame that would have been. What a shame indeed."

"Now we know how you really feel about me," Nay said. "So, what were you saying? You're skipping breakfast this morning? Fine by me. One less mouth to feed."

Quincy stammered. "Now, hold on a minute. Let's—"

Ilyawraith interrupted him. "Since you're skipping breakfast this morning, the fauglir can have yours. Will you make yourself useful and bring it to them?"

"Dammit."

— CHAPTER FORTY-FOUR —

A Brief History, Written in Bone

"So, are we inside of the bones of a dragon or something?" Nay said. The three of them sat by the blue fire of Ilyawraith's hearth, eating breakfast.

The cultivator had served them, giving Nay a break from having to cook since she spent the past day undergoing the breathing technique lesson.

She handed them bowls of skyr topped with crystal berries and drizzled with honey. The skyr was a thick, sour yogurt with a little sweetness added to it.

Nay assumed it was delicious. She ate while musing on the details of Ilyawraith's strange home.

The cultivator had referred to herself as a rebel, and Nay wondered what that meant. She also wanted people to think she was dead, and she lived all the way out on the Caraxe Strait inside the frozen remains of a kaiju.

If anyone screamed *hermit*, it was Ilyawraith.

"They say before this land was as it is now," Ilyawraith said, "before there was a sun and a moon above us, the only light from above came from the stars. So, there was a darkness here, but a natural darkness.

"There was also an Unnatural Darkness that was present here. It had leaked out of the Nether Realm and found its way to our world."

She set down her half-eaten bowl of skyr and stared into the flames of the hearth as if she was trying to look back in time. "There were things of that Unnatural Darkness that developed a jealousy and a hatred for the men that dwelt here."

"So, this thing was one of them?" Nay said, gesturing at the entombed kaiju around them.

"Let her tell the tale," Quincy said. He stood up and went to refill his bowl of skyr. He was generous when he got to the berries and honey.

"The men who toiled at the earth and fished in the sea had protectors,"

Ilyawraith said. "Contrary to what the Ligeia League may have us believe, not all creatures perceived as monsters are bad."

"But it's easy to convince a person a monster is evil when you're consuming their parts to get stronger," Quincy said.

Nay was starting to see the picture in her head.

Like back home, where greed was all the motivation one needed.

To justify destruction and death, and to make everyone feel a little bit better about the wholesale rape of the sacred when it becomes a resource, one just has to label the victims as evil.

All it took was recontextualizing the picture in order to sell it to a public who may have some initial qualms.

Which was just their humanity trying to warn them.

"The tribes of men had made an alliance and joined forces to build a Beacon. A Beacon of light that harnessed Vigor, that would have the power to illuminate the land so the men didn't always have to toil underneath the dark light of stars.

"The Unnatural Darkness despised man and hated everything they had built. They sent their unnatural army out to destroy the Beacon, the fruit of man's labor.

"At the same time, the Friends of Man, who had been present here even before man came to be, came from the lands up north to stand with them, to protect the Beacon in the upcoming conflict.

"The Unnatural Darkness had sent Entrioch, said originally be a powerful servant of the Friends of Man, once known as a slim and beautiful youth who taught cultivation secrets to the first Sects. His techniques are supposedly the foundation of the ancient First Fist Sect today.

"But after he was betrayed by the Diamond Fist, the first human here to ascend to Diamond Rank, he become corrupted and found abode with the Unnatural Darkness. Man thought he had disappeared forever. When he reappeared during the siege of Teer, he had taken the form of a monster.

"A giant demon. Three cruel horns adorned his skull. Fang-like tusks emerged from his mouth. He had two extra fingers on each hand, and they ended in sharp claws that could rend mountains.

"He could slaughter dozens of men with one swipe of his war club, a weapon forged from iron that was the length of several trees. It was studded on one end, and Entrioch used it to smash and break even the strongest cultivators with a savage ferocity.

"When the unnatural armies came for the Beacon, the alliance of men and the friends who aided them met them outside the city.

"There was fear at the sight of Entrioch, who smashed his way through the defense walls, leaving a trail of horror and rubble as he headed straight for the Beacon.

"All was thought lost, that the Unnatural Darkness would destroy the light and cast the world into a void, but the Diamond Fist appeared and met Entrioch in combat.

"It's said their battle lasted seven days and seven nights, the Diamond Fist luring Entrioch out of the city, where they fought to the land and also to the sky.

"Some say it was their battle that formed the Burning Plateau and the Charred Mountain Range.

"But Entrioch, aided by Nether Realm sorcery, had gained an advantage over the Diamond Fist and was on the precipice of finishing him when Ianthe appeared out of the sky and met Entrioch with a savagery that put fear into the dark heart of man's enemy."

Ilyawraith walked to the wall and ran her fingers along the bone protruding from the ice.

"They say Ianthe was the first mobile form to emerge from the art of Marrow Eating. She was a disciple of the Diamond Fist and had consumed a rare Delicacy called Scale of the Forlorn, activating this first mobile skill tree.

"She spent a lifetime consuming specific Marrows to augment her form and her powers, only ever to be used when Entrioch was on the verge of killing her master.

"Their fight had only lasted a day, but it contained all the ferocity and more of the previous seven days.

"Entrioch, weakened in his battle with the Diamond Fist, summoned aid.

"Nine Nether Realm Entrophists came from the under-realm, practitioners of anti-cultivation."

"*Anti-cultivators?*" Nay said.

"They gain power through anti-life," Quincy said. "They feed on souls sent to the Nether Realm to perish. They're not easily attainable; the practitioners debase themselves and will do anything to gain access to the souls."

"The battle between Ianthe, Diamond Fist, and Entrioch and the Entrophists reshaped the world," Ilyawraith said. "It was cataclysmic in scale and shifted the very nature of this planet. It caused storms and floods, and the devastation effected generations."

"They say Diamond Fist sacrificed himself to destroy the Entrophists. There are even some Loremasters who believe that this event was the spark that created the Scar.

"Ianthe carried Entrioch to the firmament, to the stars, where her final attack, all the Vigor essence she had left in her, was released. They both perished to each other's final blows. The shockwave of Vigor and anti-life shook the heavens. The outpouring, had it happened down here, would have resulted in untold destruction that would have left our world in total ruin.

"She fell from the firmament, her lifeless form crashing into the Caraxe Sea, bringing the cold of the outer darkness where the stars dwell with her. The cold spreading from her body froze the very ocean.

"And here her bones have remained, preserved in time and ice."

Nay's Second Trial, or lesson, was to be somewhere on land, a place Ilyawraith called the Frozen Vale.

They were flying on an eddy of snow and wind, Ilyawraith's preferred mode of transportation.

Nay hugged her instructor, her arms wrapped around her waist and her hands interlocked in a steel grip.

"It is okay if you let go of me," Ilyawraith said. "Or at least not hold me so tight. Even though I am Silver Rank, I still need to breathe."

The cook squinted her eyes in the rushing atmosphere of cloud mist, wind, and snow. She caught a glimpse of the geography below them racing by. The frozen and shattered sea was covered in a blizzard. They flew above the storm.

Nay was terrified she was going to be swept off this carpet ride, where the carpet was swirling snow and a blast of wind. That she would disappear in the atmosphere and turn to ice.

"I trust you," Nay said, "but at the same time, I don't know if I believe you."

"I would think by now that we would be past your fear of my intentions," Ilyawraith said.

"And what would those be?"

"To awaken your True Eye so you can truly see the world around you."

"Yeah, that's not necessary. I have an interface for that."

"Pupils of the Banshee Sect do not rely on cheats. We cultivate technique, not shortcuts."

The Frozen Vale was a large valley in the Spineshard Mountains that was once home to a city of men, but now it was just stone ruins mostly covered in ice and snow. A haunting wind moved through the remains of the temple Nay found herself in.

Ilyawraith had brought them here, to the remnants of a sacred place next to a now-frozen lake.

The vestiges of all the pillars made Nay think of being in a forest full of nothing but dead trees.

"Look up *desolate* in the dictionary and it shows you a picture of this place," Nay said.

Ilyawraith showed no sign of amusement.

"Look around you," she said.

"That's what I'm doing," Nay said.

"Do you not see them?"

"See what?"

"Your Elseworlder interface isn't showing you?"

Nay, now concerned, checked her HUD. There were no incoming prompts, and there was nothing of note on her mini-map. She looked around her and saw nothing but the cracked and crumbling stone pillars and the snow drifting between them.

"A cultivator must be able to see the traces of Vigor around them," Ilyawraith said. "They must use the True Eye."

"What's that?"

"Just as you have veins within you that are capable of cycling Vigor, you also have a True Eye that can see the Vigor around you. It can see between the material plane and the spiritual."

"Yeah, the last time I checked, I have nothing like that."

"When you were trapped in the seawater, learning the Spirit Song, didn't you see and sense the Vigor in the water?"

Nay realized she had. But her eyes had been closed. She thought that was just a vision, or a hallucination, seeing the globules of Vigor floating in the water. "I did. But I don't know how. I was focusing on my breathing, and they just appeared."

Ilyawraith didn't say anything. But there was a half-smile at the corner of her lips.

"All around us now," Ilywraith said, "flying and flitting between these pillars, are the vigama."

"Vig . . . vigama?"

"They're spirit creatures, the manifestation of Vigor," Ilyawraith said.

"They're all around us? *Right now?*" Nay said. She looked around, skeptical, not seeing any sign of them.

The cultivator nodded. "They can only be seen through the True Eye."

Ilyawraith produced an object from her pack that reminded Nay of a butterfly catcher. Then she took out a lidded glass jar. She held them out for Nay.

"What's this?"

"When you catch five vigama, then you can leave the Frozen Vale."

"*What?*"

Ilyawraith put the items in her hand.

An eddy of snow began forming around her feet, and she stepped onto it.

"You're just going to leave me here?" Nay said.

"I'll come back once you've completed the task," Ilyawraith said. The eddy floated into the air, and she rose with it.

"What if I'm not able to catch them?" Nay said. She panicked. "Then what? You're gonna abandon me out here?"

Ilyawraith just looked down her nose at her as she rose into the moonlit sky, snowdrifts blowing past her.

"How will you know?" Nay said. She shouted. "How will you know when I've caught them?!"

The leader of the Banshee Sect disappeared into the sky, riding the wind and snow.

— CHAPTER FORTY-FIVE —

The Second Trial: True Eye

Nay stood there in the snow-swept temple ruins with the jar in one hand and the net in the other. Her interface chimed with incoming notifications. She accessed the HUD.

[Quest Detected]
[Quest: Open the True Eye]
[Accept Quest Y/N?]

[Quest Detected]
[Quest: Catch 5 Vigama]
[Accept Quest Y/N?]

She sighed and accepted the quests. *I'd rather be back in the kitchen right now*, she thought. She wondered how Nom and Gracie were handling things back at the Lodge.

"So, I'm supposed to catch something I can't even see," Nay said.

She walked forward, stepping deeper into the roofless temple. All of the pillars were like trees that had their tops sliced off, ascending towards the sky and then just ending in crumbled stumps.

She tried to divine what Ilyawraith had called the vigama, but she saw nothing. She looked out into the surroundings outside of the temple.

There were maimed and disfigured statues, missing limbs, faces gone or weathered by time and the elements to the point where they just looked like scoured rock.

Nay sat down on the stone floor, setting the jar next to her, the net draped across her lap.

She thought about sensing the globules of Vigor when she was trapped in the seawater tomb. She had seen them. But her eyes had been closed because she was focused on her breathing.

That was it, she thought.

So, she closed her eyes and settled into the rhythm of the Spirit Song technique. She could sense her veins wanting more Vigor. They reached out, and she could feel herself inhaling the Vigor in the air around her, and she began cycling it through her vein pathways.

She saw the globules of glowing Vigor in the air then.

And then she saw them.

At first, she thought they were birds. But they glowed. They were bluish-white spirits flitting back and forth on fairy wings. They had ovoid-shaped bodies and faces that looked like ghost masks. There were two big dark circles as eyes and a much smaller one as the mouth. The effect was that of a face that had a perpetual surprised expression.

They looked pretty cute and innocent.

As Nay cycled the Vigor, she opened her eyes and realized she could still see the spirits.

"The vigama," she said. "I can see the vigama."

There didn't seem to be a lot of them, but she saw a few in the temple with her. They were lackadaisically hovering back and forth in little paths. They were outside, too. She saw them hovering over the frozen lake as if they were winter fireflies.

[Quest Complete!]
[Open the True Eye Quest Completed!]
[Congratulations!]
[You have been rewarded Vigor Points]

Above her she saw a line of vigama corkscrewing out of the sky. Except these seemed a bit different.

They were flying fast; in fact, they were rocketing towards her. And instead of a bluish-white, they were more of a gold color. As they got closer, she flinched and covered her face with her arms, but the vigama flew into her torso.

Then they were gone.

She didn't feel any pain. Just the usual feeling she got when she completed a quest, a slight rush that she had always just attributed to dopamine hits.

Wait a minute; did the vigama have something to do with Vigor Points?

She accessed her interface.

Vigor Rank: Base
Status to Iron: 69%

The vigama *were* Vigor Points. That meant each time she completed a quest and was rewarded with the points, vigama had flown into her from some mysterious Quest-Giver in the sky.

And although her interface was able to update her on her Vigor percentage, she hadn't been able to see the vigama because her True Eye hadn't been opened.

Now that it was, she could now observe the relationship Vigor had with this world. She saw not only the vigama but the globules of Vigor flowing through pathways in the trees, the frozen water, and in the wind.

For the first time since she had gotten here, she felt as if she was truly seeing it for the first time. There was a strange, mesmerizing beauty to it.

"All right," Nay said. "This cold is getting old. Let's work on getting out of here."

She grabbed the jar and approached the vigama nearest to her. She watched its flight pattern. It seemed to be on its own little patrol, always flying out to the same place, then turning around and coming back.

It was a loop.

So, she positioned herself at one of its turning points. She readied her net on its stick and waited for the vigama to make its way back.

As it slowly flew towards her, it didn't seem to notice her presence. If it did, perhaps it didn't care.

This is going to be easy.

Right as it turned around, she swiped the net through the air and the thing zipped off, emitting a chirp and a high-pitched mew.

The net was empty.

Nay blinked and watched the vigama race away, disappearing amongst the pillars.

"Okay, so, that's how it's gonna be," Nay said.

Two Dexterity Biscuits appeared in her hand out of her inventory. "You want to go fast, let's go fast."

She began eating.

Nay crouched near a pillar, waiting for a different vigama to fly near her.

This time, she didn't miss. She swept the net through the air, moving swifter than normal, having stacked Dexterity as much as she could from her food.

It was fast enough to catch the vigama. She felt resistance as it started thrashing like a fish in a net.

It let out singsong mews and chirps that melted Nay's heart.

"Aw, I'm sorry, little guy," Nay said. "I'm not gonna hurt you. I promise. I just need you in this jar so the crazy lady can come back and take me somewhere warm. That's understandable, right?"

She opened the jar and pushed the opening into the net. The vigama flew in, and Nay quickly covered the jar with the lid.

[Quest Log]
[Catch 5 Vigama]
[1/5]

She held the jar up, casting her face in a bluish-white glow from the vigama inside. It seemed to decrease in size a little. It flew slowly around the jar, chirping.

She had an idea then.

I wonder if I can absorb it like the vigama that represent Vigor Points.

She concentrated on her breathing, falling into the rhythm. She began to sing her Spirit Song as she focused on the technique.

She reached a hand into the jar, and the vigama landed on her palm. She took it out of the jar and the vigama mewed at her song. Then it flew into her chest.

She felt that dopamine hit, and she looked to see if she had gained any Vigor.

Vigor Rank: Base
Status to Iron: 69%

So, no uptick yet.

It probably took a bunch of them to see a change in the status.

Also, these vigama probably weren't worth as much Vigor as the golden vigama she got from completing quests.

Interesting, she thought.

She set to collecting more of the blue vigama so she could complete this quest and get out of here.

She was putting the fourth vigama in the jar with the others, where it bumped into its chirping comrades before settling into its own flight path, when she noticed something strange near the frozen lake.

She had left the temple and wandered towards the lake as she hunted vigama in the snow amongst the razed statues.

There was a stone bench near the snow-covered shore of the lake, and it appeared as if someone was sitting there with their back to her.

In the time she had been here, she hadn't heard or seen anyone except the vigama. She looked around and didn't see anyone else. She wasn't sure what to do.

If this person was dangerous, she might either be fighting or running for her life.

So, she could back away and try to find a vigama on the other side of the temple and hope that Ilyawraith would come soon after.

Or she could try and talk to the person.

She was trying to make her decision when the voice interrupted her own thought process.

"It's cold here, isn't it?" the figure on the bench said, still with their back to her. There was a melancholy tone to the voice.

"You're a mysterious stranger and you're really gonna open with a comment about the weather?" Nay said.

"You're as much a mystery to me as I must be to you."

Nay cautiously approached the bench but kept her distance. She made sure she was off to the side and not directly behind this person.

When she got parallel, she looked over to get a glimpse of the person.

It was a guy who looked like he was in his twenties. He was rake-thin with skin the color of a pale moon. Which is to say there was a silver glow to his white skin. His black hair was scraggly and dark as night, as if someone had teased not hair but the void itself.

Nay could tell when he stood, he would be tall. He was wearing a black cloak as dark and as shimmering as his hair.

When he looked at her, she couldn't tell if his eyes were blue or silver. They reminded her of the stars.

"Collecting bugs, are you?" the man said.

Nay looked at the jar of vigama in her hand.

"Something like that," Nay said. "But I doubt they like to be called bugs."

He seemed amused by that.

"I remember when this place wasn't so cold," he said.

"You do?"

"It was still cold," he said. "But its bite was nothing like this. The pupils of the Snow Sage practiced their techniques all along the shore here. The water wasn't frozen then. It was full of fish."

"Who are you?"

"I'm just a wanderer," he said. "Perhaps not so much different from you."

"I thought I was a mystery to you."

He looked at her again and then scooted over on the bench.

"Would you like to sit?" he said.

She looked at the space on the bench next to him. Although he was beautiful and she was intrigued, there was something unsettling about the man. She didn't trust him.

"I think I'm good right here," she said.

"Apologies," he said. "I can see my presence disquiets you."

He stood up, his black starry cloak billowed around his rapier-thin form. Nay was right. He was tall. Well over six feet.

"Forgive me," he said. "You take the bench. I'll stand."

He walked away from the bench, giving her space. He stood in the snow and stared out at the frozen lake.

This gesture surprised her, and she felt awkward. She didn't know what to do, but she found herself walking slowly to the bench anyways. She sat down, on the farthest end from him, but didn't look away from him.

His eyes in the dark sockets of his face seemed to twinkle like stars.

"There are other paths," he said.

"Excuse me?"

"There are other paths if you don't like the one you're on."

"And what path am I on?"

"*Cultivation.*" He sneered at the word.

"And how do you know that?"

He nodded at the jar of vigama. "You're not collecting those just to have a pretty bauble to light up your room when it's dark, are you?"

"You know, I think I'm gonna leave," Nay said. She stood up. "This conversation is getting a little weird."

At that, he crouched and touched the snow with two fingers. A starry pool of darkness formed in the snow, and black veins spread out from the pool.

Something dark began growing out of the snow. There was a shoot and black vines crawling out of the frozen ground.

It was a black rose.

It crinkled as the buds finished blossoming. Ice crystals speckled the petals.

He plucked it from the ground and held it out to her.

Part of her wanted to run, but she couldn't resist.

She cautiously stepped towards him and reached for the black rose.

He handed it to her and stepped away.

She looked at the rose, and the black petals seemed to swirl with stars, as if she was looking at a galaxy on the surface. The pistils in the center of the rose were purple.

When she looked back up, the strange man was gone, leaving her at the frozen lake by herself with the haunting wind whistling around the half-formed statues around her with a black rose in her hand.

— CHAPTER FORTY-SIX —

Doomheart

Nay had hidden the black rose from the strange man inside one of the inner pockets of her cloak. Her arms were wrapped around Ilyawraith as the eddy of snow carried them across the frigid sky.

The Wraith of the Moving Ice never asked about the man Nay had met. Nay wondered if she even knew of their meeting. She had known when she had collected the fifth vigama. Her teacher had shown up shortly after she saw the prompt on her interface.

[Quest Complete!]
[Catch 5 Vigama Completed!]
[Congratulations!]
[You have been rewarded Vigor Points]

Again, more golden vigama had descended out of the sky and flown into her, merging into her veins. Then the rush of dopamine indicating her Vigor was upticking again.

Somehow, Ilyawraith had known when she had caught all the vigama. Maybe she had put an enchantment on the jar or something that notified her when it was full. Was it possible her teacher was watching her?

Yet Ilyawraith didn't seem to know about her odd meeting with the man with void-black hair and starry eyes. Did the man have powerful magic to cloak his presence?

These were the thoughts tumbling around in Nay's head when they arrived at the iceberg, flying into the eye-socket cavern of Ianthe.

Quincy had done some ice-fishing while Nay was chasing around vigama in the Frozen Vale. There was a special area near the bottom of the berg where fishing holes had been cut out of the ice. He had placed his catch in a pool that was towards the back of the hearth chamber, where Ilyawraith kept her seafood alive and fresh.

"Let's see what you brought to me," Ilyawraith said, walking over to the pool. She pointed at each one. "Sanguine salmon. Icestone tuna. And some Darkfall yellowtail. Very nice, Quincy. I'll make a fisherman out of you yet."

"There's something peaceful about ice-fishing," Quincy said. "I can enjoy the silence without having to relive all the mistakes I've made in my head. Maybe I need to get out here more often."

Nay glanced at Quincy.

What does he mean by that? Mistakes he's made?

"If you do that, you better make sure you're never followed," Ilyawraith said. "Otherwise, I'll have to find a new place to live."

"Only a madman would come to the Caraxe Strait."

"It's the madmen that concern me," Ilyawraith said. "Especially the ones with long memories."

"They're too concerned with their politics and scheming and backstabbing on the Peninsula. The Ligeia families are too busy dealing with each other to worry about a hermit. The Grand Chessboard requires blind obsession."

"Maybe so. But the Orsonnen family does not forget."

Nay fixed herself a cup of pink coral tea and sat in front of the blue flames, warming herself. The tea was soothing, and she could sense a saltiness to it, which made her think of a good broth.

But yet it had the lightness and astringency of a pleasant green tea.

The brew method still consisted of steeping the tea in hot water, but instead of actual leaves or plant matter and herbs, it was more like mixing the water with a matcha-like substance derived from the coral. It was a pink, chalky powder.

Ilyawraith used a net to collect the fish for their meal. She bled and gutted them and packed them in ice.

Nay had dozed off, lying in front of the fire. She awoke to the sound of a spoon stirring liquid in a bowl.

Ilyawraith had a pot of rice made. Nay sat up and saw that she was stirring a sauce. She sniffed and could smell the vinegar in the air. She had probably combined it with sugar and salt to make a rice vinegar.

Her teacher had orange-pink, red-orange, and pink cubes of fish flesh sitting on the table.

Sushi!

Ilyawraith poured the vinegar mixture into her bowl of rice and started mixing it, making sure to get the vinegar on every single grain.

Nay wiped the sleep from her eyes and observed Ilyawraith assembling the rolls. She took a sheet of nori, laid it out on the table, and started scooping the rice onto the sheet.

Of course she has nori, Nay thought. *She's using dried seaweed as foot mats in this place.*

Next, Ilyawraith picked up her knife. The handle looked like it was made out of yellow coral. She began carving slashes of sanguine salmon. She placed them on top of the rice and then rolled it all together.

She even had a makisu, the woven mat to shape the roll. It didn't look like bamboo, though, but some other type of dried plant matter.

It was calming to watch her work. When she was done, she cut the rolls of sanguine salmon, icestone tuna, and Darkfall yellowtail and put them on a platter of ice.

They were all eating in front of the blue hearth.

Nay looked at her plate of sushi in awe. There was even some type of fermented sauce she could use for dipping. She dipped a pinkie finger in; she guessed it was salty like soy sauce, but the color was more of a light caramel. But it served the same purpose.

She picked up a piece of the sanguine salmon and was blown away by the striations of color on the meat. She took a bite and was hit with how fresh it was. Because of her taste buds, she couldn't appreciate it fully. But she knew this straddled that line between fishiness and vinegary tartness that all good sushi had.

If she ever wanted to cry because of her ruined taste buds, now was an appropriate time.

But she did enjoy how soft and pleasing the texture was. There was the crunch of the nori and the vinegary chewiness of the rice. Together, it was all the perfect bite.

There was no talking for a few minutes, as all of them were enjoying their food too much.

One doesn't simply interrupt the sacred moment between an eater and a tasty bite prepared expertly and with love.

Nay waited for Ilyawraith to finish before she spoke. "I didn't know this world had sushi."

"Sushi?" Ilyawraith said.

"Yeah, this dish," Nay said. "Fish and rice, as you prepared it."

"I've always just known it as hapan kalasta. Sour rice and fish."

"Oh, in my world we call it sushi."

Nay was struck with a stray thought then. On her interface, whenever Quincy appeared in the quest logs, the first time being the boss battle with the Nether Sister, his name had appeared as—

[Quincy the Doomhearted]

"Quincy," Nay said. "I have a question."

He was eating his sushi with laser focus. As if the only things that existed in the world were him and his Darkfall yellowtail roll. He merely grunted at Nay's voice and took another bite.

"Why are you called the Doomhearted?"

Quincy and Ilyawraith both stopped chewing and looked at her. Then they glanced at each other.

Quincy swallowed, pulled out of his special moment with the sushi. "Where did you hear that?"

"It's on my interface," Nay said. "That's how you're named, 'Quincy the Doomhearted.' Plus, I heard you call yourself that when we first got here."

"It's kind of heavy conversation while we eat," Ilyawraith said.

Quincy brushed flecks of rice from his mustache. "It's okay."

He set his plate next to him and wiped rice vinegar off his hands with a cloth. He got up, walked over to Ilyawraith's wine rack, and selected a green bottle of mead. He popped it open and guzzled.

When he was done, he rubbed his mouth with the back of his hand and sat down. When he finally spoke, his voice was unnaturally quiet. "My sister and I didn't come from noble blood. Far from it."

He looked into the blue fire, the flames reflecting in his pupils as he visited the past.

"We were the children of a blacksmith. We were able to become Marrow Eaters because we had enlisted in the Ligeia military and we had both risen through the ranks, becoming officers. The military was the only viable option for us to increase our social standing, because we could attain titles through service and deeds. Once we became officers, we earned the right to become Marrow Eaters through the DMA.

"After our shining service in the Ligeia League, Quella and I took two different paths. As a Marrow Eater, she had taken skill trees that veered her towards the study of stealth and assassination. She became a valuable member of the Thieves' Guild.

"Me? I became an adventurer. I craved the rush of taking monster contracts and hunting for Delicacy and Marrow. While I was making a name for myself with my party, Quella was becoming something of a feared name in the criminal underworld of the city-states on the Peninsula, specifically in Delicatessa and San Violeta.

"If you were an individual with some considerable coin and you wanted someone dead, and I mean guaranteed dead, no mess-ups, then you hired Il Fantasma, the name of an assassin spoken in whispers within the Thieves Guild and the criminal underworld."

"That was Quella," Nay said. "Il Fantasma."

Quincy nodded. The blue hearth crackled, the only noise in the silence, save for the echoing drip of water.

"My sister was stubborn. And passionate. When she wanted something, there was no talking her out of it. She was hard-headed and we had a lot of fights because of it.

"So, there was no convincing her that having an affair with Prince Furio was a bad idea. She was going to continue her romance with one of the most powerful people in San Violeta. The Furios were the family in control of the city. They represented San Violeta in the Ligeia League.

"It was only a matter of time before his wife discovered her husband's indiscretion. In response, Lady Vittoria sent all of the assassins under the employ of the Furio family after my sister.

"'The Fall of Il Fantasma' is a well-known modern tale in the Ligeia League. But my sister didn't go down without a fight. She killed six Bronze Rank Marrow Eaters in a fight that destroyed the canal district of San Violeta.

"But in the end, there were too many of them and they overwhelmed her.

"Lady Vittoria had Quella's head on display in front of Palazzo Furio for a day. But her husband, grief-stricken and still in love with my sister, had it and the pike it sat on taken down."

Quincy took another swig from the bottle. His eyes glistened with tears. Then his face hardened and he continued.

"I went to great lengths to get the one Delicacy I knew would be appropriate for my revenge."

"The Bile of the Plaguemonger," Nay said.

"There were rumors of a horrific calamity that befell the island of Vynia, that a terrible plague had run through most of the population, and sailors were warned to stay away from the island. I paid a Seer, one who had the power to observe and see and spy on places far away, to tell me what she saw.

"The cause of the plague was a man who had come to the island, a man who had the power to spread disease. He didn't even have to draw weapons or raise his fists to take over the island. Once one person got sick, it ran through the whole population. A terrible affliction of fever, exploding boils, and blood rot.

"This man made his dwelling in the deceased governor's mansion.

"I pled my case to my adventuring party, and they agreed to make him our next job.

"Half of my adventuring party died helping me take down the Plaguemonger, an Entrophist from the Phantomhead Empire, a land far from here to the south on another continent. He had come to Vynia because of some slight one of their diplomats made to him while in the Phantomhead.

"The fight . . . is not something I will ever forget. Fighting and killing monsters requires courage. But fighting and killing another person requires . . . sometimes it can require a part of your soul. It was easy for me, though, after seeing what he had done to the people of Vynia. And my heart was willing to do anything to avenge Quella.

"When the Entrophist was dead, I butchered him for the Delicacy. I bribed an Epicurist to prepare and activate it for me. He made the Bile into a red sauce I ate over a culotte, a cut severed from the cap of beef sirloin. It was Ignatius beef, extremely expensive. It was cooked on a grill over winterwood and seasoned with Vancian salt.

"It was one of the most delicious steaks I ever had.

"With the Delicacy acquired and consumed, I took the remainder of the coin I had accumulated over decades of soldiering and adventuring, and I hired the most-skilled and most-sadistic mercenaries I could find from the Company of the Black Rose."

Nay sucked in her breath at that phrase and thought of the rose tucked into the inner pocket of her cloak.

"We infiltrated Palazzo Furio during the Feast of San Violetta del Carro. Dispatching the guards was easier than I thought. I infected the first one I cut down with Gertrude. The plague spread through his comrades with surprising speed.

"By the time we were shedding blood in the dining hall, the disease and sickness I wrought spread through the Furio family, their servants, and their friends with a shocking celerity.

"Imagine that in one moment you're feasting, and the next you're being attacked by Marrow Eater mercenaries of the Black Rose. Perhaps it was overkill to rub unholy disease into their wounds.

"I killed Lady Vittoria with no hesitation or remorse. She tried to beg for her life, but I swung Gertrude before she could make her appeal. I felt no satisfaction watching her head roll down the stairs of the Palazzo Furio dining hall.

"I let her husband live. It wasn't his fault that my sister chose to love him. I watched him trip on the stairs in his wife's freshly spilled blood. He scrambled out of the hall, all dignity absent, and that's the last I ever saw of him.

"As I went to step out of the hall and leave the Palazzo, a woman's voice begged for my attention. It was Duchess Strega, Lady Vittoria's mother.

"She said, 'I curse you! I put a curse upon you for this pox you put on my family. As long as you wield your axe, as long as you wield your bow, you will be known as the Doomhearted! Your heart a day closer to death for every life you take! For each life you steal, you will be robbed of yours! Now go, Doomheart, go and take death with you!'"

"She died then, succumbing to the plague that moved through her body, turning her organs to soup."

He finished the bottle of mead.

"It's funny," Quincy said. "I think she pulled it off. Because whenever I wield Samuel and Gertrude, whenever I take a life, my heart flutters. Like a wounded bird."

— CHAPTER FORTY-SEVEN —

Then It's Iron I'll Be

Nay held Thorn in her hands, admiring the craftsmanship of the blade. But she was also marveling at the fact it was one of Quella's weapons.

Il Fantasma.

This dagger was a relic from a feared assassin. How many lives had it taken? At least six that were mentioned in Quincy's tale.

She saw the Lodge owner in a different light now. She understood why a man from the Peninsula would move to the edge of the world to run an inn and tavern, now.

It was his way of distancing himself from his past.

Why in the world had he given her his sister's blade? she thought. *I can't live up to her legacy. This belongs in the hands of someone capable. I'm just a chef.*

"Make sure you get some rest tonight," Ilyawraith said.

Nay looked up and saw that her teacher had come back to the hearth. Quincy was already sleeping in his bed.

"Another trial?" Nay said. "What am I learning this time?"

"Tomorrow, you either get to Iron Rank . . ."

"Or?"

". . . or you die."

Nay got up before everyone else and stood in the eye socket of Ianthe, looking out over the Caraxe Strait. It was a frozen wasteland. Sea spray immediately turned to icy mist in the still-dark air. The promise of the sunrise was to the east, a corona of purple light on the horizon.

"There you are."

Nay turned to see Quincy. He was holding two cups of tea. He handed her one and leaned against the orbital wall and shared the view with her.

"The Moving Ice," Quincy said. "Just when you thought we had it cold in Stitchdale, there's this cursed sea."

Nay took a sip of her tea. There was a kick to it she didn't recognize.

"It's bloodrush tea," Quincy said. "It'll get your blood flowing and keep you alert through the rest of the day."

"Guess I'm gonna need it."

"Aye, that you are."

"Why did you give me your sister's dagger?"

"What do you mean?"

"This is a relic of someone great. Wouldn't you rather have it under safekeeping?"

"Not much use in safekeeping. It's meant to be wielded."

"Quincy, I hate to break it to you, but I'm just a chef."

He turned to her then and looked her in the eye. His solemn sincerity disarmed her.

"You were never just a chef, not even in your previous life. We aren't just what our jobs are. We are trees with many branches. Being a chef is just one of your branches. Here, in my world, if you want to survive, you have to strengthen yourself."

"What about the normal people? People like Gracie or Bryja or Alric? They seem to survive just fine."

His voice lowered. Nay almost mistook it for anger. It wasn't anger. It was gravitas.

"You don't get it, girl. Those people have people like me watching over them. They have everyone at Fort Nixxiom trying to protect them from forces that mean them harm. The Base Rank people on the Peninsula? Their life is one of hardship and toil and unfair treatment by those who lord over them."

He put his scar-covered hand on her shoulder then. It radiated strength. And love.

"So, understand this now. You have the capability in you to protect the normal folk too. I see it in you. Nether hells, girl, you've already done it whether you realize it or not! Because of what you can do, the cook, the sous-chef, the farmer, the gardener, the librarian, even the miners and the lumberjacks, they may be able to live because you can be one of the guardians that's willing to stand for them and defend that which is good in this world."

Nay was stunned by his earnest conviction. She didn't know how to respond and stammered something incoherent.

"So, Thorn belongs to you now. Yeah?"

Nay clenched her jaw and nodded.

He turned to leave and then stopped. His jaw tightened. "I'm not going to tell you goodbye, because the next time I see you, you'll be an Iron."

He left her then, heading back into the iceberg. She watched him disappear on the decline as it curved out of sight.

She finished her tea, staring over the ominous wasteland of moving ice.

"Then it's Iron I'll be."

Ilyawraith took Nay to the north this time, flying deeper into the Caraxe Strait on her eddy of snow. The more distance they crossed, the darker it seemed to get. The light seemed to be blotted out here by the gray clouds and white mist.

When they began to descend, passing through the cloud cover, a treacherous ice island emerged into view. There were pillars of ice formations shooting into the sky like the fingers of a frozen god, and there were sharp contrasts in elevation.

It was as if two glaciers careened into each other, rupturing the surface into crags, peaks, and deadly chasms.

"Today, you learn about Beast Cores," Ilyawraith said, turning her head back at her.

"Beast Cores?"

"There are some creatures who also practice cultivation. Their Vigor amasses inside their bodies. This is their Core. So, when you slay them, you can take the Core and absorb it into your veins, thus gaining their Vigor. Cores can provide considerable upticks in your cultivation process."

They landed on the desolate frozen island then. Nay looked around. They had landed in a small valley next to a steep crag. Everything was dark blue. The place was empty.

"There's a beast who rules this glacier, an ice troll," Ilyawraith said. "Slay him. Your True Eye will reveal his Core. Absorbing it should get you to Iron Rank. If that's not enough, there are other creatures here you can hunt."

[Quest Detected]
[Quest: Slay Caraxus the Ice Troll]
[Accept Quest Y/N?]

[Quest Detected]
[Quest: Slay Ice Imps and Collect their Cores]
[Accept Quest Y/N?]

Nay accepted the quests. Already she was jittery with nerves.

Nay had an idea. "Can someone rank by just purchasing and absorbing Cores? Without having to do the heavy lifting of, you know, defeating the actual beasts themselves?"

Ilyawraith nodded. "There will always be those looking for the easiest and quickest route to ascendance. While they may seem impressive to non–Marrow Eaters and those still at Base Rank, boosters are frowned upon by real cultivators. They don't measure up compared to those with foundation and technique, who have bled to earn their Vigor. In my opinion, they are all cowards. Children who have no idea how to properly use their Vigor reserves or abilities."

"So, what you're saying is that's not an option for me."

Ilyawraith shook her head.

"Now show me the items in your inventory," she said.

"Really?" Nay said.

Ilyawraith waited.

She started by showing her the magical biscuits imbued with the various Buffs.

"I'm not interested in your Epicurist food," Ilyawraith said. "Those are things you have the Ability to make. I want to see any trinkets or boons you might have that you're not telling me about."

Reluctantly, Nay sighed and then pulled out Mirkwood's Eye and the seashell Lain had given her, the Nautilus of Teleportation.

Ilyawraith examined the eye and the seashell. There was no curiosity in her face. Her manner was all brass tacks. She pocketed both trinkets.

"Seriously?" Nay said.

"Iron Rank must be earned through your own ability and ingenuity," Ilyawraith said. "That is the way of the Banshee Sect." Then her face softened a bit. "You'll get them back when you're Iron."

"*If* I'm an Iron," Nay said. She looked down at the ice beneath her boots, hugging herself in the cold wind.

"I'm afraid there is no *if*. Either you are Iron, or the ice troll will be absorbing *your* Core."

An eddy of snow corkscrewed out of the sky, and Ilyawraith stepped on it.

"I will return on the next sunrise. I hope to find you here."

After she watched her teacher vanish into the mist, Nay said, "So, I have to survive the next twenty-four hours on a frozen rock in the middle of the most dangerous sea ever. Got it."

She wished Nom was with her so they could both complain and make dumb jokes in the face of almost-certain death.

Nay figured the first correct play was doing some reconnaissance. If there was an ice troll on this island who wanted to kill her and eat her energy, then she wanted to find him first and at least gain the element of surprise.

As she picked a direction towards the center of the island, she accessed her mini-map. It showed the peaks and dips of the island and the chasms nearby her.

Upon her next step, a red glowing dot appeared on the mini-map. It appeared to be in a cave towards the northern side near her.

That's gotta be it.

She followed the crag where it opened up to an incline of slippery, mountainous terrain. Her nagaskin boots were doing her well on the ice, so that was some good fortune at least.

She had the feeling something was watching her, and she looked behind her. There was nothing there but the falling snow.

She had begun her ascent on the incline when a frigid cold took her breath away. She gasped and noticed she was suddenly inside a stream of frost. She could feel the hair on her skin begin to crystallize, and her lungs went tight as the cold stole her breath.

Her instincts told her to pick a direction and roll, and that's what she did.

She came out of the roll and was wracked with violent shivers. She discovered she had stepped out of a cone of rushing cold air.

Its source was the shape of a head pressed into the wall of the crag. The ice cracked and a shape pulled itself from the wall.

The creature began to glow the blue of the glacier, and it seemed to be some sort of winged homunculus composed of ice. Almost like a sentient ice sculpture. It was only about three feet tall, but the claws on its two hands tapered into ultra-sharp icicles, its teeth a frozen bear trap. Its eyes shone with an ice-blue sentience and malevolence.

It was an ice imp.

It flew at her, a gargoyle of ice. Its claw slashed through the sleeves of her tunic and the skin beneath, drawing blood.

Nay screamed and drew Thorn, lunging at the impish ice elemental. The blade chipped its torso and it snarled, flying past her.

It began to circle her, and she turned with it, not taking her eyes off the thing.

It inhaled and exhaled more frost breath at her. She rolled again, staying away from the cold. She knew if she stood in it too long, it would give her frostbite, if not render her unconscious and frozen.

As it continued to circle her, she got an idea. She'd wait for it to fly at her again.

And it did, swiping its claws at her.

That's when she used her Chef's Thermometer Ability and conjured a ring of searing heat in front of it. It flew into the circle of raised temperature and shrieked.

One of its wings melted, and it crashed into the incline. Its ice form was turning to water, and it struggled to right itself, its skin sloughing off.

Nay rushed towards it, its head about knee level with her. She gripped Thorn and drove the skullcrusher into its face, shattering its head into slush.

There was a burst of blue light and the imp exploded, bathing Nay in slush and bits of hail-like ice.

She was certain if she hadn't blasted it with heat, that death-rattle burst would have been an explosion of shards of ice. A final attack in its death.

[Quest Complete!]
[Slay Ice Imps and Collect their Cores Quest Completed!]
[Congratulations!]
[You have been rewarded with Vigor Points]
[You have been rewarded with Ice Imp Core]
This is a repeatable Quest. Access the quest in your logs to accept.

Golden vigama raced out of the sky and flew into her chest.

She wiped the blue slush from her face and looked down at the glowing orb of Vigor at her feet.

The Core.

It was about the size of an apple and it shone a neon blue.

She exhaled and began cycling her Vigor. The Core grew brighter as her veins expanded, spiritually reaching out for the Core. She pushed it into her torso.

She staggered, the rush of dopamine almost rendering her horizontal. She put an arm against the icy incline and readied herself. Her veins expanded even more and they were filled with a burst of flowing Vigor.

It was like someone turned on a faucet inside her. She sat down and lay against the incline, letting the Vigor fill her.

Vigor Rank: Base
Status to Iron: 71%

— CHAPTER FORTY-EIGHT —

The Third Trial: Beast Core Tango

Nay was devouring the biscuits from her inventory to Buff her Strength, Dexterity, Stamina, and Spirit when she saw the red glowing dot on her mini-map begin to move.

Her mouth was dry like she had taken the Popeye's Biscuit Challenge and was seeing how long she could go without drinking anything. She opened her waterskin and guzzled, moistening her mouth with instant relief.

I have to adjust the recipe on these things so they're not so damn dry, Nay thought.

She set off towards the red dot on her mini-map, making her way across the terrain with caution. She kept low and studied the landscape and crag walls near her for the forms of ice imps, using the geography as camouflage.

Soon, she was descending down a slope and making her way into an ice dune. There were ice pillars, jagged ridges, and frozen sea spray. All in all, a turbulent topography frozen in place.

That's when she saw him.

Caraxus stood about eight feet tall. His limbs were long and muscular. His skin was the color of arctic ocean water, and white tusks curved out of his face. Long green hair fell onto his wide shoulders like kelp. He was clothed in sealskin, and there was a stone battle-axe on his back.

He stood on a ridge, studying the ocean. He sniffed at the air and turned to look behind him.

Nay stepped behind an ice column and held her breath, hoping that he didn't have some kind of super sniffer and had caught a whiff of her. She realized her hands were tightening into fists and she was clenching her jaw.

She made herself count to ten before she took another peek from behind the column.

At ten, she exhaled, then looked.

Caraxus's back was to her. He dove off the edge of the glacier into the sea.

Nay tracked the troll's movement on her mini-map. He hadn't gone far from the island, but he had dived below, heading deep into the water.

After a few minutes, he was ascending again.

Nay watched the edge of the glacier.

Caraxus burst out of the sea in an explosion of water and landed on the ice, a massive blue crab in his hands. The claws were the size of bulldozer buckets. They snapped at the air, trying to reach him. There was so much force powering the claws, it looked like they could cut a person in half with ease.

The ice troll spun and threw the giant crab like it was a discus. It smashed against a pillar of ice, cracking both the crab's shell and the ice structure. Ice crystals rained down on it.

The crab landed on its back, on its ruined shell, its pincer legs and claws pumping and snapping at the sky.

[Marrow Detected]
[Claw Meat Marrow of the Caraxian Crab]

There was a Marrow on that thing.

Caraxus swaggered to its prey, pulling the massive stone axe off its back. He swung, the stone blade bisecting the crab down the center in an explosion of juice and shell.

The thunderous crack of the axe splitting the crab and ice echoed across the island.

The troll crouched near the dying crab, waiting for its death throes to pass. After a few minutes, he picked up the halves of the crab, slung them over his back, and began the journey back to his cave.

Nay was pressed against her own pillar of ice, her back to it, hiding. She swallowed. "How am I supposed to fight *that?*"

As she obsessed over this thought, a prompt and chime interrupted her.

[Delicacy Detected]

"*What?*"

A gold dot appeared on her minimap. It was to the east, and according to the map, it wasn't on the island but in the water just off the island.

If it was a Delicacy that unlocked a martial or combat skill tree, then that was the answer to her problem. The plan formed in her head. She would go scout and see what the deal was with the Delicacy. Then she would acquire it, consume it, and hope the skill tree would be helpful when it came to slaying Caraxus.

She was getting up to head east when her mini-map pinged her. The red dot was right on top of her.

Caraxus emerged from behind the column of ice, leading with his swinging axe. The flat of the blade hit her in the face, and then there was darkness.

Nay awoke with her wrists and hands tied together. She was hanging sideways from the ceiling from hooks that were snagging the rope binding her wrists and ankles, embedded in the ice ceiling.

She was hanging with the rest of the food Caraxus had stored up here. The carcasses of giant fish, what looked like a skinned seal, and other oddities that he had caught in the cold sea.

Caraxus crouched near his campfire. He held Thorn, and in contrast to the size of his blue-skinned troll hand, it looked like its namesake for once.

"Very nice shiv," the troll said, his voice deep and guttural, a gravel baritone to it like crushed ice in a rock tumbler. Her Worldtripper Passive seemed to even translate troll. His gray eyes glanced up at Nay.

Next to him, Nay saw the halves of the giant blue crab. He had a cauldron over the fire. He was preparing to boil the crab meat.

"I could smell you before I hunt," he said. "You should have ran while you had chance. Now I save you for meals later."

"You've got me all wrong, Great One," Nay said.

Caraxus seemed startled by the way she addressed him. He cocked his head up at her, puzzled by the use of the honorary. "Great One?"

"I come here to your island to serve you," Nay said. She was taking a gamble with this approach, but she felt it was worth trying. She'd at least be able to back up her bluff.

"Serve Caraxus?" the troll said.

"Sure," Nay said. "You see, Great One, I am an Epicurist. I saw you catch that crab." She nodded at the halves of the shell. "And I'm here to tell you it contains a Marrow."

His gray eyes widened and he looked at bisected blue crab. "Marrow, you say? It is true?"

"I wouldn't lie to you," Nay said. "But if you want me to prepare and activate it so you may consume it and gain power, you should right this wrong and get me down from the ceiling. I know you didn't know I was an Epicurist, so I hold no ill will towards you."

The troll's eyes narrowed then and he stood to his full height. "How do I know you don't lie to Caraxus?"

"Tell you what," Nay said. "Let me down so I can cook for you. If you eat the Marrow and nothing happens, then you'll know I'm a liar. Then you can proceed to do what your previous plan with me was. You can eat me. That's simple and fair, right?"

"But if you are telling truth," the troll said, "I eat Marrow and I gain power. Then what Caraxus do with you?"

"I come here to serve," Nay said. "I'd be your Epicurist, so I could cook all your meals. And whenever you find more Marrow, you have your own personal chef who can activate it for you. You do realize you have a great deal here, right?"

"But why me?" Caraxus said. "Why you come all way out here? Middle of frozen ocean?"

He had her there. It made no sense why a human Epicurist would come out to a glacier way up north in the middle of the Caraxe Strait. A cook venturing out into an icy desolation? It made no sense unless the cook was committing suicide.

"Because Veritax sent me."

"Veritax?"

"To be a witness for Verity so that you may know truth."

"Truth?"

"Yes. Truth. It is said that Verity reaches even the loneliest places. So, here I am, a faithful servant."

Caraxus shrugged.

"We will see truth either way. Caraxus see if you can cook Marrow or not. If yes, then good for me and you. If not, well, bad for you."

The troll cut her down from the ceiling.

"That is Marrow?"

"Yes," Nay said. "It's in these legs."

"Not in claws?"

"No," Nay said, lying. "I'll cook claws after. For now, we cook the legs because that's the meat containing the Marrow."

"But claw is tastiest."

"You're not wrong. Which is why we'll save the best for last."

She kept the claws off to the side.

Each crab leg was easily double her height. She cut them down at their joints with Thorn. Caraxus had given her the dagger back, not concerned that she might use it against him.

She realized he didn't perceive her as a threat. She could use that to her advantage.

The cauldron was large enough to accommodate the legs.

When Caraxus wasn't looking, Nay accessed her inventory and grabbed her equivalent of Old Bay seasoning, which she kept in her spice kit there, along with some salt. She put a liberal amount of each into the pot.

While boiling the crab meat, she imbued the legs with every Debuff she had access to. When Caraxus consumed it, not only would he be astounded by the flavor, most of his stats across the board would be weakened.

Strength. Dexterity. Stamina. And Spirit.

And just for the hell of it, she put in a Debuff to give him an unquenchable thirst.

Hopefully, the Debuffs would even the playing field enough for her to slash his throat with Thorn.

While they waited for the legs to finish cooking, Nay noticed a troll skeleton lying on the floor near a darkened wall. It was decorated with seaweed and seashells. It was a shrine-like presentation.

"Who was that?" Nay said. "Someone important to you?"

Caraxus nodded. "My mate. She died, a sickness from bad shellfish. I could not help her. She was a good mate. I keep her here to remember her. Otherwise, I miss her too much."

Nay grimaced. She felt sympathy for the troll now. She did not want to feel sympathy for the troll.

Dammit.

The legs seemed to be done cooking. She was careful to pull them out of the pot, grabbing the ends sticking out of the boiling water.

She laid them before Caraxus. "I present to you the Marrow of the Caraxian Crab."

Impatient, the troll grabbed a leg, snapped it in half, and began sucking the meat out of the shell with his mouth. He chewed on the ends, crunching into the shell and making smacking sounds as his tongue searched for the seasoned crab flesh.

Nay cringed at all the mouth noises, but Caraxus didn't notice because he was in a trance of pleasure, working his way through the legs like a Southern preacher at a barbecue. He was a troll possessed. Driven by the pleasure areas in his brain.

Nay saw the Debuff icons begin to pop up over his head.

It was time.

Now or never.

Nay's hand tightened around Thorn. She casually approached him and he didn't seem to notice.

But he looked up at her before she could get behind him.

So, she slashed at his throat horizontally.

The troll jerked his head up and there was the sound of steel scraping across bone.

Instead of his throat, Nay had slashed one of his tusks.

Shit.

She jabbed forward this time and felt Thorn open up the skin on his cheek.

Caraxus howled and rose, swiping at her with his hand. The clawed fingernails slashed her thigh, and she felt a sting as her flesh opened.

Nay rolled backwards, crashing into a wall.

Caraxus went for his stone axe, and Nay used her Chef's Thermometer Ability to conjure a ring of heat around the weapon. It wouldn't be as effective if the weapon was metal, but the troll still bellowed when his hand touched hot stone.

He recoiled and looked at her in a new light.

Nay used the moment to grab a crab claw, the Marrow of the Caraxian Crab, and blink it away into her inventory. With her other hand she began conjuring her temperature rings.

It was obvious Caraxus had a resistance to cold.

So, she conjured several heat rings, one on top of him and then several around him, so no matter what direction he moved in, he would be in the heat longer.

He winced at the sudden flare of heat around him.

Nay ran.

She stumbled out of the cave.

His bellow came from within. He was in pursuit.

She had to get away.

She conjured a ring of cold the circumference of the cave entrance. Ice crystals formed in the air, and the moisture in the atmosphere froze.

A sheet of ice stretched across the entrance, materializing and then solidifying, trapping Caraxus inside.

He crashed into the ice door. It shook but did not break.

He snarled and drew his stone battle-axe and began whaling on the wall of ice.

Nay fled.

Nay had two problems.

Well, she had a lot of problems, but these were two immediate ones.

One, she was leaving a blood trail from her wound. Caraxus would be able to follow the droplets of her blood in the snow like they were breadcrumbs.

Two, she felt the approach of Vigor Sickness. Freezing over the cave exit with the Chef's Thermometer had taken too much of the little Vigor reserves she had at Base Rank.

When Caraxus found her, she would most likely be unconscious.

— CHAPTER FORTY-NINE —

The Third Trial: Icescythe

Nay had no choice but to stop for a moment and pack the wound on her thigh with snow. She had to stanch the bleeding.

She exhaled and closed her eyes and fell into the Spirit Song, cycling Vigor for a moment. She became a little less dizzy from the moment of cycling and replenishing her veins a tiny bit. Hopefully, it would be enough to hold off the Vigor Sickness.

Next, she conjured a ring of cold around her snow-packed wound, freezing over the top of the snow, converting it to ice. She gritted her teeth as she felt the skin around her wound freeze. She needed it to hold long enough so she wouldn't leak blood.

She just hoped the lasting damage wouldn't be too bad. But she would have to survive first before being allowed to worry about that.

She continued on, fleeing downwind so Caraxus couldn't follow her scent. The snow-packed wound seemed to be working. She was no longer leaving a blood trail on the ice.

But the Vigor Sickness was returning.

Even though she cycled, that last Ability cast of Chef's Thermometer was enough to make her dizzy again.

She had to find a hiding place, somewhere she could avoid Caraxus and regroup.

Nay tried to stick to the ice and avoid fresh snow. Leaving footprints was just as bad if not worse than leaving a blood trail. Both were like putting up a sign saying, *That bitch that tried to slash your throat is right here.*

She accessed her mini-map to see if she could find somewhere to hide.

Nowhere looked appealing.

There seemed to be another cave, but she thought that would be too obvious. Caraxus most definitely knew every inch of this island. This was his territory. He would know all the prime hiding spots.

She would have to create her own.

She slid down into a chasm that was full of those ice pillars reaching for the sky. They reminded her of a frozen version of the rock formations she had seen in New Mexico when she drove through during her move to Los Angeles.

She got up and chose a pillar. Once she got there, she sat down and settled into her breathing technique to cycle more Vigor, trying to keep the hum of her Spirit Song at a low volume.

As she filled her veins, that sensation of Vigor Sickness grew faint. It wasn't completely gone, but it would have to do for now.

She opened her eyes and steadied herself, boosted by the new Vigor in her passageways. She conjured a ring of heat and gestured with both of her hands, pushing it into the pillar.

The ice began to melt. A circle about the size of a doorway formed. She pushed the ring of heat further into the pillar, hollowing out a chamber large enough to house her. She felt her Vigor reserves depleting again.

She slipped into the chamber. It was still moist from the melting ice. Water was dripping everywhere.

Using the last of her reserves, she conjured a ring of cold to cover the hole with ice, covering up her tracks. Ice crystallized and refilled any trace of the hole on the outside.

She collapsed in the darkness, succumbing to the Vigor Sickness.

[Error Message]
[Error: Marrow Ability Detected at Base Rank]
[All Marrow Abilities Require Minimum of Iron Rank]
[Not Enough Vigor to Sustain Abilities]
[Please report to a DMA Agent]
[Error Message]
[Worldtripper Anomaly Detected]
[Please report to a DMA Agent]

As the error messages blinked red on her HUD, Nay, face-down on the ice floor of the chamber, trembled into her Spirit Song.

It was slow-going and she felt nauseous, like she was going to throw up, but she couldn't risk passing out with Vigor Sickness. Who knew if she would wake up again.

Eventually, she began to cycle Vigor, and the error messages went away. She continued until she stabilized.

She pulled a biscuit with a Recovery Buff out of her inventory and halfheartedly chewed on it, exhausted. She lay on the floor inside the pillar and rested.

The wound across her thigh was a nasty one. The ice-packed snow had warmed and grown dark with her blood. It had become a red slush inside the gash in her thigh and was dripping off her leg, forming a puddle on the floor.

She was going to have to do something lest it get infected. Then she would really be in trouble.

Reinvigorated, she spent some of her Vigor reserves on conjuring a ring of heat.

She held Thorn's blade in the ring. The steel absorbed the heat, its temperature rising. After a couple minutes, the blade turned red.

Nay snapped an icicle from the chamber ceiling right above her head. She put it in her mouth like it was a stick.

Her nostrils flared as she pushed air out, steeling herself for what she was about to do.

Nay bit on the icicle and pressed Thorn, glowing red with heat, against her wound.

There was a sizzle, like laying a strip of bacon in a hot pan, and a burst of searing pain.

Her teeth crushed the icicle in her mouth and she released a cry of agony, tears pouring down her cheeks, as everything went black and she passed out.

Nightfall had descended on the island. With it came ribbons of green light rippling in the sky, an aurora borealis. It cast everything on the glacier in an eerie chartreuse glow.

Nay's thigh was tender and sore from the self-cauterization, but at least she wasn't bleeding anymore. She had poured salt water on the cauterized wound, hoping the salt would kill any bacteria or potential infection.

Damn Ilyawraith, she thought. *Why'd she have to take the trinket Lain gave her?*

Nay crouched against an ice formation and watched the creature who possessed the Delicacy.

[Delicacy Detected!]
[Bladegland of the Icescythe]

Then a quest prompt appeared.

[Quest Detected]
[Quest: Separate the Delicacy from the Icescythe]

[Reward: Bladegland of the Icescythe]
[Accept Quest Y/N?]

Nay accepted the quest, knowing that separating the Delicacy from the Icescythe was going to involve slaying it.

Based off the looks of it, there would be no negotiations.

The icescythe was about Nay's height, but that's where the similarities stopped. It had scythes for arms. They were mantis-like, hinged on one joint. They seemed to be the thing's bones, except the spines on the back sides were translucent and seemed more like crystallized matter. The curved bone blades tapered off into sharp tips.

It was on all fours and was ripping at the carcass of a sea lion. Its short hind legs ended in three-clawed talons. Ice quills vibrated atop its skull, and it had a mouth that looked like the inside of a turbine.

It didn't eat so much as blend the seal flesh inside its maw.

Nay could see the Delicacy glowing gold inside its lower torso, probably best accessible through an incision via its back.

Her plan hinged on the hope that Caraxus would not be on this side of the island. Best-case scenario was that he was in his cave, sleeping and recuperating since it was nightfall.

If he found her while she was engaged with this Icescythe, it was game over.

She had tracked the creature for the past couple of hours. She observed it hunting the sea lion.

She began pulling Debuff Biscuits out of her inventory and placing them on the ice. She walked backwards towards the small cave she had found, leaving a trail of biscuits.

The "cave" was really just a medium-sized grotto in the ice where one could sit with some shelter while watching the sea. She formed a pile of the biscuits under the biggest ice stalactite here and hid behind an ice formation and waited.

If the first part of her plan revolved around Caraxus not interrupting this trap, the second part of her plan depended on the Icescythe actually being interested in the biscuits.

She had stacked her stats with the Buffs as much as she was allowed, and she had Thorn in her hand, ready to engage. Her hands were trembling from nervousness and she felt sick to her stomach.

Time moved slow. Seconds felt like minutes. It was torture.

Just when she thought that her plan wasn't working, she heard the tapping of ice and the sound of teeth grinding as they pulverized baked goods.

The Icescythe appeared in front of the grotto, scrambling across the ground and stabbing biscuits with its scythes and lifting them to its round mouth, where it hoovered the flaky bread.

Nay saw the Debuff icons appearing over its long skull.

It stopped in front of the cave, hesitating. It didn't grab the next biscuit that was sitting just past the threshold of the grotto entrance.

Nay whispered, *"C'mon, c'mon, c'mon . . ."*

But then she saw the icon of a figure with a hand on its belly appear over its head.

The Hunger Debuff.

Its artificial hunger drove it forward into the grotto, and it continued devouring the biscuits.

It reached the pile of biscuits underneath the ice stalactite.

As it started stabbing and lifting the biscuits to its mouth with both scythe-limbs, Nay conjured a ring of heat around the stalactite.

The creature didn't notice the water dripping from the ceiling onto it and the biscuits, because it was too busy eating.

But it did notice the two ice imps that appeared at the entrance of the grotto, who saw the Icescythe and responded by releasing their frost breath attacks into the grotto.

There was an earsplitting crack and the stalactite fell from the ceiling in an outpouring of ice and water.

The Icescythe leapt at the ice imps, its scythes delivering stabbing punches like it was an industrial knitting needle.

The ice stalactite crashed into the ground where it just was, missing the Icescythe by only a fraction of a second.

The grotto shook and spiderweb cracks spread across the floor of the chamber.

"No!" Nay said.

She had to attack now, while the creature was distracted.

The ice imps were flying around the Icescythe, dive-bombing it with their claws.

The Icescythe impaled one with the end of one of its scythe-arms, and the creature exploded.

Its final act in dying was its death-burst attack.

Shards of ice shrapnel hit the Icescythe in its face and neck, cutting it and drawing blood.

The monster shrieked, and blood the color of glowing blue phosphor spattered the entrance walls of the grotto.

That's when Nay drove Thorn down into the back of its ridged neck. The blade penetrated the bluish-white reptilian skin there, and she felt it scrape against the thing's spine.

She pulled her hand up and ripped Thorn out, pulling up sinew and spurting phosphor blood.

The Icescythe screamed and twisted. The spines on the back of the nearest scythe-arm scraped across her forearm, ripping skin.

Nay cried out, then found herself ducking the scythe-arm that passed over her, almost taking her head off. She backpedaled into the grotto as the Icescythe stabbed at her.

She fell into a crevice in the ice, and as the sharp end of a scythe was on the path to skewer her face, she conjured a ring of extreme cold, and the thing's spraying phosphor blood froze in a sheet across the lip of the crevice, shielding her face.

The tip of the scythe-arm embedded into its own frozen blood.

Ice chips sprayed into the air.

Its movement was erratic, and one half of its body didn't seem to be operating right. One of the scythe-arms fell limp at its side, and it slipped on one of its hind legs that seemed to lock straight out.

She must have injured it worse than she thought when she stabbed it in the neck.

It wailed in frustration, and instead of trying to break through to her, it spun around. A half dozen more ice imps appeared, and they were swarming it, blasting it with their frost breath and slashing at its exposed side.

Nay had an idea.

She melted the frozen blood and pulled herself out of the crevice; her torn arm had gone numb. She wasn't bothered by the wound on her thigh.

She had a stray thought that it must be the adrenaline.

She took a wide circle around Icescythe and the ice imps attacking it.

Soon, she was outside of the grotto, the back of the ice imps to her.

This was a play that was going to disable her with Vigor Sickness. But she considered the odds and knew it was the correct play.

She conjured a ring of heat in front of her as if it was a shield.

Heat vapor rippled in front of her.

She jabbed the first ice imp in the back of the head with Thorn's tip. The blow dealt enough damage to kill it, triggering its death burst.

Ice shards flew in all directions. They penetrated Icescythe, the shrapnel piercing one of its eyes.

The pieces of the ice imp flew at Nay and would have shredded her face, but they melted as they passed through the heat ring, showering her in ice-imp slush.

She let out a battle cry and felt adrenaline clashing with the onset of Vigor Sickness.

She only would have a few more seconds.

She attacked the ice imps, slashing horizontally and mixing in jabs. Sometimes she missed, but mostly she hit them, triggering their death bursts.

The last slash took out two at once, and the explosion of ice shredded the Icescythe's face, ripping the flesh off his skull and penetrating an artery in his throat.

Nay was showered in ice-imp slush and the blue-phosphor blood of the scythed monster as it staggered and collapsed, sighing with a gurgling death rattle as the life left its body.

[Error Message]
[Error: Marrow Ability Detected at Base Rank]
[All Marrow Abilities Require Minimum of Iron Rank]
[Not Enough Vigor to Sustain Abilities]
[Please report to a DMA Agent]
[Error Message]
[Worldtripper Anomaly Detected]
[Please report to a DMA Agent]

Nay collapsed next to the body of Icescythe, succumbing to the Vigor Sickness.

— CHAPTER FIFTY —

Cool Knife Shit

Nay fluttered in and out of consciousness, the glowing ice-imp Core rolling next to her face. The flashing red alarm on her HUD felt like an icepick going into her brain.

She moaned and managed to grab the ice-imp Core. She pulled it towards her and held it against her chest, the light vapors dancing across her face.

Nay summoned all of her remaining strength and willpower and used it to focus on her breathing. She would fall into the Spirit Song technique or she would pass out trying.

The spirit veins appeared in her mind and they were writhing, starved. The song drifted out of her at a low volume, and she crushed the ice-imp Core into her chest.

She absorbed it and her spirit veins straightened and expanded, accepting the Vigor and jump-starting the cycling process.

Consuming the Core hit her with dopamine and pulled her from the edge of Vigor Sickness.

She crawled to two other Cores, consuming them, refilling her reserves. The error message on her interface went away and she stabilized.

She was still weak and bleeding, but she was still conscious.

She sat up and collected the remaining ice-imp Cores. But she stopped herself from absorbing them. She was struck with an idea.

She put the ice-imp Cores in her inventory.

[Delicacy Detected]

She observed the Icescythe carcass, the blinking golden dot on her minimap overlaid across her vision.

Her open True Eye rendered this section of the Icescythe translucent, and she got a glimpse of the Delicacy itself, a gland the size of a peach pit connected to the underside of the skin, next to a cluster of nodes and connected to a system of nerves.

She worked fast, in front of the grotto entrance, underneath the green light of the rippling aurora.

She wished she had a set of butcher knives for this job.

Thorn was good for fighting and slaughter, but it was no paring, boning, or carving knife.

The Icescythe was like no creature she had ever butchered before, and technically, she was only cutting in to remove a gland, but she had no frame of reference for working on such a monster.

It seemed part reptile, part insect, and part ice elemental.

She supposed the closest thing would be butchering an alligator, but that still wouldn't come close.

She had cut through the scaly reptilian skin and was removing chunks of flesh to make her way to the Delicacy. Gold motes began to drift out of the wound, and she found the gland.

It was neon yellow and looked like a cluster of grapes congealed in one mass. She cut through a membrane casing and then sliced it away from the nerves and some blue-hued organ she didn't recognize in the abdomen.

She freed it from the carcass and held the Delicacy in her hand, illuminating her face in neon yellow.

[Quest Complete!]
[Separate the Delicacy from the Icescythe Completed!]
[You have been rewarded with Bladegland of the Icescythe]
[You have been rewarded with Vigor Points]

Golden vigama flew down from the aurora and entered her veins, slamming her with dopamine. Then another prompt appeared.

[Delicacy Discovered!]
[Delicacy: Bladegland of the Icescythe]
[Delicacies Unlocked 1/3]
[Would you like to Consume Delicacy Y/N?]

She closed the text menu and stored the Delicacy in her inventory. She was beginning to leave the grotto when she stopped to look at the corpse of the Icescythe one more time.

Her eyes drifted to the scythe-arms.

She knelt and examined the appendage. The bone and ice-elemental aspect of the physiology made it a sturdy and deadly weapon. Maybe not as good as forged steel but good enough to do some rather unique damage.

She thought for a moment, then she grabbed the other scythe-arm and crossed it over, manipulating the limb. She turned it so she could use the spines on the back of it like a saw.

She wasn't sure if it would work, but it was worth trying.

Nay used the spine of one arm to saw at the other, towards the end of the scythe. It ground into the limb, and matter began to flake away.

It was working. It was cutting through the bone and elemental ice.

It took her longer than expected, because the scythe was so dense, but after a half hour or so, she had removed the ice scythe to have a weapon that was slightly longer than Thorn.

It was curved, ending in the deadly tip.

She stored the ice scythe in her inventory and hurried back to her hollowed-out pillar.

Back inside her Chef's Thermometer–made chamber, Nay produced a pan from her inventory, along with the Marrow of the Caraxian Crab.

It was huge and took up most of the space inside the chamber.

"Too much," she said. She used the skullcrusher on Thorn to crack off the end of the lower pincer.

She set it inside the pan and put the rest of the Marrow back in her inventory.

She produced a pot from her inventory and filled it with water from her waterskin.

Then Nay took out the Delicacy from her inventory and placed it in the pot to soak in the water. This would remove any grit. She wished she could let it soak for a whole day, but she figured she only had a few hours until Ilyawraith would be returning to the island.

She waited, slipping into Spirit Song to cycle her Vigor until she lost patience.

Nay used her Chef's Thermometer Ability to conjure two heat rings, one for the pan, one for the pot.

She was essentially grilling the Marrow portion of the crab pincer. She would have preferred to boil it, but she hadn't been able to find a suitable container.

She removed the Delicacy from the pot and gingerly shook it dry. Then she took it a step further and used a popular method called "pressing" usually used to remove excess water from sweetbreads, or thymus glands, before cooking.

Nay took out Thorn and her ice scythe from the inventory. She set the Delicacy on the wide end of the scythe, on the flat part. She used Thorn to press down on the bladegland, squeezing out the moisture.

From the cooking kit in her inventory, she used some of the herbs she had stored in jars. Some mint, some tarragon, and some rosemary. She sprinkled and rubbed them over the gland along with some sea salt.

She took a glob of butter from her inventory and placed it on the hot pincher. She wished she had time to make some clarified butter, and perhaps she could have taken the extra time, but she was in a hurry.

She placed the bladegland Delicacy down in the pan with the melting butter and it began to sizzle.

As it seared, she used Thorn to spoon the melted butter and bathe the Delicacy as it cooked.

This was not the ideal way she had wanted to prepare a Delicacy and a Marrow, but beggars couldn't be choosers. She had to work with what she had. Some chefs liked to use flour as a breading for sweetbreads, but Nay found it unnecessary.

As long as the gland was dry, then searing it with butter would make it crispy enough.

It was the equivalent of being on one of those ridiculous cooking shows where the contestants were given weird or limited resources to create a meal under a ticking clock that would impress some judges.

Except her judge was life-or-death.

She looked over at the other pincher where the Marrow was grilling. She used Thorn to flip the portion of crab pincer over to ensure even cooking.

Then she turned over the Delicacy and bathed it in more melted butter. Golden motes began to fill the chamber, filling her little abode in neon light.

The bladegland had a nice crispness to it, and even with its bright coloration, it looked like a piece of fried liver or even a fried chicken nugget. She was surprised to find that there was no musty smell about it, which was usually the case with some organ meat.

Instead, to her surprise, it reminded her of the smell of fried treats at county fairs. It smelled a lot like a combination between funnel cake and fried chicken.

When it was almost done cooking, she pulled a biscuit with a Recovery Buff out of her inventory and ripped it in half. She set each half in the pan with the Delicacy, toasting it in the hot butter.

Nay de-conjured the heat rings and cycled more Vigor for a moment, readying herself for the experience of consuming a Delicacy.

She placed the cooked Delicacy on one half of the biscuit and admired what a little heat, seasoning, herbs, and butter could do. To think that this was a gland inside of the Icescythe just a short time ago. Now it was transformed into an appetizing meal.

"Bon appétit."

She took the first bite and was hit with a burst of flavor. The Delicacy was so powerful, it revived her sleeping taste buds.

The bladegland was at first crunchy but then gave way to a tender creaminess that was straight euphoric.

The Delicacy carried her to a rapture. A sun was birthing in her stomach, and its light spread through her body, filling her veins with pure nirvana.

After another bite, she had to lie down.

Her vision filled with the celestial firmament, and she was flying through a galaxy. Text prompts floated into her vision, the words of some heaven. They burst into existence over her flight through space.

[Delicacy Unlocked!]
[Bladegland Delicacy Unlocked!]
[2/3 Delicacies]

Then another prompt appeared.

[Marrow Ability Path Unlocked]
[Prerequisite: Yes]
[Marrow of the Bladegland]
[Rank: Base 75%]
[0/12 Ability Slots in this Tree]

Congratulations, you have unlocked a Delicacy [2/3] and have activated a second skill tree of Marrow Abilities. You may now consume Marrow to awaken Abilities [0/12] within the Marrow of the Bladegland Ability Tree.

To give your blades an extra little something for your enemies to remember you by, you've been granted the Passive Ability of Rupture.

Rupture allows you to store Kinetic Points and release them with Finishers to enhance your damage.

You've also unlocked Dire Knife, Rank 1.

Dire Knife is a Weapon Imbue that amplifies your blade attacks, and each successful delivery rewards you with one Kinetic Point.

You've also unlocked Gore, Rank 1.

Gore is a Finisher that requires Kinetic Points to activate. Once activated, it causes wounds inflicted upon the enemy by your blades to burst, delivering more damage. (Note: Watch out! Could get messier than the front row of a Gallagher show!)

Nay's speculation was right. The Delicacy had unlocked a combat-skill tree.

Her vision returned to normal but she felt weightless, as if she were still floating through a galaxy.

"Thank you," Nay said. She wasn't sure who it was directed to, maybe it was just the universe, but she wanted to express gratitude. She felt some anxiety disappear now that she had some combat abilities.

Knowing she had it made the thought of facing Caraxus again a little more bearable.

"Now time for the Marrow."

She tapped the cooked shell with Thorn's skullcrusher, cracking the shell and exposing the off-white crab meat. It was the color of clotted cream.

She grabbed some "Old Bay" seasoning from her inventory and sprinkled it on the Marrow. She grabbed a portion with her fingers. It was tender and easily separated.

It was also still hot.

She plucked the Marrow in her mouth and kept it open, blowing out steam and juggling it with her tongue until it cooled. She bit into it, releasing the sweet marine flavor over her tongue.

Strangely, there was a temperature effect, where it felt like a spritz of frost hit her in the back of the throat. It must have had something to do with the freezing waters of the Caraxe Strait. It was a welcome complexity of experience, a contrast to the hot meat.

[Marrow Consumed!]
[Crab Claw Marrow of the Caraxian Crab]
[Would you like to unlock Marrow Ability for Tongue of the Hierophant]
[OR]
[Bladegland of Icescythe]
[Choose one]

She chose the bladegland.

[Opening Delicacy Tree]
[Marrow Abilities: 3/12]
Opening Ability Tree for the Delicacy: Bladegland of Icescythe.

As with the other Marrows, she was met with a view of a human digestive system. There were cubes rotating next to the organs, indicating open Ability slots.

You have ten open slots in this Ability Tree. You have consumed Crab Claw of the Caraxian Crab. It has syncretized into the Decapitate Ability. Would you like to use slot for Decapitate [Y/N]?

She accessed the description for the Ability.

Decapitate. Much like the Caraxian Crab's favorite attack, this Ability allows you to summon a spirit pincer attack. A successful hit has the chance to multiply your damage threefold and has a chance to decapitate target. Note: Cooldown is 1 Day.

Goddamn, Nay thought. She hit *Y*, and her stomach began to burn and her body temperature rose.

As the effect of the Marrow Ability activating did the three-hundred-and-sixty-degree thing to her vision, she happily lay on the floor and let it happen.

I can do cool knife shit.

— CHAPTER FIFTY-ONE —

The Third Trial: Duel

Nay's whole body ached.
Her forearm throbbed. She had wrapped the wounds the Icescythe's spines had inflicted on her skin. She dipped the arm in seawater, hoping the salt would help prevent infection, and she had almost passed out from the searing sting. The cauterized wound on her thigh pulsated with pain, and her fingertips and toes tingled from the bite of the cold.

The recovery biscuits and all the Buffs she had been continuing to stack seemed to be keeping her on life support.

All in all, she thought death would at least be a sweet release from the misery of this glacier.

The ice formation holding up the ice boulder finished melting at its thinnest point, where Nay had thrown up the ring of heat, and the frozen boulder fell from its perch and crashed into the ice.

The boom echoed across the island, and Nay waited for Caraxus to arrive, drawn by a noise he wouldn't be able to ignore.

Nay smoked an iceflint cigarette she found in her inventory, a leftover artifact from her life at Quincy's Lodge, which felt so long ago. Gracie had rolled it for her, and she wondered how her friend was doing.

She wondered how Nom was doing and if she would ever see her friends again.

Nay had chosen a crag above the sea for the location of their duel. The viridescent aurora, although fading, signifying that dawn would be arriving in due time, danced across the sky. The rippling curtains of light created a psychedelic absinthe backdrop for their stage.

Nay's legs were hanging off the cliff as she stared at the otherworldly horizon, wondering how lucky she was to experience such a sight. How the rest of this day went would determine if she got to experience more of this world or if her journey ended here.

She saw him approaching along the cliff top, the ice troll's silhouette appearing far away. She took a hit of the iceflint, exhaling the frost over the sea stacks.

When he drew close enough that Caraxus was no longer a silhouette, Nay took one last drag of the iceflint cigarette and flicked it off the cliff. She stood, drawing Thorn. The longer ice scythe appeared in her off hand.

She had wound the blunt end in butcher twine from her inventory, creating a makeshift hilt. She wasn't sure how to use the scythe, but she figured swinging the sharp end at her opponent would be a good-enough start.

"You lie to Caraxus," the ice troll said. He was maybe fifty yards from her, standing on the edge of the cliff. "You no Epicurist."

"I'm an Epicurist," Nay said. "Just not one meant to help you."

"You come to hunt Caraxus?" he said.

Nay didn't say anything at that. She just nodded and turned the ice scythe in her hand.

"I never know you," Caraxus said. "But you come to my home, want kill me. *Why?*"

It was a fair a question.

"So that I can live," Nay said.

Caraxus understood.

"Then we see who deserve Vigor more. You . . . or me."

He drew his stone battle-axe and charged her.

She mentally clicked on her Dire Knife Ability, and Vigor auras suddenly flared up around Thorn and the ice scythe. The Weapon Imbues flickered like spirit fire, and she looked in amazement at the weapons.

A meter appeared near the center of her HUD. It was the outline of three knives. The word *Rupture* was above the icons. She knew what it was then. It was a meter to track her Kinetic Points.

And to her surprise, she found herself running to meet Caraxus instead of running away from him.

Her blood rushed to her ears, and suddenly, she was sidestepping to avoid the stone ax coming down at her vertically. It shattered the ice where her feet just were, and as Caraxus pulled his weapon out of the ground, Nay slashed the inside of his wrist, drawing first blood.

One of the dagger icons on her interface turned red as if it filled with blood. She had one Kinetic Point.

Caraxus roared and swung the ax at her with both hands, twisting his body.

Nay, taking care to pay attention to her feet and stances, took a step away, and there was a loud *crack* as the stone ax hit her ice scythe.

The vibration traveled down the bone and elemental ice matter and traveled into her hand, shooting up her arm. With the vibrations came pain. It took everything Nay had to hold on to the weapon.

Here's the thing Nay was learning about combat: that she never expected it. The toll it took on the hands. The muscles cramped, the skin blistered, the grip weakened.

Not knowing if she would be able to use the Ability again, Nay mentally activated her Gore Ability.

The Rupture icon flashed and the knife meter depleted, her Kinetic Points returning to zero as the Ability procced.

Caraxus cried out in pain as blue-phosphor blood erupted out of his wrist, the wound bursting.

That's when one of his own Abilities procced. He released a guttural roar and grew a few inches. Not just in height, but all of his muscles engorged and expanded. Tendon, bone, and sinew enlarged.

A blood-red glow spread from his Core up and down his body until he was encased in the crimson steam rising off his skin.

He had become Enraged.

He lowered his head and charged Nay like he was a bull, his tusks aimed at her.

The only move that made sense to Nay would have seemed counterintuitive to anyone watching. But she moved towards him.

He was heading up the slope of the cliff; she was going down.

And just when one would expect a horrible collision of bone and flesh, Nay slid as if she was a softball player out-juking a catcher. She hit the ice and slid leg-first underneath him and between his legs.

She didn't so much as swing but hold the ice scythe out, making sure to lock her wrist.

The point of the blade entered the side of Caraxus's ankle and partially ripped his Achilles tendon as she slid past him. The resistance of tendon and bone slingshotted her at a different angle down the slope.

It was a bad wound, but because the troll was Enraged, she might as well have been a child scraping him with a butter knife as far as pain recognition went.

He chased after her down the slope.

Nay conjured a ring of heat in front of her feet that melted the ice enough to make it slick, creating a moving Slip 'N Slide. She roostertailed wet ice down the slope.

Caraxus stepped into it and stumbled, careening. He tumbled down the slope after her. He righted himself and activated another Ability.

He held up his hand, and a spinning ball of snow appeared hovering in his palm. It grew and grew until he was holding an ice boulder.

He hurled it at Nay below him.

She looked just in time to see the boulder of ice descending towards her. She used the ice scythe like a pickaxe climber and caught the ice below her. Chips flew as the point dug in.

She used the leverage to pivot herself and change direction, sliding down the slope at another angle.

The boulder cratered the slope next to her. Shards of ice cut her face.

[Error Message]
[Error: Marrow Ability Detected at Base Rank]
[All Marrow Abilities Require Minimum of Iron Rank]
[Not Enough Vigor to Sustain Abilities]
[Please report to a DMA Agent]

The dizziness came and, when combined with the sliding and fighting, gave her immediate vertigo.

"Fuck your DMA Agent!"

An ice-imp Core appeared between her fists as she held on to her weapons. She had summoned it from her inventory. She pressed it into her chest, absorbing it.

The injection of Vigor made the error message disappear. She shook her head, trying to see straight.

She looked up to see Caraxus creating another ice boulder. She waited for him to throw it.

He took aim and lobbed it at her.

Nay halted her slide with her ice scythe, stabbing the slope. The sudden halt of momentum almost yanked her arm out of the socket.

The boulder flew over her, and Caraxus was sliding straight for her.

He saw her, her hand hanging onto the scythe dug into the ice, her other hand holding Thorn. There was no way he could stop his slide, so he aimed straight for her. He readied his legs for a kick that would smash her face.

Nay counted, timing his arrival. "One . . . two . . .

"*Three!*"

She let go of the scythe, grabbed it with her other hand, and moved Thorn to her scythe hand. Then she twisted.

It was just enough room to dodge Caraxus's rocketing body.

She thrust Thorn into his side.

The blade entered his torso and scraped along his ribs as he slid by, opening up a long gash from his abdomen to near his armpit.

Her Rupture menu upticked. More blood glow filled the second dagger icon.

She had her second Kinetic Point.

He continued by her and the dagger was out of him. He rolled down the slope, shouting.

Nay ripped the ice scythe from the slope and continued her descent, reaching the bottom of the slope. Nay rose to her feet, her body flooded with adrenaline and dopamine.

They were in a chasm with pillared ice stacks.

Caraxus got to his feet, still Enraged and glowing bright red with blue phosphor dripping out of his wounds.

"You fight like jellyfish," he said. "You seem pretty and harmless . . . but you sting Caraxus!"

He came at her then like an unstoppable train. They were on even elevation, and Nay found herself on the defensive.

His stone ax took out a chunk of ice formation next to her head. She darted and dodged as he came at her with a combo of ax swings, the ax shattering the ice stacks around them. Her agility Buff was putting in work.

She rolled backwards, the axe cutting a deep furrow into the ground.

She bobbed and weaved, keeping her neck away from the swiping axe blade.

She half-ass parried with the ice scythe, diverting the ax enough so it didn't bite into her flesh.

And though Caraxus was physically Enraged, her speed and slipperiness served to emotionally enrage him.

As he pursued her, bellowing and swinging through the ice stacks, she conjured heat rings, melting parts of the pillars above them so ice and slush would come tumbling down, creating an environment of chaos.

Every time the error message appeared on her interface, she injected herself with an ice-imp Core from her inventory.

But she was losing steam, on the precipice of becoming gassed.

And she was running out of ice-imp Cores.

She had to end this.

Caraxus got his axe stuck in an ice stack, and Nay saw her chance.

She swiped Thorn and ice scythe through the air, crossing her arms in front of her. She activated the most powerful Ability she had.

"Decapitate!"

A violet spirit pincer manifested, flowing out of her weapons and spinning through the air at Caraxus. It left a Vigor trail in its wake. They looked like ridged and razor-sharp supernatural hedge clippers twirling through the air.

She felt an outpouring of Vigor leave her body. She fell to her knees.

The spirit pincers hit Caraxus in the neck and clamped shut like a bear trap. An explosion of Vigor filled the atmosphere.

Caraxus grunted and fell to his knees.

The Decapitate chance procced, and a cut formed around his neck. His head was still intact. Blood trickled out of the thin wound around his neck.

He was still alive.

It must be because he's still Enraged. That Ability must Buff his defenses. It saved him.

He shrank a few inches then, his muscles, bones, and tendons returning to normal. That red glow dissipated.

The Enrage Ability had depleted.

His hand went to his neck and he felt the wound. He looked at his phosphor blood on his fingers. He touched the long gash on his side, and took a limping step and looked at his injured Achilles tendon.

He trembled, anger rising.

He howled and charged her, leaving his stone ax in the ice.

Nay quickly summoned the last ice-imp Core from her inventory and injected it. She screamed and swung out at him with the ice scythe.

But he backhanded the weapon away and collided into her.

She felt his tusk enter her side, scraping the edge of her ribs. The bone-on-bone sensation was so painful, it almost paralyzed her.

They crashed into the side of the chasm, and everything went black as Caraxus punched Nay in the face. She felt her nose crunch and flatten under the blow.

He hit her again, breaking her cheekbone.

He was going to beat her to death.

There was one last thing she could do before the sweet release of death ended her violent suffering.

As she spoke, the words didn't come out right. Her jaw was fucked up. But she said it when his fist was reared back for another strike. It came out and sounded like, "*Rushtur . . . moddfuzzer.*"

"*Rupture, motherfucker.*"

Gore activated, her finisher, channeling three Kinetic Points.

In simultaneous fashion, his wounds burst.

The severed Achilles tendon.

The long gash along his side, exposing his ribs.

The garrote-shaped cut around his neck.

Nay was showered in blue-phosphor blood as his wounds exploded as if a nail bomb went off inside the lacerations. His ankle disappeared in the gore, his foot falling off. His entire torso opened up on one side, cracking his ribcage open and blowing out his organs.

Lastly, his neck disappeared in a mist, and the only thing left connecting Caraxus's head to his body was his exposed spine.

His lifeless body fell against Nay, pushing her to the ground.

[Quest Complete]
[Slay Caraxus the Ice Troll Completed!]
[Congratulations]
[You have been rewarded Vigor Points]

She was crumpled on the ice with the ice troll's body on top of her. She was vaguely aware that something was wrong with her head. Everything hurt. And every time she inhaled or exhaled, she wheezed blood.

As the golden vigama flew into her, she knew she was dying.

[You have been awarded Ice-Troll Core]

Light emerged from the ice troll's still corpse. And the top of Caraxus's neon-blue Core pushed out of his physical body. It pressed into her and she leaned in to its warmth.

The Core was the size of a basketball, and as it passed out of the troll's dead body, it pushed into her. She let herself absorb it, and a neon-blue light burst across her interface.

Her Vigor Rank meter filled out her Base Rank.

[Congratulations!]
[You have cultivated enough Vigor to Rank Up!]
[Procedure from Base Rank to Iron Rank Starting . . .]
[Please Find a Safe Distance Away from Others]
[And Please Brace Yourself]
[Purging Impurities]
[Metamorphosis to Iron Rank Activated]

Her vision went from bright blue to white, and she lost control of her muscles as her body went into a seizure. There was an exhalation, and something started spraying out of all her pores before she lost consciousness, the white light blinding her.

Nay clawed her way out of some kind of embryonic sac or cocoon that was flesh-colored. Her lungs inhaled the icy air, and gray sludge poured out of the sac. Was she surrounded in that?

Her head no longer hurt and she no longer felt wrong. Her facial bones and jaw seemed normal. She looked at her forearm and thigh. Her wounds had healed into scars.

It was the same way on her thigh.

"Congratulations, *Iron*."

Nay looked up to see Ilyawraith standing above her in the chasm. There was a smile on her face.

The new Iron Rank looked around and saw the remnants of her battle with Caraxus. His body was lying next to her.

Ilyawraith called her snow eddy to ferry them back to Ianthe, but Nay took another look at Caraxus's corpse. The ice troll deserved a better resting place.

"Wait," Nay said.

Ilyawraith looked at her questionably.

Nay laid Caraxus prone next to the skeleton of his mate in his cave. She then took his stone ax, put it on his chest, and put his hands around the handle.

In her peripheral vision she knew Ilyawraith was watching her perform this grim ritual.

Nay stood there a moment, staring at the remains of the two trolls. It was awkward and she wasn't sure what to say or do. So, she settled for just nodding, knowing she had done the proper thing.

The beast whose death helped her get to Iron Rank deserved that much at least.

— CHAPTER FIFTY-TWO —

An Interlude Wherein Nom Noms

Nom was having a blast running the kitchen at the Lodge, but he missed Nay. Although he had expressed excitement about her learning how to officially cultivate, he was worried about her.

What would he do if she didn't come back? If she had failed to get to Iron?

Don't think those thoughts, Nzxthommocus III, of course she'll advance to Iron.

He'd been around enough cultivators to know she had what it took.

When he had first arrived on this world, he had recognized the Vigor for what it was: something cultivators would obsess over, just as the cultivators in his world had obsessed over *the quintessence.*

In his world, as part of the host body, he wasn't allowed to Siphon. He and the other tentacles had served the Pain Lord, who had in turn served a powerful cultivator named Cassian Carter.

Before the cultivators had come to their world to subjugate the Dread Ones, Nom's kind naturally strengthened themselves on the emotions, memories, and dreams of others. This was done by physical contact and using an Ability called Siphon.

This feeding was how he strengthened his Eldritch Void. The more he fed, the more abominable he would become. It was the Dread One equivalent of cultivating.

While his friend Nay had to go and learn how to cultivate so her Marrow Abilities wouldn't kill her, Nom had been Siphoning and strengthening his Eldritch Void to accommodate the Marrow Abilities he had been acquiring with her.

The fact was, there were a contingent of the Hounds of Tindalos who did not look kindly on cultivators.

Being subjugated by them could have that effect on a broodling.

Nom often wondered what his world would turn into if his kind had ever broken the chains of Cassius and the other cultivators.

"How are those mussels coming along, chef?"

Nom was pulled out of his thoughts by Gracie, who was looking at him from the expo table. She was tapping her foot. She blew a strand of hair out of her face, and Nom knew she was irritated.

Nom came back to the present. His attention snapped back to all the saucepans laid out in front of him on the heat rings he had conjured. They were filled with mussels from Lac Coineascar. He was sautéing them in Vancian white wine, butter, and cream with shallots and parsley.

He called them Nom's Sumptuous Shells, and he served them with the same french fries they had always made with the Fish 'n Chips. The townspeople loved the mussels and went crazy for dipping the fries in the white sauce.

He saw that the shells were open on all of them, exposing the delicious mussels inside.

"Sorry, Gracie," Nom said. "I zoned out for a bit there."

He ladled the mussels onto plates and poured the sauce over them. Then he grabbed several plates with his protuberances and sped to Gracie, setting them on the expo table.

"Were you worried about Nay again?" Gracie said.

"How could you tell?" Nom said.

"You kind of stare off into the distance, and one of your fins starts to twitch," Gracie said.

That made Nom self-conscious. He looked down at his fin protuberances.

"I'm worried about her, too," Gracie said. "With everything that's happened here, now she's left somewhere with Quincy for a few days? Makes me anxious about what's going on."

He and Gracie had developed a rapport, which is what naturally happened while working in the kitchen trenches with another person. She was doing a good job as the kitchen manager, and he had grown accustomed to her presence during work.

Nom preferred most of the humans here compared to his world.

But the social dynamics were different. Back home, he was often used as a tool of torture by his master, and if that didn't dampen tentacle-human relations, then he didn't know what did.

Of course, maybe the dynamics would have been different if he hadn't been a servant of Ormandius.

It was easier to communicate with humans when they didn't hate or fear you so much.

Bryja came in and saw her orders ready. "Finally! Was beginning to worry that Nom was slacking off back there."

"A tentacle is never completely slack, nor are we completely taut," Nom said. "We're always best somewhere in the middle."

Hilde came in next, red-faced and huffing. "I'm gonna kill him. I swear to Veritax I'm gonna kill him."

"Degnar?" Gracie said.

"If he makes one more comment about my 'copious features,' I'm gonna drown him in the Lac," Hilde said.

"Want me have a talk with him?" Nom said. "Might do him right to experience true darkness. I can show him a glimpse of the roiling rings of Tindalos. Seems to always do the trick."

"No, Nom," Hilde said. "I appreciate the offer but I can take care of myself."

Nom held his fins up and shrugged. "Of course you can. But the offer still stands."

"Thank you, Nom," Hilde said. "I'll keep that in mind." She took a tray full of mussel entrees and Nay's garlic knots out the door.

"Nom," Bryja said, putting her elbows on the expo table and her chin in both of her hands. "Do you ever get bored being cooped up in the Lodge? What do you do for fun?"

"Oh, I manage to keep myself entertained," Nom said.

Portitia giggled in the bubble bath, her hands bracing the side of the clawfoot tub in her room at the House of Saccharine Delights.

She squealed in excitement as something tickled her. A green protuberant fin appeared out of the bubbles and then disappeared back into the water.

The stitchgal squirmed and squealed again, laughing. A flash of purple muscle intertwined with her legs and then moved underneath the bubbles.

Portitia leaned back and closed her eyes, enjoying a peculiar but delightful series of sensations.

Jolf was strolling down the street, eating a winter apple, when he heard a woman's screams coming from the next block. He tossed the half-eaten apple into the mud and hurried his way towards the sound.

Then he stopped, realizing the noise was coming from the House of Saccharine Delights. They weren't screams but yelps of pleasure. The woman's voice crescendoed in volume, reached a yodeling peak that stopped foot traffic for a moment, and was then quickly forgotten as it faded into the laughter and music coming from the bordello.

Jolf shook his head. "Nether hells. Snowstroke needs to pad those damn walls."

He straightened his belt buckle before walking on, continuing his patrol.

* * *

Nom settled in to what he called his *lair*.

He couldn't help himself. As a spawn of the Hounds of Tindalos, he was compelled to have a lair.

Just like all of his kind.

His lair was a place of his own between the walls of Quincy's Lodge. It was towards the top of the structure, between the upper level and the one below it. So, not quite an attic, but he did have the green-tinged moonlight shining in through the cracks in stone and wood.

This was where he stored his collection of baubles and trinkets he had scavenged from around town. There were bits of fabric from clothing, buttons, and jewelry townsfolk had dropped in the mud or on the frigid shores of the Lac.

If Nay had seen this place, he was sure that she'd call him a magpie.

He liked to collect little pretties. As a tentacle connected to a larger host body in his previous life, he had never been allowed to own property. But now he was his own entity and could do as he pleased, to an extent.

This was also where he made his poisons.

One darkened and cobweb-strewn corner of his lair was a shrine to the art of making poisons.

There were glass tubes he had stolen from the glassblower artisan in town. Well, not stolen. He had left some of the silver coins from his money that was accumulating as an employee of the Lodge. The coins bore the mark of the Winterfist Bank, and it was the currency everyone used in Stitchdale.

But these glass tubes had labels like *Lamprey's Spit* and *Kyr-nine*. Poisons that had already been created and were ready to deploy should they ever need them.

His current experiment was a new poison recipe he had acquired when he consumed the Marrow of the Mewlipped Tode. It required catching the gray sickle spiders that dwelt in the arctax trees in the forest.

They liked to spin their webs on the lower branches so they could catch the bugs that clung to the elk and reindeer that brushed against the boughs. Nom had caught a few in jars, and he was keeping them alive.

Milking the spiders of their venom took forever, but he made sure to do it once a night so that in hopefully a few weeks, he would have the amount his recipe required.

The process involved paralyzing them with Mind Shiv and then using an electric lamprey to send a jolt of electricity into the arachnid. This would stimulate the gray sickle spiders into ejecting venom into the glass tubes he had placed them in.

The name of this new poison recipe was called Sickle Drop and required his activation when the time was ripe.

He was proud of his poison collection, and he wondered when he would be able to put it to some use again. He was particularly interested in Sickle Drop because it was meant to be spread over a blade or edged weapon as a delivery device.

As with all the others who were involved in the fight with the Nether Sister, he felt that something was coming for all of them and it was best to be prepared for anything.

Poison was a weapon, and it was of his opinion that they should have as many weapons as possible at their disposal.

He set about to his daily ritual of milking the spiders for their venom before he would set off to Siphon.

Most of the town would be asleep by then.

Nom always tried to choose the elderly and bed-bound to Siphon from.

Feeding on people's dreams and memories could leave a person feeling weak, drained, and bewildered. He didn't actually want to harm anyone, so he tried to stick to victims who wouldn't suffer as much after being fed on by him.

Picking some stitchguy who needed his energy next day to work on the mines would make him feel guilty. But sticking to someone who was already bedridden didn't make him feel so bad.

Also, people would be less likely to notice that there was an entity in town psychically draining people.

He had chosen a drunk stitchguy who was sleeping inside one of the fishing vessels that was in the dock. This person was a known drunk, so Nom felt no qualms about feeding on him.

However, he wasn't ready for the memories he saw during the Siphoning.

During these Siphoning sessions, it was inevitable that Nom would get some impression or glimpse of the memory or dream he was devouring.

Usually, it was the ephemera he had learned to expect from people.

The themes seemed universal. Speaking in public only to learn they're wearing no clothes. Dreams about teeth falling out. Some embarrassing social faux pas long buried in the subconscious.

But this drunk happened to be a sailor who had worked for Wint the Fishmonger. He had also done other odd jobs for the man.

And he was with him the night of the Night Sister attack.

Nom ceased Siphoning and explored the memory . . .

"Hurry," Wint was saying. "Before she bleeds to death. Imbecile!"

The man was trying to lift something ungainly into a boat. After some struggle, he finally half-lifted and half-rolled it in with a clunk.

It was a limp body.

Wint leaned over it, putting a hand on its face. "You're stronger than this, girl! Just hang on, damn you! I can't lose you, too! Hang on!"

When he leaned out of the way, Nom saw who it was.

It was the fishmonger's daughter.

Mishell.

She was still alive.

.

— CHAPTER FIFTY-THREE —

Banned Books

If Nay felt different since achieving Iron Rank, it was that she felt stronger, sturdier. She noticed it in the little things.

Walking up those steps to get to the cavernous eye sockets of Ianthe to enjoy a view of the Caraxe Strait?

She no longer got winded making the journey.

The cauldron Ilyawraith used to boil shellfish?

It was easier to lift.

Accidentally nicking herself with a knife while cutting potatoes?

It didn't hurt as much, bleed as much, and the cut healed noticeably faster.

She could simply *do more*, and the toll it took from her body was nothing compared to the fatigue and discomfort she would feel at Base Rank.

Not to mention she no longer had to worry about the danger of Vigor Sickness sidelining her for simply using Marrow Abilities. Ilyawraith and Quincy told her Vigor Sickness could still be a thing if she pushed her abilities to the breaking point and depleted her Vigor reserves.

But, for all intents and purposes, she could use her day-to-day abilities without worry.

In addition to leveling up her cultivator rank to Iron, Nay discovered she had received some upgrades.

Her wish about her mini-map had come true. The range had increased, but also she actually had markers for the other people around her. They appeared as smaller white dots.

There was one representing Quincy and another representing Ilyawraith.

She also discovered she could create labels next to the dots. She could conjure a spirit keyboard out of the air and type on it. Her keystrokes appeared on the interface.

She made a label for Quincy and Ilyawraith.

She also got dots for the creatures that were in the ocean around them. There was something large passing by them, probably a whale.

Her favorite discovery was an upgrade to her Chef's Delight Ability. A blinking icon appeared in its menu. It was the symbol for a book. She mentally clicked on it.

[... Accessing the Recipe Books of Jezabelle Childe]
[... Please Stand By ...]
[Granted Iron-Rank Access]
[Peruse!]

A digital recipe book was available on her interface.

Mastering the art of Epicurist Cooking. Volume 1: Cuisine of Iron.

She flipped through it, amazed. It was written in the dazzling script of Jezabelle Childe's handwriting, whoever that was.

**Candied Frog Legs. Ingredients. Frog legs: Frog legs, salt, butter, garlic, parsley. Candied Mixture: Sugar, water, gelatin strips.
Grants Jump Spell Effect. The eater can jump twice as high for the next two hours.**

Nay discovered Iron-Rank recipes could do a bit more than Base-Rank Buffs. They seemed to be legit magical spell effects. She trembled with excitement as she flipped through the pages.

**Venison Stew. Ingredients. Hindquarter deer tenderloin. Bacon. Onion. Potatoes. Rosemary, garlic, oregano, salt, pepper. Butter.
Grants Fleet-footed Spell Effect. The eater can run as fast as a gazelle through the forest for three hours.**

"Yeah," Nay said to herself. "I think I'm going to enjoy being Iron Rank."

**Pastie of Nether-Being Slaying. Ingredients. Pastry: Flour, salt, cold butter, cold water. Filling: Cubed rump steak, diced potato, diced swede, chopped onion, salt, pepper, egg.
Grants Amplified Damage against Nether Beings. The eater can consume these to make fights against beings from the Nether Realm a bit easier. Lasts one hour.**

"I'm going have to make a whole shit-ton of these pasties when I get back to the Lodge," Nay said.

"What was that?" Quincy said. He had appeared on top of the stairs inside the eye socket of Ianthe.

Nay was up here exploring the new upgrades and features in her interface.

"Why didn't we get to Iron Rank sooner?" Nay said. "I can do a lot more stuff now. Useful stuff."

"Because I didn't know it was going to become such a problem to let you be at Base Rank," Quincy said.

"You thought I was just gonna be the Lodge chef," Nay said.

"Isn't that what we both were hoping?" Quincy said.

"Yep," Nay said. "I guess I wasn't also expecting to have to fight a witch from a hell dimension. Now I can do cool knife shit."

Quincy smirked. "Show me."

Nay drew Thorn and activated the Dire Knife imbue.

The spirit aura appeared around the combat dagger.

Quincy took a closer look, intrigued. She explained the mechanic of landing strikes and building up Kinetic Points that could be released with her Gore Ability.

"Quella could do something similar," Quincy said. "What was the Delicacy you used?"

She told him about the Delicacy and Marrow she had acquired on the glacier, recounting the fight with the Icescythe. He was a bit overwhelmed with her enthusiasm in the retelling of the tale. She couldn't help it, she was excited.

"Quella's Delicacy for similar abilities was the Talon of the Phasebeast," Quincy said. "It made her a terror with daggers."

She pulled the ice scythe out of her inventory. "I figured I'd be more comfortable with two weapons instead of one, even though I really have no clue how to properly use it. It was at least useful when we were sliding down the icy slope."

Quincy examined the ice scythe, nodding. "Dual wield is the way to go with light weapons like this. But you'll have to learn proper technique and train if you want to be any good at it."

"I was good enough to beat Caraxus."

"Aye, girl," Quincy said. "That you were."

He sat down on the edge of the eye socket, letting his legs hang off the side. He produced a bottle of Rimefang Ale he had found in Ilyawraith's stash. He opened it, took a swig, and passed it to her.

"I'm proud of you," Quincy said.

She was in mid-sip when she looked over at him. She finished her swig and handed the bottle back to him. She sat next to him.

Those words of validation did something to her. She enjoyed praise, especially as a chef, but this was different.

This type of validation felt like it ran deeper.

Nay didn't say anything, just examined the ice scythe in her hands.

Quincy took another swig of the Rimefang Ale and then changed the subject. "We'll be heading back to Lucerna's End tomorrow. Green Moon Festival is coming up, and we'll be preparing a lot of the food for the event."

"Oh, a festival!" Nay said. "Sounds like a challenge, too."

"That it is," Quincy said. "So, get your recipes ready. And let's hope Nom and Gracie haven't burned the place down by the time we get back."

"What about Ilyawraith?" Nay said. "She never leaves Ianthe?"

"Sure, she leaves," Quincy said. "She leaves the Caraxe Strait for supply runs and whatever business she is tending to. But for the most part, she is the definition of *hermit*."

"Why?"

"It's not my story to tell," Quincy said. "But maybe she'll tell it to you one day."

It was to be Nay and Quincy's last night with Ilyawraith at Ianthe, so Nay wanted to make a meal that her mentors wouldn't forget.

She saw that Ilyawraith had shrimp, squid, and an octopus swimming around in her live-seafood storage pool.

She also found a short-grain rice imported from the Peninsula that reminded her of Arborio rice.

So, Nay diced up some shallots and garlic and sautéed them in oil, then added the Arborio grains to the pan.

At the same time, she heated up a jar of chicken stock Ilyawraith had and took some time spooning the stock into the rice and letting it evaporate.

Every time it evaporated, she added more stock. It took about twenty minutes to go through the stock, but it added a wonderful flavor to the rice.

Next, she grated some cheese and parsley into the risotto and began cooking the seafood.

She started with sautéing the shrimp in some oil, then added the squid rings, and after those cooked for a couple minutes, she added chopped octopus.

She had to be careful and make sure not to overcook the octopus or the squid, as those could go charred and rubbery fast.

She plated the proteins on top of the risotto and sprinkled more parsley over it all.

This was Nay's version of seafood risotto.

She served her mentors, and even Ilyawraith went for seconds, as they both couldn't get enough of the meal.

Nay always knew her food was good when the people eating were silent for a time as they concentrated on their meal.

To her surprise, she discovered she could taste again. The flavors of the shrimp and risotto were vivid inside her mouth. She chewed, stunned, thinking it was a fluke.

So, she took another bite.

She bit into the squid and octopus and was brought to tears by the caramelized sweetness of the dish, coupled with a hint of the sea.

"Are you okay?" Quincy said, who had noticed her becoming emotional.

Nay nodded. "I can . . . *I can taste again!*"

She took a sip of the Vancian white wine and was hit with the vision of flying over golden vineyards next to a rocky sea.

"Ascending Ranks can heal wounds, injuries; it can even filter out physiological impurities," Ilyawraith said.

This seafood risotto was pretty damn good. It was hard to beat how fresh the ingredients were. Filling, too.

She let her mentors finish off the leftovers. Nay was satisfied with just one bowl.

She sipped on her Vancian wine and waited for Ilyawraith to finish eating. When the woman was satisfied, setting her bowl aside, that was when Nay spoke.

"Who is Jezabelle Childe?" Nay said.

She asked Ilyawraith because if anyone was going to know that name, maybe it would be the cultivator who was a Silver.

The cultivator was lighting a green cheroot when she paused and looked at Nay, nonplussed. "How do you know that name?"

"When I became Iron, I unlocked the first volume of her cookbook series. It's in here." Nay pointed at her head.

"She lived many, many centuries ago," Ilyawraith said. "She was from Delicatessa and was one of the first Epicurists."

"So, one of my predecessors?"

Ilyawraith nodded, exhaling tobacco smoke. "Although there's been a movement to suppress her writings and ideas. She is one of the first Epicurists, but the Culinary Guild frowns upon her recipes and methods."

"Why?"

"Because she believed everyone should have access to Delicacies and Marrows, to her cooking. Not just DMA-approved Marrow Eaters. I'm also sure she had some recipes that created effects they did not approve of."

"So, I have access to a collection of banned books? Neat."

Ilyawraith and Quincy exchanged a look.

"When you reached Iron, you gained accessed to her material?" Ilyawraith said.

"That gave me access," Nay said. "But it came with an Ability called Chef's Delight. It came off a Marrow. And I only have access to the Iron volume, which means there are probably others with each Rank, right?"

"I think your guess would be right," Ilyawraith said. "It would appear that fate may have put you here for a reason. *Fate* being Ms. Childe."

Nay laughed. But no one else did.

"You're joking, right?" Nay said. "How I got to this world was chaotic and random and—"

"Maybe it's not as random as you think," Ilyawraith said.

"Are you saying this Jezabelle Childe person somehow called me here?"

"I can't say," Ilyawraith said. "But sometimes, a strange coincidence turns out not to be so strange."

"You said she was one of the first Epicurists from centuries ago," Nay said. "Is she even still alive?"

"That's something I'll have to look in to," Ilyawraith said.

"*Look in to*?" Nay said. "How? How would it be possible for her to still be alive?"

"How old do you think I am?" Ilyawraith said.

Nay looked at her, studying her. "I don't know . . . in your thirties, maybe your forties? But . . ."

"But what?"

"But I know you're older than that."

"The higher Ranks of cultivation slow the aging process," Ilyawraith said. "Jezabelle Childe was a powerful Epicurist. Definitely powerful enough to age differently."

Nay got quiet then, considering the ramifications of this revelation.

What did it mean? An Epicurist from this world trying to reach out to a chef like her?

"The next time we speak," Ilyawraith said, "perhaps I'll have some answers for you. Until then, let's enjoy the dessert I've prepared!

"It's this lovely sea salt sherbet I've been experimenting with . . ."

— CHAPTER FIFTY-FOUR —

The Nature of Truth

Nay was beginning to suspect her mysterious Quest-Giver in the sky was Jezabelle Childe.

If she was the one who lured Nay here to this world, or perhaps saw an opportunity with her arrival, then it would make sense that she was maybe the one guiding her along and making sure she was getting enough vigama, loot, and boons to stay alive and advance on this strange path she found herself on.

If it was someone or something else, she was sure curious about their motive.

With Jezabelle C., she could see maybe why she was somehow magically sponsoring an Elseworlder who had Epicurist abilities. Nay was a symbol of her beliefs that cooking Delicacies and Marrow should be available to everyone.

If this was the case, on one hand, Nay felt flattered. And on the other, hadn't Jezabelle C. essentially put a target on her back?

Good thing she was up here at the edge of the world where she didn't have to worry about the politics of the Peninsula. She craved somewhere warm, but she could live with the constant cold if it meant staying out of the blistering heat.

She had planted the black rose from the mysterious stranger in a clay pot that she kept on the windowsill in her room. She wasn't sure if it would grow as a single stem, but she would sprinkle water on it and kept a glass jar over the rose to protect it.

Nom had wanted to hear everything about her journey and the trials, and she did not omit the part with the strangely attractive man.

She hadn't said a word about him to Quincy or Ilyawraith, and although it made her feel guilty, she thought there were some things she should be able to keep to herself.

She didn't want to give them reason for alarm. She didn't think he meant her harm, but she was intrigued that he seemed to know about her. And the rose. She liked the rose and she liked taking care of it.

She didn't want to tell Nom, because she thought they could keep secrets between themselves, but she feared he would discover it anyways because of his access to her memories during his Mind Meld spell.

Plus, she needed to talk about him to someone.

And it wouldn't have been an appropriate topic of conversation with any of her other girlfriends here because, well, reasons.

"You should probably eventually tell Quincy about him," Nom had said. "He has all the signs."

"All the signs of what?"

"Being a total freak."

Nay had scoffed at that. "I don't think so. Really? No. He was just a weirdo like all the magical people are here. He was more . . . *eccentric* . . . and *mysterious* than anything."

It had been Nom's turn to scoff. "You need to take off your horny-lensed glasses—"

"Horny?!"

"You have the hots for the guy; I can smell the pheromones coming out of your pores. It smells like a sushi bar in a grocery store."

"*Nom!*"

"I'm kidding. It's more of an escargot-in-butter smell—"

"Jesus, please stop."

"Okay, okay! I'm sorry, all right? But it's possible the guy is bad news. He appears out of nowhere, seems to know things about you, presents you a weird offer, and then he just gives you a rose and disappears when you decline? Does all of that not seem like a red flag to you?"

"To be fair, both of us appeared in this world out of nowhere. And look at us! We're trustworthy people, right?"

"Trustworthy? Sure. But are we good people? We both have our secrets, and we've done enough questionable things here where I think we might be toeing the line."

"Oh, come on. We're not keeping secrets . . . we're just . . . delaying information until the time is right."

"Well, don't wait too long."

"Like you did with your little adventures in poisoning assholes in bordellos?"

"Hey, I told you right away when that happened."

"Yeah, but how long were you experimenting with poisons before you told me?"

"It was the right time."

"So, same thing with the guy I met in the Frozen Vale."

"All right," Nom had said. "Suit yourself. But I'm gonna keep an eye on that black rose. If it starts growing strange attachments like venus flytraps or poisonous spores, I'm setting it on fire."

While she had told Nom everything about her trip, he had told her everything that had transpired at the Lodge during her absence.

That the dinner services had run smoothly without any issue, unless one considered the townsfolk's addiction to white wine and butter-based sauces an issue.

Nay didn't dislike French cuisine, but while she recognized it as a bedrock of foundational knowledge for a chef, it wasn't the be-all end-all of great cuisine.

She appreciated the French more for their *brigade de cuisine* contributions to kitchen organizational and hierarchal structure than their affinity for everything being cooked in butter.

She couldn't diss them too much, as she grew up in Louisiana and the very first dishes she ever learned wouldn't exist if not for the French.

Chicken fricassee and crawfish etouffee were not only some of her first dishes but some of her favorites.

Regardless, she was anxious to introduce the townsfolk to other flavors.

Nom had told her about how he suspected that Mishell, the fishmonger's daughter, was still alive, and she had asked him why he thought that.

He told her that it was more of a premonition he had, and emphasized that they should be on guard.

She wasn't too worried about it.

Now that she was Iron Rank, she was no longer afraid of the prospect of Mishell showing her face again.

She was certain if they had a rematch, it wouldn't be an even match.

When Nay reached the Veritax chapel, which was near the edge of Lac Coineascar but on the other side of Lucerna's End from the Lodge, she stopped to observe the architecture.

Most chapels back home, especially the old ones, adhered to a cruciform floor plan and structure.

The Lucerna's End Chapel of the Veritax adhered to a hexagonal floor plan. It was made from cut stone, which made the place seem more like a mini-cathedral than some hastily constructed wooden structure, which was what Nay had been expecting.

At the top of the stone structure was that symbol Alric had branded on him, the eye within the hexagon. This was made out of metal and the eye rotated within, turning three hundred and sixty degrees throughout the day and night in alignment with the sun.

Alric had described it as a symbol of truth, but to Nay it just gave her the vibe that this deity was always watching. There was something accusatory about it that made her feel uneasy.

Maybe it was her dislike of most religions and nothing more. But in her experience, whenever she walked into a place with holy symbols, negative shit had always followed.

From being judged by the other girls in her youth group during that short stint when she was a teen when her mother decided to become a Christian, to literally being attacked by a rift spider inside of that Korean church, she couldn't help but expect some unfortunate or regrettable consequences.

Yet she stepped through the doors anyways, because she wanted to give Alric a visit.

It had been too long.

The doorway entered into one of the six arms of the chapel. This atrium was like a foyer, lit by a torch. In the center of the arm, situated across from the veils leading into the interior of the chapel, was a statue of Verity herself.

She seemed to be made of bronze.

In one hand she was holding a mirror; the other hand held a horned head. The head seemed to be a grotesque union of a man and a goat. Whatever it was, it was old and had a huge beard.

Nay stared at it for a moment and mouthed, *What the fuck?*

She had so many questions, but she continued through the veil.

Four of the six arms of the hexagon served as naves. There were chairs arranged in rows in each of the arms, and the outer ring of the center of the hexagon served as an aisle.

The altar was located in the very center of the structure, where there was a raised dais someone could speak on. That was where Alric probably pontificated from.

Torches lined the walls, and the ceiling was domed and painted with a mural of Verity holding up a giant mirror, showing a mass of people their reflection.

The arm opposite the foyer had a strange wooden booth at the end of it.

One portion opened and an elderly stitchgal emerged from it like it was a confessional.

She looked relieved about something, as if she was walking with a little lighter step than before going in there.

As she passed Nay, she smiled.

She made Nay think of a grandma who had just received some good news about something that was previously making her nervous.

Nay looked back at the box, and she had a pretty good idea that Alric was in the other compartment.

She walked up to it and entered the compartment the elderly stitchgal just got out of.

She sat down inside.

Instead of a screen divider wherein she could see Alric sitting behind in shadow, there was a mirror.

Yet he somehow saw her.

"Nay!" It was Alric's voice. "What a pleasant surprise! I thought you were still on your excursion with Quincy."

"You knew about that?" Nay said.

"Sure," Alric said. "I went to the Lodge a couple nights ago to eat, and Ulla told me you and Quincy had gone on a trip. May I ask where to?"

"So, is this like a confessional?"

"Confessional?"

"You know, where I confess to my sins and you listen and then absolve me of them."

"I'm afraid not."

"So, what is this?"

"You tell me about an event or happening that confuses you. And then I tell you the truth about the matter. As a servant of Verity, with one ear turned towards you and the other towards her."

"I see. The truth, eh?"

"Want to give it a go?"

"Oh, I don't know. Can we talk normal? I brought you some food."

"Food?"

She pulled a burrito out of her inventory. "It's a carnitas burrito. Nay and Nom's carnitas bombs. It's pork. You can eat pork, right?"

"Sure, I can eat pork. Why wouldn't I?

"In some religions in my world, the practitioners aren't supposed to eat pork. It's considered an unclean animal. Pigs wallowing in mud and all that."

"I happen to enjoy pork. I couldn't imagine going without bacon."

"One of the reasons why I'm an agnostic, bro."

"What's an agnostic?"

"Eh, someone who doesn't really believe in gods but isn't completely opposed to the idea of it per se."

"I see. Well, I'm excited about trying your pork pie!"

Nay cringed.

She composed herself. "Burrito. It's called a burrito."

"Apologies. I can't wait to try this burrito, then!"

"All right, so I'll see you on the outside?"

Alric didn't answer her at first. Instead, his voice got a little quieter. "Come on; go ahead. There's gotta be something you want to know the truth about."

Nay could see that he really wanted to demonstrate the power of his deity. And she had to admit she was a little curious.

"Sure," she said. "Why not?"

"Splendid!" Alric said. "You can take your time; think of the scenario you want me to hear."

Nay thought for a moment. Then she made up her mind. "So, when I was gone with Quincy, I met this person."

"Yes? Who were they?"

"Well, that's what I'd like to know. Maybe Verity knows."

"Go on . . ."

"They seemingly appeared out of nowhere. This person, I didn't know them. But they seemed to know me. And they wanted to offer me something."

"Which was?"

"They were talking about paths, the paths people were on, and he mentioned that I had another choice concerning my path. A different way than the one I'm currently on."

There was silence for a long and uncomfortable moment. She thought she heard Alric whispering.

"Alric?" Nay said. "You still there?"

The whispering noise stopped.

"Verity can't tell you who the man is," Alric said, "but she knows where he's from. And she knows that you're confused about whether or not you can trust him."

Nay was taken aback a little. She wasn't really expecting an answer. "Can I . . . trust him?"

"No one from the Phantomhead Empire is to be trusted."

— CHAPTER FIFTY-FIVE —

The Problem of Moon Cakes

"What do you mean, 'Phantomhead Empire'?" Nay said.
Where had she heard that name before?
When Alric spoke, his voice was deliberate and slow. There was a poise to it that unsettled Nay. "The man who gave you the black rose, grown from Entrophist thaumaturgy, is a representative of the Phantomhead Empire."

"Entrophist . . ."

The anti-cultivators.

From Ilyawraith's stories.

"They're not the sort you want visiting you unannounced," Alric said. "Or at all."

"How did you know about the rose?" Nay said. "I didn't mention anything about it to you."

"Veritax saw it," Alric said. "She sees all truthfully."

This wasn't the type of party trick that Nay enjoyed. This was getting a little too serious, a little too creepy for her liking. If Alric was trying to prove there was something *other*, something supernatural to his beliefs, it was working.

"She says that you know where the Phantomhead Empire is," Alric said. "Quincy told you it was a continent to the South of the Peninsula, across the sea. It's one of the places Marrow Eaters are not welcome."

How much did Alric know about her life from consulting with Verity? How much did he know about everyone in town?

Verity was telling him everyone's secrets.

"You ought to destroy the rose," Alric said.

"Alric, this is making me uncomfortable—"

"Burn it!"

Nay flinched. She found she had instinctively recoiled from his voice.

"Throw it into the fire and burn it!"

Nay pushed the door open and tumbled out of Verity's vault and fled towards the center off the hexagon. She ran past the altar and burst into the opposite arm, where Verity's statue was waiting. As she hurried past it, her swift movement causing the nearby torch to flicker and lean in one direction, the head atop the statue turned to watch her flee.

It spoke, the bronze lips creaking and a hollow, metallic voice sang out:

"Destroy the black rose! Sever your connection to the Entrophist!"

Nay nearly screamed in fright. She looked in horror at the animate statue and then sprinted out the door of the chapel. She ran the entire way back to the Lodge at the speed of Iron.

Nay grabbed the black rose from the windowsill and brought it downstairs to the hearth in the tavern area. She held the clay container in her hands and stared at the flames. She looked to the rose. Parts of the petal reflected the light in little coronas, as if there were twinkling stars within the material of the petal itself.

She couldn't do it. Nay couldn't throw it into the fire. She burst into the kitchen and headed for the larder.

"Afternoon, chef," Gracie said. She was sitting with Nom at the table, enjoying fried Lac clam sandwiches Nom had made for them. "There's extra if you're hungry."

"I've no appetite, Gracie," Nay said.

Nom shoved a whole sandwich into his mouth, turning a light shade of red as he chewed. That particular shade of red signified he was eating something delicious.

Nay entered the larder and headed straight for the corner underneath the window where she had an herb garden set up in a barrel. She tucked the clay pot with the black rose behind the barrel, but she positioned it so it still had access to the light coming in through the window.

She headed for the exit but then stopped in the threshold. She took one last look at the black rose, felt a mix of emotions, then left the larder.

Nay joined Nom and Gracie at the table, and Gracie slid her a fried clam sandwich. She had made fluffy, buttery rolls out of the dough used for garlic knots, and she split them vertically to create a bun for the clams. Nom had concocted a delicious tartar sauce to spread on the buns, and the whole deal was sprinkled with lemon juice and dill.

Quincy must have sensed there was delicious food available, because he wandered in from the tavern and sat down. Gracie made him a sandwich. Nom went ahead and fried more clams to accommodate Quincy's appetite. There was no way he was going to stop at just one sandwich.

"Green Moon Festival's next week," Quincy said, chewing as he spoke. There was tartar sauce stuck to his mustache.

Nay chuckled and tried to point it out, but he was too focused on the remainder of the sandwich in his hand.

"What's the Green Moon Festival celebrating, exactly?" Nay said. "Besides, uh, the green moon . . ."

"You're not wrong," Gracie said. "It's for the moon. It's at its highest and brightest next week. It's three days of food and drink and games. There's boat races on the Lac, sporting events for the lads to demonstrate strength in contests, there's dancing 'round the Lucerna tree for the ladies and children, the lighting of lanterns on the third night; why, there's a lot of festivities. It's my favorite time of year!"

"Moons are pretty neat," Nom said. "They light up the night. Also, there wouldn't be werewolves without moons, right?"

Quincy and Gracie scrunched their noses and gave Nom a weird look.

"We didn't always have a moon," Quincy said. "It's why we celebrate it."

"Before the Beacon," Gracie said, "there was nothing but stars in the sky."

"After the Beacon was almost destroyed," Quincy said, "men took it up to the sky and split it into the sun and moon so there would be light for the world during both the day and night."

"There's songs about it," Gracie said. "You'll get sick of hearing 'em before the festival is over."

"I trust that you all will come up with the best food the festival has ever seen," Quincy said. "But the main thing is we want to make sure we have enough moon cakes. We're always on the verge of running out every year, and I don't want us to have to worry this year."

"Moon cakes?" Nay said.

"They're the special treat everyone loves," Quincy said. "They're sweet, they're delicious, their texture is exquisite, and they're also only available during the festival. That was the only time Ol' Pat ever made them. Did I mention they're delicious?"

"Okay," Nay said. "I'm sure they're not hard to make. Do you know the recipe, Gracie?"

Gracie shook her head. "Ol' Pat kept it to herself. But I'm sure she has it written down in her book."

"Okay," Nay said. "I'll take a look at it today and make sure we have enough ingredients."

"These are delicacies, do you understand?" Quincy said. "It ain't the Green Moon Festival without moon cakes. If we run out of moon cakes, these people will riot and burn the town down. We *need* the delicious moon cakes."

Nay and Nom exchanged a look.

"I . . . can't wait to try one for myself, then," Nom said. "To see what all the fuss is about."

"The filling is special," Quincy said. "We better hope Ol' Pat wrote down the ingredients and her method, because if you don't get it just right, everyone will notice. And then the Green Moon Festival will be a disaster."

"All right," Nay said. "Jeez. I get the point. Let's just chill out and I'll take care of it, okay? It's me we're talking about. I'm not a pastry chef, but I've made plenty of cakes in my time. How hard could it be?"

It turned out it could be quite hard when there was no recipe to reference.

Nay had flipped through the little leather-bound recipe book at least a dozen times. There were recipes for fish and fish pie and tinned fish and smoked fish but nothing about cake or moon cakes. "You gotta be fucking kidding me," Nay said. She sat in the storeroom and looked around. "Gracie!"

After a minute, Gracie stuck her head in. "Yes, chef?"

"I'm not seeing anything about moon cakes in Ol' Pat's recipe book."

Gracie, curious, entered and walked over to Nay. She reached over her. "May I?"

Nay sat back, exasperated. She spun a pencil on the table and sighed. "Have at it."

Gracie flipped through the book. She chewed on her bottom lip as she perused. She let out a little *harrumph*. "I think you may be right."

"Describe a moon cake to me," Nay said. "And please don't use the word *delicious*. I swear to god, if Quincy had said that word one more time . . ."

The kitchen manager didn't look up from the book as she started to describe the delight. "So, they're handheld cakes about the size of a good biscuit. But the crust is golden and glossy-like. It's a thin layer and it's sticky. Got a bit of a savory taste to it. But the filling is a blue and green paste with a bit of egg yolk. It's sweet and delic—"

She stopped herself.

"It's good," Gracie said. "I can't eat more than one in a day, as they're dense-like. Hurts my tum if I eat more than one. They go great with tea. A good tea can help curb the sweetness of the cake. It's just cozy."

When she said *cozy*, her eyes were closed and she did a little shimmy before opening them.

"The filling's a paste?" Nay said.

"Yes, an elderflower paste," Gracie said. Her face was back in Ol' Pat's recipe book. "Now, what's this?"

Nay looked at her.

Gracie was tracing something with her finger on the page. She was mouthing something to herself. "I think this might be something. See this?"

She lowered the book.

On one of the pages, in Ol' Pat's scrawl, the former cook had written: *Elderflower paste. Volva Serrilda.*

"I understand elderflower paste," Nay said. "But what does *Volva Serrilda* mean?"

"Not what," Gracie said. "But who."

Nay was putting on her cloak and halfway out of the tavern area when she heard Quincy's voice calling after her. "How are the moon cakes coming along? Do you need to buy more ingredients?"

"It's fine," Nay said. "Totally under control. I'm going to the market now to make some purchases."

"That's what I like to hear," Quincy said. "We have the moon cakes; we'll have a successful festival. The town needs it, Nay. After what happened here, the townsfolk need a reason to celebrate and enjoy festivities. It will do the soul of the town good."

"There's no worries," Nay said. "You can trust me to get the job done."

Nay hunched her shoulders and cringed at herself as she exited the Lodge. "Fuck."

Nay grabbed Juniper from Bruennig, and the fauglir nuzzled against her side with affection. The chef saddled her, mounted, and then left the town, heading northwest into the forest. She consulted her mini-map where she had discovered she could plan an itinerary when Gracie was giving her the directions.

As she rode Juniper, Nay's thoughts went to Alric. She felt conflicted feelings concerning him. He was the first kind and helpful person she had met in this world, but now she felt he had ruined their friendship with what had happened in his chapel. Not that he forced his religion on her, but at the same time, she did feel he was aggressive about it.

And the whisperings and his voice and the knowledge he shared. It had scared her. She wasn't sure how she would react the next she encountered him.

But she was deep in the woods now, consulting her mini-map. She would worry about Alric later.

Volva Serrilda was an old stitchwoman who lived as a hermit in the woods. She lived in a cabin called the Ravenfeather Lodge.

She was something of a local Loremaster who knew the history of Stitchdale and Lucerna's End and the surrounding region. She was also a talented healer with herbs and salves, which made her alluring to parents who would sometimes call on her if their children were ever seriously ill. She was something of a crank and didn't like to be around people, hence the hermit cabin away from the town proper. Gracie warned her not to get on her bad side.

"She'll shun you if you piss her off," Gracie said. "And since you be needing answers from her, best to stay in her good graces."

"I got it, I got it," Nay had said.

Which is why she flinched when she finally reached Ravenfeather Lodge and a voice cried out from a window, "Your mutt is standing in my mushroom garden!"

Nay closed her eyes and sighed.

Goddammit.

— CHAPTER FIFTY-SIX —

Volva Serrilda

"Don't let her eat the mushrooms or I'll turn you both into tundra toads!"

Nay looked down at Juniper, who was munching on mushroom caps.

"Uh, Juniper," Nay said.

Juniper ignored her.

"Juniper, my dear, those aren't our mushrooms," Nay said.

Juniper looked up at her, pieces of gilled and gray mushrooms on her snout, with big innocent eyes. She then looked back down to eat some more.

"Juniper!" Nay tugged on the reins, and Juniper snorted, finally getting the message.

"I'm sorry, but we can't eat stuff that doesn't belong to us. This is someone's garden."

She piloted the fauglir out of the fungal garden and back onto the snow path leading to the Lodge.

The front door to the two-story cabin burst open, and an elderly druidic-looking stitchgal stomped out onto the wooden porch. She was using a wooden staff to help her walk. The top part of the staff branched into a Y, and there were feathers, bird claws, and . . .

Were those dried eyeballs?

. . . hanging off it.

She had thick white hair dusted in snow falling onto her shoulders. There was a strip of black paint across her eyes, from the top of one ear to the other, and when she blinked Nay saw her eyelids were painted yellow.

She was wearing the hide of some feline-type creature on top of her head. It included the creature's face, its two fangs gripping her forehead like it was biting her skull. She wore a necklace of antlers, and her fingers were covered in gold rings.

I hope to god that isn't a cat she skinned on top of her head.

"Stop!" Volva Serrilda said. "Go no further! This dwelling is protected!"

Nay climbed off Juniper and stood in the snow. "We meant no harm. I can compensate you for the mushrooms. Do you want coin as recompense?"

"I don't need your coin, girl," Volva Serrilda said. "I need you to leave me alone!"

"I would do that," Nay said, "but I'm afraid I need your help."

Volva Serrilda walked off the porch and down the steps, using her staff as a walking stick. She wielded it with alarming aggression. Soon, she was in front of Nay, examining her like a witch gazing at the cast of bone dice.

"Who are you, girl? And, what do you need my help for?"

"My name is Nay Favreau. I'm the cook at Quincy's Lodge."

Volva Serrilda's mouth crinkled and one of her eyes narrowed. "Ol' Pat's the cook at Quincy's Lodge."

"Ol' Pat's passed away."

This news surprised the crone. She seemed disturbed, as if she realized something was poking holes in the passage of time. "Passed away? But we were supposed to have a tinned-fish date. She brings the tinned fish and bread, and I make the tea and cookies."

She drew into herself then, lost in her own thoughts. She chewed on her lip, which deepened the wrinkles on her shrewd face. "The outside world appears to be passing me by."

"I'm sorry," Nay said. "I truly am. It seemed like you two were friends."

"More than friends, girl," Volva Serrilda said. "We were both old enough to remember the things everyone else in Lucerna's End seemed to have forgotten."

There was a haunting sadness on her face, and a whispering wind seemed to pick up around her, lifting her hair. The antlers on her neck knocked together, creating a sound that was not unlike wind chimes.

"Ol' Pat is actually part of the reason I came to see you."

Volva Serrilda blinked and her sad face softened, expectant and hopeful.

The Ravenfeather Lodge was nothing like Quincy's Lodge. Volva Serrilda's place was more of a cabin. It was also a familiar landmark for those who lived in Lucerna's End. To the townsfolk, it was the two-story cabin where the old hermit lady lived, a place mostly to be avoided unless someone's child needed an esoteric nature remedy. If Volva Serrilda wanted to be seen or socialize, she'd come to town.

Feathers, tails, and claws dangled from braided strings hanging from the ceiling of the porch, giving the place a wild, one-with-nature vibe. There were runes carved into tree stumps on the property, and Volva Serrilda mentioned they were to keep certain predators out. The markings were relics of the old religion of the human tribes who once lived in Stitchdale.

Because she was an old woman living alone in the woods, her defense system was a hedge of stones and thorns surrounding the lodge and the two large, half-wild fauglir named Bein and Astrid who patrolled the area.

They were brother and sister from the same litter. The fauglir lived outside and kept more tangible predators at bay, but Volva Serrilda would let them in at night to feed them dinner and let them laze in front of her hearth.

Nay left Juniper with them. "Don't wander too far off, now. I won't be too long."

Juniper sniffed Bein and Astrid; they sniffed her. Then they half-galloped, half-sprang into the trees, nipping playfully at each other.

The first floor of the cabin looked like an apothecary exploded and had never been organized again. Herbs and roots and bones were scattered across shelves and tables. Others hung from the wall and ceiling.

Precarious stacks of old tomes leaned against furniture, and the whole place was cast in a dim orange glow from the hearth. It smelled of licorice and ginger and vegetable stew.

Volva Serrilda led her to two comfy club chairs in front of the hearth. The leather was ancient and worn.

Nay stepped around the piles of books at their feet and took a seat.

The wild winter crone grabbed what looked like a raw strip of wood from a pile sitting on a rabbit pelt. She stuck the end into the hearth, lighting it.

A pleasant smell of burning pine filled the cabin as she wove the smoke wand in the air. She set it in a jar, where it continued to slowly burn. Next, she laid her staff against the wall and settled into her chair with a groan. Then she sat up, suddenly remembering something.

"I haven't offered you refreshments," Volva Serrilda said. "Where have my manners gone?"

"Oh, it's okay," Nay said. "I don't think this will take long. You see—"

"Spittle that," Volva Serrilda said. "I have warm cocoa and butter cookies."

Nay watched her get up and rattle about in her pantry. "The butter cookies are, unfortunately, a lost art in Lucerna's End. It's a maugrim recipe, and the dense stitchfolk here failed to continue the tradition of a good, buttery cookie. A light texture, crumbles in the mouth in buttery bits. If I had any say, they'd have never forgotten. Their loss, I suppose."

She grumbled as she poured warm milk from a tin into wooden mugs.

Nay could smell the chocolate as it melted in the milk. She could see the wisps of steam rising from the mugs.

Volva Serrilda came back with a tray with the warm cocoa and spread of butter cookies. Nay grabbed a mug and took two cookies, then the old woman sat down.

The cookies were shaped like dominos, and there were little crows etched into the crispy surface. They had been sprinkled with sugar crystals. Nay took a nibble from one, and it crumbled in her mouth and melted like butter across her tongue. It tasted—she could taste again!—a lot like a crispy shortbread. She swallowed. "That's very good."

Next, she took a sip of the warm cocoa and was surprised to find a frothy cream leaving a mustache above her lip. The cocoa flavor was brushed with cinnamon, and it was like drinking a nice hot chocolate. She dipped a cookie in the warm cocoa and noticed Volva Serrilda watching her with a smile.

"See," she said. "To me, they taste even better, the colder it is outside. There is a magic to it; trust me."

Nay finished her softened cookie, drank more of the warm cocoa, and then it set it aside. "Thank you. If you're so inclined, if you want to share the recipe for the cookies with me, I can make them at the Lodge and we can put them on the menu."

"That's right," Volva Serrilda said, "you are the new cook! That is a clever idea. You could even keep them in jars and have them on the bar counters for all to see!"

"Sure," Nay said. "If that's what you'd like."

"I will think about it." Volva Serrilda nibbled on a cookie, her yellow-painted eyelids winking at Nay through the wisps of pine smoke and amber light. "But something tells me you didn't come here for my cookie recipe."

"You're not totally wrong," Nay said. "I come here to inquire about another recipe."

"Oh?" Volva Serrilda straightened, intrigued. "Another recipe?"

"Moon cakes," Nay said.

The wild winter crone processed those words and then tilted her head, nodding. "The eve of the Green Moon Festival is approaching, and you need to produce moon cakes in bulk."

"Exactly," Nay said. "But the only person who seemed to know how to make the moon cakes has moved on from this world without leaving a recipe behind."

One of Volva Serrilda's hands started fidgeting with the antlers hanging from her neck and mused. "No recipe, you say?"

"That's right," Nay said. "And I have her recipe book. Nary a mention of moon cake, but I did find a curious note."

Volva Serrilda tilted her head, waiting for an explanation with widened eyes.

"Your name, next to the words *elderflower paste*."

Volva Serrilda nodded and sat back. She picked up another cookie and took a bite. "I was the one who helped her with the recipe."

"Oh," Nay said, somewhat relieved. "So, you have it? And would you share it with me?"

"I would if I could," Volva Serrilda said. "Except I didn't teach her the recipe. I just gave her directions on where to get it."

"I'm sorry," Nay said. "I'm not sure I follow."

"The recipe for the particular kind of elderflower-paste moon cakes is something of a secret," Volva Serrilda said. "It was shared with Ol' Pat, and if she didn't write it down anywhere, then it seems it still remains a secret."

"But you said you gave her directions on where to get it."

"Moon cakes were a delicacy shared with the stitchfolk by one of the Friends of Man who dwells in the mists of Maer Scathan."

"Friends of Man?"

"One of the first folk who dwelt here before anyone else."

"Okay . . ."

"Her name is Aule, and . . ." Volva Serrilda paused for a second, thinking, then continued. ". . . I can give you direction on how to find her, but there's no guarantee she'll give you the recipe."

Nay was baffled. She tried not to show her irritation. "What's the big deal about this recipe? A well-kept family secret is one thing, but I'm beginning to think the recipe must be magical."

"It may be," Volva Serrilda said. "It's a Friends of Man recipe, so it's very old. Their knowledge isn't shared very often with man today. If at all. But you can try and find her. What happens next is up to her."

"She must have liked Ol' Pat, though," Nay said, "since she shared the recipe with her."

"Ol' Pat was a loyal lass," Volva Serrilda said. "The Friends of Man can sense qualities like that on a person. It's said they can judge a person's character with a glance."

Nay swallowed.

Great. The success of the Green Moon Festival would hinge on whether or not some old being deemed me worthy or not. Just fantastic.

"Don't look so troubled," Volva Serrilda said, chuckling. "It's just a treat. The town might deserve to go without moon cakes during the festival for a while. After all, they don't seem to care about my butter cookies. The fools."

[Quest Detected]
[Quest: Find Aule in Maer Scathan]
[Accept Quest Y/N?]

— CHAPTER FIFTY-SEVEN —

Upgrades

Nom was going to accompany Nay to the mists of Maer Scathan to hunt down this Aule. If Nay didn't get the moon cake recipe, the Green Moon Festival would be a disaster. At least, that was how Quincy framed it. At the very least, it would be a major downer.

She hadn't told him what was going on, that Ol' Pat never wrote down the recipe, so she was now on this wild goose chase to acquire it for the townsfolk of Lucerna's End. As far as Quincy was concerned, Nay was still acquiring enough ingredients and was prepping to mass-produce the cakes.

Aule had approved of Ol' Pat, but the old cook let the recipe fade away with her. Now Nay was having to stand in her place for the town and earn the good graces of this Friend of Man. And Nom would be coming as her backup. Just in case things got dicey.

And, let's be honest, things for Nay always had a way of getting dicey.

So, naturally, the first matter of business was consuming more of the Marrow of the Mewlipped Tode.

Nay had defrosted one of the remaining filets of the tode Marrow, and it was salted and sitting on a rack while she prepared the ale batter. She poured some Icemarrow Ale into a bowl of flour and gave it a good mix until it was the droopy consistency of a melted milkshake. If the batter was too thick, it had a way of trapping more steam while it fried, making the fish become a soppy mess once it was in the sandwich. So, a light batter with a light touch was the play for her.

Nom was next to her, preparing his version of tartar sauce. He had made the mayonnaise himself, too, and for a delusional few minutes, they wondered if they had introduced mayo to this world.

"Probably not," Nay said. "I'm sure the Culinary Guild has stuff that we've never heard of or even conceived. So, I'm sure they figured out how to make mayo a long time ago."

Nom strained lemon juice over the mayo. Next, he added in chopped pickles, snow shallots, and cured capers. His special ingredient was crumbling these packaged crackers he had found in the pantry. He had developed an affinity for them in Nay's absence.

They came in a red-and-gold cardboard sleeve. The material looked it came from playing cards of some kind. They were labeled *Duke Umberto's Digestive Biscuits*.

Nay had tried one, and it seemed to be a cross between a Ritz cracker and a saltine cracker.

"They do miracles for my digestion," Nom had said.

"I didn't realize you had issues."

"My esophagus sphincters can always use a little attention. Skyr and these crackers have me running like a well-lubed machine."

"TMI, Nom. TMI."

"TMI?"

"Too much information."

He finished the tartar sauce off with a generous dose of dill.

"You can't forget the dill," Nom said. "Tartar sauce just isn't tartar sauce without it."

Nay wiped the excess moisture off the Marrow filet and then dredged it in flour. Putting a layer of starch on the meat would give the batter something to bond to. She dipped it in the beer batter and then slowly set it into the pan of oil. Easing it in prevented the battered fish from sticking to the bottom of the pan.

"What kind of Marrow Ability do you think it's going to be?" Nom said. "I think it would be interesting if it gave you that deadly tongue the creature had. I saw it rip off a man's head from at least three fauglir carriages away like it was grabbing a cluster of grapes off a vine."

Nay was struck with the image of the Mewlipped Tode ripping off a night watchman's head. She shook her head, wishing she could forever forget that memory and have it never be revived again.

"Sounds useful," Nay said as she watched the Marrow fry. Gold and green motes of light floated out of the oil. "Maybe if I never regained my sense of taste."

She shuddered at the thought of having a frog tongue as a weapon that could rip pieces off people and, not only that, actually having to taste everything while it was happening. Leave it to Nom to conjure disgusting images full of too many sensory details.

After a couple of minutes, the Marrow was done frying. She scooped it out and shook off the excess oil, letting it dry. The filet now had a glassy and golden layer of beer batter locking in its flavor. She found herself salivating as she prepared a bun.

"You didn't happen to save any of that Crab Marrow for me, did you?" Nom said. "I'd really like another Ability."

Nay froze. "Oh, my god, Nom! I'm such an idiot. How could I have forgotten?"

She summoned the claw of the Caraxian Crab from her inventory. She dropped the huge appendage before it fully materialized into her hands. It appeared next to them, its girth and sudden presence shoving aside the nearby tables and shelves and knocking a bunch of pots and pans from their hooks.

"I'm sorry; I was thinking about myself this whole time," Nay said.

Nom, startled, approached the massive crab claw.

"For the love of all that is precious," Nom said. "Why did you take the entire claw? Do we plan on trying to sell all the Marrow?"

"Are you crazy?" Nay said. "We're not Marrow dealers! Besides, in order to be successful at that enterprise, we'd probably have to be on the Peninsula, where we would be hunted like chemistry teachers turned meth dealers or the charming but scummy lawyers helping them."

"Huh?"

"Never mind," Nay said. "I took the whole claw because I was in a hurry. An ice troll was trying to kill me. So, I just shoved it in my inventory. Any other questions?"

"Yeah, where's the Old Bay at?"

Turned out she was hogging most of that delicious mid-Atlantic seasoning in her inventory. She retrieved a shaker of it for him and went back to assembling her fried Marrow of the Mewlipped Tode sandwich.

While she put down a nice leaf of icethaw lettuce on a homemade brioche bun and scooped multiple dollops of the tartar sauce on the other half, Nom had gotten a huge pot of water boiling and was in the process of breaking off part of the Caraxian claw.

Nay placed the golden, crispy filet onto the bed of tartar sauce and then topped it with the lettuce and the other bun, completing the Marrow sandwich. Light motes floated out of the center of the sandwich.

Nay grabbed the work of art with both hands. "Down the hatch!"

She shoved as much of the sandwich as she could into her mouth and bit down. The beer batter was the perfect crunchy touch to the sandwich. She envisioned herself biting into edible gold glass. That was the effect. It was followed by the juiciness of the Marrow, and it was probably the best faux fish filet sandwich she had ever had. The creaminess and tang of the tartar sauce, coupled with the fresh dill, really brought the bite to another level.

Bursts of light and magical text soon followed.

[Marrow Consumed!]
[Frog Leg Marrow of the Mewlipped Tode]
[Frog Leg Marrow of the Mewlipped Tode has already been used for Tongue of the Hierophant]
[Would you like to unlock Marrow Ability for Bladegland of the Icescythe Y/N?]
[Delicacy: Bladegland of the Icescythe]
[Opening Delicacy Tree]
[Marrow Abilities: 4/12]

She mentally clicked on the Y.

Opening Ability Tree for the Delicacy: Bladegland of the Icescythe.

The diorama of the human digestive system spread across her HUD, rotating, all the organs surrounded in a white aura with cubes rotating next to them, indicating open Ability slots.

One was already filled, which represented her Decapitate Ability.

You have eleven open slots in this Ability Tree. You have consumed Frog Leg Marrow of the Mewlipped Tode. It has syncretized into the Salvo of Knives Ability. Would you like to use a slot for Salvo of Knives? [Y/N?]

She accessed the description for the Ability.

**Salvo of Knives. Instantly throw both your weapons at target. A successful hit with dagger amplifies weapon damage. All other successful hits with other weapons stay at base weapon damage.
The ranged attack is also accompanied by a cluster of spirit knives that causes area-of-effect damage. Weapons return to hands after a hit or miss. Cooldown is 30 seconds.**

"Nice," Nay said. "An AOE attack."

Nom, upending almost the whole shaker of Old Bay into the pot with the crab Marrow, said, "That's something when dealing with multiple opponents . . . or monsters."

"I know that," Nay said. "I don't need your mansplaining."

"Tentacle-splaining."

"I'm not a virgin when it comes to video games."

She chose Y, and as the Salvo of Knives Ability became a part of her, she went and lay down on the floor underneath the table and got ready for the three-hundred-and-sixty-degree-vision effect to run its course. Every time she ate a Marrow, she got that glimpse of being connected to some presence that was greater than her. That sensation of being tethered to something sentient and significant.

It was here again, and she tried to perceive its nature. She drifted into her Spirit Song breathing technique to cycle Vigor, and she tried to see this presence with her True Eye. She got a glimpse of gold light but then it disappeared. Her vision returned to normal.

As she recovered from the spiritual experience, Nom pulled the Crab Claw Marrow of the Caraxian Crab out of the boiling water. Motes of red light were buzzing around the claw, and the kitchen was filled with the aroma of Old Bay seasoning.

While the Marrow had been boiling, Nom had made a huge bowl of clarified butter. The clear, yellow liquid would create the perfect dip for the crab meat.

He didn't even wait for the claw to cool. He cracked open the shell with a mallet and then shoved the entire top of his head into the cracked shell. He bit off some tender white meat and then dunked his beak into the bowl of clarified butter. He let out a little gasp at what was surely an intense flavor of crab meat and butter. His entire body flared with a red lava light glow.

The tentacle dove back into the claw, headfirst, ripping at the flesh and then dunking the meat. Clarified butter splashed everywhere.

"Jesus, Nom," Nay said. "I was gonna say we need to get you a bib, but it looks like we should have covered the floor in a plastic sheet."

Between bites he said, "I haven't seen plastic in this world yet."

After a few minutes, he lay on the floor next to Nay, and swathes of gold were rippling through him.

Nay waited a minute and then said, "So, what Ability did you just get?"

He sat up and closed his eye for a minute. He waved two of his green protuberant fins, and a bar top table materialized out of thin air. A sign hung in midair over the table. In ostentatious tavern scrawl, it said, Nom's Salty Bevs & Brews. On one side was what looked like a medieval homebrewing kit, with tubes and different-sized glass jars and containers. And there were beer and ale bottles with different labels.

Nay sat up and examined it all in awe.

One of the ale bottles was labeled *Voidbringer Lambic*. And there was a Hounds of Tindalos brewer logo. It was an illustration of Nom holding a mug of frothy beer, protuberances outspread in a welcoming gesture. On the other side, there was a frosty mug of what looked like a slushie. It was green and there was a slice of pineapple perched on the rim. There was a label, *Restorative Smoothie*.

"Holy shit dude!" Nay said. "You can summon a table full of your own brewed beer and cocktails!"

"It's not a cool combat skill like you've been getting," Nom said, "but it's still a quality-of-life Ability when it comes making food."

"Are you kidding me?! This is cool as shit! You're like an instant bartender now!"

"I mean, it's okay."

"Are you jealous I have a combat skill tree?"

"Yes, I am jealous! The next Delicacy that unlocks a combat skill tree is mine!"

"I'm okay with that."

At that moment, Quincy came through the kitchen doors and stopped in his tracks. His eyes went from the oversized crab Marrow just sitting there in the middle of the kitchen to Nay and Nom lying underneath the table in all their post-Marrow consumption hangover.

It was akin to wandering into one's kitchen at midnight and seeing a couple of stoners with the munchies raiding the fridge. It was just undignified.

"Nether hells," Quincy said. "Put that stuff away. We're gonna get raided."

"Relax," Nom said. "There's no DMA agents in Lucerna's End."

"Still!" Quincy said. "It makes me nervous having a Marrow the size of a fauglir just lying in the middle of the kitchen and leftover Marrow in the pans!"

"Do you want some?" Nay said. "I'm sorry; I've been so selfish. I didn't consider that you might want some."

"My skill trees are full," Quincy said. "I'd have to reset if I wanted to consume any more Delicacies or Marrow."

"Reset?" Nay said. "Is that possible?"

"At Bronze rank, it is. But it's also extremely expensive and can set a Marrow Eater back not just in finances but in time and power. It's wiping the slate clean and returning to zero skill trees."

"Damn," Nom said. "Seems like resetting could leave one pretty vulnerable."

"Exactly," Quincy said. "Those with the resources and need to reset make sure they have their feasts prepared and ready. And even then, they're still in a weakened state for a number of days." Quincy, irritated, waved his hands at the mess. "Now clean this up before Gracie gets back from the market!"

He exited the kitchen, leaving the doors swinging on their hinges.

— CHAPTER FIFTY-EIGHT —

Fleet-footed

Nay and Nom set out for Maer Scathan in the dark of night. They worked through dinner service—where the Voidbringer Lambic and the Red Velvet Blood of Shoggoth Shake made quite an impression—and cleaned the kitchen.

When all the servers left, and when Quincy and Gracie had retired to bed, Nay and Nom sneaked out to the boat she normally used to go to her training glade, and set out for the opposite end of the Lac.

Nay took out the brooch Volva Serrilda had given to her upon parting. It was unassuming, made out of an ancient white wood called mauralyn. The brooch was carved into the shape of a tree, a few vigama flying amongst the boughs.

"*Pin this to your chest when you set out into the mists,*" Volva Serrilda had said.

"*Why?*" Nay had asked.

"*So Aule doesn't treat you like a threat.*"

She had explained the brooch was a symbol of the Friends of Man. Someone didn't have it unless it was first given to them as a gift by one of the Friends.

Nay pinned it to her chest and then began rowing. As she had an overall stat increase leveling up from Base to Iron, taking the boat to the other end of the Lac would be more of a nice workout than anything. If she was still Base, she'd most likely be sore and exhausted by the time they got to the other side.

"I left Gracie a note that we wouldn't be available till right before dinner service tomorrow," Nay said. "I gave her directions on the menu, and she won't have to do much prep, because she'll be using some leftovers from the past couple of days."

"Good," Nom said. "Wouldn't be fair to leave her with a ton of work while we're gone. She'll have enough to do as is, and I'd rather keep her happy."

"My sentiments exactly," Nay said. "So, no matter what happens, we need to make it back in time for dinner service tomorrow. If we don't, there's no way Gracie will be able to run it by herself. It will be a disaster."

"Not to mention Quincy will know something is afoot because we're absent," Nom said.

"Can I ask you a question?"

"Shoot."

"Why didn't you just tell Quincy that we don't have the recipe for moon cakes?"

"Because I don't want him to worry. He's got other problems. This whole Nether-Sister-not-being-dead thing has him on constant alert. This moon cake situation is our problem and I can handle it."

"Don't take this the wrong way," Nom said, "but it seems like a matter of pride."

"Of course it is. I want him to know I'm totally capable of taking care of kitchen business. And this is kitchen business."

"It just seems like he'd be willing to help if you told him the truth."

"He's helped me enough. The best way I can repay him is by making myself useful and being helpful to him."

Nom sighed. "All right. This whole thing goes tits up, don't say I didn't try to say something."

"Noted."

Nom peered over into the water, scanning it. "Well, since time is of the essence, I suppose I can help speed things along."

"What do you mea—"

There was a splash as Nom jumped out of the boat into the water.

"Nom! What in the hell?!"

Nay peeked over but saw no sign of her tentacle friend in the dark, icy water.

Suddenly, the boat lurched forward. It cut through the water, picking up speed. It was leaving a wake behind it.

Nay peered over the back and saw Nom just underneath the surface of the water. His protuberances were pressed against the boat and his whole body was gyrating in circles, acting as both a propeller and a rudder.

The faster he gyrated, the more speed the boat picked up. Nay stopped rowing and let Nom transform the rowboat into a tentacle-powered motorboat.

They raced across the Lac, the light of the green-tinged moon peeking through the gentle snowfall.

"Why do I have to carry you?" Nay said.

"Because you're Iron now and you can handle the extra load," Nom said. "It's the least you could do after I saved us all that time propelling us across the Lac."

He had a point, so Nom was wrapped around her torso and lying across her shoulders as they left Lake Coineascar and headed through the pass into the adjacent valley that contained Maer Scathan.

"We should have brought Juniper with us," Nay said.

"She wouldn't have fit in the boat," Nom said.

"She could have swam."

"Across the entirety of Lac Coineascar? Then she'd be useless by the time we got to land."

They followed the Bluerun, the gentle and bubbling stream that connected Lac Coineascar to the lake in Maer Scathan. Volva Serrilda mentioned it was often populated by fishermen who wanted to stay off boats, but since it was nighttime, they saw no one else on their trek.

As they saw the valley coming up before them, Nay found a rock to sit on next to the Bluerun. She pulled various Buff Biscuits out of her inventory and shared them with Nom. Next, she pulled out the tin thermos of magical venison stew she had cooked earlier during dinner service. It had been her first time accessing a recipe from Jezabelle Childe.

She glanced again at part of the description.

Grants Fleet-footed Spell Effect. The eater can run as fast as a gazelle through the forest for three hours.

She stuck a wooden spoon into the thermos and began eating. The stew was hearty and thick, and the bacon complemented the lean venison nicely. It warmed her stomach in this cold. After a few swallows, a sensation of lightness and confidence passed through her. She cycled some Vigor to fill the reserves in her veins.

She had never felt this way before. She wasn't sure how to describe it other than that she wanted to run. An icon appeared in the top right corner of her HUD, to the left of her mini-map. It was of a foot with wings on it. She clicked on it.

[Fleet-footed]
[2:59]

Very nice.

Nom reached for the tin thermos of stew. "My turn!"

Nay handed it and the spoon to him. He began shoveling it into his mouth. After a bit, he spooned some onto a biscuit, making a sandwich. It disappeared down his hatch.

Nay saw the Fleet-footed icon appear over his head as he radiated all shades of red.

"Do you still want me to carry you?" Nay said, teasing him.

"Maybe after I test out this Fleet-footed spell!" He disappeared in a poof of snow, leaving the thermos and spoon spinning on the rock.

A serpentine trail appeared in the snow, leading towards Maer Scathan and running parallel with the Bluerun.

"Don't go too far!" Nay said. She grabbed the thermos and spoon, storing them in her inventory, and sprinted after him.

It was exhilarating.

Running as fast and as light as a deer through the wilderness was pure magic. Nay had never been much of a runner or jogger. Sometimes, back in Los Angeles, when she needed to drop pounds, she'd put the treadmill on an incline and watch Netflix.

But going for a run?

She'd rather be caught taking a depression nap than running.

But this was different. Not only was she in better shape here, she was also an Iron Rank. Her legs were stronger. Her lung capacity was better. Not only did she process pain differently, but her threshold for pain had improved.

Now, add the Fleet-footed spell to the mix?

She felt like the fastest person in the world. She ran down the trail, hopping over patches of ice and logs and rocks, and each time landing with a grace that could only be possible with magic. She followed the furrow Nom had left in the snow.

She could see him zooming ahead of her, leaving a roostertail of snow in his wake. Nay pushed herself to run faster; the Bluerun became a blur next to her. She was closing the distance between her and Nom. She attributed her extra percentage of speed to the fact that she was Iron.

Soon they were side by side, racing into the valley of Maer Scathan.

Volva Serrilda had told her to head for the mists in the northwest. She said she wouldn't miss them.

"Follow me!" Nay said. She bounded past Nom and consulted her minimap. There were dots demarcating groups of elk and reindeer. There was even a bear nearby.

And there was something racing up next to them from the east.

That's when the white stag leapt in front of them, steam flaring out of its nostrils, leading the way where the path ended and into the alpine forest. Nay and Nom followed, both curious to see if they could surpass the stag. The trees became a haze in her peripheral vision as she focused on the stag.

Soon they noticed the mist drifting through the forest, giving the landscape a dreamlike effect. It grew thicker and thicker as they continued on, the stag becoming harder and harder to see until only they could see its horns bobbing through the fog.

They were sprinting and leaping through a glen of birch trees, their white bark blending in with the mist. Nay found herself having to dodge them at the last second, strafing and darting side to side.

Suddenly, they both skidded to a halt.

The stag was waiting for them in the middle of a clearing. The moon shone down on it, casting it in a natural spotlight.

It snorted. Curls of steam shot out of its nose, lingering in the cold. Then it turned and walked into the whiteout mist, disappearing.

"You bear our brooch," the voice said, startling them.

It seemed to be coming from the west. But when she turned to face it, there was just mist.

"Yes," Nay said. "We come seeking Aule!"

This time, the voice seemed to come from the other side, the east. "Who gave you the brooch?"

Nay and Nom turned in circles, trying to catch the owner of the voice.

"She calls herself Volva Serrilda," Nay said. "The hermit of Lucerna's End."

She thought she saw movement out of the corner of her eye. She pivoted to face it.

Just more mist.

Then the voice came from behind her. "Why do you seek Aule?"

They spun again, only to be greeted by more mist. Nay thought she saw the horns of the stag streak by them.

"I understand you once gave a recipe to a cook named Ol' Pat," Nay said. "Also from Lucerna's End. I come seeking the same recipe."

There was a giggle. It seemed to come from all directions. "Ah, yes! The moon cakes of Auledern!"

"Yes," Nay said. "The moon cake recipe. You see, I've taken Ol' Pat's place as a cook at Lucerna's End after she passed. And with the Green Moon Festival coming up—"

"In six moons."

"Yes, in six moons. I'm supposed to have moon cakes ready for the town. But she didn't write the recipe down, so—"

"Oh, one must never write the recipe down."

Nay paused. "I'm sorry?"

"That's one of the rules. We don't write recipes down."

"Okay . . . so, I've come here to ask if you can teach me the recipe."

"I *can* teach you. But *will* I teach you?"

Nay and Nom exchanged a look.

"I guess that's up to you," Nay said.

"Ol' Pat was a helpful woman. She helped me find something dear to me that was lost. Maybe you can help me with a favor as well."

"I can help you. We can help you. What do you need?"

"The moon cake recipe requires elderflowers. But lately, the elderflowers that used to grow in my secret garden here have all been poisoned. Changed into toxic things, twisted versions of their true form. Maybe you can find the source that has been poisoning my elderflowers."

"I suppose that's fair."

"It's a nasty pest that's been living in the winter burrows underneath the forest."

A child stepped out of the mist, then, what appeared to be a little girl.

"If you fetch me its heart, I'll share the moon cake recipe with you."

— CHAPTER FIFTY-NINE —

Congealed Salad

Nay took a step back, in surprise, fright, and awe. The child was glowing, and Nay could see the vigama flowing inside of her.

[Quest Complete!]
[Find Aule in Maer Scathan Completed!]
[You have been rewarded Vigor Points]

Aule watched the golden vigama fly into Nay and clapped.

The Friend of Men's skin was translucent, and they could see the interior of her physiognomy's different systems. The circulatory, the nervous, and every pathway had a corkscrew helix of miniscule golden vigama flowing around them. She was pure Vigor.

Nay blinked, and this view into the child's interior spiritual systems went away, shifting back to opaque porcelain skin emitting a gold aura. Ringlets of gold and red hair fell to her shoulders. There were crystallized blue flowers poking out of the ringlets.

Looking at her longer now, she wasn't a child but merely smaller in stature. Her facial features weren't completely human either. Her eyes were large and almost feline in nature. Green pupils rimmed in a gold ring. The nose was fox-like, and she had three fox tails pluming out of her garments. She was clothed in a white robe like she was some monk of the mist.

"Do not be frightened," Aule said. "I will do you no harm."

"Sorry," Nay said. "You just weren't what I was expecting."

"And what were you expecting?" Aule said.

"To be honest?" Nay said. "I guess I was expecting someone a little taller."

Aule laughed then, a shrill feral giggle and half-bark. "That's what men in this age always expect. They have forgotten about us." Her voice became sad for a second. "Now that our numbers have dwindled."

Then she looked at Nom and walked over to him. "Now, this is a curious one." She appraised him with her strange eyes. "Most curious indeed. The void is your Vigor."

Nom flinched at that, his eye darting to Nay and then going back to Aule.

"But I don't sense malevolence and disdain for beauty in you," Aule said. "We should schedule a teatime, as I'd like to talk to you more. But now is not the time, is it? I sense urgency in both of you."

"Yeah," Nay said. "We could really use that recipe."

"It is not our way to freely give gifts," Aule said. "It is only proper to exchange gifts. That's the way it's always been."

"Okay," Nay said. "You mentioned something about a nasty creature. And us fetching its heart?"

"That could be your gift to me," Aule said. "Then I could exchange the recipe as a gift to you."

"Sounds like a fair-enough trade to me," Nom said. "Where is the creature and what is it?"

"There's a series of burrows underneath this region," Aule said. "The creature lives in a warren connected to these burrows. It managed to get into my secret garden through its subterranean digging. My elderflowers bloom once a month, every full moon. And every full moon, without fail, the creature has been feeding on my flowers before I can harvest them."

Nay had claustrophobic visions of delving underneath the earth to hunt some creature and she shuddered. "Okay, but what kind of creature is it?"

"I do not know," Aule said. "I've yet to see it."

"You haven't tried to deal with it yourself?" Nom said.

It was a good question. Aule, with all her Vigor, seemed capable of handling things like this herself.

Why does she need us? Nay thought.

"It is a complicated matter of time," Aule said. "It is our way to patrol several outposts," Aule said. "This is one of many for me. Eventually, I would have dealt with this. But now you're here, willing to take care of it for me."

[Quest Detected]
[Quest: Slay Vampra and Retrieve Its Heart]
[Accept Quest Y/N?]

Nay looked at Nom.
Well?
He gave her a curt nod. She accepted the quest.

As she did so, Aule seemed to pulse with vigama glow for a moment. She smiled.

Oddly, her teeth weren't fanged.

Nay had been expecting fangs for some reason.

"We'll hunt this thing," Nay said. "If we're successful, you'll give us the moon cake recipe."

"A fair trade indeed!"

Aule brought them to a knot of entwined birch trees. There were a dozen of them, twisted around each other like massive vines. The effect, if viewed from farther away in the mist, was that of one massive tree.

Their root systems were intertwined, sticking out of the earth and snow like fallen leviathans. They had fused together into a network. There was an opening in the center of the ground, flanked by a crescent of stones. It led into the earth. It looked a lot like the entrance to a dungeon.

"I'm confident if you enter through here," Aule said, "you'll eventually find the culprit."

Nom gazed into the darkness, unfazed. "You don't want to come with us? Just out of curiosity?"

"I have to tend to another outpost, far from here," Aule said.

"How will we find you when we're done?" Nay said.

"I shall return with the first rays of the sun."

Nay consulted her mini-map and saw a winding passageway leading into further tunnels underneath the earth. When she pulled out of the map, she discovered Aule was gone.

"Where'd she go?"

Nom looked around, just noticing that that she had disappeared. They were alone again in the whiteout mist. The wind whistled through the birch trees, an eerie tune.

"Figures," Nom said. "Shall we enter this dungeon and get this side quest over with?"

Nay pulled a torch out of her inventory. She applied a ring of heat to it with Chef's Thermometer, lighting it.

A flame whooshed to life.

"Clock's ticking."

There were earthen steps leading underneath the forest. As they descended, Nay handed Nom the torch. "You carry this." She drew *Thorn* out of its sheath, and the ice scythe materialized in her other hand. Vigor spirit energy bloomed around the blades as Dire Knife activated.

Nom looked at the weapons and the Vigor imbue in wonder. "I can't wait until I get to unlock a combat tree."

"Keep a lookout for Delicacies, then," Nay said. "Who knows, maybe we'll find one down here."

"There's not a part of you that thinks this is a trap?" Nom said.

"Of course there's part of me that thinks this is a trap," Nay said. "I'm not one just to take enchanting yet weird fox girls who dwell in the middle of a snow forest at their word."

"So, what's the backup plan?"

"The backup plan is the same as my normal plan."

"Which is?"

"Stabby stab stab stab."

"She gets a combat tree, and suddenly she thinks she can solve every problem with knives."

"What about you? What's your backup plan?"

"This stew makes me run fast as fuck."

They were well under the earth now. The tunnel they found themselves in had cold dirt walls, with the roots visible in the strata and running along the ceiling. Nay opened her mini-map and could see the network of tunnels branch off a few times, but it was all connected. The burrows all led to a large chamber that must have been the warren.

There was a blinking red dot in the warren. That must be Vampra.

"It's kind of weird that this thing's crime is destroying flowers but the fox girl wants its fucking heart."

"It does kind of seem like overkill."

"But then again, people get protective over their gardens."

"Yeah, Vampra has done fucked up."

"Vampra?"

"It's the name of this thing up ahead."

"Not sure I like the sound of it, but I'm ready to get this over with so we can get back to the Lodge. Maybe I can catch a few hours' worth of sleep before dinner service."

"Yeah, there's no reason we shouldn't be able to speed-run through this side quest. Can you get the torch up here? There's a fork coming up."

Nay reached the fork and there was still no response. "Come on, Nom. Did you hear me?"

Again, no response. Unless one counted the torch light extinguishing as a response.

So, she whipped around only to see Nom seemingly frozen in midair. He was gently vibrating, trying to move, but that's when Nay noticed the clear pile of light green jelly he was encased in. The torch had been snuffed inside it. Which meant there was no oxygen.

Nom was stuck inside of a slime like a piece of fruit in a congealed Jello salad.

"What fresh hell is this?" Nay said, disturbed. Remnants of the slime were dripping from the ceiling. It looked like it had been hiding in the crevices of the roots before dropping down on Nom.

"Hold your breath bud," Nay said. "I'm gonna cut you out!"

Nay stepped up to the sludge, slashing down with the ice scythe. It looked like Nom was trying to shake his head *no*. But her intent was to slice open the gelatinous bubble and free him.

Instead, the ice scythe entered the slime and got stuck. It wasn't a strike, so Nay got zero Kinetic Points. She yanked on the weapon, trying to pull it out, but it got sucked into the blob. It threatened to pull her hand in with it, so she let go.

It quivered inside the slime with Nom.

"Uh, that's no bueno," Nay said. "What the hell do I do? *Think, Nay. Think.*"

Nom was trying to mouth something inside of the goo, but Nay had never been very good at reading lips, much less beaked mouth holes. When the tentacle opened his mouth, it just filled with slime.

"I'm sorry about this, broski," Nay said. "But it's about to get cold."

She used Chef's Thermometer to conjure a ring of freezing cold, making it big enough to contain the slime and Nom. There was a dry-ice reaction, and the skin of the slime started to make a screeching sound as it frosted over. It was like watching Vaseline harden and freeze.

Not that Nay had ever seen Vaseline harden and freeze, but if she had, she was sure it would've looked like this. The blob of slime finished its metamorphosis into a giant ice cube, with Nom frozen in dismay within. Nay struck the frozen slime with the skullcrusher end of Thorn, using it like an icepick.

Cracks spread along the surface of the slimesicle, and her next strike broke it apart like it was a giant ice cube. Nay pulled chunks of icy slime out of the way and was able to grab Nom, who was extremely cold to the touch.

As Nay pulled him out, the rest of the frozen slime crumbled, an ice sculpture shattering and falling to the floor. She scooped the ice scythe out of the icy debris and put a hand to Nom's face. He felt like a pickle that had been chilled in ice.

Nay used Chef's Thermometer to warm him, pulling him out of his frozen and dormant state. He coughed, his breath fogging the air between them. He was shivering, his teeth chattering. "You . . . y-you, y-ou . . . . *you bitch!*"

"I said I was sorry!" Nay said. "What else should I have done?"

Nom blew several cold breaths, warming up in the ring. "Y-you did . . . the right thing. Still, so cold."

Nay rubbed her hands across him, using touch and friction to generate heat. "If I used heat, there was a chance I would have burned you too bad. We know that extreme cold just puts you to sleep."

"Doesn't mean I like it!"

"You were inside a slime!"

That's when she noticed movement at her feet.

She looked down and saw the frozen chunks of slime were starting to melt. Little half-frozen blobs of slime were moving across the floor towards them. Nay helped Nom up. "We gotta get outta here."

Nom looked down at the one slime that was now dozens of smaller slimes. "I don't think I like this side quest anymore."

They hurried towards the warren, away from the multitude of slime.

— CHAPTER SIXTY —

Vampra

Nay pulled another torch out of her inventory and handed it to Nom. She led them by mini-map, choosing directions at the forked tunnels, making it to the warren. She checked the remaining time left on the Fleet-footed spell.

[Fleet-footed]
[1:34]

The first thing they noticed about entering the warren was the change in temperature. It was warm down here, which meant something or someone was generating heat.

The main hollow of the warren was nothing like she was expecting. Instead of some hollowed-out and darkened burrow in the earth, there appeared to be a well-tended garden in here with bioluminescent lichen light.

It was a bizarre botanical garden.

The green leaves and stems of root crops were poking up out of the ground. They were spotted with mold.

Lichen clung to the root ceiling above, providing light. Moisture dripped onto the plants.

The vines here were not green but the color of flesh. There was an assortment of strange pitcher plants, the leaves dark as night with red veins running along the plant matter. There was a swollenness to them that reminded Nay of overfed slugs.

There were *Dionaea*-style snap traps that looked like they had human teeth. Other growths had strange leaves and filaments and even pink tongues.

These plants were arranged in grids. Nay concluded that meant there was a gardener who had designed this layout and was tending to all this.

Nom whispered. "Are there any magic pictures to go with your magic words describing Vampra?"

"I've got nothing describing Vampra."

"What good are these quest logs when you don't have any sort of monster or creature codex to go with it?"

"Sorry, next time my interface gets upgraded, I'll ask them to install it. I didn't have time to ask at the interface dealership during my last visit."

They made their way through the garden and passed a large plant that stopped them in their tracks by its sheer vibes.

It was a *Dionaea*-style snap-jaw plant, but it was massive. Its coloration was that of a purple bruise. There was a giant bladder on the stalk, and it drooped towards the ground. They could see through the green and crimson plant-fiber membrane. It provided them a glimpse of the bladder contents.

There was an entire deer inside of the plant. It was half-digested.

"How the hell did a deer get down here?" Nay said.

"Maybe it got lost," Nom said.

"Or something brought it in here."

"Okay, now I'm having second thoughts again."

They kept walking and got a clear view of the back of the warren.

Vampra was chilling in a carrot pitch, nibbling on one of the vegetables. Upon first glance it looked like a giant rabbit, but sharp claws poked out of its cute, furry feet.

There was a death's-head marking on its chest. It looked like a tribal tattoo of sorts. Its ears swiveled on its head, tracking their movement. They pulsed with a red glow.

[Delicacy Detected]
[Death's-Head of Vampra]

Then a quest prompt appeared.

[Quest Detected!]
[Quest: Separate the Delicacy from Vampra]
[Reward: Death's-Head of Vampra]
[Accept Quest Y/N?]

"It has a Delicacy," Nom said. He trembled with anticipation. He became more focused.

It stirred upon their presence.

The white-furred chest opened up, revealing a porcelain humanoid form within. It reminded Nay of a young version of the Steksis. It, too, was female and the face had enough human features to make Nay feel a mixture of sympathy and horror. They shared the same uncanny-valley effect, a bewitching revulsion.

"Ah," Vampra said. "Have you come to see my garden of delights?"

She perched on her hind legs, gazing at them with inhuman eyes.

That's when Nay got a prompt.

[Reputations Menu]
[Factions]
[The Scar: Friendly]

Vampra's origin was the Scar, just like the Steksis. No wonder she was getting similar vibes.

"Have you come here to help tend to my garden?" Vampra said. "Corpse shade could use a gardener with a tender touch."

She gestured to the massive snap-jaw plant with the bladder containing the deer corpse.

"I don't really have time to explain," Nay said. "You're the mini-dungeon boss here. I need to defeat you for your loot. But do you just wanna cut through all the bullshit and just give it to us?"

[Reputations Menu]
[Factions]
[The Scar: Unfriendly]

The corpse shade rose up behind them and whipped forward, striking. The snap trap struck the ground, shaking the warren, closing its jaws over Nom.

"Didn't think so," Nay said.

The stalk lifted up, and Nay could see Nom flailing inside, his body pressing against the plant matter, making it bulge.

Nay drew Thorn and the ice scythe, the Dire Knife imbue flaring around the blades.

She moved to engage the grotesque *Dionaea*. She felt a searing pain on her shoulder and side and was suddenly flying through the air. She crashed into the earthen wall, dazed. Part of her cloak and tunic had been obliterated and her exposed skin was burned.

The hell?

She looked at Vampra, who was charging up some type of energy attack with her bunny ears. The ends glowed laser red, and there was the charge of electricity in the air.

"Oh, shit—"

A beam of energy blasted out of the bunny ears and lasered at her. She did a rising handspring and dove out of the way.

If it wasn't for the Fleet-footed spell, she would have been smoked. The blast blew a crater into the earth and rock.

In front of her, Nay noticed the leaves and stems of the root vegetables shuddering and vibrating. They were moving. Little brown and flesh-colored root arms exploded out of the soil. They were root-tendril appendages. They pressed against the earth. With a *pop*, the bulbous and gnarled root bodies emerged.

They had faces with glowing red eyes, the vivid hue of maraschino cherries. They had little brown noses and pouty mouths that made the things look constipated in perpetuity. They were filled with sharp thorn-teeth.

Vampra mandrakes.

There were a dozen of the vicious mandrakes. They leapt onto her like a pack of piranhas, their roots scraping at her, trying to twine around her. Their teeth gnashed and nipped at her, tearing flesh through her clothes. They bit the back of her legs, her back. One tried to bite her ear.

She screamed and rolled across the garden, tearing up posts and barreling through the stalks of plants. She used the moment to do a kip-up, launching herself back to her feet. Mandrakes popped up into the air from her movement. She sliced one in half with Thorn. Pink entrails and green goo spilled out of its top half, and it released a high-pitched mew.

Three of them hit the ground, scrambling right side up before charging her. She swung with the ice scythe, taking their heads off like a reaper come to harvest, separating wheat from chaff. Mandrake heads rolled across the ground, leaking green goo, the pouty mouths pouting even more, the maraschino eyes rolling around in the sockets, their thorn teeth chittering.

She scrambled away as the others righted themselves. They were joined by more Vampra mandrakes pulling themselves out of the ground. A self-induced harvest because they sensed fresh meat. Another Vampra ray blast flew over her shoulder, its heat singeing the ends of her hair. She ducked and twisted, moving away from the little army of mandrakes running at her.

It would almost be comical if she wasn't already torn and bleeding from their attacks.

"This is no way to treat a lady!"

She raised Thorn and the ice scythe and went to throw them, activating Salvo of Knives. Mid-motion, the weapons disappeared out of her hands and reappeared across from her. Thorn was now in the forehead of the mandrake, its hilt quivering. The ice scythe spun in a crescent pattern, cutting through several of the mandrakes at their waists, slicing them in half.

A cluster of spirit daggers rained from the ceiling, hitting the mandrakes near Thorn's target, impaling them to the dirt or just passing through their root-shaped bodies, immobilizing them. Some of them coughed green goo as they died, their maraschino-cherry eyes bulging in their last moments. A few of them let out pitiful mews.

"No, don't make pitiful noises! Why are you trying to be cute now?!" Nay said. "I don't feel sorry for any of you. Y'all are assholes!"

Her weapons disappeared again, only to reappear in her hands. "Whoa."

And that's when she saw Vampra hopping towards her. For a moment, time slowed for her, just to feature a giant monster bunny rabbit leaping in slow motion. It was majestic. It planted its forearms in the ground and threw its lower body forward at her, kicking at her with its clawed hind legs.

Nay sprinted to the side, dodging the nasty-looking claws. Vampra hopped high into the air and twisted, landing on her bottom, sliding away from Nay like a dog dragging its ass along a carpet. Its two bunny ears began to glow red, charging up.

"Fuck that," Nay said.

She lunged towards Vampra and swung the ice scythe. It was a backhanded swing. Right as the blast of energy was going to laser her down, the ice scythe severed the bunny ears, prematurely releasing the burst of energy in an explosion.

Nay was airborne again for a brief moment. She landed at the stalk of the corpse shade plant.

There was a screech as the blast took off part of Vampra's face. The creature twisted to the ground, falling into a patch of its carnivorous flowers.

Above Nay, there was some type of serpentine struggle happening in the bowels of the corpse shade. She could hear Nom crying in anger inside. "I don't wanna . . . but I gotta!"

There was a wail. "Damn you!"

There was a gnashing of teeth. There was a great tearing of plant matter, right where the mutant flower's sphincter was located. Normally used for secreting pollen and the waste juices of its prey, it currently had the tip of a tentacle bursting through it. Nom's head popped out of the sphincter, his fins poking through the vegetable and flesh matter, tearing the orifice open wider. A brutal reverse osmosis.

Chlorophyll and other botany juices drenched Nay. She squirmed, totally grossed out.

Nom slid out of the back end of the corpse shade, drooping down to the floor, contained inside a membrane. It was like a baby giraffe still inside the embryonic sac falling out of its mother. Nay used Thorn to cut Nom out of the stomach lining membrane.

"These moon cakes better be fucking delicious!" Nom said. "I just chewed my way out of that thing's asshole!"

Corpse Shade shrieked, its thorny vines flailing. It twisted on its stalk, and hate radiated off its snap-trap visage, sensing Nay. It reared its head back as if it was a giant serpent, preparing to strike.

And strike it did.

With a rush of air, its trap mouth opened and it whipped towards Nay. She swung an underside swing with the ice scythe, and the curved blade entered the corpse shade's lower jaw, penetrated its mouth, and punctured its upper palate, skewering the whole apparatus.

Nay, utilizing her Iron Rank strength, held the head in place, stopping the strike. With her other hand, she used an overhand grip to stab Thorn into its throat. She pulled the combat dagger down, ripping the corpse shade's throat open in a vertical slit. Brown-and-green plant juice spilled out of the wound.

The odor of rotting flesh hit her full in the face and she gagged. But the thing went limp, impaled on the ice scythe.

"Another Delicacy," Nay said.

She yanked the ice scythe out of it and spun. The corpse shade hit the ground, lifeless. Nay made eye contact with Vampra. The top of the bunny monster's skull was gone, part of its brain exposed to the world.

It was an odd Mexican standoff, between human girl and Scar monstrosity. And it only lasted about a second before Nay threw her blades at it, activating Salvo of Knives again since it was off cooldown.

But instead of appearing inside the monster like she expected—and she had really hoped one of the blades would be poking out of its exposed brain—Vampra rose into the air and held its forelegs in the air as if signaling a touchdown. Under-flaps of chitinous scales fell from its armpits as if they were wings. They gave off a silver sheen.

Nay's weapons appeared. The scales reflected the blades, turning the attack back on Nay. They flew back towards her, blade and points first. To make matters worse, the salvo of spirit knives that fell from above were reflected as well. Suddenly, they were falling towards Nay and Nom.

Nay sprinted, crashing into Nom and pushing him away from the volley of blades. Thorn and the ice scythe flew past her. The combat dagger hit the bladder of the plant, releasing a toxic pollen gas into the warren. The ice scythe took the heads off some flowers and embedded in a root protruding out of the wall.

"Are you okay?" Nay said. She inspected Nom. He sat up, and he was knife-wound-free.

"Nay!" Nom said, warning her.

She turned her head just in time to see Vampra hopping at her. It pushed its lower half out to claw her with its hind legs again. She was about to get turned into a Nay-kabob. But then the bunny creature froze in the air. It was gently vibrating, held in place by an invisible psychic force.

Nom was using his Mind Shiv spell on Vampra. "Finish it!"

Nay didn't hesitate. She sliced off the hind feet and claws with the ice scythe and drove Thorn into Vampra's exposed brain. Her Kinetic Point meter was full. She activated Gore.

Its wounds ruptured from within. Its stumps where its feet had been showered Nay's torso in gore. Its brain exploded, splattering Nay and Nom's faces. The cut on its side blossomed, spurting liquefied viscera.

Nay and Nom stood there in the botanical garden from hell, covered in the innards, secretions, and juices of the creatures that dwelt here.

"I'm beginning to think a Bathe Ability would be really useful," Nay said.

— CHAPTER SIXTY-ONE —

Seed

Nom hovered over Vampra's body. The bizarre bunny creature didn't look peaceful in death. It was a bloody mess.

"I think we just soured our relations with creatures from the Scar," Nay said.

"The Scar?" Nom said.

"My interface told me that's where it came from," Nay said. "Just like the Steksis."

Nom seemed pensive for a second, but only for a second. It looked like he was ready to dive into the corpse for the Delicacy.

Nay could see the gold glow of the Delicacy within Vampra. It was the death's-head markings on the fur.

"Part of the hide," Nom said. "I'm thinking some kind of cracklings or seasoning. What do you think?"

Nay looked around the warren. At the bodies of the mandrakes, the strange carnivorous plants. At the green toxic cloud just lingering over an area of the garden. It was slowly spreading and dispersing through the warren. She frowned.

"I'm thinking we can worry about how to cook the Delicacy later," Nay said. "Let's take it and the heart and get out of here."

Nom noticed the noxious cloud as well.

Nay used Thorn to cut through the bunny skin and hide. She traced a circle around the death's-head marking with the tip of the blade first, then she started sawing through the circle like she was cutting a hole in a pumpkin.

The strange reflective layer of scales underneath the armpits was actually a separate flap that pressed up against the other side. It was tough, and luckily, she was able to shove it aside and keep it retracted so she didn't have to deal with it.

There was a gold aura flickering around the death's-head marking. She finally got it separated from the chest.

[Quest Complete!]
[Separate the Delicacy from Vampra Completed!]
[You have been rewarded with Death's-Head of Vampra]
[You have been rewarded with Vigor Points]

Golden vigama emerged out of the root ceiling and flew into Nay's chest. She enjoyed the quick dopamine hit of Vigor.

[Delicacy Discovered!]
[Delicacy: Death's-Head of Vampra]
[Delicacies Unlocked 2/3]
[Would you like to Consume Delicacy Y/N?]

Nom reached for it. "I want to carry it."

"Why don't I just put it in my inventory?" Nay said. "It's safer there."

Nom seemed reluctant. "All right, I guess you're right. Frees me up, too."

"What's the matter?" Nay said. "I'm not going to hide it from you. It's your Delicacy as much as mine, if not more. Don't worry; you can consume it when we get back to the Lodge, all right?"

"Yeah," Nom said. "Sorry. I'm just anxious to finally get a new skill tree!"

"I know you are. It's all good."

Nay stored the Delicacy in her inventory and then focused on the unpleasant butchery of retrieving Vampra's heart. Cutting into a monster bunny thing was one thing, but this part of the creature was humanoid.

It made her feel like she was performing an autopsy rather than performing a butcher task.

She made an incision underneath one of the porcelain-white breasts.

Were all creatures that came from the Scar some unholy fusion of humans and monsters? Was it supposed to symbolize a mockery of humanity and nature?

She cut in through the side because she figured she would be able to reach the heart without cracking the ribcage open. She pulled down the layers of skin, revealing the meat and bone underneath. The flesh was covered in a bluish membrane.

There was the white of a lung.

She grimaced and reached a hand in, pushing the lung to the side. There was the heart, nestled behind the lung and sternum. It looked like a red artichoke, ready to be plucked from its stalk.

She reached in with Thorn and cut through muscular tissue, tendons, and membranes, severing it from the body. She pulled it out. It was about the size of a pomegranate.

[Quest Complete!]
[Slay Vampra and Retrieve Its Heart Completed]
[Congratulations!]
[You have been rewarded Vigor Points]

More of the quest vigama appeared and flew into Nay, stimulating a release of serotonin in her brain.

"What do you think Aule is going to do with that?" Nom said. "Eat it?"

Nay stored the Vampra heart in her inventory.

"No clue," Nay said. "As long as she gives us the moon cake recipe, she can do whatever she wants with it."

She glanced at the Fleet-footed timer.

[Fleet-footed]
[55:02]

Just under an hour left.

They were headed for the exit when they saw the blob of slime waiting for them at the entrance of the tunnel.

"This jellied asshole again," Nay said.

They navigated their way around the wisps of toxic green cloud dispersing through the warren. Nay covered her mouth and nose with the collar of her tunic just in case. Not that any time was a great time to breathe in poison, but to do it now after they had gotten their loot would be a comedy of errors.

"Let's freeze it," Nay said.

"Already on it," Nom said.

Both of them used their Chef's Thermometer rings of cold, plunging the temperature on top of the slime. There was that dry-ice effect again and it solidified, turning into a block of ice.

Except there was one problem. There was now a frozen block of slime blocking their exit. The tendrils of toxic plant gas crept towards them.

"I guess we should have waited," Nom said.

"Nah," Nay said.

She struck the frozen slime with Thorn's skullcrusher. It shattered, falling in a cascade of broken pieces, clearing their way. They hurried into the tunnel. Nom turned.

"What are you doing?" Nay said.

Nom froze over the opening as high as he could with his Chef's Thermometer Ability. It was still open at the top, but if the slime thawed, it would take it even more time to ascend and squeeze through. They Fleet-footed through the tunnel system, moving twice as fast as they had compared to when they had first entered the earthen dungeon.

"Nom," Nay said, as they raced towards the surface.

"Eh?"

"How are your Vigor reserves?"

"What do you mean?"

"Well, you must have expended a lot of energy to freeze that opening over. Trust me, I know. I guess I'm just wondering how you're not getting Vigor Sickness."

"I don't use Vigor."

"Huh?"

"I'm not a cultivator like you."

"Oh, but you're still a Marrow Eater."

"I guess I'm just using a different battery than Vigor."

"Weird."

Nay side-eyed him for a second and had the thought that maybe one day, someone capable might study him to figure out what resource he was using, if any. Maybe it just had something to with his particular race.

I guess anything is possible.

But then those thoughts were gone as they reached the steps to the surface world.

They had both fallen asleep in the shelter of a cluster of trees.

Nay awoke to the first rays of sunlight penetrating the mist in the birch-tree forest. With it, Aule was there, sitting cross-legged on a stump, smoking a pipe. For a moment, still stuck in that liminal state between dreams and being awake, Nay thought she was in *Alice in Wonderland*, watching the caterpillar smoke on top of a mushroom.

She groaned and sat up, extricating herself from Nom, who had snuggled up close to her for warmth. She left his cloak on him and then rubbed her eyes.

"The light of the dawn blesses you with its warmth," Aule said.

Nay realized there was some sunlight shining on her. She could indeed feel its warmth.

"The deed is done," Nay said. The heart of Vampra materialized out of her inventory and appeared in her hand.

Aule smiled slyly, her pupils homing in on the heart.

There was a sudden breeze. Nay blinked and the heart was no longer in her hand. Instead, Aule was now holding it in hers, examining the organ. Her two fox tails on each side of the middle one were subtly twitching.

What the hell?

The breeze was gone.

Did she just move so fast, snatch the heart out of my hand, and return to her seat in the blink of an eye?

"This will do just fine," Aule said. She placed Vampra's heart inside a leather sack and cinched it tight.

"You're not curious as to what or who that heart belonged to?" Nay said.

"It was a pest that didn't belong here," Aule said. "It crawled out of a crack from a place it should have stayed."

"You mean the Scar?" Nay said.

"It's more like a festering wound that cuts deep into our world," Aule said. "Every now and then, something foul pours out of it and leaks into our affairs."

So, she did know.

"There's no way to bandage this wound?" Nay said. "To heal it or cover it up?"

"Many of my people have died trying," Aule said. "The best we can do is stanch the flow until the day it erupts."

"And what happens then?"

"Then, as Friends of Man, we hope man is ready."

"It seems like more people should be worried about the Scar, then."

Aule nodded. "You're a wise girl for acknowledging that. Unfortunately, most of your kind is too busy worrying about each other instead of what lurks on the other side of that wound."

There was a rustling, and Nom poked his head out of Nay's cloak and the snow. He sat up, waving his green fins and releasing a yawn. He rubbed sleep from his eye and then became aware of Aule and Nay. He shook himself out of his haze. "What did I miss?"

"Nothing, my strange friend," Aule said. She took a hit of her pipe and blew a series of smoke rings at the tentacle. The smoke smelled like maple and cinnamon. "Perhaps I will visit you in the future and we can chat."

"Sure," Nom said. His eye darted away from her. He fidgeted some. "Not sure I'm as interesting as you think."

"Nonsense!" Aule said. "It's not every day one gets to converse with an eldritch being! Much less one who is congenial!" She let out that half-bark, half-giggle again, her tails swaying behind her.

"There's much I'd like to learn of your kind," Aule said. Then she looked at Nay. "You gave me my gift. Now I believe I owe you yours."

Suddenly, Aule appeared right in front of them, bringing a breeze with her, the cinnamon scent of her tobacco smoke now in their faces as if someone was holding up a plate of cinnamon-sprinkled French toast to them.

But the Friend of Men was holding a round pastry in each hand. The outer layer was brown with a golden glaze, but the filling looked like a mint-colored paste. The elderflower paste. They were moon cakes.

She gestured for them to take them. They both reached out and grabbed their moon cakes.

Nay couldn't discern if there was anything super special about it other than that it looked super tasty. It reminded her of red bean pastries she had enjoyed before. The pastry was a little moist and sticky, and there were decorations of a moon cycle and leaves on the top and bottom.

Nom bit into his and immediately turned a mint green. "Oh . . . *oh, my* . . ." He let out a groan of delight as he chewed and ate some more.

Nay turned her attention back to the cake in her hand. She sniffed it. It smelled like marshmallows and burnt graham crackers. She took a bite, sinking her teeth through the pastry and into the thick inner filling.

She was hit with a plethora of sweet and salty flavors. There was the saltiness crumble of the pastry, and then the cool sweetness of the elderflower paste. There was a hint of floral tones to the flavor, but the main thing she noticed was that it was just the right amount of sweetness.

It wasn't overpowering like some pastries. And it didn't need any more sugar. It was at just the right amount to bring total satisfaction.

Nay couldn't think of anything else to follow this up with. It was the type of dessert you end a multiple-course meal with. Perhaps some green tea or matcha tea, or even a cappuccino or shot of espresso. But that's it.

Somehow, she had the knowledge of how to make this. She shook her head, taking another bite. She knew the exact ingredients and the amount and the techniques to use.

She looked for icons and Buffs on her HUD, regarding the moon cake, but there were none. She used True Eye to study the cake yet didn't see anything out of the ordinary. Nay looked at Aule in wonderment. "The recipe is in my head now."

"And there it shall stay," Aule said.

The fox girl handed her a wooden box. There was a moon carved into the white wood. Was it more mauralyn? She opened it.

Inside, there were seeds.

"Elderflower seeds, my friend," Aule said. "From my own flowers from my garden before they were tainted. Plant them somewhere where they will get plenty of moonlight. Pour them water from the melted snow, and they will yield you a harvest that should be enough for your moon cakes."

"I don't know how to thank you," Nay said.

"You don't have to thank me," Aule said. "We exchanged gifts, and that is thanks enough. Now go, return and get to baking!"

Aule stepped away from them, extinguishing her pipe. "Oh, one last thing. Do make Volva Serrilda's butter cookies for your townsfolk. They really are quite nice!"

The Friend of Men disappeared, leaving the hint of breeze and the smell of cinnamon and maple in her departure.

— CHAPTER SIXTY-TWO —

Death's-Head White Chocolate

They tried to eat more of the venison stew granting the Fleet-footed spell, but there was no effect. It turned out that they could only use the spell once a day. Which meant the stew wouldn't have any other effects except for filling an empty stomach until after midnight.

So, they had to trek back the old-fashioned way, which was by foot at a normal speed.

And since Nay was Iron Rank and had the convenience of legs, she found herself carrying Nom along the Bluerun back to their boat.

"Strange girl, that one," Nom said.

"She seems interested in you," Nay said.

"What can I say? I do have a way with the ladies."

"I wonder how many like her are left."

"Who knows? Doesn't sound like many. If her kind were the first ones who inhabited this world, I wonder what happened to decrease their numbers."

Nay considered this. "She mentioned patrolling 'outposts.' What do you think she meant by that?"

"They're monitoring the affairs here, keeping watch. As for what they're watching for specifically? Wouldn't be able to say without flat-out asking her."

"Maybe you should do that when you two have your 'chat.'"

"Seems fair."

By the time Nay had rowed across Lac Coineascar, it was past lunch and they would have a few hours to kill before dinner. Nay had wanted to nap, but Nom begged her about the Delicacy. "Sleep later; cook and eat Delicacy now!" he had said.

They had been following the directions from the activation recipe granted to Nay by her Chef's Kiss Passive, which was the Ability that granted Nay the power to be an Epicurist. She had discovered a section in Jezabelle Childe's cookbook volume titled

[Recommended Delicacy Recipes].

She found the Death's-Head Delicacy listed under desserts. The recipe was as such:

Death's-Head White Chocolate Strawberry.

Scrape Death's-Head marking off hide with the edge of a blade. Use a mortar and pestle to grind Death's-Head Delicacy into a powder. Take note: One Delicacy will only yield one serving.
Melt white chocolate in a bowl. Add the Death's-Head powder until the Delicacy is blended and incorporated.
Dip a strawberry (or fruit of your choice) into the white chocolate mixture and place on a parchment-lined baking sheet to dry. Slowly cool until the chocolate is hardened.

They had to use their chef's knives to scrape the Death's-Head marking off the piece of Vampra hide. It flaked off like pieces of dried paint. They collected all the pieces into a bowl. By the time they had ground the Delicacy down with a mortar and pestle, they were only left with a tablespoon or two of Death's-Head powder.

Since the Delicacy would only yield one serving, then only one of them would be able to eat it.

So, since Nay already had two Delicacies activated, it was only fair that the Death's-Head Delicacy go to Nom. Plus, he was so excited about unlocking another skill tree, there was no way Nay was going to take that away from him. But she did help him prepare the Delicacy for activation.

They used a bar of white chocolate that had been imported from the city of Delicatessa on the Peninsula. Quincy had told her all the best chocolatiers operated in Delicatessa. In fact, it was the capital which housed the Culinary Guild, so all food produced there was of the best quality.

She tried a bite and Quincy was right. It was the best white chocolate she ever had. It was sweet and milky in just the right way, which she liked as she was more of a milk-chocolate girl than a dark-chocolate girl. The white chocolate had that taste that came from creamy, coagulated butter. It was smooth and melty with hints of vanilla and honey.

She gently warmed a bowl with her Chef's Thermometer Ability to melt the chocolate. She watched the solid bar, missing a corner from where she had taken a nibble, melt into a white puddle.

Nom upturned the stone mortar bowl, pouring the Death's-Head powder into the melted white chocolate. He stirred it with a wooden spatula, mixing the powder into the chocolate. He watched the gray powder become one with the white chocolate. Gray motes of light bubbled out of the chocolate, denoting the magical properties of the Delicacy.

They didn't have any strawberries, so Nom chose a winter apple. Since there was only enough for one portion, he cut off a slice and dipped it into the melted white chocolate. He set it on a baking sheet and used Chef's Thermometer to chill the piece of fruit, hardening the Death's-Head white chocolate into a magic shell. White motes of light rose off the piece of fruit, giving the desert almost a beatific and holy aura.

"Well, are you going to eat it, or are you just going to stare at it all day?" Nay said.

"It's just so beautiful," Nom said. "I want to savor and remember this moment."

"It's a shame we don't have phones here," Nay said. "Kind of a basic tool for a foodie to have, to take photos of all their meals, recording visuals of their dining experiences."

"There's gotta be some magical object here that does the same thing," Nom said.

"If we ever meet a gnome tinkerer, we'll have to commission them to make a camera. How else can we be proper foodies?"

Nom grabbed the Delicacy and consumed the white-chocolate-covered winter apple. As he chewed, his color began changing, from purple to violet to gray and then back through to purple and to red. He looked like one of those cabochon carnival light boards, blinking from color to color as his biology absorbed the Delicacy and it worked its magic, birthing another skill tree inside of him.

He lowered himself to the floor and curled up in a spiral as the changes happened. His eye remained wide open, and Nay thought she could see a galaxy zooming by within his pupil. She went and fetched him some water. She held a flagon up to his beak and he drank greedily. "Well?" Nay said. "What'd you get?"

Nom rose up, his body finally settling to his normal purple color. He grabbed a winter melon and put it in one of the unlit fire alcoves. Then he came back to where he was. He tilted his head forward. The tip of his head stalk began to glow red. Nay felt a charge of electricity in the air as energy gathered around Nom.

Then a red beam blasted out of the top of the tentacle, the ray lasering across the kitchen and hitting the melon. The fruit exploded in the alcove. Nom's headed shifted from red to purple again.

"Holy shit," Nay said. "So, you did unlock a combat skill tree!"

It was like Vampra's bunny-ear blast.

"It's a Disintegration Ray," Nom said.

"That will be useful," Nay said. "Ranged attacks are great."

Nom handed her his chef's knife. "Throw this at me."

Nay looked at the knife in his fin. "No, I'm not doing that."

"C'mon."

"No, because I don't want to ruin your chef's knife. If it hits the floor and chips, then that's not cool. We gotta be respectful of our tools."

"Oh, good point."

Nom thought for a second, looking around. He grabbed an eggplant out of a vegetable basket. "Use this."

Nay took the eggplant. She walked to the other side of the kitchen.

"Now chuck it at me," Nom said. "Throw it hard. Really try to hit me. No mercy."

"All right," Nay said. "Don't get mad at me when I bean you."

She gripped the eggplant like it was a boomerang. She reared back for a throw and then released it with all of the power and momentum her Iron Rank could muster. The eggplant spun end over end like a tomahawk. Right before it hit Nom, his purple skin took on a silver sheen. Silver scales seemed to shimmer for a moment in the light.

There was the thud of eggplant against metal, and suddenly, the vegetable was flying end over end through the air right back at Nay. Nom had reflected the projectile back at its thrower.

It would have beaned her if not for her Iron-enhanced speed.

"Oh, thank Celestia both of you are—"

The eggplant splattered against the hearth wall and exploded, splattering Nay and Gracie, who happened to be walking through the kitchen door just as the vegetable burst upon impact. She stopped in the threshold, startled. Purple-and-yellow squash mush speckled across her cheek, chin, and hair.

All three of them looked between each other, stunned.

After dinner service, Nay was dead tired. Traveling to Maer Scathan, doing a dungeon dive, fighting monsters, and then traveling all the way back to work a full dinner service at the Lodge had taken enough energy to exhaust her at Iron Rank.

During the service, Quincy had reminded her that she needed to stay on top of the moon cake production. She was reminded again in her quest log.

[Quest: Bake Moon Cakes]
[Accept Quest Y/N?]

So, she couldn't go to bed quite yet. There was one last bit of business to take care of. She accepted the quest and headed outside.

Nay found a place behind the Lodge that was higher up on the cliff facing Lac Coineascar. It was out of view of the cobblestone street leading towards the Lodge and the path that led towards the back where the kitchen was. There was a plot up here next to the red-leafed mountain ash that towered and bloomed over the Lodge. Covered in constant snow, it was quite a beautiful sight, with hints of the vermilion leaves peeking out from underneath the white powder.

She had carried some lumber planks that Quincy had stored in the stables, and she arranged a makeshift rectangle in the soil. She'd come back later and assemble a better raised garden bed, but for now she just needed to mark off the area. She used a trowel to dig a hole in the soil. The surface was hard, almost frozen over, so it took her a minute to make an adequate break in the surface. The dirt underneath was soft and fertile, a decent area for planting.

She pulled the box Aule gave to her out of her inventory. She opened it and poured the elderflower seeds into her palm. She planted the seeds in the holes she dug, then used her bare hands to swipe dirt back into the holes, covering them up. She crouched, looking up at the green-tinged moon, the ribbon of magenta gas decorating the outer space around it.

"That's plenty of moonlight," Nay said.

She grabbed handfuls of snow and used Chef's Thermometer to melt it into water, sprinkling it over the freshly dug garden. She whispered at the seeds buried in the earth. "Grow."

— CHAPTER SIXTY-THREE —

Something Strange Is Afoot

Nay and Gracie were at a table in the tavern area, going over the menu list for the Green Moon Festival. It was in four moons, or four days, and Nay wanted to get the list settled and the supply of ingredients in order.

"So, let's see," Nay said. "We have more than enough fish for fish 'n chips, pork for char siu bowls, beef for sliders, and crab for the baskets of steamed crab. Proteins don't seem to be an issue."

"Traditionally," Gracie said, "the Green Moon fest is also a time farmers like to show off their season's harvest. Tundra pumpkins, chestnuts, persimmons, frostshrooms."

"I already know what I'm gonna do for those," Nay said. "Wine-braised frostshrooms with chestnuts. Tundra-pumpkin soup, and tundra pumpkin pie and persimmon pudding. Just a few of my ideas."

Gracie wiggled in her seat and smiled. "I'm getting hungry just hearing about it."

Quincy reached into the jar of butter cookies sitting on the bar. He grabbed one and munched on it, getting cookie crumbs in his mustache. Nay noticed he had made a considerable dent in the jar of cookies. She had made them from Volva Serrilda's recipe. "Save some for our customers there, boss."

Quincy took another bite, making a loud crunch. He waved her off. "I don't know if I can help myself when they're right in front of me like this."

"Never took you for a sweets man," Gracie said.

"There were hardly ever any good ones to eat," Quincy said. "I swear I've gained a stone since you two have been running the kitchen."

Nay went down the list she had assembled. "There's an order from Icerend Orchards of chestnuts, persimmons, and frostshrooms today. Several barrels of each. Tundra pumpkins . . . okay, tomorrow, there's a shipment from Snowdew Farms . . . yep, we're getting some tundra pumpkins from them . . ."

"And we're fine on Icemarrow Ale," Quincy said from behind the bar. "Did you ever talk to Alric about getting us some Frostbite Ale? Would be good to have multiple ales."

Nay realized she was frowning.

Things were now weird between Alric and her. She had been so busy, it felt easier just to avoid him, but she supposed she'd have to talk to him sooner or later. She'd only be able to avoid him for so long.

"It's on the list," Nay said.

She looked up to see Quincy observing her. There was no way he could know about her bizarre encounter with Alric at the Veritax chapel.

"Our shipment of rice flour hasn't arrived yet from Moonglum Farms," Gracie said.

Nay stopped. "We need that rice flour for the moon cakes."

Quincy stopped polishing one of the beer glasses he was working on. "Maybe they're just running behind?"

"We'll give them another couple of hours," Nay said. "If the order isn't here by then, we can check in with Don."

"I can make a visit to the farm if need be," Quincy said. "Because, honestly, we can be short on everything else, but if we don't have enough moon cakes . . ."

"Yes," Nay said, trying not to sigh. "Disaster."

"Disaster," Quincy echoed.

"The good news is we have enough inventory to keep the townsfolk fed throughout the fest," Nay said. "But we do need that rice flour, as the moon cake production begins tomorrow."

When Nay went to go check on the elderflower seeds she had planted, she was both surprised and relieved to discover that this stretch of cliff had been transformed into a field of elderflowers. They had spread past the rectangle of wood she had arranged as planters, refusing to be contained.

Unlike the species of elderflower she knew from back home, which were clusters of miniscule star-shaped white flowers, these were more substantial mint-green and light-pink flowers. They were about the size of orchids. They had pushed through the layer of snow, looking fresh and luscious. There was definitely magic to these flowers Aule had given her. She used True Eye and saw that they were abundant with motes of Vigor.

She looked in amazement at all of them. Coupled with the ash tree looming overhead, this section behind the Lodge was now quite the sight. She ran back to the Lodge and grabbed two baskets. She returned and started harvesting the elderflowers. She needed the petals, pistils, stems, and all for the elderflower paste.

* * *

Nay had left a few of the elderflowers underneath the ash tree and was sure by morning the field would be taken over again. She was storing her current harvest in barrels when Quincy came into the kitchen.

"Don still hasn't arrived with the shipment," Quincy said. "I was gonna take a ride to the farm to look in to this, and I was thinking you might want to accompany me if you're not too busy."

At that, a quest prompt appeared on her interface.

[Quest Detected]
[Quest: Investigate Moonglum Farms]
[Reward: Rice Flour]
[Accept Quest Y/N?]

That was odd. So, there was definitely something going on at the farm that was delaying the shipment.

It wouldn't be until tomorrow when the serious prep work and baking would begin, and Nay knew she could kill a couple of hours before dinner service. Nom was quick with prep work and could run things himself. She accepted the quest. "All right, let's go."

Nay and Quincy were on their respective fauglir mounts, Juniper and Al, and were heading outside of town towards Moonglum Farms. It was another gray and cold day in Stitchdale, with moments of alpine beauty depending on which direction one looked and when.

Nay didn't grow up in places with snow, so she was still struck by the beauty of it covering the evergreen trees and mountains. The way icicles hung on the banks of cold, bubbling creeks did something to her heart. Gentle snowfall on bodies of water was a sight that never ceased to amaze her.

Quincy breathed in the fresh air and exhaled. "Sometimes, it just helps to step outside."

"The Lodge getting stuffy for you?" Nay said.

"I love the Lodge," Quincy said. "But I need my moments with the wind and snow on my face."

"Does it snow on the Peninsula?"

"In the mountainous regions, it does, but nothing like here. On the Peninsula, the snow comes in thin layers. It's cold but not frigid. Most of the year, it's hot and dry. Unless you're on the coast."

"Do you miss it?"

"Sometimes, I miss the coast of the Vancian Sea. Sitting on the cliffs and watching the gulls above the waves while drinking a nice wine. I miss the sunsets in the Hills of Buscan. It happens right after dinner, sometimes right as you're enjoying dessert. Eating a lemon ricotta cake and watching the sky turn into a burst of orange haze before ushering in the night. I miss the countryside, not the people."

That seemed understandable, Nay thought. Sometimes, she missed back home but more for the memories and the sensations than the people. Hiking in Joshua Tree during the fall. Smoking a joint while taking a stroll around Venice Beach.

Then again, Quincy probably couldn't go back for more practical reasons. After hearing about his past, it sounded like he and Ilyawraith still had many enemies there.

"Do you ever worry about people from the Peninsula coming to look for you?" Nay ventured to ask.

"You mean my enemies?" he said.

Nay nodded.

"At first, some of them tried," he said. "But then they discovered it wasn't worth it."

Nay knew that he meant that they had decided it wasn't worth their lives. She wondered how many people he killed who came looking for him after the events of the Massacre at Palazzo Furio.

"As the things stand now, it feels like we're kind of at a truce," he said. "I don't set foot down there; they don't set foot up here."

"What happens when the truce ends?" Nay said. "Do you ever wonder if danger would come to the Lodge?"

"Are you concerned about old enemies of mine endangering the Lodge and the lives of the people in Lucerna's End?"

"Well, now that you bring it up, yeah."

"You let me and Ilyawraith worry about that," Quincy said.

"Ilyawraith?"

"You don't think she doesn't monitor Stitchdale, do you? It's close enough to the Caraxe Strait to concern her. She'll know if there's a threat as soon as it steps foot into the valley. And if one does get brave? They better hope they're Silver Rank."

Nay processed this. So, Ilyawraith was somehow surveilling or had some type of system in place for watching their backs.

Then how come she didn't see the strange man who visited her in the Frozen Vale?

"Is the Phantomhead Empire evil?" Nay said.

Quincy looked at her. "You're just full of questions today, aren't you?"

"I'm just curious about the world. And you've mentioned them . . ."

"They're ruled by Entrophists who feed on souls, robbing those souls of an afterlife. Does that seem evil to you?"

"What if I don't believe in souls?"

"Whether you believe in souls or not, it's how they gain their power."

"What stops them from crossing the sea and annexing the Peninsula?"

"Well, to do that, they'd have to face the might of the Ligeia League and their Marrow Eaters. It would be a surefire way for them to overextend their reach. And overextending like that could turn out to be a fatal mistake."

"So, I take it Entrophists are unwelcome here and cultivators are unwelcome there?"

"That's the way it's always been, far as I know," Quincy said. "But they haven't conquered all of their own continent. That's another reason we're not really in their sights: they have enough to worry about on their own borders."

"They must have strange powers compared to Marrow Eaters."

"It is a dark art. But they need fresh souls to fill their reserves. That's their weakness. Souls aren't easily attainable and come with a high price. With us, we just have to replenish our Vigor."

"So, there's not any chance there could be like . . . a good Entrophist?"

Quincy looked at her again. "Why the sudden interest?"

"I don't know," Nay said. She was uncomfortable under his gaze. Her thoughts went to the black rose she was keeping a secret. "It just seems kind of one-dimensional, you know?

"One-dimensional how?"

"Marrow Eaters can be either good or bad. The source of their magic doesn't define their morality. At least it doesn't seem like it."

"Our," Quincy said, correcting her. "*Our* magic."

"Right, our magic. But by definition of the Entrophist method, they're evil."

"Because they kill and steal to gain their power."

"Couldn't the same thing be said about Marrow Eaters? We kill monsters for their parts and consume them to gain abilities. We also take their Cores and absorb them into our bodies. How often are the monsters or beasts willing participants?"

Quincy chuckled, both impressed and annoyed by her line of questioning. "I'm not going to justify it. But I'd say it's complicated. And there's clearly a difference between hunting monsters and consuming souls meant for the afterlife. If you really want to know about the Phantomhead Empire, you should hear some of the atrocities they've done to nations they've conquered. I can say with some certainty, at least concerning those running the ship over there, that they are not good people."

She saw his point, and maybe their nation was evil. Or their leaders were evil. But surely, there had to be some good eggs.

At least that was what she told herself as she justified keeping her rose-giver a secret.

As Moonglum Farms became visible when they reached the top of the hill, Quincy pointed something out.

"Do you hear that?"

Nay listened and studied the farm before them. There was a main compound and stable and then the fields surrounding it.

"I don't hear anything," Nay said.

"Exactly," Quincy said. "There's not even wind."

Nay realized he was right. Usually, there was always the hint of a cold wind whispering around them. No sounds of birds or any other animal that populated the area.

There was just eerie silence.

Quincy opened a bag on the side of Al and took out his battle-axe and crossbow. He unclasped and removed the sheath from the blade of the axe and slung the weapon over his back. He placed the crossbow in front of him on the saddle. He nudged Al forward and Nay followed.

They descended towards the farm.

"Stay alert," Quincy said. "Something strange is afoot."

— CHAPTER SIXTY-FOUR —

Netherlings

Moonglum Farms was owned and operated by Don Moonglum, and it had been in his family for generations. There was the farmhouse where his family lived. He had a wife and a trio of stitchchildren, two young girls and an older boy, who all helped run the family business.

There were the stables and animal pens, a greenhouse, an orchard, and then the fields for the animals and various crops. All of the livestock were of the sturdy Stitchdale variety, a species that was fine with the harsh cold; they just needed a little extra feed.

Usually, on such farms, there would be the noise of animal activity. Chickens and roosters. The squeal and grunting of pigs. The occasional mooing and snorting of cows. The bleating of goats.

There was no such sound or activity as Nay and Quincy approached the farm. Not even wind. It was unnaturally still save for the soft snowfall. The branches of the various fruit and nut trees in the orchards didn't stir.

Nay consulted her mini-map and saw a mass of dots, all in the barn. She stopped Juniper and stared at the image on her interface. There was a red dot in there, signifying some kind of threat presence.

"What is it?" Quincy said, keeping his voice low.

"They're all in the barn," Nay said, whispering. "There's something in there with them."

"Do you know what it is?"

Nay shook her head.

"Do you know if they're alive?"

"I think so; otherwise, I don't think I'd see them marked on the map."

Quincy studied the farm, observing the stables. He pulled out his spyglass, extended it, and took a look. He scanned the buildings and then grunted, slamming the spyglass closed. "I see dead animals."

"What's the play?" Nay said.

"We scout out the stables," Quincy said. "Slowly. Stay by me and keep your eyes peeled."

He nudged Al forward, but the fauglir let out a whine, not wanting to go in that direction.

Nay noticed that Juniper didn't want to get any closer to the farm either. The fauglir looked up at her and whined.

"This isn't good," Quincy said. He lowered his mouth to Al's ear. "What is it, boy? What do you sense on that farm?"

Al licked Quincy's face and then looked at the farm, letting out a growl.

Quincy picked up his crossbow and kept it in his hand, finger near the trigger. "It's all right, boy. Be brave now; I won't let anything happen to you."

He nudged the fauglir forward and Al obeyed, cautiously stalking closer to the property, hackles half-raised.

Nay leaned down and spoke to Juniper. "Stay close to 'em, girl. Don't worry now; you're safe with us." Her words seemed to embolden Juniper, and the fauglir followed their companions.

There were feathers and blood in the snow between the farmhouse and barn. Something had gotten to the chickens. The roost entrance was smeared with blood. There was a severed chicken talon poking out of the snow near the entrance.

Quincy, who had gotten off Al, took a peek in. "Whatever did this didn't do it because it was hungry."

Nay climbed off Juniper and joined him at the entrance. The roost was littered with the torn and shredded bodies of chickens. "It did so to kill."

Quincy looked at the stables. "We need to get in there and hope it's not too late for the Moonglums."

He headed for the stables and Nay followed, but a noise caught her attention. Quincy stopped and he listened. He heard it too.

There was a strange tearing sound coming from the stables.

Nay, compelled, walked over. She noticed that a nearby trough was full of blood. It looked like there were teeth floating in it. "Quincy . . ."

He looked at the trough and his face hardened.

Nay reached the stables. It was an A-frame building with open pens. At first, she didn't understand what she was looking at.

There was a sow pig, laid out on the ground. Its head was jerking as if it was nodding in conversation with someone. There was darkness in front of it, like there was a tear in reality, as if there was a void covering the length of its body. Then she noticed motion, and Nay flinched, stepping back. There were white teeth stained red hanging in the air.

They belonged to the darkness.

A snarl came out of the mouth, and Nay realized it was some type of four-legged creature made of the nether dark. It released the pig, revealing the torn abdomen on the sow. The nether creature charged at her, scampering across the ground on all fours like a reptile made out of the night.

Thorn and the ice scythe appeared in her hands, the Dire Knife weapon imbues flaring to life around the blades. There was an explosion of snow and motion as it leapt at her.

Suddenly, a crossbow bolt hit the creature, impaling it to the earth. It squealed, gnashing its white teeth, tendrils of nether dark floating off it like ink. Quincy wielded his crossbow, Samuel. He gritted his teeth in disgust. "*Netherlings.*"

Nay remembered something. She pulled two items out of her inventory and held one out to Quincy. "Take it and eat it!"

Quincy took the item. It was a pastry. "What is it?"

Nay took a bite out of hers and chewed quickly, forcing herself to swallow the savory pasty and steak filling. "It's a Pastie of Nether-Being Slaying."

Quincy immediately took a bite, wolfing it down. "How long does it last?"

"An hour."

That's when they both noticed a dark shadow moving underneath the snow. Nay thought it was some type of oil spill racing across the ground. The shadow exploded out of the snow, taking a tangible, corporeal form, its materializing mass throwing Quincy into the air.

The larger nether beast shot into the sky like a giant reptile scrambling out of the earth. It was about the size of a van. It reached its apex above the barn and then crashed back onto the ground. The ground shook when it landed.

Nay got a prompt on her interface.

[Quest Detected]
[Quest: Slay the Netherspawn Mother]
[Reward: Loot is involved!]
[Accept Quest Y/N?]

"You really don't give me much of a choice with this one, do you?" Nay said. She accepted the quest.

Midair, Quincy pointed Samuel at the large Netherspawn Mother and pulled the trigger, unleashing a burst of fléchettes that exploded upon contact with the nether monster, sending flames up and down its body.

Quincy landed on his back in the snow and immediately went to reloading the crossbow.

The small netherling next to Nay had its two hands on the back of its head, gripping the bolt that impaled it to the ground. It was trying to rip it out of the earth. Nay decapitated it with the ice scythe. The body collapsed, but the hands were still holding on to the bolt. Black-and-violet smoke poured out of the neck stump.

"So, that's how shadows bleed," Nay said. These things were from the Nether Realm. She wondered if that meant the Nether Sister was here.

She spun around and her eyes widened.

More netherlings were coming out of the stables, a tide of darkness spreading towards her.

She turned to run, and Juniper was there. Nay jumped on the fauglir's back, mounting her. The closest netherling swiped at her, its shadow talons raking through the air.

Quincy threw his axe, Gertrude.

Two noxious spirit axes formed on either side of the battle-axe. The trio of blades spun through the air, crashing into the tide of netherlings. Gertrude bit into the netherling reaching for her, splitting its corporeal skull. The spirit axes crashed into the tide of netherlings behind it, releasing an unholy poison into their targets.

The big netherspawn, the brood mother, charged Quincy, who was now on his feet.

Juniper, frightened to get away from the outpouring of netherlings, was running for her life. Straight towards Quincy and the Netherspawn Mother.

Nay lowered the ice scythe to the side as the Netherspawn Mother grew closer. She swung, the elemental bone and blade piercing a back haunch of the beast. The scythe ripped through its strange flesh, releasing black-and-violet smoke.

She racked up a Kinetic Point on the creature.

The Netherspawn Mother roared and spun towards Nay, but Juniper was too fast.

Quincy shot it with another round of fléchettes. It flinched and flames licked at its flesh. Behind it, Quincy's magical poison was spreading through the wave of netherlings. Black boils were bursting into explosions of nether smoke. They were on their sides, screaming, their limbs thrashing at the snow.

The Netherspawn Mother collided with Quincy, grabbing him with its hands and lifting him into the sky. At that moment, Gertrude reappeared in Quincy's hand. With both hands, he raised it over his head and swung the axe into the Netherspawn Mother's face. It turned its head, and the axe embedded in the side of its head.

Noxious green smoke began pouring out of the wound, and it snarled, throwing Quincy. He hit a tree, his crash shaking all the snow off its limbs.

The monster put a hand to the axe wound in its face, at the black boils forming there. It ground its teeth and strained all its muscles. Green smoke and venom poured out of the wound. It was pushing the poison out of its body.

The cut scabbed over with its fast-coagulating blood, a clump of keratin forming over the wound like extra armor. It spun towards Quincy, hate burning in its violet nether eyes.

Suddenly, there was a commotion coming from the barn. Frightened screams came from within. Presumably, they were the cries of the Moonglum family. The double doors burst open and there was an animalistic roar.

Nay didn't understand what she was seeing at first. There was a white mass of claws, teeth and fur turning in circles and wrestling with a clutch of netherlings.

Is that a fucking polar bear?

It was.

It was indeed a polar bear, standing on its hind legs, ripping the netherlings from itself and tossing them to and fro, snarling. Nay noticed an odd detail. The bear had what looked like a leather belt around its waist, and it was wearing the remnants of a tattered loincloth. There was a cluster of slivermoon trout hanging by their tails off the belt.

What the hell?

The polar bear ripped the head off a netherling with its teeth. Black-and-violet smoke sprayed into its face and the bear coughed, throwing both halves of the netherling to the ground. The polar bear grabbed another one off its back and slammed it repeatedly against one of the barn doors until it went limp in its hands.

Meanwhile, Quincy was dodging swipes from the Netherspawn Mother. He slashed it across the stomach with Gertrude. More of that smoke spilled out as the two opponents circled each other.

The polar bear saw the Netherspawn Mother fighting Quincy and roared. It fell onto all fours and loped across the ground, barreling towards them.

"Quincy!" Nay shouted.

He looked up to see the new contender approaching.

She moved to unleash Salvo of Knives on the polar bear but hesitated. It had been fighting the netherlings with them. Was it really going to attack Quincy?

The bear crashed into the Netherspawn Mother from behind with a loud *smack*. They rolled across the snow in a massive ball. Both creatures bellowed as they scratched and bit at each other.

Quincy pointed Samuel at the wrestling beasts. He took aim. He didn't seem to care if he hit both of them.

A voice surprised both him and Nay.

"Don't shoot the bear!"

Don Moonglum was poking his head out of the barn. "It's on our side!"

— CHAPTER SIXTY-FIVE —

Tuk-Tuk

Sentient polar bears? And it was on our side? Was it the mobile form of a fellow Marrow Eater?

Nay looked between the bear rolling with the Netherspawn Mother and Don Moonglum.

"How did you know to come here?" Don said.

"We didn't," Nay said. "You missed our shipment of rice flour, and we wanted to see what was going on. It's unlike you to miss an order."

"I hope you understand, now that you see the circumstances," Don said. "I'm relieved to see you, if it wasn't for—"

At that moment, a netherling loosed itself from the shadow of the barn and charged towards Don. Nay released Salvo of Knives, and the netherling was instantly pinned to the ground as soon as Thorn appeared in its body. Don flinched and recoiled in fright. The spirit knives raining from above immobilized the other netherlings that had emerged from the shadows to attack him.

"Are there any other of those things in there with you?" Nay said.

Don shook his head, staring at the netherling corpses in shock.

"Stay in there with your family and lock the doors," Nay said.

Don nodded and retreated into the barn, pulling the doors closed after him. There was the clattering of a chain and the clasp of a lock snapping into place.

Nay tapped Juniper with her heels and nudged her towards Quincy. When she reached him, she hopped off the fauglir. Thorn reappeared back in her hand.

The Netherspawn Mother managed to extricate itself from the polar bear. It scrambled onto all fours and a roiling black cloud appeared over its head. It started sucking in wind. The monster flickered with a violet glow, lightning in a storm cloud.

All the air around them started flowing towards the cloud above the nether monster. Molecules of snow, one by one, started to fly towards the vortex. Nay felt herself being pulled towards the creature. The same thing was happening to the polar bear, which was already near the Netherspawn Mother, and Quincy.

Quincy swung Gertrude into a tree, creating an anchor. He grasped the handle of his axe and held a hand out towards Nay. "Take it!"

Nay grabbed his hand, and his fingers closed around her whole hand and wrist, pulling her closer to him.

"Hold on to me!"

She tried to wrap her arms around him, but he was so big, she just dug her hands into his clothing and leather armor, finding a grip.

The polar bear roared in frustration, but the vacuuming wind was too strong. It fell head over heels, tumbling towards the Netherspawn Mother.

Gertrude's blade creaked in the flesh of the tree. The top half of the evergreen bent towards the vortex, the hole in reality, over the Netherspawn Mother.

The polar bear rolled into the radius of the monster.

There was a chaotic charge of energy in the air, then a booming violet flash. Forks of violet lightning shot out of the cloud vortex. A violent blast of energy exploded off the creature in all directions.

The polar bear was airborne.

Nay watched it cartwheel over the barn and disappear on the other side as if it were nothing but debris in a tornado. The reversal of energy shattered the tree, and Quincy and Nay went tumbling, carried on the blast wave. They landed in the snow close to the farmhouse.

Nay shook off the disorientation and looked up just in time to see the Netherspawn Mother charging them.

Nay did a kip-up just as Quincy fired Gertrude. The bolt was accompanied by a wall of spirit bolts materializing around it. The projectiles shredded into the nether monster. Spatters of black-and-violet smoke streamed from the holes pierced through the creature.

It fell to one knee and slipped, then righted itself and kept coming.

Nay lunged, sinking Thorn into its side, racking up another Kinetic Point. It whipped around to face her, opening its maw wide. It snapped at her. But a pair of white paws caught the mouth, protecting her from the bite. Nay caught a strong whiff of fish and blood and dirty fur.

The polar bear stepped in front of her, holding the Netherspawn Mother's mouth open with its powerful paws. The bear pushed forward on its hind legs. It held the upper jaw and lower jaw like it was trying to snap a wishbone in two, forcing the mouth open wider.

A huge axe blade appeared in the Netherspawn Mother's back. Quincy had leapt on the thing and had driven Gertrude into its spine.

Nay swiped the ice scythe in a backhanded swing, slicing the nether monster's chest. She had three Kinetic Points. As the polar bear roared, Quincy ripped Gertrude out of the creature's spine and made for another swing.

Gertrude chunked into the spine again, and as the polar bear lunged, wrapping its own jaws around the neck off the beast, Nay activated Gore. There was an explosion inside of the three cuts she made. Black-and-violet smoke billowed out of the holes, and the Netherspawn Mother collapsed onto her stomach.

The polar bear ripped its throat out.

Quincy ripped Gertrude out and swung at the thing's neck, lopping its head off.

[Quest Completed]
[Slay the Netherspawn Mother Complete!]
[You have been rewarded Vigor Points]
[You have been rewarded Loot]

As its life poured out of it, the death cries of the remaining netherlings sang a haunting chorus over the land. Gold vigama descended out of the sky. Nay absorbed the Vigor points.

Quincy hopped off its back and joined Nay. "Were you hurt?"

"I'm fine," Nay said.

They looked at the polar bear, who stood there heaving, catching its breath. There were dark red patches of fur where it had been bleeding.

"And you are?" Quincy said to the bear.

Surprisingly, the polar bear spoke. And it was in a human voice. "Tulutuktuk," the bear said. Then he shifted into his human form. He was bare-chested and brown-skinned. Long brown hair fell to the middle of his back.

Nay couldn't help but think of a Native American kid. Or an Inuk in Alaska. He couldn't have been much older than nineteen or twenty, Nay thought.

"My friends call me Tuk-Tuk," he said.

"You're with the Twelve Tribes?" Quincy said.

The boy nodded. "I am of the Volinaqq Tribe."

"What are you doing all the way down here?" Quincy said.

"Tracking this thing," he said. He spat on the remains. "Thirteen moons back, it and its spawn attacked my tribe. It killed several people. I was part of a hunting party pursuing it."

"Where's the rest of your party?" Nay said.

"Dead."

"I'm sorry to hear that," Nay said.

"We weren't the only hunting party. Nor was this the only creature. There were other attacks on the tribes. They took children."

Quincy and Nay exchanged a look.

Tuk-Tuk knelt next to the shadowy remains. He collected the teeth and put them in a leather pouch. "A trophy to show my people when I return to them."

Nay walked over to the barn and banged her fist on the doors. "It's over! You can come out!"

After a moment, there was the unclasping of a lock and the rattling of chains. The doors opened.

Don Moonglum stood there, peeking around her to see if it really was safe. His middle-aged stitchgal wife and his three children were in the middle of the barn. Two young girls and a teen boy. They were all holding farm instruments as weapons. Pitchforks, shovels, and even a bullwhip. They looked frightened but otherwise all right.

"The monsters?" Don said.

"Alive no longer," Nay said. "Can you tell us what happened?"

Don and his family walked out of the barn, looking at the corpses of the netherlings and the Netherspawn Mother in a mixture of fascination, relief, and horror. "My son and I were packing the orders for the town into the wagon when there was a commotion from the animals," Don said. "Weirdest thing, though."

"What's that?" Quincy said.

"Before they attacked, there was absolutely no sound," Don said. "No wind; not even the animals were making a squeak. That's how I first knew that something evil was near. Are they truly from the Nether Realm?"

"Aye," Quincy said, nodding.

"My Angakkuq says they've come to our realm to collect for a blood ritual," Tuk-Tuk said.

"Blood ritual?" Nay said.

Tuk-Tuk nodded. "They want to awaken the One in the Black Ice."

"What's that?" Nay said.

"An old legend," Quincy said. He was suddenly looking at Tuk-Tuk with interest. "Your people really believe that?"

Tuk-Tuk shrugged. "There's a great stirring in the spiritual realm. Something recently opened the doorway between our realm and the Nether for a reason."

[Quest Completed!]
[Investigate Moonglum Farms Completed]
[You have been rewarded Vigor Points]

Quincy pulled on one end of his mustache, processing this. Then he walked over to Don and put a hand on his shoulder. "Are you okay?"

"As long as there's no more of these things around," he said.

Tuk-Tuk was turning his head, looking around. "Your farm is clear now."

Nay watched Tuk-Tuk. Did he have some kind of True Eye like her? But one that could see Nether Realm happenings?

"I owe all of you for protecting me and my family," Don said.

"Killing it was reward enough for me," Tuk-Tuk said.

"You owe us nothing," Quincy said.

Don looked like he could cry. His son was helping his wife and daughters get back to the farmhouse.

Nay could no longer ignore the blinking Loot icon, and she opened it up.

Vortex Bomb of the Netherspawn Mother. When you need to gather your enemies into one spot, why not use this handheld Vortex Bomb? It's the suction power of a thousand netherling mouths inhaling at once.
Useful if you need to keep multiple pesky enemies in one place or make them congregate to combo with a nifty AOE attack.
Three uses.

Nay pulled the loot item out of her inventory. It was a dark bracelet with a glittering black-and-violet cloud hewn out of onyx and amethyst. She was tempted to wear it now, but she didn't want to actually trigger a Vortex Bomb. That would be embarrassing. She put the Vortex Bomb of the Netherspawn Mother back into her inventory.

"We ought to get back to the Lodge," Quincy said. "I have some arrangements to make."

Nay wondered what arrangements those might be. He clearly seemed bothered by the attack and what Tuk-Tuk had said about the nether-being activity. She was struck with a thought.

Was he going to contact the Gloom Rangers? Or consult with Ilyawraith?

"All right, we can take some of the rice flour with us now, if that's not a problem," Nay said. "I'd like to get started on the moon cakes during dinner service tonight."

"Sure," Don said. "I'll give you a few sacks for now. And I'll deliver the rest later once my family is settled and safe. In fact, we might come to town for the night to stay at the Lodge just to feel safe."

He went to go tend to his family and get the rice flour.

Quincy and Nay moved to get their fauglir.

"Wait, you guys run a tavern?" Tuk-Tuk said.

Nay nodded.

"What of it?" Quincy said.

"I could use a place to stay before I begin my trek back. I don't have any coin, but I'll work in exchange for lodging."

"You can stay free of charge," Quincy said, "if you let me ask you more questions while you stay. I'd like to know more about the happenings amongst the Twelve Tribes."

"Sure," Tuk-Tuk said. "But it doesn't sit well with me to stay for free. Let me pay you somehow."

"Do you have any skills?" Quincy said.

"I'm not bad around a frying pan," Tuk-Tuk said.

"We've already got cooks," Quincy said.

"I'm a great fisherman." He grabbed the fishing rod next to his belongings against the wall.

"And there's an abundance of fishermen."

"Well," Tuk-Tuk said. He bit his lower lip with his bottom teeth. He leaned forward and said, "I can wash dishes. I'll be the best dishwasher you've ever seen."

Quincy looked at Nay. *Up to you.*

"I suppose we could always use a good dishwasher."

Tuk-Tuk smiled, relieved. He grabbed his stuff and joined them.

Quincy and Nay climbed atop their fauglir. "I suppose we'll have to trek back slow."

"No, you can go at whatever speed you like," Tuk-Tuk said. "I can keep up."

And with that, he shifted into polar-bear form. His bag was on his back, and he held the fishing rod in his mouth. He trotted past them, a happy bounce in his chonky steps.

— CHAPTER SIXTY-SIX —

To New Friends

There were only three more moons until the Green Moon Festival.
The key to making the elderflower paste involved sautéing the elderflowers with a knob of butter and then simmering with Green Moon wine and reducing. But the kicker was one couldn't use a metal pan.

It had to be done with green clay.

Quincy told Nay that green clay was harvested from the earth deep in the Viridian Forest, or the First Forest, as some Loremasters called it. It was known as being the area where the Friends of Man had first gathered. Supposedly, they had a dwelling there. A city built amongst the boughs of the trees.

Luckily, Nay had found Ol' Pat's stash of green-clay cookware in one of the storage chests in the larder. The green clay was used in some of the structures in the Peninsula cities, often packed into the foundation because people believed it brought good luck. Some people believed in this so much, there were even Marrow Eaters who used weapons made out of the clay because they believed it gave them a lucky edge in battle. The same for trinkets. People were willing to pay a handsome fee for such items.

Nay melted the butter in the green-clay pans and sprinkled in the elderflowers. She added some fresh mint leaves and then poured some of the Green Moon wine into the pan. She brought the concoction to a simmer and waited for them to reduce. After reduction, the next step was pouring the mixture into the gnomish blenders and blending to break apart the flowers.

The blended elderflowers were then poured through strainers, and the liquid was collected in jars to eventually be mixed with rice flour, sugar, and eggs.

[Quest Detected]
[Quest: Make a Thousand Moon Cakes]
[Accept Quest Y/N?]

Nay had accepted the quest, and for the rest of the day, she, Nom, and Gracie would be making the paste and storing everything inside the walk-in cooler.

It turned out that Tuk-Tuk was also a beast as a dishie.

Not that he shifted into his bear form to take command of the dish pit but that he was fast and efficient. He was also thorough. Every plate, pan, and pot was cleaned with nary a speck of food residue or dirt to be found on them.

The previous night, upon arriving at the Lodge, after he had taken a bath and cleaned himself of the blood from the battle with the Netherspawn, he was brought to family dinner, where he met the rest of the staff.

And Nom.

Nay had prepared him as best as she could. "Don't be alarmed. The sous-chef isn't of the human variety."

The tribesman had raised an eyebrow at that, but it was clear that whatever he was expecting didn't line up with the reality. He had stopped in the threshold to the kitchen to stare.

"You must be the Bear!" Nom said. "Come and join us! I made some fried venison hearts and roasted potatoes. Should replenish you, and you can tell me all about how you saved Moonglum Farms!"

Tuk-Tuk looked from him to the servers and to Nay. When he realized that everyone was calm, enjoying their meal, and showing no sign that anything was wrong while dining with a talking tentacle, he relaxed some.

"Go on, don't be scared," Nom said, scooting over. "I don't bite.

"Hard," Nom added, after a moment.

Bryja and Ulla laughed.

Tuk-Tuk sat down next to Nom. He seemed stiff as a board, unsure how he should present himself, so he was defaulting to his stoic mode.

Nay served him a plate of the food and then grabbed a plateful for herself. She sat down across from him, next to the girls.

Tuk-Tuk grabbed a portion of the slivered and fried deer heart with his bare hands and took a bite. His demeanor of suspicious caution melted away to one of pleasure. He was impressed by the taste and continued to eat, amazed.

Bryja and Ulla giggled while watching him eat. They didn't bother hiding their attraction to the youthful and mysterious hunter from the Twelve Tribes. Nay smirked.

"You know," Nom said, "if it wasn't for our new friend here, we wouldn't have the rice flour to make the moon cakes for the festival. In fact, the Moonglum family might not even be alive."

The server girls observed Tuk-Tuk with renewed interest. But the Northern hunter was too busy focusing on the meal. As one does when eating Epicurist-quality cooking.

"It's true," Nay said, as she made her way through the roasted veggies. "Some monsters attacked the farm, but Tuk-Tuk was there to defend them. Isn't that right, Tuk-Tuk?"

Tuk-Tuk was having a moment with his food, going for seconds.

"Right, Tuk-Tuk?"

He realized everyone else had been talking. He set his plate down and nodded. "I was hunting it from the North. I tracked it to the farm and was able to confront it. Although I don't know if I would have succeeded in protecting the family if it wasn't for you and Quincy. You're as much to thank as me."

The servers looked at Nay.

"Well," Nay said, unsure how to act or what to say, "Quincy's a former adventurer. He's had plenty of experience dealing with monsters."

"If I recall," Tuk-Tuk said, "you didn't seem to have any qualms about getting close to it and stabbing it with knives."

Nay glanced at the servers, who were looking at her, impressed and ever-curious about the chef. "Anyone else who was there would have done the same."

Tuk-Tuk observed her, a bit puzzled to why she was downplaying her role. But then he let it go and turned his attention back to the deer hearts. "I must thank you for the meal. It's nice to eat with others again."

"How long were you traveling alone?" Nom said.

"It's been seven moons since the last member of my hunting party perished," Tuk-Tuk said.

Nom nodded with respect. "I'm sorry to hear that."

"My people have been having problems with these things," Tuk-Tuk said. "Is it the same here?"

Everyone looked at each other.

"We've had our share of troubles," Nay said.

"Dark days, then," Tuk-Tuk said. "We share the same land and ought to protect each other. As long as I'm here, I will keep an eye out for you."

"And we for you, friend," Nom said. The tentacle got up and retrieved a Void Lambic from his conjured table. He set the frothy beer in front of Tuk-Tuk. Tuk-Tuk picked it up and Nom bumped his drink into his. "To new friends and an end to the darkness!"

Tuk-Tuk watched Nom down his drink in one gulp. He was impressed.

The brown-haired hunter threw his head back and slammed the Void Lambic without taking a breath. When he was done chugging, he slammed his flagon on the table.

"All right!" Nom said.

Tuk-Tuk wiped the beer froth off his lips with the back of his hand and looked sheepishly at the servers watching him. Bryja and Ulla smiled back, turning red. The chillwind faun slowly adjusted herself until she was hiding behind her flagon, but Ulla just started laughing.

Dinner service rolled around and everyone was at their different stations, back of the house and front of the house, all going about their different jobs. Occasionally, their orbits would intersect.

As Nay and Nom concentrated on cooking pasta, working with careful timing to move the noodles into their pans of venison sauce where they would ladle a little pasta water and let things mix together, she glanced back at the dish room and gestured at Tuk-Tuk, who was crushing the dishes like a man on a mission.

"Better watch the front-of-the-house girls with him," Nay said. "He's the type of dishie whom servers and hostesses can't help but fall for."

"He does have a certain mystique about him," Nom said. "I wonder if the polar-bear thing is a plus or a minus."

"Definitely a plus. He can basically turn into a warm bed."

"I'm a little jealous," Nom said.

"Don't be," Nay said. "He's unique, like you. To paraphrase the words of a great writer, he's one of God's own prototypes. A high-powered mutant of some kind never considered for mass production. Too weird to live and too rare to die."

"You're saying I'm weird?"

"In a good way. But to tell the truth, I think we're all weird here."

Nom didn't argue with that. As he monitored his pan of venison sauce and ditali noodles, he went to reach for a sprinkle of parsley and realized he was out. "Need more herbs here."

"I'll grab them," Nay said.

She went into the pantry where the barrel herb garden was. She went to pluck a few handfuls of parsley from where it was growing, and a voice startled her.

"There you are."

She froze and spun around. There was no one behind her at the door.

There was a chuckle.

"Not there. *Here.*"

Nay turned and looked at the black rose tucked behind the barrels of herbs. It had grown much bigger from when she last saw it. The shimmering-galaxy black petals gestured at her, and there was sap or some type of secretion dripping from the tips of the thorns. And strangest of all, there was a mouth formed out of purple plant matter at the center of the black rose.

It spoke again.

"I've been looking for you," the voice said, coming out of the mouth.

She recognized it then. It was the voice of the mysterious Entrophist.

"Have you been avoiding me on purpose?"

Nay glanced behind her again, to make sure no one was nearby. Then she leaned closer and whispered, "No, I haven't been avoiding you. I've been busy."

That chuckle again.

"I'm glad you decided to let the Rose of Distant Voices grow."

"So, that's what this thing is called."

"I gave it to you so we could communicate, should you choose to let it grow. I'm glad you did."

"You know, I was about to throw it in the fire."

"And why would you do that?"

"Because I have every reason to believe you're a bad man."

There was an exclamation of mock offense.

"Me? A bad man?"

"You're from the Phantomhead Empire."

"You're right about one thing. The other is a matter of opinion, you'll find."

"So, you're not bad?"

"It depends on who you talk to about me."

"So, give me a reason not to cut off our communication and destroy this . . . Rose of Distant Voices."

"I suppose that's fair. What do you want to know?"

"Well, a name would be a good start."

"Nikolai Dragavei."

"Okay, Nikolai. How did you find me in the Frozen Vale?"

"Scrying."

"And how did you elude the attention of those watching the vale?"

"It's really not that interesting."

"Humor me."

"A powerful cloaking glamour."

"What is it that you want with me?"

"It's not what I want with you. It's what I can offer you."

"And what's that? I'm not interested in doing what you do."

"And what is it that I do?"

"I know what you are. You feed on souls."

There was silence for a moment. Nay was sure this was the end of the conversation that spanned the geography and an ocean.

"Some of us, like me, only feed on the souls of the willing," Nikolai said.

"What does that mean?"

"You assume all of us kill and steal souls. Am I right?"

"Well, isn't that what you do?"

"There are some of us who refuse to take a life. We only feed on those who have offered their souls to us. Those too sick to live. Those too old to live. They're all on the cusp of death and want to dedicate their lives to a cause greater than them."

"And what cause is that? Expanding your empire?"

"There are those of us who might want to topple the empire."

This threw Nay for a loop.

"So, you said you could offer me something. What did you mean by that?"

"What if I told you there was a way to return to your world?"

Nay stared at the black rose, thunderstruck by that question. As her thoughts raced, there was a bang and the air filled with torn black petals imprinted with a galaxy. The black rose exploded in pieces, pierced by a crossbow bolt.

Nay turned around and Quincy was in the doorway, holding Gertrude, his face twitching with anger.

— CHAPTER SIXTY-SEVEN —

No More Secrets

Before Quincy shut the door behind him, he shouted, "Nom! Take over for a bit!"

"But the parsley—"

Quincy grabbed a bunch of herbs with his huge hand and ripped them out of the soil in the barrel. He shoved them in a basket and slid it into the kitchen. He closed the door.

He stepped next to Nay and looked at the remains of the black rose. The torn pieces were already turning gray and wilting, the galaxies on the petals winking out, extinguished.

The part that was shaped like a mouth drooped and curled in on itself.

Nay stood there, mortified, afraid to even move.

"How long was it growing back here?" Quincy said, his cadence deliberate and slow, his voice low.

"Ever since we got back from my training," Nay said.

"And how did it get here?"

Nay closed her eyes, not wanting to tell him. She hadn't expected her secret to be discovered like this. "I brought it here."

Quincy turned to face her. She couldn't meet his eyes. She was too ashamed. She wanted to hide, to shrink into herself and disappear.

"And where did you find it?" Quincy said.

His calmness was the worst part. It was simmering. She felt that at any moment, he might explode, unable to contain his anger.

Nay looked down. "It was given to me."

Nay was in Quincy's small office full of his trophies and adventuring artifacts. She had been patched into Ilyawraith's communication Ability. A prompt appeared on Nay's interface.

[You have an incoming Party Invite]
[From Ilyawraith]
[You have been invited to Banshee Sect]
[Accept Ilyawraith's Party Invite?]
[Y/N]

"You should feel or become aware that Ilyawraith is trying to contact you. That's her Whispering Wind Ability. Give her permission."

Nay obeyed and accepted the Party Invite.

[Vigor Link Established]
[You have joined Banshee Sect Party]
[Incoming Whispering Wind Call from Ilyawraith]
[Accept Y/N?]

Nay accepted.

An eidolon of Ilyawraith appeared in the office with them. She was levitating in the lotus position. There was a spectral nature to her image. She was translucent and cast in a blue hue.

It was like a holographic party chat. There were options for just voices or texts, but this one was already sent to a holographic feed. It took Nay a moment to adjust to the experience. She wondered how the Ability prompts appeared for the natives of this world, for the ones who didn't have her convenient videogame interface. She was sure it was also probably intuitive to them in its own way that made sense to them.

"Start from the beginning," Ilyawraith said.

So, Nay told them about her encounter with Nikolai in the Frozen Vale. It was like she was finally getting to confess. It was liberating in a way, to tell them the truth. When she was done, Ilyawraith and Quincy exchanged a look.

"You realize you should have told us about this man earlier," Ilyawraith said.

"I know," Nay said. "I'm not proud of it."

"Why keep it a secret?" Quincy said. "This could have ended much worse. We may still be in danger because of your actions."

"I didn't feel like he meant me harm," Nay said. "I know you probably don't believe me, but I think I have a pretty good read on people. And I don't think this person had ill intentions."

"There are skilled spies who are trained to make people think that," Ilyawraith said. "This man could be a spy for the Phantomhead Empire."

"But why choose me?" Nay said. "I'm no one here. Unless . . . unless he was trying to get information on you two."

Ilyawraith spoke to Quincy. "She's right. If they're using her, it would be to get to us. The only problem with that theory is that Entrophists don't have any reason to spy on me. I've never had dealings with the Phantomhead."

Quincy fidgeted with his mustache. "Maybe someone is seeking retribution against me for the man I killed in Vynia."

"Do you have any other enemies who have connection to the Phantomhead?" Ilyawraith asked.

Quincy thought for a long moment, scouring his memories. "I may have angered or had a lot of disagreements with many people, but I can't think of anyone . . . Wait. . ."

Nay looked at him with anticipation.

"What is it?" Ilyawraith said.

"After what happened at Palazzo Furio . . . there was fallout. One of the mercenaries I hired from the Black Rose. Bounty hunters hired by Vittoria's family found and killed him. He had some family, a sister, children. He had bought them time to escape when he faced the hunters. They've disappeared. Maybe they're still out there somewhere and hold me responsible for his death . . ."

"I can sympathize with their sentiment, but it seems too many degrees separated to be connected," Ilyawraith said.

"Still," Quincy said, "there's something about it that's always nagged at me. Guilt, maybe." He shrugged. "You're right, though. They're not connected with the Phantomhead."

"What gives me pause, that gives credence to Nay's instincts," Ilyawraith said, "is the mention of dissension in the Empire. An Entrophist justifying their methods is one thing, but suggesting there are elements that might not be happy with the Empire's current leadership is intriguing. If he's manipulating Nay, of course he would try to present himself as amenable. But if he's not manipulating her in that sense, then maybe there's about to be a play for power there."

"But why choose me to contact?" Nay said.

"The only other thing I can think of is that it's because he knows you're an Elseworlder," Ilyawraith said. "He did tell you that there might be a way for you to return to your world, didn't he? What did he say exactly?"

"He asked me . . . what would I think if there was a way to return to my world?"

"What *do* you think if there was a way to return to your world?" Quincy said. "Is that something you want?"

"I mean, it throws me for a loop, for sure," Nay said. "But is it something I've wanted? I guess I've wondered if it was a possibility. But I haven't exactly been looking to return. Feels a bit . . . been there, done that, you know what I mean?"

"You don't have any family that you would want to see again?" Ilyawraith said.

"It would be nice to see my mother again," Nay said. "I never got to tell her goodbye."

She thought more about it. "If I got to choose, signing over control of my taco-truck business to my old sous-chef Remi would be a proper move. But is it even possible? Is it possible to travel back to my world?"

"You traveled from your world to ours," Ilyawraith said, "so there would be some logic in getting to reverse the trip. But such magic is beyond my knowledge or understanding."

"He said something else interesting, too," Nay said.

They looked at her expectantly.

"He said that he only used willing souls, people who were already on the brink of death who gave him permission before they died."

"I don't pretend to understand their culture," Ilyawraith said, "but in all the recorded encounters between Marrow Eaters and the Phantomhead Empire, the Entrophists have always been evil."

"Regardless of the way he presented himself," Quincy said, "we need to worry about his intentions. He's interested in Elseworlders. We need to be wary of why. He's not to be trusted."

Nay began to speak. "I don't—"

"We don't know what he wants," Ilyawraith said. "And until we do, that's a good reason to be wary and keep our guard up. If he tries to contact you again somehow, you will tell me immediately."

They were right. They were being rational. Of course she should be cautious. But why was part of her open about giving Nikolai a chance still? She was intrigued by him.

"You will tell us immediately, yes?" Ilyawraith said.

Nay nodded. "You're both right. I'm sorry for keeping it a secret from you both."

"It was incredibly stupid, Nay," Quincy said. "Allowing our passions to override our conscience can lead to things worse than heartbreak. I speak from experience."

"Wait," Nay said. "You think . . . you think I'm romantically interested in . . ." She sputtered, embarrassed.

"Protect your heart," Ilyawraith said. "Even out of all the knowledge I can teach you about cultivation, this is the best advice I can give you."

"His manner intrigued me," Nay said. "You have to understand that everything I've encountered here has been terrifying in some way. But if I had just run away from every person I met, I wouldn't be here with you two. But I trusted my instincts. I really believe he didn't mean me harm."

"Maybe so," Quincy said, "but think about all the people you care about. You can't keep secrets. You're not just protecting yourself anymore."

He was right, of course, but Nay felt herself turning red. She was ashamed. "Are we done here?"

She turned to leave but Quincy grabbed her hand. He didn't grasp it hard. He held it softly. He didn't look at her. He just said, "No more secrets, okay?"

"No more secrets."

Nay fled out of his office.

Nay fed pieces of the black rose, now gray and shriveled, to the small fire in the oven alcove. She watched them burn to ash in the flames.

She regretted hiding the rose from them. She felt stupid for putting her friends at risk. But part of her also wondered if she would ever hear from Nikolai again. She wanted to know if he knew a way to travel between the two worlds.

She wanted to know more about his life and his people. But she also wanted to become strong enough to defend herself if there were forces in the Phantomhead that were conspiring against her and her friends.

She dropped the last petal into the flames. The stalk was still attached to it. She watched it burn and curl and turn to nothing. She whispered into the flames.

"Until we meet again, strange friend."

Nay took a break from prepping the vats of moon cake pastry dough. She stepped into the tavern to make herself some tea from behind the bar.

That was when the doors opened. The cold wind and snow blew into the entrance. There were footsteps, and Rolf, one of the Brothers Bouldershield, entered the tavern.

Nay nodded at him. "Sheriff. Care for some tea? I'm about to put on a kettle."

"That would be proper swell," Rolf said. He took a seat at the bar and looked around.

"Quincy here?"

"He's around somewhere," Nay said. "I'm sure if you linger around here long enough, he'll show up."

Gracie stepped out into the tavern area and saw Rolf. Some color appeared in her cheeks. "Morning, sheriff."

Rolf turned to look at her. "Morning, lass." He smiled. "Have we met before?"

"Not officially," Gracie said. "But I know who you are."

"And yet I don't know your name."

Gracie couldn't help but smile back. Then she looked away, still smiling. She realized she was kneading her dress with her fingers, and she made herself stop.

"Are you truly going to make me fish for your name?" Rolf said. "What should I call you? Oh, yes, I got it! Beauty of the Lodge! How's that?"

Gracie blushed and turned, not knowing what to do with herself. She bumped into a table. Then she looked him in the eye. "Gracie, sheriff. My name's Gracie."

"Well, Gracie," Rolf said, "it's a pleasure to meet you."

"Gracie is the kitchen manager here in the Lodge," Nay said.

"Is that right?" Rolf said. "Keeping all these chickens in a row, eh?"

"She's excellent at her job," Nay said. "Keeps this place running smooth as silk."

"I'm glad to see you're healing well," Gracie said. "Sheriff."

"Stop with this *sheriff* nonsense! Call me Rolf."

Gracie couldn't contain her joy. She was practically beaming.

"Yes," Rolf said. He touched his cheek. "The Gloom Ranger healer saved my looks. It's like you can't even tell I was on the wrong end of a pack of toothy bastards. They tried to make me as ugly as them."

"You could never be ugly," Gracie said.

But she had said it so quiet, only Nay had heard it.

"Hm?" Rolf said. "What was that?"

Gracie realized she said a thought aloud and turned to escape.

But then Rolf's voice interrupted her. He had remembered something. "That's actually why I'm here. I wanted to deliver some news to Quincy. From Fort Nixxiom."

"What news?" Nay said.

"We received a winter raven," Rolf said. "Seems like there's been some turmoil at Scarwatch. One of their own has gone missing."

Nay and Gracie looked at each other.

"Oh?" Nay said.

"Martygan," Rolf said. "The righteous lad with the crossbows and sword. The one who saved my life. He was still recovering from the events here . . ."

"And?"

"He's disappeared."

— CHAPTER SIXTY-EIGHT —

The Legend of the Winterband of Heroes

With only two moons until the Green Moon Festival, the kitchen at Quincy's Lodge was a hive of activity. For Nay, this was the equivalent of catering prep for a big event. She always loved serving at food festivals back home, but this event brought the extra pressure.

It was like being in charge of the food at a wedding. If she fucked up, it could ruin someone's special day. There was a layer of tradition involved, and her job was to enhance and not mar the experience.

Nay and Nom were mixing batches of pastry dough for the moon cakes. Tuk-Tuk was in the kitchen with them. He had volunteered to help prep for some of the other dishes. At the moment, he was butchering some pork for the char siu bowls.

"Tuk-Tuk, you know this isn't required of you," Nay said. "You don't have to help."

"I would like to stay a little longer and experience this Green Moon Festival," Tuk-Tuk said. "If I am going to partake, it is only right I contribute."

Nay had learned that the men and women of the Twelve Tribes were big into doing their part and paying their way. Nothing was freely given, and nothing was freely taken. It was a culture of reciprocation and exchange, and she wondered if his people were all like him, bound to their honor.

"Suit yourself, then," Nay said. "I appreciate your help."

She watched him cut strips of pork and set them in the marinade. He knew his way around a butcher's knife.

"Won't your people miss you, though?" Nay said. "You've been gone for a while, right?"

Tuk-Tuk continued with his work without looking at her. "It is my job to protect the land. Your town is part of the land. It is important I bring back knowledge to my people so that we may act and prepare accordingly. I will return after the Green Moon Festival has concluded."

Nay heard giggling and looked up and saw Bryja and Ulla peeking through the kitchen doors, watching Tuk-Tuk. When they noticed Nay looking at them, they scattered.

"You seem to have admirers," Nay said.

Tuk-Tuk glanced at her and then looked out into the tavern. He returned back to the work of cutting the pork and half-smiled.

"Can I ask you a question about something you said earlier?" Nay said.

Tuk-Tuk nodded. "Of course. Part of the agreement I made with Quincy was sharing my people's knowledge with him."

"Back at the Moonglums', you mentioned something about the One in the Black Ice."

Tuk-Tuk put a lid over the bin of the pork and marinade and went over and set it on the rack in the walk-in cooler. He came back and washed his hands in the sink. "Do you mind if we go out back so I can smoke my pipe while we talk?"

After Nay had finished prepping a tray of moon cakes and storing them in the walk-in, she met Tuk-Tuk out back. He was already up on the cliff part near the ash tree, puffing his pipe and observing the elderflowers.

"These are flowers of the First Ones," Tuk-Tuk said. "Teriannaq. We call them the Fox People."

"Yes, they were a gift from one," Nay said.

"You must have done something impressive to earn this gift, especially if it was from a Teriannaq," Tuk-Tuk said.

"There were some hoops to jump through, yes," Nay said. She remembered Vampra and the bizarre botanical garden. She felt like her skin was covered in goo just thinking of it.

"The First Ones are the ones who entombed the One in the Black Ice," Tuk-Tuk said. "Most people just think it's an old legend. But we in the Twelve Tribes know it to be truth. I've been on the border of that cursed land and have seen the taint of the Black Ice from afar."

"What is it?" Nay said.

"Kigatilik," Tuk-Tuk said. "A Nether Lord. It came to our realm, seeking a lost artifact said to have fallen from the sky. That land was home to a flourishing hub of trade where all the tribes would gather. Now it is called the Black Ice Waste.

"It's a cursed and haunted land. As children, we are told stories about the things that roam there. The land itself is tainted. Many have disappeared there. So, we know to stay away."

"So, the Nether Lord tainted the land?"

Tuk-Tuk nodded. "With the Nether Lord came his tower and his nether minions. They cut into the ice and earth, searching for this artifact, their machines tainting the land and creating the Black Ice. Their arrival disrupted the peace. There were many incursions of these foul creatures into the land of the tribes.

"This didn't just upset my ancestors but also the First Ones. It was decided that an alliance of First Ones and tribesmen would confront this Nether Lord. The Winterband of Heroes. Except the Nether Lord wouldn't meet them out in the open. He hid like a coward at the top of his tower. While these heroes ascended the tower to face him, their forces met with the Nether Lord's forces on the battlefield before the tower. The Battle of Icelorn Fields.

"The alliance half-succeeded. While the battle was at a standstill, neither side gaining an advantage over the other, the tower fell, thanks to the efforts of the Winterband of Heroes. They had ousted the Nether Lord. But he was too strong. The Friends of Man performed magic to trap the Nether Lord in the Black Ice, but it would be with consequence. Several of the heroes became trapped in the ice with him."

"What was the artifact he was originally looking for?" Nay said.

"A weapon."

"What kind of a weapon?"

"I do not know. I only know the name. It was called Dark Brother."

"And you and your people think someone or something is conspiring to free this Nether Lord?"

"That's what my Angakkuq says. That children are being taken, their lives needed to perform the dark ritual that will melt the Black Ice."

"And are your people doing something to stop it?"

"The Twelve Tribes have been preparing for war. Already we have parties patrolling the border of the Black Ice Wastes. We also have scouts inside. We will confront whatever forces we meet."

She should get word to the Gloom Rangers. If everything Tuk-Tuk was saying was true, then there was evil brewing on their borders. It was also their job to protect Stitchdale from the Scar. But surely, they would be interested in another powerful and monstrous threat so close to them.

"And Quincy knows all this?"

Tuk-Tuk nodded. "Just as my people watch over the land, he does as well. He's watching for signs in this town."

He had probably already sent word to Fort Nixx and also to Ilyawraith.

"Do not worry," Tuk-Tuk said. "My people will stop this event from happening. Every generation has been preparing for it in some way. We have guarded the Black Ice Wastes. There have been other attempts that didn't succeed, thanks to the Twelve Tribes."

* * *

Nay found Quincy behind the bar, taste-testing some of the brews from Nom's conjured table. He had a notepad next to him. He took a sip of a beer labeled Nom's Milk Stout. His face contorted and he forced himself to swallow.

He coughed into a napkin and then scribbled on his notepad next to Nom's Milk Stout, *No*.

"I don't like milk stouts," Quincy said. He coughed again, clearing his throat. Nay took a seat at the bar in front of him.

"So, what are we gonna do about what's happening at the Black Ice Wastes?"

"We stay here for now," Quincy said.

"But what if Tuk-Tuk's people need help? We can't just sit around here while some crazy Nether occultists try to free something trapped in the ice!"

Quincy could see she was quite serious about this. He set down the new beer he grabbed. This one was labeled *Nom's Cthonic Cider*. He pushed it to the side. "Ilyawraith is doing reconnaissance to see if there's any truth to this tale."

"You don't believe Tuk-Tuk?"

"The Twelve Tribes have many myths and legends. Some of it is based on fact, but usually they're just stories told to their children to teach them things. Parables and such."

"There was no tower and no battle with a Nether Lord?"

"If there was, it happened so long ago, any recollection of it has been distorted."

"But we can't just ignore it . . ."

"I agree. That's why Ilyawraith is scouting. To gather firsthand information to see if there's any truth to the situation."

"And then what?"

"For now, we tend to our town and our people. We enjoy the festivities the Green Moon celebration has to offer. And we stay alert for any happenings. If Ilyawraith reports back and there's truth in this matter, then we will take the appropriate action."

Nay thought about it and found herself agreeing. Let Ilyawraith see first, then act if needed. It made sense. For now, the best way to look after Lucerna's End was to be present here.

"The Eldritch IPA is my favorite," Nay said. She headed for the kitchen.

Quincy grabbed a flagon of the Eldritch IPA and took a sip. He made an *mmmm* sound and did a double-take at the liquid, reacting to the hoppiness. He picked up his pencil and went to jot down his notes.

There was a trick, preparing the eggs for the moon cakes. It required boiling the egg just long enough for the yolk to still be runny. But she had made herself enough ramen with the type of boiled eggs with the runny yolk that she knew the method. Just the fact that she was doing it in bulk was a little disconcerting. It created a challenge.

It was a matter of temperature and timing. With her Chef's Thermometer Ability, the temperature wasn't a problem. She just had to be alert with the timing. Even a few seconds too long, and the eggs would be overcooked.

The next step was rolling the paste around the egg and then setting the whole thing in the cake-mold trays, where the pastry was waiting for the filling. Then the final piece of pastry was placed over the top, and then into the ovens they went.

She and Nom were baking around the clock, and the racks full of cooling moon cakes were taking up most of the free space in the kitchen.

It was an assembly line of sorts.

As she worked, her thoughts went back to the Gloom Rangers and how Martygan was missing. The last time she saw him, he was in a coma from his fight with the Nether Sister. She recalled the stalks that had sprouted from the Nether Sister's wrist stump had been inserted into Martygan's mouth and throat.

What if it implanted him with something? Was that why he was in a coma?

That night was so chaotic, but what had happened to him was one of the more-traumatic images burned into her brain.

She wished she could speak with Lain. Ilyawraith's Whispering Winds Ability would be a fine thing to have right now. Lain would be one of the people patched in to her party. She wanted to know what exactly was going on at Fort Nixx.

She pulled the last tray of moon cakes out of the oven. When she did, she was hit with an interface prompt.

[Quest Complete!]
[Prepare One Thousand Moon Cakes Completed!]
[Congratulations!]
[You have been rewarded Vigor Points]

Thank Christ. The moon cakes were done and there were enough of them for the people of Lucerna's End to have a proper nosh.

Now it was just a matter of getting everything to the beach at Lac Coineascar and working the Green Moon Festival itself. With mysterious happenings brewing at Fort Nixxiom and to the barren north, it would be a challenge to focus solely on celebrating.

But she would try.

— CHAPTER SIXTY-NINE —

The Green Moon Festival

The catering contingent from Quincy's Lodge had pop-up tents set up on the Lac Coineascar beachhead next to the rows of the long feasting and drinking tables. Poles bearing torches had been planted into the ground, and strings hanging with moon-shaped green lanterns crisscrossed above from pole to pole. Nay watched the boats gather for the Green Moon Race in the water as she prepared bowls of Char Siu and braised chestnuts.

These were placed next to the assortment of sliders, fish 'n chips and baskets of steamed crab. Tuk-Tuk was monitoring the pots. He wore an apron. Tongs and ladles and other kitchen utensils hung off his belt. He was in charge of steaming the silver and blue Coineascar crabs that were caught in the Lac.

Town councilman Durfin was at Gracie's table, where the townsfolk could peruse and order their food. "How delightful! I am actually seeing choices that aren't just fish! I'm afraid I won't be able to make up my mind, though. So, I'll have one of everything!"

Councilman Durfin waddled back to his table, carrying an overflowing tray of food in both hands. It was so full and piled so high, he had to peek around a tower of food to navigate the crowd.

There was a considerable group of men and a few women gathered around Quincy's bar setup. Nom's conjured table of exotic brews and curious cocktails was next to him, the tentacle himself nowhere to be seen. Nay knew he was around somewhere, staying out of sight. Hopefully, he would manage to stay out of mischief, too. Though that was a tall order.

Already, his new drinks were turning some of those with a penchant for drink into budding craft-beer snobs. They were gathered around the table with the sign Nom's Tasty Bevs & Brews.

"The Eldritch IPA has accents of barley and tastes like a strong bitter beer washing the blood off your bleeding gums after an energetic bar fight," one of the miners turned beer connoisseurs said.

"The IPA is okay," another freshly converted connoisseur said. "I'm partial to the Shoggoth Sour. I'm not a fan of a mouthful of hops."

"Mixing the Lurker Lager with this sparkling lemonade, though," another new craft beer snob said, "is just downright refreshing."

"There's already a brew like that on the table," yet another said. He held up a beer bottle labeled R'lyehian Radler. There was an illustration of a dark ocean and a tentacle poking out of the waves holding a brewski.

"Lord," Nay said. She had enough char siu set up, and she made a survey of the other dishes, satisfied at how smoothly the operation was running. Everyone seemed to be happy.

All of the townsfolk were out enjoying the festivities. Stitchkids chased each other along the Lac, Volva Serrilda's butter cookies in their hands, and the band, Minekeeper's Daughter, played songs about the beauty of the green moon.

The Green Moon of Vermira
watches in the night
when you think you're lost
look up to the sky
and know love can't be gone
where there's light

There were baskets of overflowing moon cakes next to Gracie's table so people could grab them as they put in their orders. She saw several people try them out. Their faces were pleased as punch, and they grabbed extra to eat when the Green Moon herself reached her apex. By that account, the festival was already a success.

Nay passed by Gracie and told her, "Good job."

That's when a familiar face startled her. It was Alric. She tried to turn around but he had her out in the open. "Nay," he said. "Is it possible if I could have a word with you?"

Nay looked around. Besides the remainder of the line, most of the people already had their food. Gracie and the girls would be okay for a few minutes. "Fine," she said.

Nay met with Alric on the snow-laden shore near the Moonpole, where many stitchgals and children were dancing. Night was on the verge of replacing the dusk, and the Green Moon was approaching her zenith.

"The food today has been astounding," Alric said, breaking the ice.

"You didn't ask to talk to me to praise the food," Nay said.

"You're right. I wanted to apologize for what happened the other day," Alric said. "The veritas booth can be uncomfortable, especially the first time."

"Uncomfortable?" Nay said. "That's one way putting of it."

"I don't make excuses for Veritax's manner," Alric said. "But she frightened you, and for that I apologize. She is directly opposed to the Phantomhead and their deity."

"Who's their deity?"

"Mortem, the god of death."

"Of course it is," Nay said, sighing. "Why wouldn't it be?"

"In her way, she was trying to protect you," Alric said. "I shouldn't have been so enthusiastic about getting you to participate. I just figured since you were already in the booth, you wouldn't mind giving it a go. It's usually a peaceful experience for people."

"It was unsettling."

"Your business is your business. I'm sorry I pried."

"Really? You're not concerned about me talking to someone from the Phantomhead?"

"Of course I'm concerned. But you already have friends here who would be concerned as well. I'm sure they would have talked sense into you."

Nay chuckled. "You're right about that. They were quick to intervene, and I'm constantly reminded of my choices."

As Alric was about to respond, they were interrupted by the screams of men out on the water. Everyone's attention turned to the Lac. Despite the light of the Green Moon and all the lantern light, whatever was happening was out of sight in the darkness.

Nay had caught Quincy on the shore. He produced his spyglass and looked out into the water. "Oh, no . . ."

"What?" Nay said. "What is it?"

He handed her the spyglass. She pointed it in the same direction and gazed through the eyeglass. Out in the Lac, just out of the radius of light, she saw overturned boats. An appendage of inky blackness erupted out of the water and smashed down onto a boat. Water, men, and splintering wood flew everywhere.

She could tell by the crackles of violet light in the dark form of the monster that it was a nether being.

Rolf and Jolf ran up onto shore next to them.

"Get the watchmen and militia gathered," Quincy said. "It's another Nether Realm attack."

* * *

Quincy and Nay wolfed down Pasties of Nether-Being Slaying. Tuk-Tuk appeared and Nay pulled another pastie out of her inventory and held it out to him.

"I'm not hungry," Tuk-Tuk said. "How can you eat when your town is under attack?"

She shoved it in his hands. "Just eat it."

"Trust the lass," Quincy said.

Tuk-Tuk looked at the pastie and took a bite. As the taste wowed him, he looked at the treat in a new light. He shoved the whole thing into his mouth and chewed.

Nay also took out a basket of candied frog legs and a thermos of venison stew from her inventory. She passed them around with Buff biscuits so they could Buff up and augment themselves.

"The candied frog legs will allow you to jump twice as high for the next two hours," Nay said. "The venison stew will make you be able to run as fast as a deer for three hours."

Tuk-Tuk bit into a candied frog leg. "I run fast as a bear."

"Not in your human form, you don't," Nay said.

"Quickly," Quincy said, swallowing some stew. "I need to get out onto the Lac and help those on the water. You two deal with the netherlings coming out of the Lac onto the shore. The watchmen and the militia are gathering."

"Everyone!" Quincy shouted, catching the attention of the townsfolk in the vicinity. "Everyone get back to your homes! Lock and barricade your doors! Spread the word!"

The people, scared and confused, began to scatter.

Quincy sprinted towards the dock, enhanced by the Fleet-footed spell. He leapt into the air and landed in a boat. He began rowing for the men dealing with the Netherspawn Mother in the water.

Two coils of netherlings burst out of the water and were coming up on shore, little nightmares scrambling like lizards through the snow.

Nay's blades materialized in her hands, the aura imbues lighting up with a sizzle. She whipped around, releasing the blades at the shore. "Salvo of knives!"

The two weapons skewered two netherlings each. The spirit salvo raining from above finished off the rest of the coil.

Tuk-Tuk shifted into his polar bear form and stampeded into the other coil. He used a swipe attack with his paws, ripping through the group of netherlings. Black-and-violet smoke fizzled into the air.

All along the shore, more of the netherlings emerged out of the Lac. There were screams as the townsfolk who dared to remain saw the monsters. They turn and fled then, the nether beings chasing after them.

A man's voice broke through the screams, and Rolf and Jolf emerged through the crowd, coming onto the beachhead. They wore their armor and were wielding their spears and battle-hammers.

Behind them, the watchmen ran onto the beachhead to engage the netherlings. Across from them, the town's militia, hastily geared and armed, arrived and met their own wave of nether beings.

As Nay's blades returned to her hands, she scythed through a stray netherling leaping at her, cutting it down.

Up on the field before the beachhead, she saw a burst of red light streak in a horizontal line and a resultant shriek as the energy blast fried the netherling.

"Nom," Nay said. She headed in that direction, hoping to meet up with her friend. They could protect each other while fighting to protect the townsfolk.

She leapt into the air, aided by the spell from the candied frog legs, clearing the beachhead and landing in the snow field along the tree line. It was exhilarating, jumping that high into the sky. And with Fleet-footed, she flew towards where she had seen Nom's Disintegration Ray.

She thought she heard something.

She turned to see a white wolf running parallel with her. There was something familiar about it. Its eyes glowed violet.

It kept pace with her and adjusted to run at an angle, heading straight for her. It snarled and leapt to intercept her. Nay jumped into the air. It leapt with her and nipped at her, but she avoided its jaws.

When she landed, it was on the other side of her. Her pace didn't slow as she landed. She increased her speed and the wolf increased its speed, on a collision course for her. She readied herself to engage, blades ready.

But before she could fend it off with her blades, a massive white blur collided with the wolf. There were a roar and a growl and an explosion of snow. The polar bear and the wolf were rolling across the ground, snarling and gnashing at each other in a frenzy.

It was Tuk-Tuk.

The polar bear went to bite for the wolf's throat, but the wolf darted away and shifted into the form of a human.

It was Martygan, the Gloom Ranger.

Except there was something different about him. His eyes had changed from brown to violet, and the veins underneath his pale flesh were blackened. He looked tainted. He looked possessed.

Tuk-Tuk, still in bear form, charged Martygan. But the Gloom Ranger punched the bear in the face, stunning him. The Bronze-enhanced Ranger hit the bear with a combo of punches, knocking him end over end. They were approaching a cliff.

When Tuk-Tuk got up, the Ranger closed the distance in the blur. When he reappeared, energy Vigor burst from his body in a stun attack. The blast of Vigor energy sent Tuk-Tuk flying off the cliff.

"No!" Nay said. She looked over and saw the polar bear just miss the rocks below, landing in the dark water in a big splash.

Martygan turned to her. "You can come with me conscious, or you can come with me unconscious, your choice."

"I don't like either of those choices."

She swung the ice scythe at him, but he deflected the blade easily with his now-drawn smallsword. He was amused. "An Epicurist who can fight!"

She lunged at him with *Thorn*. He easily sidestepped her. "You really think your undisciplined Iron attacks can hurt me?"

"I can try."

She swung again, this time slashing down with the ice scythe and following with a stab from *Thorn*. Steel rang against steel twice, Martygan's sword meeting each of her attacks.

Nay circled him. Martygan stood in the same place, just turning to slightly face her, his body always at an angle to her. "You show promise, but I'm trained in the Way of the Ranger."

Frustrated, she went in for another attack.

She slashed. *Clang!* She jabbed. *Clang!* His sword was always there to meet her blades. He was doing it all with only his wrist.

"You fight with anger; that's good."

He swept her blades aside. He moved so fast, she couldn't keep up with him. His foot kicked the inside of her calf. She lost her balance.

As she tried to regain it, his shoulder planted in her chest, pushing her back. Her sliding feet left tracks in the snow. There was something about how easily he was handling her that angered her. He was toying with her.

"Parry this!" Nay said.

She swung, crossing her arms together, activating her Decapitate Ability. The Vigor spirit blades spun towards Martygan. Her eyes barely registered him moving. He sliced the spirit blades in half with a vertical slash. The halves of the spirit blades flew past him on both sides. They stuck in the snow, smoldering. Then they turned into vigama and fluttered away.

"Interesting," Martygan said. "But playtime is over."

He blurred and appeared right next to her, the Vigor blast radiating from his body. She took the brunt of it and was swept off her feet. She was hit with momentum he had kept stored, the equivalent of rereleasing the energy of a car crash into a single blow.

By the time she hit the ground, the world had gone black.

— CHAPTER SEVENTY —

Nether Bond

Nay regained consciousness to a blinking prompt in her vision. The world around her was hazy, so she focused on the prompt until the words came into focus.

[Marrow Detected]
[Liver Marrow of the Frostfang Yeti]

She stared at her mini-map, rubbing her head, until she could see it clearly. She saw a red dot near a green dot. "Huh?" Then she remembered her last moments before everything went dark.

The red dot was Martygan. He was going after Marrow, somewhere close to her.

She groaned and discovered she was nestled between the roots of a giant tree, lying on a blanket of snow. She looked around and discovered she was in some type of strange forest.

The trees here were ancient and massive. Instead of the usual evergreens, these trees were gnarled with black and twisted branches. Their presence made the dark, snowy forest seem haunted.

There was a campfire nearby, pots and pans hanging from a wooden stand. The carcass of a hare was draped across it.

Nay heard heavy breathing and snarling. The fighting was nearby. She rose to her feet and peeked out from behind the tree to see a large humanoid swiping with a white-furred claw at Martygan.

It was a yeti. About nine feet tall with blue-and-white fur. It had green eyes and sharp teeth. Its fur was marred with its own blood, already bleeding from half a dozen cuts.

The possessed Gloom Ranger easily leaned away from the swipe, and he drove his short sword into the yeti's belly. The yeti let out a mournful howl, and Martygan twisted his sword and yanked it out the side, tearing the monster's torso open and freeing its entrails.

The hot innards hit the snow and steam blasted into the air. Nay caught a whiff of the foul stench.

The poor creature tried to hold its insides in. It fell to its knees and howled. Its lonesome cry cut short as Martygan sliced the monster's head off. He examined his butchery, exhaling hot breath into the cold air.

The center of the yeti's chest began to glow, and the curvature of a blue bubble began to emerge out of the dead yeti's chest. It was a Beast Core. As Martygan knelt to retrieve it, Nay realized that she should use the moment to flee.

[Quest Detected]
[Quest: Escape Martygan]
[Accept Quest Y/N?]

There was something wrong with the Gloom Ranger. He had changed somehow after emerging from his coma. The last time Nay saw him conscious, he had a part of the Nether Sister shoved into his throat. That's when she remembered something the witch had said: *"I've been looking for new thralls."*

Motherfucker, he has been turned into a thrall of the Nether Sister.

She ran through the forest. She pulled the thermos of the venison stew out of her inventory. If she ever needed the Fleet-footed spell, it was now. Also, if it was off cooldown, that meant she had been unconscious for at least a day.

As she unscrewed the lid, there was a whooshing sound behind her. Something hit her in the calves, entangling her legs. She tripped and fell, sliding through the snow. She lost her grip on the thermos of magical venison stew. It spilled across the snow. She looked at her feet, and there were cords attached to weighted balls entangling her ankles.

Martygan was holding one of his crossbows in the distance. He had shot bolas at her. And he was in pursuit.

Thorn appeared in her hand, and she cut through the cords, slipping out of the bolas. She got up and ran.

She felt a shift in the air around her, and suddenly Martygan was next to her, grabbing her. She tried to stab him but he caught her wrist. Her Iron-level strength was easily subdued by his Bronze grip.

"I wouldn't stray too far from me, little bird," Martygan said.

Nay spat in his face. "Fuck you."

Her saliva spattered his cheek and above his eyebrow. Her spit ran down his pale skin, dripping off his elegantly formed cheekbone. He closed his eyes and wiped the saliva off his face with the back of his leather glove.

His fingers squeezed her upper arm. Although it hurt, there was something electric about his touch. With his other hand, he pushed a finger near the center of her chest, between her breasts. "See this?"

She looked down and realized her tunic was torn, exposing the skin on her chest. There was a black mark on her chest that he was poking. It looked like the tattoo of a nether creature. A pinwheel of arms sprouting off the round body. Every time Martygan applied pressure to the mark, she thought she saw the tattoo move underneath her skin.

"You bear a Nether Bond to me," Martygan said. "If you stray too far, the Flesh Wight will grow and erupt out of your back, drilling a hole through your heart as it eats its way out. To leave me is to die."

"You lie!"

"Don't believe me?" Martygan released her. "Then fly, little bird. Fly away."

She grimaced and shook her arms, brushing at herself as if she was wiping away the stain of his lingering touch. She began walking away from him, not taking her eyes off him, stumbling in the snow. Then she turned around and picked up speed until she was running.

When she was about fifty yards away, an uncomfortable sensation radiated from her chest. With each step, the discomfort increased until it was outright pain. She looked down at her skin and saw the Flesh Wight had grown in size, its appendages rippling, making her skin undulate. She kept going though until she felt something was stabbing away inside of her, touching her breastbone.

She cried out and stumbled, falling to one knee. A hand flew to her chest. In another hand, Thorn appeared. She was going to carve the Flesh Wight out of her.

As she prepared to cut into her skin, she noticed two shadows racing across the ground towards her. Netherlings erupted out of the shadows. They rushed at her and she turned to defend herself.

She slashed them down with Thorn and looked back to her chest.

"Stop!" Martygan was walking towards her, the ground before him rippling with shadows. It seemed like he could command netherlings. "I'll release them if you don't. You may be able to defend yourself for a while, but how many waves do you think you can stop?"

"Let's find out," Nay said. The ice scythe appeared in her other hand, and she turned to face him. Another wave of pain from the Flesh Wight made her see double. She activated Salvo of Knives and threw her weapons at Martygan.

His short sword appeared in his hand, and the air wavered around him, some shifting of Bronze-level power. As the weapons appeared to impale him, he backstepped and swiped the blades away with his short sword. They disappeared into the ether.

Spirit knives emerged out of the sky above him, and without looking, he held his sword above his head and parried each knife away. "Your stubborn thick-headedness will be the end of you, girl."

He blinked forward, halving the distance between them. He swung his sword, and the air pressure reversed and Nay fell forward, carried by a rush of wind. Some close-the-distance Ability dragged Nay towards Martygan. She rolled and tumbled through the snow, stopping at his feet.

The intensity of the pain at her chest disappeared and she gasped. The Flesh Wight was shrinking now that she was within range of her captor. "Don't be stupid," Martygan said. "You're no use to me dead."

Nay sat on one of the massive tree roots by Martygan's campfire as he absorbed the Beast Core. She was biding her time, racking her brain for an opportunity to escape. He was too powerful for her to beat in combat, so that wasn't an option. Her heart would basically explode if she got too far from him. So, she had to do something about their Nether Bond.

He had stopped her from cutting the Flesh Wight out of her flesh, so it seemed that could work. But she had to do it at a time he couldn't intervene. At the same time, part of her was curious as to why he had taken her. What was he trying to do, or rather, what was the Nether Sister using him for?

[Quest Detected]
[Quest: Gather Information About Nether Sister's Plan from Martygan]
[Accept Quest Y/N?]

Martygan's chest glowed for a second as his body took in the Core. He grunted at the surge of Vigor. Then he dug up the raw and bloody Marrow that he had packed in the snow. He tossed it onto Nay's root. A fleck of blood hit her arm.

It was the yeti's liver. Green motes swirled within and around it.

[Marrow Detected]
[Liver Marrow of the Frostfang Yeti]
[Consume Y/N?]

"Activate this," Martygan said.

She played dumb. "I'm sorry. Activate what?"

"Don't play dumb, girl," Martygan said. His voice had lowered into a growl. "I know what you can do. *She* showed me."

"I'm sorry. I don't follow."

"Cook the Marrow so I may eat it."

"Ew! You want me to cook this organ for you? That seems unsanitary."

Martygan took a step towards her. Shadows formed on the ground around him and on the trunks of the trees. Netherling heads poked out of the shadows, watching her with their violet eyes.

"If you value the lives of the people you care about in Lucerna's End, you will obey me," Martygan said. "So, end this mummer's farce and cook the damn Marrow. *Epicurist*."

She eyed him and his netherling familiars. "Fine."

A pan and cutting board appeared in her hands from her inventory. She grabbed the Marrow and set up her prep station on the massive root next to the campfire. The shadows disappeared, and Martygan sat down across from her, his face smoldering with a feral intensity.

She cleaned the yeti liver with water from her waterskin. "Aren't you concerned about your brothers and sisters from Fort Nixxiom hunting you?"

Martygan sneered. "I have too much of a head start."

"If you needed an Epicurist, why didn't you just use yours at the Fort?"

"There was too much resistance with too many eyes watching."

"So, you came to Lucerna's End instead. It was you who summoned the netherlings to attack the town, wasn't it? You needed a distraction so you could take me."

He didn't deny it. "Chaos is always the best distraction."

"So, here we are. You have your pet Epicurist so you can hunt your Marrows and power up."

After a moment of silence, she continued. "What do you need to power up so badly for? Your new master must have you on a helluva honey-do list."

"*Honey-do list?*"

"A list of tasks whisked together by the Nether Sister to give to her fetch boy."

"I would mind your mouth, girl."

"So, what is it that she has planned, Fetch Boy?"

"Nothing you need concern yourself about."

"It's too late for that, Fetch Boy."

"Be quiet and cook the damn Marrow!"

He had stood up and unsheathed his short sword from the scabbard on his back. His violet eyes smoldered in their sockets, and his jaw was clenched. His hand was tight around the hilt of his blade. It looked like he was trying to resist the urge to run her through.

She shut her mouth and looked back to the task at hand. As she prepared to cook the yeti liver, she realized she could cook it without activating and he wouldn't know the difference until he ate it and nothing happened. As she took her seasonings out of her inventory, a pouch appeared on the root next to them.

She blinked and saw something slither and retract back into the snow.

Nom.

Not only had he somehow tracked and found her, but he had just given her poison.

— CHAPTER SEVENTY-ONE —

A Generous Sprinkle of Kyr-nine

As Nay pretended to organize her seasonings, she read the label on the pouch of poison Nom had slipped to her. It read, *Kyr-nine*.

Was this a reference to Vonnegut? If the cheeky bastard had read Vonnegut, how? There was no way Kurt Vonnegut books were available in his world.

Nay examined the Marrow.

[Liver Marrow of the Frostfang Yeti]

Nay pulled an onion out of her inventory.

"You don't happen to have any milk on you, do you?" she said.

"Does it look like I'm carrying milk with me?" Martygan said.

She looked at him and his meager supplies around the campfire. Then she looked to his fauglir, surely recently stolen, that had a saddlebag draped across its back. That was probably how he transported her when she was unconscious.

"Forgive me; just thought I'd ask," Nay said.

"Do you need it for your recipe to activate the Delicacy?" Martygan said.

She thought about answering yes if it meant stalling his plans and buying her more time. He'd have to drag her along to go find milk somewhere. Then she looked at the poison Nom slipped to her. Too many things could go wrong if he dragged her somewhere. Best to poison him here and get it over with. She wondered if killing him would break their Nether Bond. What would happen to the Flesh Wight? Would the poison kill him or just immobilize him?

Nay guessed she was about to find out. "Milk is not necessary, but the liver will be much more pleasant to eat if it's been soaked in milk for some time. There could be excess blood or urine in the organ. It will also make the texture softer to chew."

"I don't care about how it tastes," Martygan said. Just the Marrow Ability."
"Suit yourself."

Nay got to work. She consulted the Jezabelle Childe cookbook for the best way to prepare this Marrow because she was curious. She found it under a subsection for **[Offal & Sweetbreads]**.

Jezabelle's Lovely Liver Pâté. The secret to a good pate is a good cognac and a good toasted bread to spread it out. For cognac, I am quite partial to the Count Crispin's Reserve label. It has an autumn aroma characterized by toffee and truffle aromas, which I am particularly fond of.
For the bread, ciabatta from any baker working in the city of Crescentia will do. But if you're in a pinch, a Sassissi sourdough won't upset your fancy. Make sure to toast it, but don't forget a drizzle of olive oil, which will enhance both the taste of the bread and the pâté. In a saucepan, combine the livers with shallots, garlic, bay leaf, thyme, and salt. Add enough water to bring to a simmer. Cover and reduce heat. After the liver has only a slight pinkness, remove and cool. Discard the bay leaf but spoon everything else along with the livers into a blender or masher. Add the cognac, season with salt and pepper, and blend or mash. Store the pâté in the container and store in a cooler until firm. Enjoy!

She didn't have shallots or cognac or a blender; best she could do was a pan-fry with butter, flour and onion. And a generous sprinkling of kyr-nine. That was now her most important ingredient, other than the Marrow itself. But Jezabelle's recipe wasn't required for activating the Marrow; it was just a recommendation on the best way to cook it.

Activation was up to Nay, and she could cook the hell out of this and make it delicious without having to activate, which was the plan. She diced up an onion and seasoned a bowl of flour with salt and pepper. She also emptied the pouch of kyr-nine into the flour mixture without looking at Martygan. She went ahead and got a saucepan going with her Chef's Thermometer Ability.

She cut the yeti liver into strips and coated them in the flour mixture. Then she threw a knob of butter on the pan and tossed in the diced onions.

[Incoming Whispering Wind Call from Ilyawraith]

Nay didn't accept the call but saw she had an option to send a text back. A translucent phantom keyboard appeared in the air before her, and she quickly typed in:

A little busy atm. Call back in 5.

She sent it and swiped the keyboard out of the air. After the onions had been sautéed, she placed in the strips of liver and they sizzled when they hit the hot pan. They cooked quickly and she made sure not to turn them too much. Just a quick turn and then a toss of the pan was enough.

The Marrow's green motes floated out of the saucepan, and Martygan moved closer to watch, practically licking his lips. Nay was pretty sure she heard his stomach growl. So, the possessed Gloom Ranger had an appetite and was hungry. He'd get to enjoy the taste for a short while until the poison kicked in. At least that was what Nay assumed.

She had been careful not to activate the Marrow while cooking it. By his demeanor, she knew he couldn't tell the difference. She lifted the pan from her heat ring and gave the contents a gentle toss with a roll of her wrist. Then she tilted the pan and poured the yeti liver and onions into a bowl.

She lifted the bowl with one hand and ran her hand through the steam and green motes floating from it, taking in the scent. "Smells delicious, don't ya think?"

She looked at Martygan and he was licking his lips, eyes locked on the Marrow. She placed a Debuff biscuit in the bowl with the entree. This particular biscuit would nick his stamina.

"Enough!" Martygan said. He grabbed the bowl of liver and onion from her, the Debuff biscuit sticking out of the dish. Steam rose out of the bowl, speckled with the glowing green motes of the Marrow.

He walked over to where he had been sitting and started wolfing it down.

"Bon appétit," Nay said.

She watched him eat with anticipation. She braced herself, getting ready for anything. She wondered how long the poison was going to take. He was ravenous and ate without hardly taking a breath, shoveling the food into his mouth. Not even a thank you for cooking the food, either. She knew he was possessed or bewitched or infected, but the rudeness still irked her.

"You're welcome," Nay said.

But he ignored her and kept eating. He finished all the food, scraping the bottom of the bowl. He stared at the empty bowl and set it aside. Then he closed his eyes and waited.

Nay watched him, uncomfortable.

Now would be a great time for the poison to do its thing.

"You've tricked me," Martygan said, opening his eyes. "You failed to activate the Marrow, didn't you?"

"I'm not sure what you're talking about," Nay said. "Perhaps if you just wait another minute—"

He stood, drawing his short sword.

Shit.

He blinked and appeared on her side of the campfire.

"You won't kill me," Nay said. "You need what I can do too much."

"Maybe so," Martygan said. "But there are parts of you that you don't need for cooking. I think I'll remove one for wasting this Marrow."

He raised his short sword, and Nay had drawn her weapons from her inventory when Martygan coughed and blood splattered her face. They both paused in a sort of Mexican standoff. Nay touched her face with a finger and then looked at the blood on her hand.

Martygan put a hand to his stomach, sensing something was wrong. Then he lurched forward and projectile-vomited blood at Nay. She skittered back but not without getting drenched in the face and all over the front of her clothes.

He looked at her, accusatorily, a dark understanding dawning on his face. He opened his mouth and managed to say, "You cun—" before he made a horrible retching sound and was racked with another seizure of projectile-vomiting blood. He fell to his hands and knees and spewed blood into the snow. The stream stopped after a moment. But he barely had time to catch his breath before the fountain began again.

From behind him, a form emerged out of the woods. It was a polar bear. Wait, no two forms. Because there was something on top of the polar bear. It was a tentacle.

Tuk-Tuk walked into the camp in bear form with Nom atop his back. They cautiously approached as Martygan was busy dying.

"Well, well," Nom said. "It looks like kyr-nine lends to quite the dramatic death."

Nay felt a pang in her chest, and she looked down at the Flesh Wight. The black creature was squirming and turning gray. It was working. Martygan dying meant that the Flesh Wight was dying and that their Nether Bond would be terminated.

She felt conflicted about letting the Gloom Ranger die and wished there was another way. If there had been a way to remove the hold the Nether Sister had him on, she would have preferred that. And although he had saved her once before and had helped save Lucerna's End, he had been turned into something else.

Nom hopped off Tuk-Tuk's back and slithered his way to Nay. "What do you think, huh? It's useful to have a master poisoner as your friend, isn't it? Correction: maybe I'm not a master yet. But you know what I mean."

The polar bear shifted into Tuk-Tuk's human form. He looked down at the grisly scene of Martygan vomiting into the snow with disdain. "This is a bad death."

"How the hell are your poisons strong enough to kill someone at Bronze Rank, anyways?" Nay said. She started gathering her things to get out of there.

"I couldn't tell you," Nom said. "I guess I'm just that good."

"He is a Bronze?" Tuk-Tuk said. He was suddenly alarmed.

Nay nodded.

Tuk-Tuk drew the hand axe from his belt and swung it at the back of Martygan's neck. At that moment, Martygan rose up and vomited blood into the sky. The axe hit the back of his neck but didn't break skin. It was stopped by some Bronze-enhanced defensive Marrow Eater Ability, some kind of bark skin that seemed to manifest itself.

Martygan's blackened veins spread across his body, and a Vigor aura formed around him. His fists clenched and then liquid began to spray out of all his pores.

Everyone jumped away from him. It wasn't blood that was spraying out of him but some type of green-tinged liquid. It had a nacreous sheen to it and it was making the snow melt, filling the air with steam.

"It's the poison!" Nom said. "He's pushing the poison out of his system! Kill him!"

That's when they all attacked the still-very-much-alive Gloom Ranger. Nom blasted him with a Disintegration Ray beam. Tuk-Tuk shifted into a polar bear and swiped at him. Nay went to drive the skullcrusher end of Thorn into his head.

But his Bronze-level defensive shell ate all of their attacks. Nom's Disintegration Ray disappeared into the Vigor aura. Tuk-Tuk's paw scraped across the Vigor aura and bark skin body shield. Thorn's skullcrusher chipped the bark skin but nothing more. All of their damage had been eaten.

Shadows formed in the snow around Martygan. There was also movement in the pools and streaks of blood he had vomited into the snow. Creatures slicked in blood pulled themselves from red snow. These were nether-infused blood imps.

Netherlings burst from the ground, joining the blood imps, who made chittering sounds, turning their heads in the direction towards Nay and her companions. They didn't have eyes, their faces a smooth bubble on the top half. The lower half was all teeth.

The swarm of familiars formed a circle around Martygan as he cleansed himself of the remaining poison. The entire half of his lower face was stained red. When he opened his eyes, they were aflame with violet light.

And worst of all, the Flesh Wight in Nay's chest wiggled underneath her skin with renewed life. The Nether Bond had rejuvenated.

"Well, this backfired spectacularly," Nom said.

"It was a good plan A," Nay said.

"Now, what's plan B?"

"Survive."

— CHAPTER SEVENTY-TWO —

Flesh Wight

The swarm of blood imps and netherlings dispersed towards them. Martygan was still recovering, but it was happening fast, and by the looks of it, he would be a huge problem again.

Nom and Tuk-Tuk circled around towards Nay.

Nay produced the item from her inventory. Nom saw the dark bracelet with the glittering cloud made out of onyx and amethyst appear. "What the hell is that? How is jewelry going to help us?"

"It's a Vortex Bomb," Nay said.

She referenced the trinket's description in her interface.

Vortex Bomb of the Netherspawn Mother. When you need to gather your enemies into one spot, why not use this handheld Vortex Bomb? It's the suction power of a thousand netherling mouths inhaling at once.
Useful if you need to keep multiple pesky enemies in one place or make them congregate to combo with a nifty AOE attack.
Three uses.

She twisted one of the pieces of onyx on the trinket, and a bomb in the shape of a black-and-purple ball appeared in her hand. It was about the size of a grapefruit. There was a red smiley face on the side.

She tossed it over Martygan's head.

The Vortex Bomb imploded over the Gloom Ranger. A black cloud spun into existence, and there was a deafening roar as the air began to be sucked into the cloud.

"Maybe we should have thought about anchoring ourselves before setting it off!" Nom said.

Air, snow, and debris began to rattle and shift towards the cloud and Martygan.

Netherlings and blood imps tried to step or lurch forward, but despite their efforts, they started sliding back towards whence they came. They clawed at the snow and tried to find purchase, but it was no use. The dispersed swarm tumbled and flew backwards towards the black cloud.

Nay grabbed Tuk-Tuk's fur. Nom coiled around one of the polar bear's legs. The bear itself managed to get behind a tree and hugged it, using the tree as a barrier between all of them and the devouring vortex cloud.

Martygan rose up into the air next to the cloud vortex, and his swarm of familiars were caught there in a giant ball hovering in the air. All of the tree branches in the vicinity bent towards the vortex. Even some birds that had been nearby were pulled into the ball of monsters.

It was like a giant magnet had been activated and everything that wasn't held down had been pulled towards it.

Nay activated Salvo of Knives and aimed at Martygan and the mass of his familiars. Nom blasted the writhing ball of monsters with a Disintegration Ray. Many of the creatures were lasered into ash or were eliminated by the spirit knives raining down from above. However, Martygan's bark skin still kept him safe.

The sound of rushing wind began to lessen as the Vortex reached the end of its duration. Martygan and the reduced swarm of familiars fell to the ground. Tree branches snapped back into place.

"How many more times can you use that thing?" Nom said, looking at the vortex trinket on Nay's wrist. "Or is it empty already?"

"Two more times," Nay said. "We should get further away for the next one."

"It's working against the Ranger's pets," Nom said, "but what are we supposed to do about him?"

He was right. They had no way of defeating Martygan. They weren't strong enough nor were their powers. To complicate the matter, Nay couldn't just run. The Flesh Wight would kill her. Unless . . .

"Tuk-Tuk," Nay said. The polar bear looked at her and grunted. "Can you get us deeper into the forest, away from all this?"

Tuk-Tuk nodded, understanding.

"And when I say stop, will you stop?"

Tuk-Tuk nodded again.

"All right," Nay said. She climbed onto the polar's bear back and Nom joined her. "Go!"

Tuk-Tuk sprang forward, away from the tree they were using for cover, and began loping away from their enemies. Nom, atop Tuk-Tuk's back, blasted the Disintegration Ray into the groups of blood imps and netherlings the second it came off cooldown. Nay released another Salvo of Knives into the familiars in pursuit. A group of surviving blood imps scrambled past their fallen comrades and made for the retreating companions.

[Incoming Whispering Wind Call from Ilyawraith]

Nay answered just as she ice-scythed the group of blood imps. Ilyawraith's image appeared in the air in front of her, floating in the lotus position. The image moved along with Nay so it was always in front of her.

"Nay, what's going on?" Ilyawraith said. "Where are you?"

Tuk-Tuk swiped a trio of blood imps as they leapt at them, swatting them hard into the snow.

Nay consulted her mini-map to try and get a read on their location in relation to Lucerna's End. She couldn't tell.

"Tell her we're in Black Tree Forest!" Nom said.

"Martygan, the Gloom Ranger who had gone missing, he kidnapped me!" Nay said. "There's something wrong with him; I think he's been possessed by the Nether Sister! Or is under her control somehow!"

"He has you now?" Ilyawraith, said, alarmed.

"He did, but I got away. I don't know for how long!" She dug her heels into Tuk-Tuk and shouted, "Okay, now! Stop!"

Tuk-Tuk slid to a stop. Nay turned around and produced the second vortex bomb by twisting the amethyst on the bracelet. It appeared in her hand, and she held it and reared her arm back, waiting for the familiars in pursuit to get a little closer.

"What's that—" Ilyarwaith said, but Nay tossed the vortex bomb, enhanced by her rank of Iron. It spun through the air and imploded, sprouting the cloud right before the familiars.

"Okay, now go!" Nay said. Underneath her, Tuk-Tuk bucked and ran, putting distance between them and the range of the vortex bomb.

The familiars were sucked forward and pulled into the air by the vortex.

Nay looked back at Ilyawraith. "I can't run from him." She pulled her tunic down and showed her.

"A Nether Bond," Ilyawraith said.

"Okay, Tuk-Tuk, this is good," Nay said. She felt the Flesh Wight becoming agitated at the distance. It had grown some and was kicking underneath her skin, sending little stabs of pain into the nerves there.

Ilywraith said, "Before you do anything—"

Nay hopped off Tuk-Tuk and drove Thorn's tip into her skin, carving into her flesh around the Flesh Wight. She cried out, startling Nom and Tuk-Tuk. The latter shifted back into his human form and said, "What are you doing?!"

Nay fell to her knees and ripped the gory mess out of her, the flap of skin pulled down and hanging there. She threw the Flesh Wight onto the snow and conjured a ring of heat on top of it with Chef's Thermometer.

"—do not remove it from your body!" Ilyawraith finished saying.

The Flesh Wight started to grow. When it came out of Nay, it was about the size of a scorpion, but now it was the size of a dog and it was growing bigger by the second.

"Uh, what is that?" Nom said.

The Flesh Wight screamed at the heat and its unfortunate, premature birth. It looked like a mass of flesh tumors that were knotted together in a central ganglion. Multiple arms curved off its body; each had one joint, giving the monster the shape of a pinwheel. Its skin was brown and yellowed, pocked with lesions and open sores and disgusting, fizzing warts.

"They eat their way through the heart when they are birthed!" Ilyawraith said. "If pulled out of a host without a heart to feast on, they will go on a rampage with a hunger that cannot be satiated!"

Even though Nay was an Iron, cutting out a skin flap and pulling the Flesh Wight out of herself hurt like a motherfucker. She leaned against a tree, wincing. "Now you tell me!"

Nom blasted the growing Flesh Wight with his ray, destroying one of its many arms, and it shrieked, spinning towards the tentacle.

Nay conjured a heat ring onto Thorn's blade so she could cauterize her wound, but one of the many writhing arms of the Flesh Wight whipped it out of her hands. She cried out in surprise.

The Flesh Wight grabbed Nom with one of its arms, and the tentacle twined around the appendage. Nom was trying to lock its joint so it was stiff-armed.

Nay fell onto her knees and her blood loss was beginning to make her lightheaded. And soon, Martygan might be on them with his remaining familiars. She looked at the image of Ilyawraith.

"We're outnumbered and the Gloom Ranger is Bronze," Nay said. "What do I do, teacher?"

Ilyawraith knew the situation was dire. She rose to her feet. "I'm coming."

"I'll be pushing up daisies by the time you get here."

"The shell in your inventory," Ilyawraith said. "Use it."

Of course. Lain. She could help.

As Ilyawraith rose into the air, her image disappeared as she burst into flight.

[Whispering Wind Call with Ilyawraith Ended]

She produced the nautilus from her inventory and blew into it. Her breath spiraled into the shell.

A wind blew through the trees, and a golden portal spun to life in front of her. A silhouette appeared in the light, growing closer.

Lain stepped out of the portal. "Nay!"

She hurried to Nay while at the same time assessing the situation around her. "What have you gotten yourself into?" the healer said.

"It's Martygan," Nay said. "This is all his doing."

Lain's eyes narrowed, and she looked between Nay's wound and the growing and singed Flesh Wight that was currently trying to catch Nom, who was scrambling across its bulging back. "He's been compromised by the Nether Sister. It put something that's been gestating inside of him."

A golden flower blossomed in Lain's palm. It was made out of Vigor spirit and vigama. She blew the petals from it, and they fluttered onto Nay's wound, bursting into golden flashes atop the wound. Nay felt Lain's soothing healing power mend her bloody flesh. The pain disappeared. As the light faded, Nay's skin was smooth again.

When Nay looked up she saw a coil of netherlings churning through the snow towards them. "Come with me," Nay said. She pulled Lain along with her and produced the last vortex bomb. She threw it behind them and ran.

The netherlings were pulled back towards the new vortex.

Lain's sudden presence and her calming voice were a welcome addition to this party. Tuk-Tuk had shifted back into his polar-bear form and was attacking the Flesh Wight.

As the thing tried to shake Nom from it, he shot another Disintegration Ray at point-blank range into its warty hide, its five remaining arms pinwheeled around, and Tuk-Tuk caught one in his teeth and yanked. The Flesh Wight stopped spinning and jerked. It turned its attention to Tuk-Tuk and started attacking the bear with all five of its arms.

"That was inside you?" Lain said.

"Martygan put it in me," Nay said. "A Nether Bond."

Lain processed this. "Why you?"

"I'm afraid I've been keeping a secret from you. I'm an Epicurist. And I've been training as a Marrow Eater."

Lain's eyes widened and she looked at Nay in a new light. But she didn't have time to fully appreciate this new knowledge as the Flesh Wight shrieked.

One of Lain's golden hoops appeared in her hand. It shot a red beam of devastating energy at the Flesh Wight. The blast blew off one of its arms. It looked up at Lain, who started throwing bursts of gold healing at Tuk-Tuk and Nom.

It shoved Tuk-Tuk to the side, its form now so big, it splintered a tree as it turned to face Lain. It screeched at her, its many tongues and skin flaps undulating. Lain stood her ground and grabbed the other razor-sharp hoop off her back. She spun and threw it like a discus at the charging creature.

The hoop severed one of its legs at the ankle and it stumbled, falling in the snow.

Nom hit it with another Disintegration Ray in the back of the head. His Ability attack was nothing more than an annoyance to the tough creature. But the attack had seemed to enrage it more than Lain's debilitating attacks. It turned around, grabbed Nom from its back, and shoved the tentacle into its mouth.

"No!" Nay said.

She scooped up Thorn and charged the Flesh Wight.

— CHAPTER SEVENTY-THREE —

Bronze Meets Bronze

Nay reached the Flesh Wight and it spun, its arms spinning to clobber her. She slid underneath the clubs of flesh as one of Lain's hoops razored into two of them, taking the massive three-fingered hands off the wrists. Nay stabbed up with Thorn, slicing through the thick underbelly of the Flesh Wight.

She dinged up a Kinetic Point. The belly opened, and chunks of yellow flesh spilled out in congealed strings of blood. It looked like the unholy fusion of lychee fruit and blood pudding. She gagged at the smell.

The monster let out a bellow. "Mommy!"

Nay's blood ran cold at the voice. And she cringed at the word *Mommy*. *What the fuck?* Did the thing identify her as its mother? It made some sense, as she did kind of birth it out of her body.

It planted the knuckles of its hands from three remaining arms into the snow and straightened its arms, lifting up like a flying saucer on a tripod. Its tumor-like head swiveled on a wrinkled neck truck, bending down and underneath its body to observe her.

Nay stared in horror into a face where everything was in the wrong place. Eyes, nose, slanted mouth. As if assembly had gone wrong in the womb.

"Why ... Mommy ... hurt ... me?" it asked, drool and blood and other fluid falling in strings from its pointed teeth. It was about to say something else, but its neck bulged. It was Nom pressing against the inner walls of the neck.

Nay could hear the strains of her friend's muffled voice. "Why do I always have to end up inside things?!"

Nay drove Thorn into one of the Flesh Wight's yellow eyes. Another Kinetic Point. It shrieked, spraying Nay with the stank of its hot breath and spittle. It retracted its neck to move its head.

Nay drove the ice scythe up and into the back of the massive trunk, hooking it. A third Kinetic Point. She was lifted into the air with the neck. One of the three-fingered hands wrapped around her and squeezed.

The pressure was immense. It was an intense crushing Nay had never experienced before, nor would she want to experience it again. She felt some of her ribs crack and her spine began to compress. She started to scream in pain.

"I pop Mommy!" the Flesh Wight said.

There was a blinding gold light. One of Lain's hoops appeared above her and was shooting a healing beam onto her. Nay closed her eyes and the pain disappeared.

Lain's other hoop sliced through the knuckle joint of one of the fingers holding her, and the pressure was suddenly gone. The Flesh Wight released Nay and she fell to the snow.

Renewed and rejuvenated by Lain's healing, Nay produced a candied frog leg from her inventory and tore into it with her teeth. Tuk-Tuk rolled away from one of the Flesh Wight's arms and stopped next to her. She touched the back of his neck and held another candied frog leg up to his snout. He licked her hand and consumed the frog leg.

Nay saw the Jump icon appear over his head.

[Frog Ups]
[02:00]

Nay leapt into the air and landed on the Flesh Wight's back. The beast's hide was rough with warts the size of speed bumps. The back shuddered. Tuk-Tuk had landed next to her. He grunted and nodded at her. They both began moving forward towards the neck.

Nay used the warty mounds as handholds so she didn't get thrown off.

Tuk-Tuk found a soft patch of skin near what looked like the bumps of the spinal column underneath. Then he roared and activated some kind of berserker-frenzy attack and started clawing at the skin like he was digging into a beehive for honey. Flesh and blood filled the air around him.

The Flesh Wight cried underneath them. Nay could see Martygan, rejuvenated, approaching them, led by his swarm of remaining familiars. He was taking the crossbows off his belt.

Nay activated Gore, spending her Kinetic Points. The wounds she had made on the Flesh Wight ruptured. Its belly opened up. The top of its face where its ruined eye was exploded. And its neck wound widened, the skin flapping with the released energy.

The Flesh Wight wailed and toppled, crashing into the first wave of netherlings and blood imps. Nay and Tuk-Tuk, shifting back into his human form, rolled off its back and landed in the snow.

Lain held both her hoops and jumped on the back of the trunk-like neck of the Flesh Wight. Steam came out of the thing's nostrils and it let out a pained sigh. "Mommy . . ."

Lain placed the razor edges underneath the neck and then pulled back, decapitating the beast. The head of the Flesh Wight fell into the snow, and a green fin emerged out of the neck stump. A purple tentacle appeared. Nom pulled himself out and shook all the gore from him like a dog shaking off water.

"I'm ready for that Bathe Ability," Nom said. "This is getting out of hand."

Lain looked at Nay with a new appreciation. "How long have you been training in combat?"

"Since the last time I saw you."

Something hit Tuk-Tuk in the side. The boy gasped and looked down at the crossbow bolt sticking out of his side. Everyone looked up to see Martygan approaching. The Gloom Ranger's crossbows were pointed at them.

Lain tossed a healing arc towards Tuk-Tuk. As the object spun through the air, Nay saw it was a golden acorn. It hit the boy and a wave of healing spread over him. The bolt popped out and the wound mended. But, pissed that he had been shot, Tuk-Tuk shifted into bear form and ran straight at Martygan.

"No!" Lain said. She tried to grab the bear, but he was already thundering across the snow. Another bolt appeared in the side of the bear. He merely grunted and ran straight at the Ranger.

Nay yelled, "Tuk-Tuk!"

Martygan fired his other crossbow, and Tuk-Tuk went to swat the projectile, but it pierced straight through his paw. The bear roared again and continued his charge. The Ranger went to reload his crossbows with a different sort of projectile. His hands started to give off a Vigor glow. Nay had seen what he and those weapons could do, and she had a feeling he was preparing for his Vigor-enhanced rapid-fire attacks.

"Tuk-Tuk, take cover!" Nay said.

But it was too late; the Ranger came up with his crossbows and a stream of projectiles shot forth. *Chuk-chuk-chuk*: the sound they made as he mowed the polar bear down.

Tuk-Tuk put up one of his paws again, and he took the stream of bolts across his foreleg and in his shoulder. He ducked his head and crashed into the snow, and his back turned red.

Nay screamed and threw her Salvo of Knives at Martygan. Thorn and the ice scythe appeared in his shoulders. But her Iron-enhanced attacks were just an irritant for the Ranger. The spirit knives rained down on him, and he turned, sweeping his crossbows in Nay's direction.

She took cover behind a tree. The stream of bolts chewed up the other side of the tree, spraying bark and wood chips everywhere.

Lain threw one of her hoops into the air, and it charged up, releasing a beam of red energy at Martygan. It seared one side of his face and the arm he used to shield himself. Since Lain was Bronze also, the attack did some damage, and Nay could hear his grunts of pain.

Martygan leaned forward to run and disappeared in a blink. He reappeared in front of Lain, his crossbows on his belt and his short sword in hand. Vigor blasted off him. His stun attack. The energy hit Lain and pushed her back.

The corrupted Ranger lunged with his sword, but Lain caught the tip of the weapon in the hoop in her hand. She shoved the sword aside. But Martygan pressed forward, both hands on his sword, and drove it towards Lain's torso.

Nom popped out of the snow and wrapped around Martygan's leg, holding him back, so his thrust entered Lain's stomach but didn't run her all the way through.

Lain gasped in pain and looked down at the sword tip inside her. Then she looked back up and gazed into Martygan's face, his betrayal seeming to hurt her more than his weapon. "Where have you gone, my friend? Is there no part of you that remains?"

Martygan sneered at her. "You were an annoying companion. Ever since the commander paired us, I have barely tolerated your company."

He pulled the sword out of her and Lain crumpled to the snow. Her hands began to glow gold and she held them to her stomach. Martygan raised his sword above his head to deliver the coup de grace, but Nom coiled around both of his wrists and arms, the end of his body swatting Martygan in the face.

It was more of an annoyance for the Ranger, but it bought enough time for Nay to land next to Lain. She picked Lain up with her Iron-enhanced strength and leapt away, thanks to the frog-jump spell.

Martygan managed to shake Nom off, and the tentacle went flying. The Ranger saw Lain was in Nay's arms, and he commanded his familiars to stop them. The swarm moved towards them.

The worst of her wound self-healed, Lain stood. Nay and she faced the approaching swarm. Both of Lain's hoops hovered in front of her, and the red beams swept into the netherlings and blood imps, burning them to bits. Nay helped with Salvo of Knives.

A noxious cloud started to move through the tide of netherlings and blood. It started on the far end, and Nay noticed the creatures shriveling and bursting. Their bodies turned green and started erupting with boils, the juices and gas spreading onto the ones around them. It was a plague.

"It's Quincy!" Nom said. "He's come to aid us!"

Nay and the others looked to where Nom was pointing with one of his green fins. Sure enough, there was a figure atop a fauglir that was riding around the edge of the swarm, intermittently swinging his double-bladed axe into the familiars.

Martygan aimed a crossbow at Quincy and fired. There was a clang as Quincy blocked the bolt with Gertrude. The Ranger fired again, and Quincy knocked that bolt aside as well.

As Al, the fauglir, reached Martygan, Quincy swung Gertrude. There was a massive clang of steel on steel as the Gloom Ranger's short sword met the axe. Quincy leapt off the fauglir and rolled in the snow, popping up to face Martygan.

The Bronze-ranked men circled each other.

Martygan blinked forward, and there was the ring of steel on steel as the Ranger's short sword was met each time by Gertrude. The air shimmered around them, their use of Vigor affecting the atmosphere as they moved through it. The Ranger came in again, shifting from swings that went low to high. Speed and agility were the Ranger's bread and butter, and he managed to slip through with an attack.

But Quincy just grunted and took the cut along the side of his torso. He was a hearty brawler and almost seemed to relish being struck. This time, Quincy swung. Martygan dodged, but he was baited right into Quincy's headbutt. It bloodied the Ranger's nose.

They separated.

"Stand down and end this madness!" Quincy said.

Martygan wiped the blood from his nose and looked at it on his hand. He smirked. "Finally, a worthy opponent."

And with that, he activated Blade of the Ranger. An aura began to form around his short sword, and a piece of metal seemed to materialize out of nowhere, connecting to the sword. It was going to form into a bigger, deadlier blade. As more metal appeared, spinning in the air around Martygan, Quincy swiped forward with a hooking swing. The air flow reversed and pulled the Ranger forward.

Suddenly, he was in the air, Quincy's hand wrapped around the corrupted Ranger's throat. The light show ended and the parts of the sword fell away, only halfway formed. The former adventurer had interrupted the attack. He disarmed the Ranger and slammed him into the ground. He straddled the smaller man and laid his axe handle against his throat, pinning him.

"Stand down, Martygan," Quincy said. "I don't want to hurt you."

Martygan spat at him.

Quincy applied pressure across his throat. "Yield!"

Martygan snarled at him.

"There must be some way to help him!" Quincy said to the others. "To break the hold of the Nether Sister!"

Lain shook her head, forlorn. "We tried everything at Fort Nixx to break the enchantment. Nothing has cured the corruption. The knowledge eludes us. I fear the Martygan I once knew and loved is gone."

Nay looked at her and put a hand on her shoulder reassuringly.

"Damn it to the nether hells," Quincy said. He hung his head and his face darkened.

"Wait," Nay said. She knelt so she was closer to Martygan. "Why have you been wanting to power up? What does the Nether Sister want?"

Marytgan looked at her and his violet eyes glinted. He smiled a smile that wasn't totally his. There was a twisted derangement about him, and it freaked Nay out a little. "He Who Slumbers must be awakened."

Nay and Quincy exchanged a look.

"What does that mean?" Nay said.

"In my experience," Nom said, "nothing good."

"His return is imminent and I must prepare the way!" Martygan said, spittle flying out of his mouth. "The Tower will be reformed and Dark Brother will be found, and nothing you can do will stop him!"

[Quest Completed!]
[Gather Information About Nether Sister's Plan from Martygan Completed!]
[You have been rewarded Vigor Points]

At that, his jaw tightened and he bit down on something in his mouth.

Quincy grabbed his jaw and forced his mouth open. There was a detached tooth on Martygan's tongue he was biting down on. It was his molar. It looked like he had pushed it from the socket with his tongue and bitten into it, releasing something.

"Poison?" Nom said.

Martygan started laughing even with Quincy squeezing his mouth open. A black foam spilled out of the cracked molar and started bubbling out of his mouth. He continued laughing even though he was choking on the foam. Then the foam formed into a swirling disc. It was a Nether Portal, similar to the one Nay had seen the Nether Sister use.

But as this one spun and grew and expanded, Martygan's head disappeared. Quincy stumbled back, and soon the nebulous darkness was big enough to make the rest of Martygan's body disappear. It rotated faster, growing in speed, then imploded, disappearing, taking the Gloom Ranger with it.

Martygan's deranged laughter echoed as the last of the smoky darkness dispersed.

"Well," Nom said, "that's one way to exit stage left."

— CHAPTER SEVENTY-FOUR —

A Feast and a Plan

[Quest Complete]
[Escape Martygan Completed!]
[You have been rewarded Vigor Points]

The golden vigama flew into Nay, and she expanded her spirit veins to accept them. After such a battle, the dopamine hit made her feel euphoric.

They found Tuk-Tuk still in polar-bear form, bleeding into the snow. He was barely breathing, his breaths slow and laborious. His nostrils exhaled steam and his eyes were closed. At Nay's touch he let out a pitiful groan. His body was riddled with Martygan's crossbow bolts.

Lain knelt next to him, and she put a hand on his head. "It's not your time to join the sky spirits just yet, young warrior. Not if I can help it."

She placed one of her hoops above him and healing light shone from it, encasing him. A golden ball of light appeared in her hand, and she blew it towards Tuk-Tuk. It turned into the image of an elk and approached him. It lowered its head so the antlers were about to touch the bear, then it separated into gold motes that washed over Tuk-Tuk.

The healing squeezed the bolts out of his flesh, and the light filled the wounds with healing Vigor. The injuries closed up, mending. When it was done, the hoop flew back to Lain and she leaned against a tree, showing signs of tiredness. All the healing had depleted her Vigor reserves.

A wind blew through the black branches of the gnarled trees. They looked up and saw a cloud appear above the tree cover. It lowered, a mist entering the forest. But then Nay saw the silhouette of a person atop the cloud.

Ilyawraith landed in the forest, a staff made of multicolored coral in her hand.

"You're late," Quincy said. He walked up to her and smiled.

"If someone had told me to come sooner instead of insisting that they could take care of things," Ilyawraith said, "I might have been able to prevent all this."

"I didn't want to risk ruining you being seen," Quincy said.

"I can handle my affairs while tending to my pupil just fine," Ilyawraith said.

She walked up to Nay and looked her up and down. "A few scratches and bruises, but you are relatively unscathed."

"We have a healer with us," Nay said. She nodded at Lain.

"So, you've survived Bronze-rank attacks and"—she looked around at the remains of the netherlings and blood imps—"the familiars borne from the Nether Realm."

"Quincy was the one who put an end to it," Nay said. "If he and Lain hadn't arrived, it would be a different story."

Tuk-Tuk shifted back into human form, catching everyone's attention. He examined his healed body in amazement, then looked at Lain. "You are a powerful healer."

"Next time a Gloom Ranger is pointing crossbows at you, think about finding cover," Lain said. "When we choose to attack is sometimes more important than how."

"I can't help it. When I'm a bear, sometimes everything I see turns red and I can't think straight. I can only think of the one who caused the pain."

Tuk-Tuk pulled something out of his belt. It was a leather tube.

"What's that?" Nay said.

"Something the Ranger dropped during the fight," Tuk-Tuk said. "I found it in the snow."

He held it out and Quincy took it. Quincy found a cap on the end it and opened it. It was a cylindrical case. He peeked inside and then pulled out a rolled-up parchment. Was it a scroll? He unrolled the parchment, revealing a map of Stitchdale and the surrounding environs, including the Black Ice Waste.

"A map," Nay said.

They all gathered around Quincy to study it. Nay could see markings. Some areas were circled, and there were notes in the margins.

"It's the locations of monsters containing Marrow and Delicacies," Quincy said.

"That's why he took me," Nay said. "He was wanting me to cook them so he could power up."

Quincy mumbled as he read some of Martygan's scribblings. "Blue-spotted frost cat, ice harpy, tundra wolf, Bjorbane . . ."

Ilyawraith noticed a marking in the Black Ice Wastes. "He planned to slay these creatures on his way north"—she pointed at the area of the map—"before joining with his co-conspirators."

"For what?" Nom said.

"To awaken the One Who Slumbers," Ilyawraith said.

They were able to get back to Lucerna's End quicker than Nay thought. They had only been a day's travel by fauglir into the wilderness from the town. Tuk-Tuk carried Nay and Nom on his back, while Lain shifted to her mobile elk form. To speed up the trip, Ilyawraith ferried them one by one on her cloud, starting with Quincy. After dropping him off at the Lodge, she flew back and grabbed another. After Quincy were Nay and Nom, then Tuk-Tuk, and finally Lain.

Somehow, Lucerna's End had suffered only a handful of casualties from the attack, three of them coming from the Netherspawn Mother attack out on the Lac. The fourth and last came from one of the watchmen who were fighting off the netherlings on the shore. It was an older stitchguy who died of a heart attack during the fight.

There were considerably more injured; Lain did her rounds, tending to the wounded, and all were healed.

The joy and celebration of the Green Moon Festival had been disrupted by Martygan's attack. He was the one responsible for summoning the creatures to cause chaos so he could snatch Nay. As such, she couldn't help but feel partially responsible for what had happened to the town. She compensated by having meals delivered to the houses of the families of the fallen and the injured. It was her way of caring for the townspeople and lifting her conscience. She made sure to include extra moon cakes in every care package.

It was nighttime, and the Bouldershield Brothers had made sure there were extra watchmen patrolling the streets in case of another event. But their presence was more to put the townspeople at ease.

In Quincy's Lodge, at a long table near the tavern hearth, the Marrow Eaters held a sort of council meeting over a feast of roasted pig. It was a private affair, and the tavern had been closed to all other townsfolk.

Ilyawraith headed one end of the table, and Quincy sat on the other. Along the sides were Nay, Lain, Tuk-Tuk, and Nom. Nom was hoarding a bowl of cracklings, loudly munching on the crispy pig skin.

For sides Nay had made a creamy deviled egg–style potato salad. It was a favorite of hers as a child in Louisiana, and she knew it would go well with the pig roast. Nom had fried up a ridiculous amount of onion rings. The batter wasn't too sweet, and once fried, it provided a ton of crunch. Nay had also made a slaw out of purple cabbage, the key ingredients being skyr, apple cider vinegar, and some sugar. It was creamy and had the perfect blend of sugar and acidity.

Quincy liked it so much, he had made a sandwich out of one of the rolls and a bit of roast pork, topped with the purple slaw. He also had an entire bowl of the macaroni and cheese she had thrown together. It used an absurd amount of cheese and butter and bacon. She warned Quincy not to get too savage with it or he'd be having stomach issues later.

She also had made a cornbread with some spicy tundra peppers. The secret ingredient to her cornbread was sour cream. She used a bit of buttermilk as well, but the sour cream really added a tangier flavor to the bread, and it helped the baking soda achieve an even greater rise. The extra fat did wonders to help keep the cornbread moist and tender.

Tuk-Tuk had taken a whole iron pan of the stuff and was using it to wipe his plate clean. He had eaten a whole bowl of the baked snow beans, and she had heard Nom make the comment "Wouldn't want to be sleeping in the same room as him tonight."

Once everyone was a plate or two deep, satisfying their appetites, which were considerable after fighting a corrupted Gloom Ranger and an army of nether critters and one Flesh Wight, Ilyawraith began the proceedings.

"So, it appears we have something brewing in the far North that we cannot ignore," Ilyawraith said.

Everyone looked up from their plates to give her attention. Nay could see Nom perk his head from a bowl of potato salad he had been going to town on next to her.

The highest-level Marrow Eater in the room looked at Tuk-Tuk. "The Twelve Tribes have been right. I've seen it for myself. Their legend that something nefarious has been sleeping, trapped in the black ice, is real. And there are forces and things in our realm that are working, as we speak, to free it from the ice. Already, Lucerna's End is experiencing the far-reaching tendrils of this darkness, just as Tuk-Tuk's people have. It can no longer be ignored."

Tuk-Tuk nodded, and his eyes were full of renewed interest for Ilyawraith. It must have felt good to hear someone confirm a belief others had scoffed at or discarded as mere myth.

"What have you seen?" Nay asked.

"I've flown over the Black Ice Waste and have seen a force gathering near the chasms where the black ice is the thickest," Ilyawraith said. "What was once barren is now showing signs of stirring."

"A force of what?" Lain asked.

"That, I'm not sure," she said. "I would have to consult with historical archives or meet with someone from the Twelve Tribes who possesses a better knowledge about the history of the area. But they appear to be maugrim in stature and in appearance, except they are pale of skin with eyes that freeze with the heart of ice. I couldn't get too close, because they were watching the skies."

"Do you know what they are, Tuk-Tuk?" Nay said.

Tuk-Tuk shook his head. "The things that dwell in the Black Ice Wastes are of the dark."

"What do you propose?" Lain said. "I can request a squad of Gloom Rangers to travel to the border for more surveillance. Maybe even a scouting party to investigate further."

Ilyawraith took a sip of wine and set the half-empty glass on the table. "I propose all of us travel to Tuk-Tuk's settlement to consult with the leaders of the Twelve Tribe."

"Why all of us?" Nay said.

"I'm sure there are many great warriors like Tuk-Tuk amongst the tribesmen," Ilyawraith said. "But they will also need support because of our particular skillset."

"Who's going to run the Lodge?" Nay said.

"Gracie and the girls can keep the place in business while we are gone," Quincy said. "Customers might complain, but the menu can go back to baked fish for a bit."

"I can leave her with some simple recipes," Nay said. "We have enough crab and fish for steamed crab and fish 'n chips. Just because I'll be gone doesn't mean the diners have to suffer."

"Gracie's cooking has gotten much better than you're giving her credit for," Nom said. "I taught her a few things while you were away for your training."

"I still have a lot more training to do," Nay said. "Especially for something like this."

"If you are worried," Ilyawraith said, "know that we'll be making a few stops in order to branch out your Delicacy trees on our way up north." She tapped on the leather case containing Martygan's map, the one marked with the monsters containing Marrows and Delicacies.

"You once asked me what we were going to do about this threat in the North," Quincy said. "This is it. We will stop Martygan and the Nether Sister's plans to disturb this thing entombed in the black ice. If we ignore it and don't lend help to the Twelve Tribes, it could mean the end of Lucerna's End."

"I will send word to Fort Nixx immediately," Lain said. She excused herself and headed out of the tavern.

"Get back in time for dessert," Nay said. "I have crystal-berry cobbler."

"It's all hands on deck," Quincy said. "We'll settle our affairs here and then leave in two days' time."

Epilogue

They had left Lucerna's End before the sun had risen, under the cover of darkness. Nay, Quincy, and Ilyawraith atop fauglir and Lain and Tuk-Tuk in their mobile forms of elk and polar bear. Their first destination was the location of the tundra wolf so they could slay it and extract the Marrow. But that was over a day away.

They took camp the first day on a rock formation that was part of a duo of hills called Lornetop, where the ruins of a watchtower had been left to erode. It was once used to patrol the Lorne Plateau by the men and women of Stitchdale. Now it bore the remnants of camps that had been used by travelers over the years.

For a party like this, traveling with two stellar cooks and one who could store a lot of supplies in a magical inventory, it went without saying that they didn't have to worry about eating well. Nay cooked them all tomahawk steaks on that first night with garlic mashed potatoes and roasted vegetables. She cooked the meat medium rare, except for Tuk-Tuk, who had asked for rare.

"If one of you had asked for well done," Nay said, "we would have had problems."

"Is that something that would happen in restaurants in your world?" Quincy said.

"All the time," Nay said. "Had a guy once come in and order the ribeye. He told the waiter he wanted it well done. Okay, so I make it well done. Waiter brings it out, and the guy looks at it, doesn't even cut into it, and says 'I asked for well done.' The waiter tells him it's well done. The guy says he can clearly see it isn't. So, the waiter brings it back. *What the hell?* I think. I throw it back on the flames for a few minutes. When I'm done, I'm sure there's no blood nor flavor left; everything is brown. Waiter brings it back out. Same thing. Guy sends it back. It's not well done *enough* for him. If I was irritated before, now I'm pissed off. So, I throw the thing in the microwave and nuke it. Then I throw it in one of the fryers and leave it there and forget about it for a while. When I pull it back out, it's black as a hockey puck. The waiter brings it out and the guy smiles. He eats the whole thing. At the end of his meal, after he's left, the waiter discovers he's written on the check, *This is the best steak I've ever had.*"

Nom laughed the hardest while the others chuckled.

"What's a microwave?" Quincy said.

"Oh, it's a device in my world that runs off electricity," Nay said. "It's a small box with a door. But the door has a window you can see inside. You put food inside and tell it how long you want it to cook. And it heats the food really fast, using microwave radiation. It's a type of energy that causes the water inside of food to vibrate. That's how it cooks it. It's mostly for heating up leftovers when you want to save some time. More of a device for convenience. The food doesn't taste as good after, but hey, it's warm."

"Electricity?" Quincy said.

"It's a type of energy my world uses to power things like devices and lights," Nay said. "Pretty much everything is connected so it has access to electricity. We run wires and cables underneath the ground or on poles in the air so everyone has access."

"So, it's like Vigor?" Tuk-Tuk said.

"Not exactly," Nay said. "People can't really harness it like Vigor can be harnessed. It's science, not magic."

"Seems magical to me," Quincy said.

For dessert, they had some of the leftover crystal-berry cobbler from the feast a couple nights ago. Nay found a nice perch to sit and eat on while she looked out over the snow-swept plateau. It was a commanding view, and Nay could see why a watchtower once existed here. She could even see the lights of Lucerna's End in the distance.

Quincy joined her with two plates of the cobbler for himself. Between mouthfuls he said, "The clans that once existed here used this as a focal point to monitor Stitchdale. It was easy to send word here in any direction, as you can see."

"What happened to the clans?" Nay said.

"They bred with the maugrim," Quincy said. "The stitchmen are their descendants."

"Maybe they should rebuild part of the tower and have watchmen out here," Nay said. "With current events and all."

"With current events and all," Quincy said, "it's not a bad idea."

"Have you met with the Twelve Tribes before?" she said.

Quincy licked one of his plates clean and began on the other. He shook his head. "Never. This is a first for me."

"A new adventure," Nay said.

"So it seems," Quincy said. "I'll tell you one thing, though. I never ate this good on the road when I was adventuring." He shoveled down his last bite of cobbler and burped.

Acknowledgments

I cannot express how very much it means to me that you read this book. As the wife of the author, I am going to do my best to thank everyone he would have wanted to. Please, please forgive any oversight. This book is an ode to Terrell's love of isekai fantasy and cooking. He had such a passion for storytelling! Every day that he could write, he was living well. The sorrow of having to continue his journey without him cannot be articulated. What I can give on his behalf is thanks. Nathan Ingle, one of Terrell's best friends, who helped me every step of the way in making sure this book still was published; I thank you, I thank you, I thank you. To his beloved sister, Kristina, who would cry with me on Marco Polo almost daily and gave me the strength to see this through; I thank you, dearest. To my own best friend and brother, Blake, who was a rock in my storm of grief, I love you. To Terrell's brother, Alex, who carries on his love of worlds and gaming; thank you. To Terrell's father, who passed a month after him; we miss you. To our children, the very reason he worked so hard; we love you eternally. To all the special souls at Podium; thank you for making his dreams come true. To Mela Lee, who sent Terrell a recording of her reading a portion of *Monster Menu*, so he heard his words come alive; you'll never know how much that meant to us both. To the fantastic people at Royal Road, who saw him first. To his Patreon supporters, who made him feel like a million bucks. To every person who brought me love and help during this unimaginable loss; I thank you.

Bree Garrett
March 20, 2023

About the Author

Terrell Garrett is the author of slice-of-life LitRPG *Monster Menu* and the coauthor of indie comic *Wolverton, Thief of Impossible Objects*. Originally from Georgia, he most recently resided in Long Beach, California, where he wrote screenplays that were included on the Hit List and the Young & Hungry List. In 2016, he was invited to the Sundance Film Festival as the recipient of the Cassian Elwes Independent Screenwriting Fellowship and had been commissioned by Elwes to adapt Alistair MacLean's novel *Fear Is the Key*. Garrett passed away in 2023.

Podium

DISCOVER
STORIES UNBOUND

PodiumAudio.com

Printed in Great Britain
by Amazon